'It is fortuitous that the epigraph in Barry Gilder's novel, The List, is taken from TS Eliot, the poet who once observed that the people couldn't bear very much reality. Gilder has done wonders with his story. While majorly set in a dystopian future, the narrative weaves in and out of the reality of our blasphemed past and alerts us to the fact that what we have not addressed will certainly rise up to menace us, if not us, then certainly our children and their progeny. His evocation of the hidden world of espionage and manipulation, heroism and cravenness, double-dealing and integrity, ingredients baked in with the bitter bread of the New South Africa, has given us memorable characters. It will be difficult – after reading this book – to encounter an individual on the street and not imagine the journeys he or she must have taken towards the making or the unmaking of our fair democracy. It's a must-read.'
– MANDLA LANGA

By the same author

Songs & Secrets: South Africa from Liberation to Governance

The List

[signature: Barry Gilder]

Barry Gilder

CIEP Conference 2024
Birmingham
September 2024.

First published by Jacana Media (Pty) Ltd in 2018

10 Orange Street
Sunnyside
Auckland Park 2092
South Africa
+2711 628 3200
www.jacana.co.za

© Barry Gilder, 2018

All rights reserved.

ISBN 978-1-4314-2667-6

Cover artwork © Neo Gilder
Cover design by Shawn Paikin
Editing by Sean Fraser
Proofreading by Megan Mance
Set in Sabon 10.5/14pt
Job no. 003352

See a complete list of Jacana titles at www.jacana.co.za

Printed by novus print, a Novus Holdings company

*For Reneva, Thandi, Molly,
Neo and Cadi Lerato*

The blood-dimmed tide is loosed, and everywhere
The ceremony of innocence is drowned;
The best lack all conviction, while the worst
Are full of passionate intensity.
— WB Yeats, 'The Second Coming'

Note No. 1

> I. *The Burial of the Dead*
> *April is the cruellest month, breeding*
> *Lilacs out of the dead land, mixing*
> *Memory and desire, stirring*
> *Dull roots with spring rain.*
> – TS Eliot, 'The Waste Land'

April 2020
I tell this story now in the knowledge – sound, I'm sure – that the telling is too late. Too late to go back. Too late to tell it again, differently.

I, and those with whom I shared pathways through anger and hope, over our clutched glasses of wine, would certainly have wished to start the story over again. For we knew how it began; we knew how it unfolded; and we thought we knew how it would end.

But history has overtaken us, flashed past us while our gaze was elsewhere, just when we thought we had left it far behind. It has returned. And now there is no retelling of the story. No rewrites. Sekwenzekile!

I tell this story now because I was there. Because I am safe now – relatively, anyway – and once more in drizzling London, an obscure survivor. I scratch this tale with red pen into this red notebook on this antique desk below the cracked window with dirty lime curtains in my Kilburn bedsit. I transmit this tale to the future, for no one who frequents The Old Bell down the road, around the corner from the stone church, would listen to a bent-shouldered, ashen-haired man with gnarled fingers curled too tightly around his pint of bitter, who speaks in fuzzy tones of intrigue and conspiracy.

They would not listen, for the country of which I would speak is far away. Far away in space, and any interest in it now far away in time. Few, anyway, of my pub's clientele would be old enough to remember when Trafalgar Square was filled with crowds calling freedom for Nelson Mandela. None would remember when Wembley Stadium echoed with music and song and fiery speeches in celebration of the legend's seventieth birthday. And for those not now too young, the memory of his final freedom and the democratic honeymoon that followed would have faded. And most of the inhabitants of Kilburn now are not London-born – other dark-skinned émigrés with their own tales to tell of other faraway places.

Yes, I was there when *The Signs* showed themselves. Not that they did so in ways that said, *We are Signs*, of course, but there was a logic to the road. And the signs were there, not pointing anywhere, just asking to be seen. I was one of the few who pointed them out as we hurtled past, but most said we were imagining them, that we were seeing signs where there were just naked poles.

And, yes, I was there on that unusually icy and wet February 2020 day in the gallery of the Houses of Parliament off Plein Street in Cape Town, when the mist rose up off the crags and slid down from the heavens, obscuring the flat-topped mountain. We were gathered to hear President Moloi deliver his state of the nation address in opening this second session of parliament a year after his rise, some said miraculously, to office. The colours, the daring clothing, the old-world pomp and the new-world singing and ululations. All of us gathered to celebrate the first anniversary of what some called a new beginning. Awoken from the fitful, confused slumber of early democracy, of compromise and prevarication and slow capitulation and decay.

And so I was there when, not many minutes into the president's speech, a man rose from the benches in the centre of the house and stabbed the president eleven times with a blade concealed in a mobile phone.

It could be said that history regurgitated twice on this day. First in this stabbing in cynical aping of the assassination of the architect of apartheid, Hendrik Verwoerd, back in 1966, and secondly in ironic deference to the demise of Lee Harvey Oswald, when in the confusion the perpetrator – in making his escape through the front of the house onto the piazza overlooking Plein Street – was shot by a sniper from a building across the street.

And, yes, I was there, hardly a year before this presidenticide, when Comrade Vladimir recruited me into his very special, very secret task team to investigate *The Signs*. I thought at the time that this at last was the beginning of the proper ending of the story – a proper rewrite, ruthless red pen bouncing across the pages of history, deleting the impossible, circling the improbable, reinserting the expurgated.

Chapter 1

October 1979
The road, narrow, winding through groves and koppies, seemed endless. The tyres of Otto Bester's stone-pocked Cressida hummed on the dry rough tar, an insistent whirring of purposefulness. This was his life – itinerant. Each journey across the backroads of the Eastern Transvaal culminating in another assignation, another testing of his ability to reach across the human, the cultural, the racial, the age divides of the intricate mix that was South Africa at the end of the 1970s.

'At the very next town,' he told himself, 'I will stop. I don't have to, but I need a Coke and some greasy chips.' And the thought saw him through the next seventy kilometres. As the red sign loomed up ahead, instructing him to decelerate to 80kph, he wound down his window an open hand's width and lit a cigarette, careful to exhale through the gap. As he passed the first of the 60kph speed signs, he lifted his foot off the accelerator and touched the brakes to get the reluctant car to obey the law.

He found the café, parked, and extricated the thick brown file from the space between seat and console. Inside the café, he found an isolated table and sat with his back to the wall mounted with a large black-and-white image of God's Window, his face to the door.

From the point of view of the lone waitress, this was a man you served immediately and deferentially, not from around here, probably from the big city, sullen, engrossed in the file on the table before him. She harangued the chef in the kitchen to make haste and delivered the Coke, bending her knees slightly as she placed it in arm's reach.

Bester put his hand out for the Coke without looking up. This was going to be an interesting one. Lots of promise. Long-term prospects if he played it right. Right age. Right credentials. Malleable attitudes. Good networks. He could go far.

Like an actor for whom stage fright had long dissipated into no more than a tightening of the stomach muscles and a tingling of the palms, Bester felt the stab of anticipation begin to well, a necessary spur to his forthcoming appearance on his own, un-public stage. He rehearsed scenarios in his head, and, as a warm-up, engaged the waitress as she returned with his chips.

'Lots of grease, hey?'

'Yes, oom.'

'You worked here long?'

'Since I left school, oom. Last year.'

'You finish school?'

'Standard eight, oom.'

'What do they call you at home?'

'Annetjie, oom.'

'You must finish school, Annetjie. Then maybe you can get a better job.'

Bester looked into her eyes and smiled the smile. He lifted a chip to his mouth.

'Yes, oom.'

She bent her knees again and backed away, wiping her palms down the front of her apron, the bottom edge of which hung below the hem of her miniskirt, pushed back the strand of blonde hair that had fallen over her eyes, then turned and walked away.

Pretty, thought Bester. He put another chip in his mouth and turned back to his file. He was almost ready. The contents were committed to memory. He was warmed up. There was just enough time to finish his chips and Coke, smoke a cigarette, and traverse the last stretch of road to make it on time to the desolate spot he had chosen.

Chapter 2

October 1979
S'bu Dlamini untucked the soiled shirt from his trousers and pulled the hem up to wipe the sweat from his forehead. He leaned the shovel against a tree and shifted his weight from his shorter leg. He looked down. The hole was wide and deep enough. The bag of hand grenades and AK ammunition was properly sealed, as he'd been taught, duct-taped thoroughly, so no air or soil could render the contents unusable or dangerous for whoever came to pick them up.

He took in the forest of sparse trees, the intermittent boulders poking their heads out of the soil as if coming up for air, the struggling grass. A hundred metres away was the winding dirt road that led to the village where his mother still lived. To his right, it led to the tarred road that unwound in one direction to the nearby town and in the other – eventually – to the big cities, to Pretoria and Johannesburg. He had selected this place wisely, he thought, scratching at the back of his thick neck where the sweat tickled and then kneading a muscle that had tightened.

Yes, he had chosen this place carefully. Far away from Nelspruit where he worked in the small factory, prising plastic crockery from the mould of the hissing, clanking, white man's machine that gave a thunderous rhythm to his long days and a disturbing echo to his nights in bed next to Lizzy as he tried to summon sleep in their back room in KaNyamazane. Also, hopefully, too far away, if his buried treasure was discovered, to be linked to him. Perhaps too close to his home village, but in this he had no choice. While the factory was on strike, he had come home to the village to spend some time with his mother and – although he should, perhaps, have stayed back in Nelspruit to wave placards outside the factory gates with his comrades – to attend to this other, more secret, duty. Being in his village with no transport other than the rattling black bicycle borrowed from his cousin, he had no choice but this place, his short, uneven, thick legs pedalling arrhythmically, with the rucksack of grenades and bullets bouncing against his back and the shovel strapped with rough rope to the bicycle crossbar. He had chosen this burial site not too far from the dirt road to make it easier for a quick pick-up by whoever came to retrieve the revolutionary treasure. He would have to pace the distance to the road from this spot and place his signs.

He smelled the dust before he heard the sound of tyres on gravel followed by the whine of the engine as the car struggled its way up the gradient some distance away. He snatched at the shovel and stood with it sideways behind the tree, listening for the clatter of the car cresting the incline. Then, through the gap in the foliage, he dared a peek around the tree towards the road just where it flattened out and descended on its way past his spot. A white car. Looked like a Toyota, the big one – what's it called? With a C ... Yes, Cressida. It came closer. Not from around here. TP – Pretoria number plates. White man at the wheel! He pulled his head back behind the tree.

Now he dared not wipe the sweat trickling down his nose, the taste of salt on his lips. He closed his eyes and exhaled. The car sped on, then slowed and appeared to stop perhaps seven hundred paces down the road. He heard a door open and then slam shut, the sound reverberating through his skin, and then another metallic, creaking sound he could not interpret.

What now? If he was found with open hole, shovel and duct-taped bag it was over; he'd be dragged to a police station, beaten until he named names, became *impimpi*. And, if he survived, perhaps the rest of his life on Robben Island. His mother would never forgive him.

No! He could not be found with the evidence. He listened. No sound other than the gasping of the wind through the undergrowth. He knelt down, dropped the bag into the hole and swept the dirt over it – the sound, startling, of the first fall of sand on the hard plastic, like the first soil dropped onto a lowered coffin.

At last the hole was filled. Still on his knees, he placed the tufts of grass dug out earlier on top, along with twigs and leaves. He stilled himself for a moment, drew his forearm across his brow and listened. Nothing. Without daring to move from his kneeling position, he stretched out for the marked boulder and placed it where the hole had been. He grasped the shovel and crawled away until he found a small bush and pushed the shovel inside.

Still on hands and knees, he crawled until he felt it safe to stand and brush the soil and twigs from his knees. He wiped his face, kneaded the back of his neck. He walked parallel to the road, the slight unevenness of his gait long a mannerism rather than a disability. He moved in the direction from which the invasive car from Pretoria had come, towards the spot where he had hidden the bicycle. He would have to come back when it was safe, to do his pacing of distance from road to buried bag, put the agreed mark alongside the road and retrieve the shovel.

And then he heard the second car, from the same direction. He stopped behind a tree, but this time lay flat on the ground, facing the road, eyes fixed through the clearing to the crest of the incline. The sound of this car was deeper, more muscular. White again. Bakkie. Number plates? Hey! His uncle, William 'Baba' Dlamini's pick-up. What was he doing here on a school day, so far from the school where he was headmaster? He caught a glimpse of his uncle's face as the vehicle passed. Stern, as always. Focused. Determined. Perhaps on his way back home to the village. A family errand, perhaps.

He heard the bakkie slow and stop. Strange … He rose and limped quickly to the road, found a tree from behind which he could see the road. All was clear so he crossed and dropped into the shallow donga on the other side, deep enough to allow him to move half-bent parallel to the road to where he guessed the cars had stopped.

The sound of voices told him he was almost there. He crept out of the donga and into the forest, found a large boulder, settled behind it and raised his head. His uncle and the white man were standing just off the road on the other side, talking. The bonnet of the boer's car was propped open. Perhaps he had had a breakdown and Uncle had stopped to help him. But why weren't they standing over the exposed engine? Instead, they stood some distance away, between the two parked cars, on the far side of the road, in conversation too deep for car-repair advice.

Then he saw the exchange of envelopes between them.

Chapter 3

October 1979
Bester's preparations had been thorough, although he was confident that he knew enough about the enemy to wonder whether his fastidiousness was altogether necessary. But that was the nature of the game: be prepared, always, for an omniscient adversary. He looked over the room one more time, noted the African mask on the wall over the bed and the bushveld painting on the opposite wall, the wooden figurine on the round table at which he'd carefully positioned the two chairs.

For Bester, this room in this lodge was an operational choice – a secluded, standalone chalet where his guest could enter unobserved and they could converse undisturbed, avoiding the inevitable suspicion of a black youth entering a chalet in a whites-only lodge. He checked the supply of Cokes and biltong and beer, as well as the bottle of whiskey should circumstances require. One last time he tested the microphone under the table and checked the wire leading down the table leg, under the heavy-weave rug, to the tape recorder in the cupboard of the bedside table. He flipped through the notes in his file once more, elbow on table, hand supporting his brow like a plinth, one finger absently scratching at the tight off-blond curls.

He closed the file, slipped it back under the mattress, smoothed down the bedspread with one rough hand, glancing at the watch on the other, and settled himself in a chair at the table, back to the French doors that led to the patio.

Nothing for it now but to wait. He was sure the boy would come.

And the boy did come, by way of a gentle tapping on the glass of the sliding doors. Bester turned to see a tall, dark, skinny shadow silhouetted against the too-green lawn and over-manicured shrubs.

Like an actor who had been waiting in the wings for his cue, Bester rose, bent to the bedside cabinet to switch on the recorder, slid open the door and ushered the boy into the room with a flourish of his left arm, a rigorous shake with his right, and the smile pulled up from the toolbox of his trade. His trained eye assessed the boy: half-sultry, half-angry eyes, prematurely receding hairline, larger-than-life eyebrows.

'Welcome, Amos. Welcome. Come in.' He ushered the boy to the chair facing the window. 'Come. Sit down. Here, take this chair.'

'Thank you, meneer. Thank you.'

'Bester, my name is Bester, but you can call me Otto.'

Bester nudged the bowl of biltong across the table and offered Amos a Coke, opening one for himself and drinking from the bottle.

Amos ignored the Coke. 'Sorry sir, but I'm not used to calling a white man by his first name.'

'Don't think of me as a white man then.'

'Then what are you? How should I think of you, sir?'

The eyebrows twitched. Bester was pleased. Amos had spirit.

'I am just a man.'

Amos's hand inched towards the bowl on the table, hesitated, then slipped forward again and took a chunk of biltong. His hand started to his mouth, but dropped to the table again as he spoke. 'I am sorry, sir, but you know that in South Africa no one is just a man.'

Amos was suddenly decisive and put the biltong to his mouth. He bit off a piece and began chewing, looking past Bester to the garden beyond, his eyes narrowing against the light.

He continued. 'Or just a woman, for that matter, sir. No one is really just a child or just a student, or just a carpenter or just anything. In South Africa you are a black or a white something ... somebody.'

Bester pushed back his chair. 'You want something stronger than Coke? We have beer. There's whiskey. We even have a bottle of wine ... red.'

Amos turned away from the window to look in the direction in which Bester pointed. He put the rest of the biltong in his mouth, chewed for a while, then spoke. 'Perhaps, sir, I should have a beer?'

'You sure, Amos? You don't want something stronger?'

Amos rubbed an eyebrow. 'A beer is fine, sir. Thank you.'

'How d'you take it?'

'Take it, sir?'

'I mean, in the bottle or a glass?'

'The bottle, please, sir.'

Bester stood and moved to the sideboard. He scooped a generous handful of ice from the ice bucket ordered from room service a safe half-hour before Amos arrived, poured himself a double whiskey. He bent to the bar fridge and hooked his fingers around a bottle of Castle for Amos. He left the whiskey bottle where it was, to give him an opportunity to pause for thought when he needed to top up.

He placed the beer in front of Amos, sat down and looked directly into the boy's eyes. 'I don't see people in terms of race, Amos. I just see a young man sitting in front of me, sharing a drink with me.'

'Then you are blind, or you are not a South African, sir.'

'Ha ha! I am a South African all right. Maybe just a different one.'

Amos lifted the bottle to his lips, his eyes still on Bester. He helped himself to another piece of biltong, his teeth ripping at the meat, putting a hold on conversation. Bester noted the eyes: calm, intelligent, with a wisp of a smile without the help of the mouth busy with the meat. This one, he thought, is different from the others. Confident. A leader. He could go far. He now wished, too late, that he had set up a hidden camera. He could have had the new-fangled psycho-experts at headquarters analyse the way the boy spoke, the way he moved, expressions – body language, they called it. And video footage would have helped him sell his new protégé to his superiors. He took a gulp of whiskey.

'Mr Dlamini, your headmaster, explained why I asked to meet you, Amos?' Another sip of whiskey, eyes on Amos, who took his time, finishing his piece of biltong, right hand unmoving around the bottle on the table.

'What do you mean, sir?'

'I mean, did your headmaster not tell you why we're meeting?'

'No, I mean what do you mean you're a different South African?'

'Oh, that? I mean that I don't believe in this apartheid thing. I believe one of these days we will all govern South Africa together, black and white.'

'I thought you didn't believe in black and white, sir, only people.'

'Well, yes, you've got me there. But I suppose we have to use apartheid terms to describe an alternative future. You want another beer?'

'I'm still okay.'

Bester moved back to the sideboard, poured himself another

whiskey, taking his time, allowing the liquid to crackle the fresh handful of ice.

Amos took another swig as Bester settled back into his chair. 'You don't look like an apartheid opponent.'

'I don't? What do I look like?'

'You look like a boer, sir.'

'Ha! If you mean farmer, you're not far off. My father was a farmer – here, in Eastern Transvaal. But I became a city boy when I left the farm to do my high school in Pretoria.'

'No. I don't mean farmer, sir.' He sipped at his beer and put it down slowly. 'I mean you look like a typical Afrikaner, a supporter of apartheid.'

'Well, young Amos, I don't know if values reflect in our appearance. Don't judge a book, as they say.'

Bester helped himself to a small piece of biltong and washed it down with another gulp of whiskey.

'Yes, Mr Bester, Baba Dlamini told me you may have an opportunity for me.'

'Yes? Oh yes … Indeed. Change of subject. Good. Cheers.'

Bester lifted his glass up to Amos, who lifted his bottle, clinked it to Bester's glass, then put it down without drinking. He kept his eyes on Bester, averting them occasionally to the bottle or the bowl of biltong when the light disturbed him.

'Mr Dlamini tells me you're the brightest kid in the school.'

'I get good marks.'

'No, marks aren't always the measure of brightness. He says you're wise – that's the word he used. Very wise for your age. You in matric?'

'Yes.'

'He says you engage with the subjects, know stuff outside the syllabus. You're active in the debating society, read a lot, write well.'

Amos took another drink of beer. He smiled, suddenly. 'What's the opportunity, sir?'

'Sorry?'

'The opportunity. Baba Dlamini said you wanted to discuss an opportunity with me. Do you mind if I smoke, sir?'

'No, of course not. You smoke?'

'Only when I'm drinking.'

'You drink a lot?'

'No, sir. Only when I'm smoking.'

Bester couldn't hold the guffaw. He stood, pushed back his chair and walked over for another refill.

Amos took a single Lucky Strike, a matchstick and the torn-off side of a matchbox from his shirt pocket. He lit the cigarette, narrowing his eyes for the smoke, blowing out the match and dropping it into the ashtray Bester rushed over from the sideboard. Amos picked up the bottle and let the remainder of the beer run down his throat. Bester took out his pack of Courtleighs and his Zippo lighter.

'Those are girls' cigarettes, sir.'

'Well, yes ... no. I used to smoke Texan, you know, non-filter. But I coughed a lot – bad chest. Doctor said I should stop smoking or smoke something lighter. So, yes, I smoke girls' cigarettes now. Don't you hold that against me.'

'That opportunity, sir?'

'What?'

'The opportunity. Sorry. What is the opportunity you have for me?'

'Oh, yes. Well, I work for Unisa, the University of South Africa.'

Amos nodded.

'Okay. Yes. I work on a special project for the university.'

'You don't look like a university someone, sir.'

'Oh, yes? My looks again. What do I look like?'

'You look like a soldier.' That smile, in the eyes and in the mouth too this time.

'Ha! Well, if you mean I look tough, I told you, I'm the son of a farmer. But actually, I'm not really an academic. I don't teach. I work on this project, employed by the university.'

'What's the project?'

'Yes, I was coming to that. We look for the brightest kids – black kids – around the country who are finishing school, the brightest ones, to give them an opportunity to study further, to advance themselves, all expenses paid.'

'Black kids only?'

'Yes, black kids. White kids already have opportunities.'

Amos pushed his empty bottle across the table. Bester reprimanded himself; he was usually alert to guests' drinks, but now he needed to keep his eyes on Amos's all the time, to try to fathom their ambiguity. He moved to the sideboard, considered bringing the whiskey bottle over to the table, but changed his mind and reached down to the fridge for the beer.

Amos spoke to Bester's back. 'So, sir, you admit there is a difference between black kids and white kids. They're not all just kids.'

Bester turned from the fridge, the bottle in hand, and offered his best smile – big-mouthed, full-toothed, with dimples. 'It's a difference of opportunity, not race.'

'Yes, sir, but race determines opportunity.'

'Okay, Amos, you win. Jeez! Race determines opportunity. I give in. But that's just it. We're adjusting the scales, correcting the imbalance, giving opportunity where it's been limited. And, please, stop calling me "sir". Call me Otto.'

'Why?'

'Why what, Amos?'

'Why? What's in it for you?'

'In it for me? Calling me Otto?'

'No. Not that. This opportunity thing ... What's in it for you. And I can't call you by your first name. It's hard enough not calling you "baas".'

'There's nothing in it for me.'

'No, not you personally, for you and your project and the university. What's in it for you, plural?'

'Me plural, hey? I mean us, us plural. What's in it for us? Well, we're just a group of forward-looking Afrikaners. We know apartheid can't last. We know that one day we must all govern together, run the country, the economy, play sports together, live together. We know that.'

'You do? When?'

'When what?'

'When will apartheid end, sir?'

Bester lifted the glass to his mouth and poured the neat whiskey down his throat with head tilted back, but eyes still on Amos. He stood up, nearly tipping over his chair, and made his way to the bottle, bringing it with him to the table, along with the ice bucket in which just a few diminished cubes now swished about. He dipped his hand into the icy water to retrieve some blocks, poured himself another shot and pointed the whiskey bottle at Amos. Amos shook his head, drained his second Castle, then walked over to the mini-bar for another.

Bester watched Amos's progress. 'I'm not ... we're not soothsayers. But the day will come. Apartheid will end. That I'm sure of.'

Amos seemed more relaxed now, less combative. Perhaps it was the beer. Bester held out his glass for another toast. Amos clinked with eyes averted, and drank.

'How?'

'How what?'

'How will apartheid end, Mr Bester?'

'Oh ... When enough people like you and me, like us, come together to build an alternative.'

'I see. And what about the ANC?'

'The ANC?'

'Yes, the African National Congress.'

'I know what the ANC is. You a supporter?'

'Are you?'

'Me? Huh! I have a lot of sympathy for the ANC, at least for its history. But not the armed struggle, no. I don't support the armed struggle. Or the communists. The ANC has been taken over by the communists.'

'The communists?'

'Yes. Are you a communist?'

'Me? I'm not sure I'd know if ... No, I'm not a communist. I'm black consciousness.'

'Ah, a Biko man.'

'You killed him, Mr Bester. Steve Biko.'

'Yes. They did. That was bad.'

'They?'

'Yes, *they*. I didn't kill him. The university didn't kill him.' Bester paused, watching the boy's face, his eyes. 'Well? Are you?'

'Am I what?'

'A Steve Biko man.'

'Sort of. But beyond that, I believe black South Africans have to unite to get rid of apartheid. Freedom will not be given to us as a gift.'

'No?'

'No. And maybe the ANC is the only organisation that can unite us, communists or no communists, Mr Bester.'

'You want to join the ANC?'

'Is that an option, sir?'

'Not legally, no.'

'Then why do you ask? Are you trying to trap me, sir?'

'Otto, please.'

'Are you trying to trap me, Mr Bester?'

'No. No, of course not. I was just trying to understand your thinking.'

There was a long silence. Amos looked past Bester. Bester turned and followed his gaze to the greenness outside. Behind the trimmed bushes loomed the larger, more ancient trees whose dominance of this space must have long preceded the construction of the lodge, or the settlement of the species that had built it. The shadows were stretching.

Amos took out another cigarette. Bester followed suit. They sat for a long time like that, Amos looking past Bester to the world beyond this room, Bester half-turned in his chair, wondering when to pounce. He glanced at his watch. He needed to make sure the conversation ended before the recorder ran out of tape. He didn't want anything 'off the record'. He needed to haul the line in.

'So? What do you say?' Bester pushed his glass away.

Amos started and turned his eyes back to Bester. 'To what?'

'To the opportunity, Amos. To the chance to further your studies, all expenses paid.'

Amos drained his beer. Bester gestured towards the fridge, but Amos simply shook his head and stubbed out his cigarette. 'The opportunity, Mr Bester. Yes. Who wouldn't be interested in an opportunity? To better himself? All expenses paid? To help end apartheid? Who wouldn't be interested, sir?'

'Good. That's good. Excellent, Amos. And, of course, you'd be helping yourself. Creating opportunities. Preparing your future.'

Amos smiled. Bester recognised the moment. 'Look, I have to get back to Pretoria, but we can meet again – to discuss details. You still have some months of school left.'

'I thought we would discuss details today, Mr Bester.'

'Yes ... no. Today I just wanted to get the measure of you, to get to know you. Our selection process is very cautious. Funds are limited, so we must choose well. And you are not the only one I'm meeting.'

'And?'

'And what?'

'The measure, sir? What measure did you get of me?'

'Oh, yes. No. Very good. I'm very impressed. You're very intelligent. Very pleasant. Very committed to your people. And ...' Bester nodded at the boy's empty bottle on the table, 'you're a sensible drinker.'

'My people, Mr Bester?'

'Sorry. *The* people. The people.'

Amos stood up. Bester pushed his chair back, slipped his hand into his pocket, stood and offered Amos five twenty-rand notes.

'What's this for, sir?'

'Your expenses.'

'It only cost me a few rand to get here.'

'No, no. Not just for today. For the future. We'll have to meet again to discuss details and maybe you'll need to come to Pretoria. Please take it.'

Amos's hand hovered mid-air, poised halfway across the table between them. He looked at Bester, who smiled with the dimples. For a nanosecond, Amos's eyes oscillated between sultriness and anger, but he eventually held out his hand, took the money, folded the notes and squeezed them into the back pocket of his jeans.

'Good, Amos. Good.'

Amos moved towards the door, stepped onto the patio. Bester followed him, then patted him on the back. Amos winced.

'Sorry, Amos. Sorry. I almost forgot. Mmm ... I would have been in trouble. I just need you to do me one little favour. I have to account to the university for the money we spend on this project. I just need you to sign so I can account for it. You just have to sign that you received it, then you can spend it as you like. You don't need to give me receipts or anything.'

Bester moved back into the room, tore off a sheet from the notepad provided by the lodge and wrote the date, 'Received from O. Bester R100' and Amos's name.

'There, just sign above your name. Sorry about this. Bureaucracy.'

Amos hesitated, looked at Bester's smiling face, looked back out over the garden and bush beyond, went back to the table, bent over and, in slow, studied penmanship, inscribed his signature, and then he was gone.

Chapter 4

Now the reason the enlightened prince and the wise general conquer the enemy whenever they move and their achievements surpass those of ordinary men is foreknowledge.
– Sun Tzu, The Art of War

June 2019
'Intelligence is not a game ...'

Vladimir Masilela looked up over the lectern, bent his head to look over his spectacles at the young faces that looked back up at him. An array of expressions – interest, awe, boredom, respect, bemusement, curiosity – each lodged as if sculpted there in the thirty sets of eyes in the lecture theatre.

'Intelligence is not a movie. It is not fast cars and fast women and evildoers with misshapen bodies and grotesquely scarred faces. It is not gunfights and car chases and skydiving from exploding planes.'

He paused, looked down at his notes for a well-judged moment, sensing the anticipation of a shift from the negative. He shuffled his notes as if looking for the answer to the question he had planted in the minds of these young recruits into the intelligence service. And when he judged the moment as right, he looked up again. He stepped away from behind the lectern and began to pace.

'So?' He stopped and faced the banked rows, mouth turned down, eyebrows raised. 'So ... what then is intelligence?'

They looked at him, expressions dissolved by doubt. But waited for him to respond to his own question.

'No. I'm asking *you*! What do *you* think intelligence is?'

The fidgeting began, the scribbling in notebooks, the averted eyes. He smiled, stepped back toward the lectern, rearranged his notes, rested his hands on the lectern rim and leaned forward like a preacher.

One hand shot up – a young woman, face too innocent for a career in intelligence, framed by a green-and-gold headscarf.

'Yes, ntombazana. I see we have one future intelligence officer of courage. A good trait. Yes? What is intelligence?'

She stood up, hands gesticulating. 'Intelligence, sir, is spying, getting to know other people's secrets.'

Masilela ran his hand over the top of his head, clean-shaven to hide the white hair, then took off his spectacles and wiped the lenses on his Madiba shirt. 'Mmm? Getting to know other people's secrets? Yes? Is that it? What people?'

She pulled at the edges of the scarf, glanced down at her notebook and around to her fellow students.

'Enemies, sir!' The young man, hair in dreadlocks, now put up his hand.

Masilela frowned, not so much at the apparent disrespect, but at the youthful impetuousness of this new generation of intelligence officers. They were so different from the generation that had first come into the services out of exile, the underground, prison and general activism. He let the frown dissolve and once more wiped his hand over his scalp. 'Yes, young man. Thank you.'

The boy stood up.

'And how do we decide who are our enemies? Who decides?'

'We decide, chief. We decide. Anyone who is opposed to the government.'

'We?'

'Yes, chief. We. The intelligence service.'

'I see. We decide? That is, *you* decide. I retired from the Service … oh …' – he looked at his watch – '… five years ago. You decide that anyone who opposes the government is an enemy? And we steal their secrets?'

A slender arm raised itself in the back row. A young woman, dressed in a knitted burgundy-and-pink striped dress, stood up.

'Yes, young lady. You have a different view?'

Only now did Masilela recognise her. Jeremy and Bongi Whitehead's daughter, Nadine. So she had joined the Service. Jerry had said she was thinking about it. Good for her. Good for Jerry and Bongi. He smiled cautiously, to disguise the connection.

'Yes, my dear. What's your view?'

'Thanks, DG. I think that if we decided that everyone who is opposed to the government is an enemy we would have to spy on opposition parties.'

He grinned at her use of the form of address, DG, director-general, the post he had held in the Service. It was still used by those who remembered him as such, including Jeremy's wife, Bongi. And sometimes by Jeremy himself when he wanted to feign deference or, perhaps, to return briefly to the time he had deputised Masilela. He admired the young woman's easy statement of the obvious. Jeremy and Bongi had raised her well.

'Indeed. What's your name?'

She hesitated, looked around for a long moment. 'Nadine, sir, Nadine Whitehead.'

He immediately realised his mistake. Some in the room may recognise the surname as that of his former deputy, or perhaps already knew. Certainly, Marlena Botes, the course facilitator from the training academy, would have known, or would now make the connection. Botes was an Afrikaner woman, probably in her mid-forties, inherited from the predecessor apartheid service. (He was pretty sure she had flirted with him when she picked him up at the Mpumalanga Airport earlier in the day.) She sat now on the edge of the back row, observing and taking notes.

He was distracted by the muffled sounds of feet scuffling beyond the swing doors at the back of the lecture room, which now swung open with the suggestion of rusty hinges. He looked up to see Ntombi, his secretary when he had headed the Service, and now personal assistant to the principal of the academy, hurry across to him clutching a cell phone. She whispered in his ear.

'DG, the Minister is trying to get hold of you.'

'The Minister? Intelligence Minister?'

'Yes, DG'.

'Can't it wait until after the class, Ntombi?'

'Sorry, DG. He said he's going into a meeting so won't be available for a while.'

'Did he say it's urgent?'

'He didn't say, DG. He just asked if you could call him in the next ten minutes.'

What on earth could Comrade Sandile want from him now, and in the next ten minutes? Except for the congratulatory text message and the wry reply of 'congratulations or commiserations?', he'd had no contact with him since his appointment a few months ago.

He nodded to Ntombi and turned back to the class. 'I'm sorry, students. I'm told I have to take an urgent phone call. Give some thought to our discussion. I'll be back in a moment.'

He motioned to Ntombi and followed her out the room. She didn't stop in the foyer as expected, but led him outside to the manicured garden with its stone pathways and benches, a birdbath, small indigenous shrubs, recently planted still skinny trees and the imitation granite plinth with the bronze bust of Comrade Joe, the first minister of the post-1994 intelligence services. The bust did no justice to the memory of him except for the permanently furrowed forehead.

Ntombi quickly thumbed the keys on her phone and handed it to him. He was surprised when the Minister himself answered.

'Comrade Vladimir. Thanks for calling back so quickly. Apologies for the interruption. Where are you? I believe at the academy? Which campus?'

'Mpumalanga, Minister.'

'Oh dear. That's far. I'm in Cape Town. Listen, I need to see you. How soon can you get here?'

Masilela felt the creasing of his brow. He had hardly got into the swing of his lecture. The journey to Cape Town involved a road trip and two flights. And he was supposed to have the kids this weekend. Doreen would send one of her bitter WhatsApp messages if he reneged on the precise custody arrangement. He could think of only one reason Sandile would want to see him, and Vladimir could much more easily and quickly say no right here on the phone. He was not going to be brought back into the Service. There was no need for him to fly all the way to Cape Town to turn down the offer.

'Is it urgent, Minister?'

Sandile went silent for a moment.

'Well, Comrade Vladimir, I'm travelling abroad the day after tomorrow and I'll be gone for a week. I'd like to chat before then.'

'We can't chat on the phone? Or Skype?'

'No, Vladimir.'

Masilela calculated. End his lecture now. Be at the airport in 45 minutes. Be in Jo'burg by lunchtime. Flight to Cape Town landing around 3pm. With Minister by 4pm. Thirty minutes to say no thanks to the job offer and the 7pm flight back. Doreen would be silenced.

'Okay, Comrade Sandile. Let me see what I can wangle.'

Masilela took the phone from his ear and was about to hang up, but Ndaba continued to speak.

'Vladimir, can you keep this quiet for now? You know the protocol.'

Masilela hung up and passed the phone back to Ntombi. He was struggling to process the import of the call. Yes, he had surmised the purpose, but that didn't quite make sense. There was nothing urgent or secret about an attempt to recruit – or bring back – a head of service ... Confidential, yes, for a while; time-constrained in terms of the bureaucratic processes, maybe; but certainly nothing to justify an immediate and inconvenient rush to the far end of the country. But Sandile was, of course, more than a distant minister of state. He knew him, trusted him; they'd spent long, late nights around a bottle in Lusaka sharing things that cadres of the struggle were not supposed to share, were supposed to keep private, the dreaded NTK – Need To Know.

Masilela took a quick decision to accept, for now, Sandile's bona fides. Back in the lecture theatre, he moved to the lectern and turned to the students. 'People, I'm sorry. That was bad news. A family member has been in an accident. I have to get back to Pretoria quickly. We will have to reschedule this talk.'

He was touched by the collective look of disappointment.

'Look, rather than waste the remaining hour of this session, let me leave you with some thoughts. You can discuss them amongst yourselves under the supervision of Ms Botes over there. And when I come back I will interrogate you fully. Okay?'

Some smiled at the choice of word. Others glared. A few nodded.

'Okay ... Some thoughts. Intelligence is not just about spying. Think about that. It's not just about secrets. Think about that too. And "enemies" is not a good word. We're not at war. We don't have enemies. Perhaps think about the word "adversaries". Yes, and the intelligence services are not supposed to decide on their own who the adversaries are. Ask yourselves who is. And, yes, the young lady at the back there was correct – opposition to the government is not a legitimate reason to apply the very powerful and sensitive tools of your trade the law allows you. Please think about that particularly.

Sorry again. Thanks. Until next time.'

Masilela gathered his papers, looked up at the students. All were scribbling in their notebooks, some whispering to their neighbours for a reminder of the list of questions he had rattled off to them.

He moved up the steps to the back of the hall. At the door he paused and turned. 'And another thing ...' They turned slowly, quietened down.

'Think about this. Your government is emerging from a very difficult time. It has been accused of corruption, nepotism, capture by private interests. In the public discourse, in the media, in living rooms, the judgements were based on the old faithfuls of good and evil, dark and light. But life is not like that. The world doesn't work so simply. Think about that and the role of intelligence in understanding the forces, the dynamics, the dialectics beneath the surface. What makes your country tick?'

All eyes, heads and torsos were turned to him. No one wrote in notebooks. Botes's head was tilted to one side, her eyebrows raised, a dim smile bent her lips, half standing to escort him out. Masilela tucked his document bag under his arm, waved at the room, turned and was gone.

Chapter 5

June 2019
Sandile Ndaba was not – in any sense of the word, he felt – mystical or reductionist, *destined* to be South Africa's minister of intelligence. He was not born to the calling. It was not by any means a career choice. It was certainly not an ambition. His aspirations had lain elsewhere. If at all for high office, it should at least have been one in which he could make life better for his people. He had much preferred, in spite of the lesser rank, his previous term as deputy minister for social development. Now, with his return in 2016 from his second exile as ambassador to France, a posting precipitated by his fall from grace when his party tore itself asunder in 2007, he came home to a moment of renewal.

The dramatic reduction of his party's majority in the 2016 municipal elections and the loss of key cities had been the necessary dose of good old-fashioned shock therapy. At its national conference in 2017 a new leadership had been elected. And he, emerging from the shadows so to speak, was elected back onto the national executive committee.

And thus, with the general election a few months ago, his name back in a respectable spot on the electoral list, a new president, a new cabinet, circumstance and history had brought him to this point, a point he suspected was going to test the limits of his integrity and resolve, for – in spite of the renewal of the party – things still did not sit easy in the country.

※

In spite of his speculation on the hidden purpose of this call, and his slight discomfort at the formality now required of his relationship with Sandile, Vladimir Masilela crossed the carpeted floor of the eighteenth-floor office of the Plein Street ministerial building to give

Sandile the three-part hug and the whisper of an ancient greeting. He took in once more the minister of intelligence's office with its 180-degree view of the parliamentary precinct and Cape Town and its harbour beyond. He took the seat offered to him on the sofa, at right angles to the chair into which Sandile lowered himself. The personal assistant hovered at the door.

'Good of you to pop in, Mr Masilela. I didn't realise you were in Cape Town. Always good to see an old friend. I don't have much time, I'm afraid.'

The minister nodded at the personal assistant who backed out the door.

Masilela lifted his face to Sandile, smiled with one side of his mouth and spoke just as the assistant paused at the door to close it. 'It's good to see you, Minister. I thought that, while I'm passing through, I should pop in to congratulate you personally.'

Masilela leaned forward to help himself to coffee. He looked up from over his spectacles at the minister and offered to pour him some.

'No, no, Comrade Vladimir, but you help yourself. I've already had. Was with the president just now, in a meeting with the Americans. He read them the riot act. Go ahead.'

Masilela poured his coffee to the lip of the cup, took the sweetener dispenser and allowed one tablet to drop in, then stirred for some time, his eyes fixed on the hypnotic micro-whirlpool in the cup. He was about to speak when Ndaba raised his palm, lifted his eyes to the heavens and shook his head.

'How are you, Comrade Vladimir? You still use that name? After all this time?'

'I'm good, Sandile. Yes, I do. So do you, don't you? You weren't born Sandile.'

'Ha! Yes, I do. Except when I go back to my village. They still call me Jabu.'

Ndaba stood up, took the long walk back to the desk, unlocked a drawer and slipped something into the pocket of his jacket. 'Com, I know you told me the story in one of our drinking sessions in Lusaka, but remind me how you got your chimurenga name. Me, I took mine from the uncle who introduced me to ANC politics when I was a boy.'

'Well, when they asked me to choose an MK name when I got to Maputo, I immediately said "Vladimir Ilyich". I assumed it would be taken, but surprisingly it wasn't. The "Ilyich" has fallen away.'

Ndaba shifted in his chair. 'And people don't complain that you're not using an African name?'

'Yes, some do. But I'm proud of my name. Some of us still wear our struggle names like war wounds that prove we were there. But, what did you want to—'

Ndaba held up his hand, then put his index finger to his lips and raised his eyes to the heavens again. Masilela looked up as if expecting to see someone staring down at them. Sandile leaned forward, refilled Masilela's coffee cup and slipped a folded piece of paper under the saucer.

'Yes, Comrade Vladimir, the chief gave the Americans a hard time. It was a speech I wish we could make public. Told them that after twenty-five years of democracy, we had not moved far enough, nor fast enough. It was time for decisive action and time to stop kow-towing to international pressure to moderate our economic programme to their neoliberal views. Well, he didn't use that term, but the message was clear.'

Masilela dropped another sweetener into the cup. He thought he knew now what was going on. Or at least what was not going on. If he had been called in to be asked to come back into the Service, there would be no need for this subterfuge. He would need to be patient to hear why he had endured two plane trips and the probable ire of Doreen to heed this sudden call.

'Yes, com, he told them that we are going to follow India's example of manufacturing our own cheap generic medicines, and that they should please keep their pharmaceutical dogs at bay, and that we are going to renew our independent views in multilateral forums, will not support their interventions in Africa and the East. We will intensify our campaigns for a fairer world trade dispensation, a reformed UN system.'

Masilela kept his eyes on the minister, flicked the teaspoon from his saucer and let if fall to the floor; he bent to pick it up and unfolded the piece of paper, read it between his ankles. He offered occasional sounds of interest and agreement.

Thanks for coming. Sorry for the ambush.
We can't talk here.

> *Meet me for dinner tonight at 7:30.*
> *Blues in Camps Bay.*
> *I'll be sitting inside, right at the back.*

Masilela sighed. There was no chance of a return flight tonight. He would have to check into a hotel and find a good excuse for Doreen regarding the kids. He looked up, smiled and nodded, then shrugged his shoulders in vague capitulation to whatever deep secret this old comrade and friend and new minister so carefully guarded. He was tired of secrets. Molecular infestations of the mind that clogged the pathway between self and world. Secrets required a persona that held itself remote from the interactions around it. They manufactured an inner world that at times seemed more complicated, more populated than the outer.

'Yes, Comrade Vladimir, things are different now. Things are changing. The chief is not like his predecessors. And he has the support of the NEC, a good bunch of comrades – experience and freshness and, yes, a better record of integrity. He has some radical ideas for setting an example, for combatting inequality. But you will have to wait to see. He will announce soon. And, tell me, how is retirement? I believe you refused an ambassadorial post?'

'Yes, Minister. Good. Retirement is good. Doing a lot of reading, some writing. Spending time with the kids and seeing old friends and comrades from whom work pressure kept me away for nearly twenty years. Yes, I declined the posting. I needed a break from government. Maybe later, when … if … I get bored with retirement.'

Sandile rose from his chair, moved over to the desk and lifted the phone. 'Mr Masilela is leaving now. Give me a few minutes before my next appointment.'

Masilela stood, smiled with some sorrow, and put out his hand for the treble handshake. The assistant returned silently to the room.

'Thank you, Mr Masilela. Very good to see you again. Perhaps we can meet socially if you are in Cape Town for a while.'

Ndaba made his way over to the desk, lowered himself into his chair, took a file from the in-tray and looked up with a last smile and raise of the right hand to the forehead in pale imitation of the MK salute.

'I'm pretty sure, Comrade Vladimir, that I'm under surveillance.'

By way of emphasis, and perhaps to draw a crisp border between idle dinner conversation and real business, Sandile pushed forward his plate now emptied of everything except the prawn shells and the uneaten green peppers. He lifted the glass of wine to his lips and looked at Masilela, wrinkles appearing at the corners of his eyes as if he were looking into a bright light. His face a darker shade against the purple velvet of the booth. Masilela's plate had long been set aside, leaving no trace apart from a convoluted pattern of leftover juices of the pepper steak and potato wedges. He poured himself another glass of wine. He closed his eyes for a moment, partly to escape Ndaba's stare, but mostly to draw his own frontier between banality and the thing that was now to come.

With eyes closed, other senses usurped consciousness. The sounds of subdued conversations, the clatter of cutlery on crockery, the whiff of delicately grilled meat, steaming vegetables, catch of the day, all a background score to the quiet drama at their table. And beneath it all the tactile rumble of the sea as waves broke against Camps Bay beach below. He opened his eyes and looked around for any nearby diners worthy of operational note.

'Why, Sandile?'

Sandile took his phone from the breast pocket of his dark blue suit; the phone from which he had removed the battery just as they had sat down to dinner. He reinserted the battery, switched the phone on and stared at the screen. He pressed some keys, frowned, removed the battery again, replaced the phone and returned his eyes to Masilela's.

'Why am I being followed or why do I *think* I'm being followed?'

Masilela tipped his glass. 'Both, I guess.'

'You forget I was also trained in Moscow – skills I actually haven't had to use for a long time, until now, this job.'

'But why, Sandile? Who?'

'Who? Well, for one, I suspect the bodyguards the Service assigned to me. That's why I gave them the slip tonight. But who knows? The Service, the Hawks, some private entity?' Sandile filled his glass. 'Dessert?'

Masilela looked around for a waiter. They were all otherwise occupied. 'Later perhaps. But on whose behalf?'

Sandile waved his hand in the air without turning from Masilela.

'On whose behalf? The coalition of the de-captured is my best guess.'

'The what?' Masilela didn't notice the hovering waiter until Sandile's face turned away from him. He ordered ice cream and hot chocolate sauce, Sandile the crème brûlée. He poured more wine for Masilela, waved the empty bottle at the departing waiter.

'The coalition of the de-captured. It's obvious, Vladimir: those in the party, the state, businesses captured by the corrupters ousted at the 2017 conference. We always said, didn't we, that they wouldn't give up easily?'

'I guess, we did. But are they all ousted? You sure of that?'

'Ha! That's why you're here, Vladimir. That's why I called you.'

The waiter returning with the bottle of wine allowed Masilela a moment to process this. As he observed the ritual of the proffered label, the nod, the deft removal of the cork, the pouring of the taster, the swirling and holding up to the light, he struggled to fathom what his role may be in this scenario of surveillance and de-capture. He watched the back of the departing waiter. 'You know, Comrade Sandile, when you called me so urgently to Cape Town, I jumped to the conclusion that you were going to recruit me back into the Service.'

'Ha, Vladimir! Would you have accepted if I had?'

'I spent most of the trip composing a "no thank you" speech.'

'Well, no, Vladimir. I do need to change the Service leadership soon. I really don't trust this Brixton fellow.'

'You shouldn't.'

'Shouldn't what?'

'Trust Brixton Mthembu. I don't.'

'Good. We agree. And, yes, it would be good to work with you again. We go back a long way and going back a long way brings trust. But this thing I called you for is even more important.'

'More important?'

'Yes, more important. Strange things are going on. Very strange.' His eyes scanned the room for the waiter and he raised his hand, palm up. The waiter nodded and rushed back to the kitchen. 'You know, Vladimir, President Moloi has hardly been in office a month and there are already calls for his recall, from factions or forces … well, we don't know really where they come from.'

The waiter arrived with the desserts. Sandile picked at his brûlée while he explained the mission to Masilela. And he did so just as they had been trained to: clearly articulating the overall mission, the objectives, the battlefield conditions, the nature, strengths and weaknesses of the enemy, of own forces, the resources at hand, the constraints, the operational conditions. Masilela listened, raising his eyes now and then from the ice cream, sucking on the spoon, eyes widened. He felt as if he should be taking notes, an old habit not appropriate now, so he conjured up a mnemonic for each distinct point that Sandile made. At last Sandile went quiet and turned his attention to the remains of his dessert.

'You done, Minister?'

'Yes, Masilela, I'm done.'

'Hell, Comrade Sandile, this is tough.' Masilela poured himself more wine. 'You are asking me to lead an investigation without the resources of the Service, without the knowledge of the Service, without the knowledge of anyone apart from you, and my team, and the president, of course. Shit! That's all I can say. Excuse my language, Comrade Minister.'

'I'm afraid so, Vladimir. That's about it. I'm sure you understand there is no other way. We can't use the Service. Some of the people we're worried about are there. And we are traversing tricky ground – people's reputations, lives are at stake, and, of course, the future of our postponed revolution.'

'But where do I start?'

'Hey, Vladimir! I called on you because you're the one person the president and I could think of who would know where to start.'

'But I had resources before … The whole of the Service – agent handlers, analysts, surveillance teams, technical resources, the works. We even had better resources than you're offering me now when we were in exile.'

'You'll start with *The List*.'

Masilela put down his glass.

'The List? Which list?'

Sandile drained his wine. 'Mandela's list.'

'Mandela's list? The one the boers are supposed to have given him of their agents? We have it?'

Sandile reached into the inside pocket of his jacket and removed a roughly rolled sheaf of papers that had caused an incongruous bulge in his otherwise trim apparel that Masilela had not failed to notice. He had assumed that the minister, having eluded his bodyguards for this assignation, had been carrying a firearm. He took the papers Sandile passed him under the table and, having no suitable pocket in his Madiba shirt, slipped it into the front of his slacks and let the shirt fall back over them. The document pressed against his groin with a discomforting presence.

'Treat the list, Vladimir, with circumspection, as you know. Ignore, of course, the ones who are late and those who are out of active politics, except of course if they may lead to others still involved. We're only interested in those who are still active in the party or government or related organisations, maybe even in business if they wield influence.'

Masilela weighed the doubts in his mind, like a juggler tossing flaming torches through the air, but aware that, in the very momentum of the circling torches, there is an inescapable constant – the obligation to catch. Once again he had got the call. It had come many times in his life and he had always been compelled to answer it. Yes, he had turned down an ambassadorial posting and the call to stand for the new national executive; these were calls that others could answer to. But this one depended on the specificity of him.

And so he agreed, indicating his consent by raising his glass to Sandile and draining it in the hope that it would bring their meeting to a close. He needed to think, to readjust his life, to develop a back story for family, friends and comrades that would explain his sudden trip to Cape Town and much of the unexplainable that would follow.

'What about your team, Comrade Vladimir? Any ideas yet?'

'Only one, for now – Comrade Jerry.'

'Jerry?'

'Jeremy … Jeremy Whitehead.'

'Of course. Good choice. You trust him?'

Masilela laughed. 'Trust? Trust is a spiral staircase leading from a basement to a penthouse.'

'Huh?'

'Yes. In the basement is distrust. Actually, there is a level below that, a second basement: hatred. Distrust is still relative – you are not sure, but once you know someone is impimpi you simply hate them.'

'Whatever their reason for selling out?'

'The act of selling out is absolute. The reasons might be relative.'

'Okay. And after the basement?'

'Ground floor: tolerance.'

'Tolerance?' Sandile scratched his nose.

'Yes, tolerance. You know you can't really trust someone but circumstance dictates that you tolerate them. Like we had to do with the boers in the Service when we amalgamated.'

Masilela picked up the wine bottle, held it to the light, tipped it over. It was empty. 'Next comes acceptance. You have no concrete reason to doubt someone so you accept their bona fides until proved otherwise.'

'And next?'

'Friendship.'

'Huh? How did friendship get onto this staircase?'

'Friendship is close to the penthouse. I mean real friendship, when you share intimate things, like you and I had in those Lusaka years. You don't believe that someone like that could be impimpi.' Masilela began to peel the label off the bottle. 'But, you and I know … We have had friends who turned out to be sell-outs. That is the worst betrayal. Those are the ones who descend to the second basement.'

Sandile folded his napkin. 'So? Which floor is Whitehead on?'

'Same as you, chief. Friendship. Just below the penthouse.'

'I see. Neither of us has reached the top. What do you have to do to get to the penthouse?'

'Die.'

'Die?' Sandile's eyes widened.

'Yes, the highest form of trust is death.'

'Death?'

'Yes, you know you can trust someone who has given their life to the cause.'

'Vladimir, you should write a book on trust. Thanks for that. So, Jerry is in. What's he doing now?'

'He's retired, like me. Doing some writing, he says.'

'Anyone else?'

'No, not yet. I'll have to think about it. I'll approach Jerry first and discuss possibilities with him. Maybe his wife, Bongi. She's in the Service, a manager in analysis. She could get us access to Service information.'

33

'Yes, I know Bongi. Good. Keeping it in the family?'

'Well, not consciously.'

Sandile called for the bill. 'The List is just a start, Vladimir. I'll arrange access for you to the Green House records.'

'Huh? We still have them? Where are they?'

'They're safe. Don't you worry. They've been kept all these years out of the state or Service archives, or the ANC ones at Luthuli House or Fort Hare. Perhaps we anticipated a day like this.'

Masilela's response was interrupted by the waiter returning with the bill. Ndaba started to take out his credit card, then slipped it back and took out cash – a lot of it. Masilela smiled. Ndaba reached into his pocket again and handed Masilela a bulky envelope.

'There, that's the refund for your flight and accommodation.'

On the drive in the hired car back into the CBD, Masilela stuck to the coastal route; it was not the quickest, but passed through Clifton, Bantry Bay and Beach Road through Sea Point. He turned left at the lights near the lighthouse and continued on to Mouille Point. He stopped the car and parked opposite the apartment block where he'd had his director-general's flat when he was head of the Service, for those frequent trips from Pretoria to Cape Town when parliament was in session.

Masilela climbed out of the car and walked over to his old spot overlooking the rocks below and the sea beyond. He had come here often during those days of high stress, just to think. He stood at the railing, arms stretched either side of him and hands clasped on the cold metal. Behind him the lights of the darkened city shimmered, with more garish lighting offending the night from the Waterfront mall just this side of the breakwater. The sea was too dark to see the breaking of the waves. But they came to him as an oscillation of light and dark, a deep arrhythmic roll and crack of water against rock. He breathed in. The scent of the sea mingled with car fumes and rotting seaweed.

As he stood there, eyes closed, the southeaster suddenly arose, blowing hard, whistling through the buildings and bending the trees along the embankment.

His hands tightened on the railings. He leaned forward.

Chapter 6

October 1979

The day after his meeting with Bester, Amos used some of the money to persuade a cousin to drive him back to the village. He didn't want to hitchhike back as he had done to get to the meeting with the white man. Impatience perhaps, or indulgence of his temporary wealth.

When approached along the road of summer dust as it crests the escarpment and begins its descent into the greener valley, Amos Vilakazi's village appears lost among the trees and koppies. Mud-and-grass huts appear more scattered than they could really be if this was indeed a village. On modest heights there appear more modern houses of brick with asbestos roofs.

The descent is long, whether by motor, horse-drawn cart, bicycle or on foot. The road is not kind to travellers, winding not by any logic of topography, but to skirt trees or rocks its builders were perhaps too impatient, too lazy or not committed enough to remove. But as you come nearer, the spaces between houses and huts fill up with dusty roads and arbitrary paths, modern though dilapidated shops and roadside stalls, a modest church whose wooden spire only becomes visible as you finally reach level ground, a community centre of some kind, and – as you make your way along what must be a main street – the realisation comes upon you as a feeble epiphany that this is not a village at all. It is a town, a small town to be sure. But its inhabitants still insist on calling it a village.

Once back, Amos dropped in at the family home to greet and then took the narrow path down to the river to ponder the strangeness of his meeting with Bester. He needed to be alone, to be quiet. He knew the river would not yet be flowing at this time of year, but it remained, even now, his thinking spot, the dry riverbed containing still the memory and promise of flow.

As he descended the bank and emerged from the dense thorn

scrub he heard the laughter of the children. There they were, about ten of them, impish, barely clothed, laughter cutting through the bush, some astride the large fallen tree with which nature or some enterprising villagers had bridged the river, some exploring the riverbed with makeshift instruments of excavation, and one boy perched incongruously on homemade stilts.

Amos watched for a while before they noticed him.

'Hey, Bra Amos!'

'Yebo.'

'Where you from?'

'Town.'

'What for?'

'Errand for Baba.'

'You see your girlfriend there?'

'Which girlfriend?'

'Hehe, Bra Amos. You have so many?'

The kids tittered. Barely whispered intelligence was exchanged about Amos's envied way with girls. The boy on stilts dismounted by leaning over and falling with a thump and squeal onto a swathe of river sand. Amos clucked his annoyance and walked off to find a rock to seat himself, took out the recently bought packet of Lucky Strikes and lit up, watching the smoke drift. A cleft in the riverbed below a brackish pool of water, left over from the time of flow, threw his reflection back at him. He grimaced back.

He replayed yesterday's meeting with Bester; the conversation word for word, the atmospherics: the dark room, the glare of the light from the window that masked Bester's expressions, the bowl of biltong before him, the whiskey glass and beer bottle, the Coke, the half-full ashtray, and a sense – just a sense – in the corner of his eye, of a mask on the wall.

Did he trust the white man? Generally, no. Specifically, maybe. He did not trust white people. They were a distant and onerous presence in his life, impinging not so much as individuals but as a collective of imposed superiority. But this man? Well, he was engaging, perhaps Amos's first insight into an individual who did not easily fit the collective image.

Amos caught his reflection in the pool of water below as he tossed his cigarette butt into it, reached again for the packet and lit another.

He remembered a conversation in the shebeen over beer and cheap whiskey with friends.

'You see, Amos, the boers are different. You know where you stand with them. Not like the English. With the boers you know they're racist. They don't hide behind smiles and pretences like the English. The boers, at least the ones around here, on the farms, have learned our language. They may talk down to us but in our own words.'

'That makes them better?'

'Hey! No white man is better than the other! But with the boers you can understand better. And, you know, they fought their own liberation struggle, against the English. They may have lost on the battlefield, but they won eventually through politics and economics. Maybe that's how we will win one day.'

Amos clambered off the rock, made his way over to a dying tree and tore off a long branch, swiping his hand along it to clear the brittle leaves. He went back to the rock and twirled the stick in the pool below. A swarm of tiny miggies scattered off the surface. Tadpoles dashed away to avoid the probing of the stick. His mind wandered. He mulled over the praise of the white man for his intelligence.

Amos, himself, had discovered that he was brighter than most in his third year of school when at year end the teacher handed out report cards. 'And first in the class is Amos Vilakazi.' Until that moment he'd had no sense of academic competition. As far as he knew, he hadn't tried any harder than his classmates. He read books because he liked to. He remembered things he'd read always, and assumed that was how everyone's brain worked.

But he was not just a bookworm. He played sports, such as they had at their village school, mainly soccer on the dusty field with goalposts of rough wood severed from local trees bound together by rope and side and centre lines constantly rescraped into the hard earth. He savoured the feel of his bare feet speeding over the ground, cajoling the ball into his sphere of influence, and scoring goals, although inappropriate to his position of play.

He twirled the stick in the pool, watching the ripples spread outwards and extend the boundaries of the water.

Now, too, he had been singled out, as he saw it; drawn out from his closed world to enter the other one, like an emissary. Was this not significant? He knew, young as he was, from his reading, school debates, shebeen arguments, discussions around fires with uncles and peers, that apartheid would not – could not – end with a ridding of the white man. There would be no pushing into the sea, or herding into aeroplanes to go back from whence they'd come centuries before. *Black Man, you are on your own.* And so they were, but only insofar as they needed to free themselves, without charity, entreaties, petitions for their freedom from those who withheld it. And when it finally came it would need to be a shared freedom, a hard-to-imagine living together, a settlement – yes, a settlement – agreement on the boundaries and content of a new South Africa in which distinctions of race would be supplanted by distinctions normal in the democracies he had read of – of ability, intelligence, diligence and means.

He struck the water.

Yes, he would take the opportunity offered by the white man, to better himself and, in so doing, better the chances for his people; an emissary, yes, to the future. And he would assess as he went along.

Baba Dlamini, in setting up the meeting, had warned him to keep it between themselves, against the danger of jealousy or worse. Wait until everything is settled, he had advised. If you need to talk, talk to me. And he did need to talk, but who among his peers or his elders would understand, would have the insights to advise him better than he could counsel himself?

He took a last long drag on the cigarette, tossed the stick as far as he could upriver, slid down from the rock and, this time, ground the butt hard into the riverbed.

Chapter 7

October 1979

As S'bu Dlamini approached the factory gates, he paused on the opposite side of the road, watching his comrades gathered outside, talkative, ebullient and, finally, singing – a song of victory: the strike was over; the bosses had given in, or at least a compromise had been reached; it was time to earn wages again. S'bu limped across the street and joined the throng, throwing himself mid-verse into the song, and stamping his feet with the others, quite happy for a delay in the 7am opening of the factory gates and the return to that incessant machine. His co-workers greeted him, some with a question in widened eyes as to where their shop steward had been all this time.

The police in their armoured vehicles kept a watchful distance, perhaps not keen to provoke any further violence now that the strike was officially over, but still ready to pounce should the celebration get out of hand.

A hand on S'bu's arm told him to stop his victory dance and remove his alto voice from the song. It was Patrick, signalling that they should move away from the throng. S'bu followed Patrick to a quieter spot.

'Com, we're in trouble.'

'Yini, Patrick?'

Patrick's eyes darted, his lips moistened, his hands fiddling with his belt buckle. 'Tloks has been arrested. Last night.'

'Shit! How?'

'We not sure. We heard it from his girlfriend. The boers came to their shack in the small hours, many of them, armed, searched the place and took Tloks away.'

'Did they find anything?'

'She doesn't think so. It was dark, but she didn't see them carry anything away, except Tloks.'

S'bu had read the pamphlet on military combat work produced abroad by the Communist Party and smuggled into the country by the ANC. And he had had the training by Patrick, hours spent in the bush on weekends when the factory was closed. He had learned how to use, dismantle and clean a Makarov and an AK, how to toss a hand grenade. He was taught how to bury weapons. And he learned the rules of secret communication, of checking for surveillance, working in underground cells where only those who needed to know knew who was who.

By rights, he shouldn't have even known Tloks, but it was Tloks who had introduced him to Patrick, who became his official contact with the ANC underground. For all he knew at the time, Tloks wasn't in the underground, the introduction to Patrick just a social thing, although once Patrick had inducted him he had his suspicions. This was confirmation that the introduction was anything but social, that Tloks, whatever his other involvements might have been, had been responsible for 'spotting' S'bu.

'You know the drill, Comrade S'bu. Tloks knows me. He knows you. As we were taught, we have to assume he will break, eventually. The boers will moer him bad.'

'I know, comrade, but are we sure he was picked up for his underground work? Maybe it was something else.'

'Tloks dropped out of above-ground work when he was recruited into the underground. We have to assume the worst.'

'But how? How did the boers find out?'

'We don't know. Impimpi maybe. Maybe the boers traced something back to him. We can't take a chance.'

'So now what?'

'We have to disappear. Go deep. Give it a few days and see what happens. Maybe we'll have to skip the country.'

Patrick took something out of his pocket and slipped it into S'bu's hand. 'Instructions. About how to leave the country. Contacts of people in Soweto who will help.'

'But work?' S'bu nodded towards the factory gates that were now being dragged open by the white foremen, their eyes cast down to avoid those of the workers.

'We can't go in there, com. That's the first place the boers will look for us. And stay away from your place in KaNyamazane, or just run there now to fetch some stuff. And don't go to the village.'

'But my mother? And Lizzy?'

'Sorry, S'bu. You'll have to get a message to your family later. The boers will look for you there if they don't find you here or in the location. It's better your mother doesn't know where you are. You have to move quickly. When we don't clock in now, our absence will be noticed. The other comrades have seen us here. Questions will be asked.'

'But where?'

Patrick pointed at S'bu's pocket. 'There. On the paper. There's an address of comrades in Soweto who will look after you for now. You got money to get to Jozi?'

'I've still got some of the ops funds you gave me. Should be enough.'

'Sharp. You manage to DLB the grenades and stuff?'

S'bu reached into his pocket. 'Here, com. The instructions are here. But there was something—'

Patrick raised his hand palm outwards. 'No, com. Not now. We need to move. I'll try to get this to the comrades in Swaziland before I disappear. Now you go. Now!'

Chapter 8

November 1979

'Hey, you blerry idiot! You going to burn the meat! That fire's still too hot.'

Bester stepped back from the braai, waving the long-handled spatula at Van Zyl in mock protest. Marie smiled inwardly: the dynamics of the men.

'No, kaptein. It'll be okay. Called "flame-grilled". It's lekker like that.'

Van Zyl ignored Bester's protest and asserted his seniority by pouring beer from the bottle in his hand onto the fire, spilling some onto the sizzling steaks.

'Jeez, kaptein. Now you've drowned the meat.'

'They'll taste better like that, lieutenant.'

Van Zyl moved away from the braai and joined the rest of the unit sitting in a semicircle on white plastic chairs, scuffed and stained from many similar social gatherings on the outskirts of Pretoria. This meat and alcohol fest was the preferred sport of this elite unit on these Wednesday afternoons, reserved traditionally by all the security services for sports.

Marie took in the familiar setting. The nonchalant habits of power. A white plastic table with one broken leg propped up with a stick fastened with duct tape stood in the space between the two ends of the semicircle. On it stood bottles of brandy, empty beer bottles, a clutch of mismatched glasses, a pile of paper plates, plastic cutlery, paper napkins, two loaves of white bread and a bowl of potato salad, prepared and brought, as usual, by herself. Jutting out from under the table was a large plastic cooler box with Cokes, beers and ice.

Marie turned her eyes to the late Transvaal sun as it dipped below the tops of the trees, refracting light in chaotic patterns across the scrub, the smattering of stubborn boulders, off the surface of the lake and on the faces of the seven men and herself seated facing the plastic table as if it were an altar. Glasses and bottles moved rhythmically to lips. Legs were crossed and uncrossed. Heads were turned to Bester at the braai and then back to a neighbour for a whispered comment, or to Van Zyl each time he spoke, and now and then someone rose to replenish a beer or fill a glass with brandy and Coke, pausing at the braai on the way back to check on the meat's progress.

'Oh, kaptein, give Lieutenant Bester a break. He's the best braaier in the unit. You know that.'

Van Zyl turned his head towards Marie. She sensed his resentment – permanent resentment, it seemed, given that she had spurned his advances three times. But, at this moment, it was spurred by her defence of Otto.

'You think so, Marie? The best, hey? It's just that these other bastards are too damn lazy to braai after a hard day's work.' Van Zyl swept his hand with the beer bottle around the semicircle.

'Yes, kaptein. And he's your best officer.' Marie smiled at the others. Their grimaces transformed into wan smiles. Bester turned the meat.

'My best officer? Why? Because he knows how to talk nicely to kaffirs?'

The men laughed. Glasses and bottles were clinked. Marie smiled again. 'But, kaptein, how else are you going to catch terrorists?'

'Marie, I know my trade. But Bester, he is too ambitious.'

Bester tilted his head to catch the words over the sizzling of the fire. He grinned at the steaks.

'Too ambitious?' Marie frowned.

'No, Marie, I don't mean he's after my job. I mean this bloody project of his, it's too long term. I need hard intelligence now. Who's leaving the country? Who's coming back? Where are the weapons? Where are the underground cells? Who's protesting? Who's throwing stones? Who's throwing petrol bombs?'

'Meat's ready.' Bester turned to his colleagues.

They all stood, fetched paper plates from the table and gathered around the braai. Bester placed a steak and wors on each plate, with a quiet word and his signature smile to each. When all had been served, he fetched a plate for himself, took meat and headed over to the table for bread, salad and a brandy and Coke. He took a seat between

Marie and Van Zyl, placed his glass on the ground beside him and ate with his fingers, every now and then wiping his hand with a napkin before bending to pick up his glass. Apart from a few reluctant praises for the meat, conversation was stilled now. The silence let in the hum of the distant, home-going traffic from the Pretoria streets, a mellow consciousness of the world from which they had temporarily escaped.

'So, ja, Bester, what's your story?' Willie Oberholzer turned from the table where he had placed his empty plate and took another bottle of beer from the cooler box, snapping the top off on the edge of the table. He moved quickly back to his chair, sat, stretched his legs out in front of him.

Bester looked up from his plate, again wiped a hand on the napkin and bent to pick up his glass. 'My story? What story? There's no story.' He glanced at Marie and then back at Oberholzer.

'What kaptein was saying. This long-term blerry thing.'

'Hey, Willie, this war can go on for a long time. We need to get our people into the terrorist leadership. The higher they go the more we'll know.'

'Ha! You think this war will go on long? There's no way, man. We too damn strong.'

'The war will go on until the politicians find a way of accommodating the blacks.'

'Accommodate the kaffirs? Haven't we done enough? Jirre, Bester!'

'Well, if we'd done enough there wouldn't be a war, né?'

Oberholzer leapt to his feet. Marie flinched, but all he did was down the rest of his beer in one swift movement, walk back to the table, rummage noisily in the cooler box and slam the cap off another one. Bester shifted in his chair, lifted his heels off the ground to balance his plate more stably on his lap, took a bite of his wors and turned on the smile.

Van Zyl rose slowly and moved to the table as he spoke. 'Hey, Oberholzer, give Bester a break. He's got a bloody good network going. I just need results now. We might all be dead before some of his projects pay off.'

Graham Kline, the only English-speaking member of the unit, shifted in his seat, coughed falsely as he always did to get attention, his eyes darting to Marie as he spoke. 'But Otto has a point, captain. All conflicts have to end in some sort of negotiation.'

'Jirre, rooinek, we don't negotiate with terrorists!'

Kline turned to Sergeant Booysens who had interrupted him, and then back at Marie. He bent to pour another shot from the whiskey bottle on the ground next to him, swirling the remaining ice in his glass. 'No, sergeant, but if we didn't have terrorists we wouldn't have a war. Sooner or later the war has to come to an end and all wars end with some kind of settlement, even if we're the winners. Look at what's happening now. The Rhodesians are talking to their terrorists at Lancaster House right this moment.'

'The Rhodesians are blerry stupid!'

Kline ignored him. 'And the more of our people we have in the ANC, the higher they are in the ranks, the more chance of a settlement being in our favour.'

'And beyond.' Bester lifted his glass in salute to Kline.

'Beyond?'

'Ja, kaptein, beyond. If the settlement Kline is talking about involves maybe bringing the ANC into government, we could have our people on both sides of the government, so to speak.'

'Yissus! You guys are crazy. You want to govern with communists!' Oberholzer banged his beer bottle on the side of the chair.

Bester went over for more brandy, speaking over his shoulder. 'Not all ANC are communists.'

'The communists run the bloody ANC.'

'Maybe, for now. But if we get our people in we can change that. That's what the schools project is all about, isn't it?'

'Okay, Bester! That's enough. Need to know. I'm not going to allow these sports afternoon sessions to turn into a secrets exchange.' Van Zyl went to check whether there was any more meat on the grill.

'Sorry, kaptein.'

Silence. Marie looked around. The sun dipped now below the horizon. Shadows stretched like indolent cats. She rose and collected plates and cutlery and placed them in a large black plastic bag. Glasses and bottles were drained with a flourish.

Bester placed an open photo album on the thighs of the still naked Marie. He ran his fingers over the smudges of sweat in the fine hairs of her belly.

'See here, Marie, see this one? This is Pa's farm at the dam.

Actually, more of a water hole than a dam, or a reservoir. Pa built it to store water from the river for the dry spells. That's me on the right. Must be about seven. A boy still, innocent, ignorant, happy. Yes, happy. The farm was my world. I didn't know anything beyond, although Pa used to take me sometimes to town for supplies, but I sat in the bakkie mostly, while Pa did the shopping. He was always very quick. Made a list before he went into town, then in and out the shops – grocer, hardware, bottle store … In with his lists and out with his bags and boxes.

'See there in the background beyond the trees, the small forest – although for me it was a wild jungle – see, there, you can just glimpse the curve of the river and over there in the top left corner the little bridge and the road that took us to town and to church on Sunday, every Sunday.'

Marie hoisted herself a little higher on her elbow and bent over the picture. 'And who's that swimming next to you?'

'That? That's Tshepo. Yes, Tshepo. My little black friend. I forget the surname – Sotho name. He was the son of one of Pa's workers. Imported from the Orange Free State. More reliable than the local workers, Pa used to say. Forget his name too. But Tshepo, Tshepo was my friend. My best friend, actually. My only friend back then. That was before I knew the difference. I was very young. But we were very close. Very close. Played together every day.

'I can't remember who took the photo. Another farm kid maybe. I stole – no, I mean, borrowed – Pa's camera. We took other photos on that day. But this is the only one I found among Pa's things after the funeral. I didn't even know Pa had had the film developed, never mind that he kept any of the photos, especially this one – me and Tshepo.'

Bester leaned back, shoulders against the headboard.

'So, ja, I had a black friend when I was a laaitie. But not long after this photo was taken Pa fired Tshepo's father … or maybe he died, I can't remember. Yes, I think Tshepo and his mother left, moved to Soweto maybe. I don't know. Pa was always firing workers, and shouting at them. Always just shouting. But maybe this time it was death. Anyways, Tshepo and his family were gone. Never saw him again. He did come to say goodbye, though, and … jirre, we cried.'

Marie lay back. Otto's eyes drifted and then returned with a shudder and shake of his shoulders, a forced laugh.

'Ja, Marie, perhaps Tshepo's a terrorist now, fighting to take the farm he was kicked off of. Maybe one day I'll be the one to arrest him and lock him up. That would be a story, hey?'

Note No. 2

June 2020
If you ever read this, Vladimir, you will know what I am doing, sitting here in a dark corner of this London pub, shielding my eyes with one hand from the neon glare of the lights over the bar counter. My other hand pens into this notebook that I now call 'The Red Book'. I am deconstructing, comrade. Taking all apart. Reverse-engineering history.

And, in the old movie reel I run over and over in my head, Comrade Vladimir, you are, as usual, seated on the edge of the sofa long discoloured and thread-loosened by similar evening assignations that always end close to dawn. I say 'old', but it is just a year ago – June last year, 2019. It seems all my memories now are seared with age, covered in a grey dust that coagulates between synapses.

Yes, there is perhaps a reason this memory unwinds before me now. I see it all. Your fingers are curled around your whiskey glass on the low table before us, the glass that I seem never to see you lift to your lips, as I scoop up in my hand more ice and drop it tinkling into my glass, now misty from the drink that has been. I look into your eyes that do not leave mine as you recount your tales. It is all so clear, suddenly, your round-cheeked face, with the long jutting chin – the whole shaped like a pear; a pear with drill-bit eyes, ever-sardonic mouth.

I hear Bongi in the open-plan kitchen, around the corner, clinking the instruments of her expertise, the crunch of the pepper grinder, the swish of spice shakers, the smell of fresh-cut garlic, the squeak of the oven knob. My nose anticipates already the grilled chops, lending an edge to our drinking and our conversation.

Bongi always does this when you visit. She knows that I will tire long before you have finished your tales of the corridors of power we both trod. We both know you will out-drink me. And she knows that, for us old revolutionaries, trained by the Russians in the proper art – among other arts – of serious drinking, alcohol must be accompanied by food. Soon she will join us and will argue passionately with you, while I lean back and listen, sipping at my drink far more often than either of you.

But this night is different. Your war stories are not idle. They are the setting of mood, a precursor to something specific. I am not sure how I know this. Perhaps it is your glances towards the wall behind which Bongi prepares our food. Perhaps the thoughtful pauses that do not follow the logic of your storytelling, or the sighs that indicate an anxiety or excitement that is unusual for you. Maybe your even slower-than-usual drinking, or the more intense looking into my eyes as if trying to fathom there whether I am ready for you to get to the point.

I think it is particularly in your choice of stories on this evening. They are not the usual, casual stories, flitting from one to another as the logic of one leads to the next, or the further memory spurred by an interjection. Tonight your tales are not simply the shared memories of the Angolan bush, or the drinking sessions in Kabwata in Lusaka. Nor are they the back-home stories, at the after-tears for a comrade buried, or our usual fare of narrations of the frustrations and obfuscations of governing our partially liberated country and the idiosyncrasies of the ministers and presidents we served. Tonight I can think of only one word for the common thread of your stories: signs. You are talking *The Signs*, although you don't, and you never have, liked that term. Too mystical, you said, for your taste.

Now you are telling once more how the current head of the Service, the oddly named Brixton Mthembu, your successor, was suspected during the struggle days of being a sell-out. Interesting. 'Suspected'? In your previous, more idle iterations of this story he was a 'confirmed' impimpi. And tonight your recounting of this tale has less of the emotion, less of the frustration and sardonicism of previous tellings. It is more 'scientific', more academic, a reminder, perhaps, of the mountains we climbed.

Now the aroma and the sizzling of the chops snake around the corner of the dividing wall, I hear Bongi retrieving plates from the cupboard with the broken hinge and the rattle of cutlery from the stainless steel holder. You, again a little unusually, drain the remains of your drink and reach for the bottle and the jug of water. I am intrigued by your pressed beige chino slacks, which seem never to crease, in spite of your back-and-forth movement on the sofa as you reach for your drink or lean back to continue the conversation, or occasionally cross your legs.

Bongi comes in with a platter in one hand, the meat still whispering off the heat of the oven, and three side plates with precariously balanced crockery in the other. She bends to lower her burden onto the low table in front of us, her skirt of browns, beiges and yellows catching on the side of the sofa where you sit. Her hands released, she quickly smooths down her skirt, acknowledges the smile from you, looks without expression at me, and disappears again.

We both lean forward, help ourselves to chops with our fingers, ignoring, as always, the cutlery. Bongi comes back with paper napkins and a board with thick slices of white bread, which she doesn't allow me. She always makes exceptions for you, Comrade Vladimir; breaks the rules of the house, reverts to the traditional African woman. I confess I like it sometimes, but not as an alternative to the fiercely gender-conscious Bongi, the young, lithe, hot-headed woman I fell despairingly in love with in London – or was it Lusaka? – all those memories ago. Now, in her early sixties, the years kind to her face and eyes, though now spread comfortably around her hips and thighs, she remains in my mind's eye as she's always been – an abstraction and a particularity.

She returns with a chair retrieved from the dining table and we both half-stand to offer help, which she dismisses with a shake of the head and a contrived pout. She helps herself to meat and bread, takes up cutlery, looks at us, and reverts to her hands. You beat me to pouring her a whiskey, which, like you, she dashes with water.

The perceived path of your conversation disappears, interrupted by the demands of meat and perhaps the presence of Bongi, although this has never silenced you before. You speak. To her. 'How's our Service?'

'It's okay, DG. Still the same. Same problems. Same shenanigans. But okay. We move along. Everyone's waiting for Sandile to make his moves. God knows we need some change.'

Your smile stretches a few millimetres beyond sardonicism. 'Oh, I almost forgot. I see Nadine has joined. Like mother like daughter?'

'And father,' I object.

'Hey, Jerry, you and I are long gone from the Service. Old furniture.'

'How do you know?' Bongi wipes a hand on a napkin.

'I saw her. A few days ago. At the academy. I was giving "my talk".' You gesture the quotations marks on either side of your head with a half-eaten chop still in your right hand and the whiskey glass in the other.

I take a chop out of my mouth. 'Oh … The Talk. Did anyone learn anything?'

'Actually, she did. Nadine. She gave the only sensible answer to a question I asked.'

Bongi giggles, the other thing about her that has not aged. I lift my glass to the air in front of us and you and she clink with me. 'Okay, like father like daughter too.' We clink again.

And now we talk again, more idly, as before, between the chewing and the sipping and the stretching for another chop and another slice of bread. We talk about the new president and the new cabinet – the new party leadership. We wonder whether it will make any difference to the fortunes of the country with which all three of our lives are so complexly interwoven. Bongi is optimistic. You are not quite there yet, but hopeful. I am quiet as usual, reserving my opinion until, perhaps, the whiskey gives cause.

We push our plates away. You thank Bongi in the language you share. She leans back in the dining chair, glass in both hands held by still dainty fingers. You fall back into the sofa, wiping your mouth and hands with a napkin that you then scrunch up and toss (accurately) back to your abandoned plate. I offer more whiskey. You decline with your hand out like a traffic cop.

'Sisi, I'm sorry. I need to speak to Jerry.'

Bongi's brow furrows. She looks at me. I shrug, looking back at you and then back to her. This has never happened before. Bongi has never been excluded from our drinking and gossiping sessions, at least not since we worked together, when you sometimes dropped in on your way home from the office to conclude a discussion we had not been able to finish at work.

'No problem, DG. I've got some admin to do. I'll go sit in the study.' She rises, leaves her unfinished glass on the table before us, perhaps as a reminder that her place remains here with us, or as an act of protest.

'What's up, Vladimir? It's a long time since we've had secrets from Bongi.'

'Hey, Jerry, it's a long time since we've had secrets full stop, except for the ones we carry to the grave.'

You lean forward, push your also unemptied glass away to rest close to Bongi's. I light a cigarette and stand up to slide open the French doors behind me. You smile and take a cigar from the breast pocket of your long-sleeved guayabera, a cigar clipper and reach for my lighter. The silence as I wait for you to finally get the end of your cigar glowing allows the sound of Bongi's fingers clicking on the keyboard to drift into the room.

'You remember *The List*, Comrade Jerry?'

'The list? What list?'

'*The List*. The one the boers are said to have given Madiba when he became president.'

'That list. *The List*. The one with the supposed names of boer agents in the ANC?'

'Yes, Jerry. That list.'

'Does it really exist? Why's it coming up now? Twenty-five years later?'

'Wait, Jerry. Let me go back.'

Your cigar has gone out. You flick at the lighter, which always ignites first time for you, and suck in your cheeks heavily as you goad the cigar back to a glowing end. 'I was called this week by the Minister.'

'Which minister?'

'Sandile. He called me in the middle of my lecture. I had to leave the lecture and make my way from Mpumalanga to Cape Town.'

'Don't tell me he wants you back, to take over the Service again – from the sell-out.'

'Ha! Actually, that's what I thought when he called.'

And why are you telling me this, I ask myself. Please don't tell me he wants me back, I think. I'm too old for this shit.

'He wants me to set up a task team. You were the first name I gave him.'

'A task team? For what?'

'Wait, Jerry, let me finish. You're getting like Bongi now.'

'You don't mind when she interrupts you.'

'Well, she's prettier than you.'

'Hah! Okay, chief. Carry on.'

And so you do, Comrade Vladimir – carry on. For three hours we talk, or you do, mostly. The light from the waning Highveld dusk long gone and the sounds of the traffic in the distant street slowly dying. Bongi comes back once to offer coffee. You ask for a glass of ice water. I pour myself another whiskey. Finally she comes back again to wish us goodnight, kissing me on the bald patch at the top of my head, which she knows I hate, and takes your hand with her left hand touched to her right forearm and does the little bending of the knees that she does only for you now, as she had used to do for her late father (and occasionally as a sarcastic gesture to me when we made up after an argument).

You know, Vladimir, that my memory is not good – certainly not as good as yours. I retain gist. I lose detail. Not a good trait for an intelligence officer, I suppose. But now, in this June of 2020, moved from the pub back to this dank Kilburn flat, feeding coins into the old-fashioned electricity meter, passion and panic inject sparks into dormant neurons. I remember our conversation on that June evening almost word for word.

'The Minister said the president is concerned, Jerry.'

'About?'

'About old apartheid networks persisting in the party and government.'

'Indeed? He's concerned now? We raised those concerns in the late nineties and beyond.'

'I know.'

'And we were told then that we were being too conspiratorial, blaming our own weaknesses on an imagined enemy.'

'Yes, Jerry, I know. And there was truth in that. We had some serious weaknesses. But we also need to think about who was telling us that?'

'Meaning?'

'Meaning that perhaps it was largely the purveyors of our weaknesses who were telling us that; diverting our attention, maybe.'

You relight the stub of your Cohiba with hardly any space left for your fingers to hold it. You were never one to waste a good Cuban.

'We said that too at the time.'

'I know, Jerry. I know. Stop being triumphalist. Let me finish.'

I pour another whiskey and take the empty bottle to the kitchen and return with another. But I am not feeling drunk, just argumentative. I return to my armchair, fall back into it and gesture to you to continue.

'The president is determined, with the support of a good number of comrades in the NEC and the new cabinet, to lead a decisive turnaround. He wants to deal with corruption, state capture and the excessive materialism that goes with it, service delivery failures and a much more radical transformation of the economy.'

'As was decided at every ANC conference for the last quarter-century.'

'Yes, Jerry, but it seems serious this time.'

'Why this time? What makes this time any different?'

'Sandile says there'll be announcements soon.'

'Well, that's good to know. But will he succeed?'

'Exactly, Jerry. That's the point. The chief is concerned about the effect of the old networks on our ability to implement our programmes. He wants to know which of the people we rely on in the party and government have other masters.'

'*The Signs.*'

You look at me with that look of generosity that I shall always remember you by. Your hand goes out to the whiskey bottle, but changes its mind, and you fall back onto the sofa, leaning forward quickly again to scrunch the tiny stub of your cigar into the saucer Bongi has provided as an ashtray. 'Whatever, Comrade Jerry. Whatever. And we have been tasked to investigate, as a special task team, small and very secretive.' You sigh.

'And the list?'

'Huh?'

'*The List.* You started off by talking about Madiba's list.'

'Yes, we start there. But you know very well we can't rely on it. It's probable that some if not all of the names on it were put there by the boers to sow division and distrust. But that in itself might give us an idea, a starting point. It is likely that we are looking for people who are not on the list.'

And so, Comrade Vladimir, I accept the task. Because it comes from you. Because I trust Sandile. Because I give the president the benefit of the doubt. And because it is a vindication of my suspicions since 1994, perhaps even further back, when we discussed the future in Green House as the negotiations with the regime progressed and our minds lurched towards the future.

We – the two of us – discuss the task team, the methods we will use, our future communications and precautions, and I accompany you to the front door, out to the driveway and open the gate for you as you slip into the small-hour streets. I go back inside and slip into bed beside Bongi, who stirs, and moulds herself to my back, while I wonder how I am going to deal with the fact that I once more have a secret to keep from her.

Chapter 9

June 2019
'How's your family member, Mr Masilela?'

Marlena Botes smiled at Masilela, taking his overnight bag from him despite his protest, with a slight brush of his hand. She matched her pace to his as they made their way through the airport concourse. He held onto his soft leather document bag, moving it from his left to his right hand on the other side from where she walked. He took in the African motif of the Kruger-Mpumalanga International Airport with its browns and creams and beiges. He glanced up at the high, dark wood-beamed ceiling and down at the smooth-tiled orange-brown floor with the darker dividing patterns. He breathed the smell of wood and thatch mingling with the perfumes and deodorants of passing passengers. He heard the sounds of feet on tile, hushed and hurried voices, disturbed now and then by the tinny tannoy announcements of the comings and goings from and to other places.

He turned to Marlena. 'Family member?'

'Yes, the accident.'

'The accident? Oh yes, thank you for asking, Marlena. He'll be okay. Mostly broken bones. He's still in hospital. My nephew actually. My sister's son.'

'I'm sorry to hear that. I'm glad he's going to be okay.'

She placed her hand on Masilela's elbow to guide him toward the exit. They passed through the doors and out under the high thatched overhang with its wooden beams and struts, subtly reflecting in their grain the low but still warm winter sun. She ushered him towards the parking lot and her compact, fuel-cell-powered car. Having stowed his overnight bag in the boot, she offered to take his document bag, but he switched it to his other hand and moved to the front passenger door, climbed in and wedged the bag between his feet. As she turned her head to reverse, he watched her face. Her skin was still smooth for her age. She must be in her late forties, he thought, revising his initial estimate. Green eyes. Hair unusually dark, with perfect streaks of grey he was not sure whether nature or art had put there. A long thin neck, inviting the eyes to the shoulders hidden beneath a light, cream-coloured jersey.

She finished her reverse manoeuvre, and turned her head back to the front, catching his eyes on her. 'I've booked you into a lodge, DG. It's very comfortable. I'm afraid the VIP accommodation on campus is occupied. Mr Mthembu is here to meet management and the new intake. You can check in after the lecture, if you like.'

'That will be fine, Marlena. Thanks.'

'I was wondering, DG.' She placed her hand on his lower arm. 'I was wondering if you'd like for us to have dinner together tonight, after the lecture.' She removed the hand.

Her eyes faced ahead, but there was a hint on the side of her face of a dimple brought on by a smile.

'Thank you, Marlena. That is thoughtful of you. Let's see how things pan out this evening.'

There were plenty of his old colleagues working at the academy with whom he could share a drink and some gossip this evening. But Mthembu was here and he needed to avoid time with him. Apart from anything else, there was always an awkwardness between a predecessor and his successor.

They fell into silence for the twenty-kilometre drive north, passed White River and then the left turn west onto the road, still being tarred, towards the new satellite campus of the intelligence service's training academy. The campus had been decided on, land acquired and the complex designed under Masilela's watch, a special facility for the training of new recruits, to keep them away from older, perhaps compromised, hands. One of his last acts before retirement had been to come out here to celebrate the laying of the foundations. Now, as they entered the gates, the security guards dressed in smart new uniforms hoisted the boom with a smile and a salute of recognition. He marvelled again at the structures that had been no more than drawings on an architect's sheet just a few years ago, when they had designed, redesigned, tweaked and scrunched this campus into something both functional and pleasing to the eye. Perhaps an architect, or a builder, would have been a better profession, he thought, as the spreading buildings of the campus came into view ... trimmed thatched roofs, rough-hewn beams and pillars of local wood, stone paving and stone walls.

Marlena eased the silent car backward into the bay in the VIP parking area in front of the main administration building. He wondered if the reverse parking was a hangover from her days in the field, always ready for a quick getaway; he assumed she must have spent time in the field perhaps even when he was her target or in more recent democratic days. He noted again the impressive entrance to the building and wondered suddenly at its similarity to the entrance at the airport they'd just left.

'Your lecture is in an hour, DG. Did you eat on the plane or shall I organise something? Do you want to perhaps meet with the principal before your talk, or the DG?'

'I'm fine, Marlena, thanks. I'd just like some coffee. I want to freshen up my notes for the lecture. I can sit in the lounge until then. I can greet later.'

In the lounge, the mug of coffee on the low table before him, Masilela did not work on refreshing his lecture notes. He was not one, anyway, for copious preparation for his talks. Not here at the academy, or his pep talks to his officers in his days in the service, or his fiery political speeches in the days of exile and after. He spoke off the cuff. More engaging. More dialectical. And, in that way, he often surprised himself at the ability of his brain to bring forth ideas and phrasing drawn somehow from aeons of experience and observation.

But he did have a few pages of notes for his lecture, which he now took from his bag and placed on the table in front of him. The pages consisted of single circled words with question marks beside them scrawled at different angles across the paper: *Intelligence? Secrets? Enemies? Power? Insights? Uniqueness? Tools? Priorities? Constitution? Laws? Rules?* And, interspersed between these scribblings, there were more conventional paragraphs in his meticulous handwriting – quotations copied from some of his favourite thinkers. His all-time favourite was Sun Tzu and his *Art of War*. He also liked to quote his namesake – Lenin – but, depending on his audience, he would not attribute such quotations, simply introducing them with a *someone once said*.

Before he reached into his briefcase to pull out another document, he checked the room to confirm he was alone. The paper was a list of names with, here and there, a short paragraph under a few of the entries. With pen in hand and highlighter between his teeth, he worked through the list, placing red crosses next to some names as a preliminary elimination of those no longer among the living. For others, though, whose reach might extend beyond the grave, he took the highlighter from his mouth and marked them along with the red cross. Done, he turned back to the first page and this time swiped the yellow highlighter across a selection of names and, for a few, added a red-penned asterisk. Every now and then he sipped at his coffee, ran a hand over his scalp, and, on the back of his lecture notes, made an obscure note to himself.

A soft hand touched his shoulder. Immediately, he turned the document face down and placed it on his lap.

'It's time, DG.'

'Thanks, Marlena. Sorry, I was deep in thought.'

'Still got secrets, DG?'

'Sorry?'

'You turned your document over when I came over.'

'Oh that? No. Old habits, Marlena. Ancient instincts. I was going over notes from the talk I gave to management when I started as DG. I thought I could use some of it today.' He gathered his papers together and slipped them into the briefcase. 'Let's go.'

She escorted him to the lecture theatre, where she pushed open the swing doors to let him through, then quickly stepped past to lead the way down to the front. After some hesitation, the students stood, some turning and nodding to him. Marlena introduced and welcomed him, and moved off to her seat in a row near the back.

'Good afternoon, young intelligence officers. I'm back.' He took off his glasses and wiped them on the hem of his guayabera and squinted around the room. 'Again, apologies for my hasty departure last time.'

He reached into his bag and ruffled his notes on the lectern. 'My nephew is fine, by the way.' Puzzled faces looked back at him. 'My nephew, who was in the accident that called me away last time. Well, he's not fine, but he's out of danger.'

The young man with the dreadlocks murmured: 'That's good, chief.'

'Okay. Before I beat a hasty retreat last time I left you with some questions to discuss. Did you discuss them?'

Fidgeting, heads turned to look at one another.

'Yes, they did, sir.' Marlena spoke from her seat. She smiled a private smile.

'Good. Who's going to report back, then?'

Dreadlocks eventually broke through the resumption of fidgeting. 'I will, chief.'

'Good. Okay. Sukuma, ndoda.'

Dreadlocks stood, gathered the locks tied into a thick ponytail at the back of his head, and moved them to one side over his left shoulder. He began to speak, initially with the assumed confidence of arrogance, then more falteringly, turning every now and then to his classmates for affirmation, or referring to his notebook in which, as far as Masilela could see, there were no notes.

Masilela's mind wandered. He caught words and phrases, much like the question-marked words in his sparse lecture notes: *secrets, agents, tasking, spying*. But in his head other words were drifting by, names from a list and names for further consideration, a potage of strategies and methodologies skimming across his brain like pebbles on a smooth lake, hardly creating ripples until they plopped back down, submerged. And then a small explosion of noise as the doors at the back of the lecture theatre swung open.

A man and a woman entered. The woman was Dineo, principal of the academy, an old friend and comrade. They had done their intelligence training together in Moscow a long time back. He had appointed her to head the academy. The man he recognised with less pleasure. His youthful face contradicted the tinges of grey in close-cropped, tight-curled hair, small, ever-darting eyes, dressed (inappropriately) in a dark suit with navy blue tie and a matching handkerchief protruding from his breast pocket.

Masilela clapped his hands. 'Stand up, students. Do you not recognise your director-general?'

Marlena was the first to get to her feet. The rest of the class stood with some lethargy. Mthembu indicated that the lecture should continue. He and the principal slipped into the back row.

'Right. Welcome, director-general. Welcome, principal. We've just started. This young man was reporting back on a task I gave the class last time I was here.'

'I was finished, chief.'

'You were? Was that all?'

'Yes, chief.'

'Okay. Anyone want to add anything?'

Nadine Whitehead put up her hand, more confidently than the last time.

'Yes, young lady. Please go ahead.'

He smiled at her, perhaps too warmly. He looked over at the director-general. He would certainly know of Masilela's connection with the young woman, but the man was whispering to the principal. Instead of drawing him to her words, the sound of Nadine's voice triggered a reminder of his recent evening with Jeremy and Bongi and the troubling choices he and Jeremy would have to make. The sudden silence disturbed him.

'I'm done, sir.'

'Good. Good, ntombazana. Thank you. Anyone else want to add?'

The students looked at him blankly. The director-general stared at him with narrowed eyes and that signature twist of the right side of his mouth.

'No? Okay. Good.' Masilela shuffled his notes and wiped his spectacles again.

'We talked last time, and you discussed after I left, the question of enemies and adversaries, about legitimate and illegitimate targets for intelligence-gathering, about collecting secrets and so on. I want now to talk a bit about intelligence as insight. That's a good word: "insight". Seeing into things. Seeing behind the obvious, the apparent.'

Masilela spoke at length, but at some distance from this time and place, the words escaping from his mouth as though from a digital recorder lodged somewhere in his head, while the fleshy part of his brain focused on other, more urgent things. This absence of engagement was unlike him, but still the digital device droned on.

He spoke of the need for the intelligence service to have insight, beyond the everyday, to understand what it was that made the social conglomerations of the human species tick, the causality of human interaction and the evolution of human society. Jeremy had liked to tease him: 'You mean, DG, we need an ideology.' He would laugh, a glint in his eyes: 'Yes, comrade, if by that you mean a system of ideas.'

He came back from his reverie into this auditorium.

'You see, young officers of our democratic intelligence service, when you look around at our country, at some of the strange things that have happened – are still happening – it may not be enough to go out there and try to gather secrets.'

He looked up at them and realised only then that he had been speaking with his eyes cast down to his notes. He saw Marlena hold up her arm with the face of her watch pointed at him. He took his phone out of the pocket of his guayabera to check the time and quickly put it back when he realised his mistake – he was not supposed to bring his phone into the lecture room; all signalling devices were banned from the meeting rooms of the Service. The students fidgeted.

'I see time's up. Sorry about that. I have left no time for questions or discussion. Perhaps next time.'

He nodded at the students, looked at Mthembu, and spoke with a tinge of sarcasm, drawing on an old deference from his days in MK: 'Permission to conclude the lecture, director-general?'

Mthembu made a flourish with his right hand, his face expressionless. Masilela packed up his notes, slipped them into his bag and, with a wave of his hand to the students, walked to the back of the room to greet Mthembu and Dineo. Marlena rose as he passed and followed behind him. Mthembu pointed to the door, dismissing Dineo with a nod, motioned to Marlena to wait behind and led Masilela out into the courtyard.

'How are you, Vladimir?'

'Good, thank you, DG. And you?'

'Ah, I'm surviving. Things are tough. This new president is putting on a lot of pressure.'

'Apparently. He's got big ideas, I hear.'

'Indeed. So, my brother, I see you haven't shaken off your Marxism.'

'My Marxism? You mean my talk? Didn't mention Marx once. And didn't know Marxism was something that needed to be shaken off, like dust?'

'No, no, Masilela. No need to be defensive. Just not sure if your ideas are appropriate in this day and age.'

'An understanding, DG, of what makes society tick is always appropriate.'

'Yes, yes. Of course.' Mthembu took Masilela by the upper arm and guided him further into the courtyard. 'I believe you had a meeting with my minister.'

Masilela noted the possessive pronoun. Mthembu was not appointed by Sandile; he had been inherited by the minister. He did not have the same background as Masilela, Ndaba and others. He had not gone into exile. He had been an activist inside the country during the days of struggle, with a reputation for fiery and sometimes provocative activism. In 1994 he was drawn by the ANC into the process of creating the new intelligence services and held a middle management position in the service for a few years until he left to take up a post in a state-owned company. He was parachuted into the top position in the Service by the previous president after Masilela's retirement. His appointment had not been popular, but perhaps the president thought he needed a manager with corporate experience at the head of his intelligence department.

'A meeting? No, it wasn't a meeting. I was in Cape Town on other business and I popped in to greet and to congratulate him on his appointment.'

'I didn't know you were in business now.'

'No, no, not that kind of business. It was family business.'

'Family? You mean the Party? Are you still a member of the Communist Party?'

'Ha! Actually, I meant my personal family. My nephew was in a car accident and I had to go down to brief my sister who was tied up with the parliamentary session. And, yes, I am still a member of the Party. Is that a problem?'

'It's a free country, my brother. And what did he say?'

'Who?'

'The minister.'

'No, nothing. Idle chatter. Told me the president has some radical ideas, but said I must wait to find out what.'

'He didn't try to recruit you? To bring you back?'

Masilela's mouth took a shape closer to a grimace than a smile. He looked straight into the director-general's eyes. 'No, not at all, DG. We didn't discuss the Service at all. Even if he had tried to bring me back, I would have refused. I've done my bit. It's time for the younger generation.' The grimace softened to a smile.

Students thronged past them and Marlena hovered at a respectful distance. Mthembu adjusted the handkerchief in his breast pocket, looked quizzically at Masilela, took his phone out of his shirt pocket, put it back.

'You want to join us for a drink and maybe a meal later? We can chat some more.'

'Thanks, DG. Actually, I'm really tired. The travelling, the family issues. Many late nights. I think I'll just go to my hotel, eat, and read for a bit.'

'Okay, Masilela. That's fine. We can meet for a chat in Pretoria some time.'

As Mthembu strode off, Masilela noticed two bodyguards in dark suits, standing a few metres away, step up to accompany their charge. Unnecessary here, thought Masilela. He had only used his obligatory bodyguards as drivers, allowing him to prepare for meetings in the back seat of the car. He dismissed them on evenings, weekends and holidays.

Marlena approached, touched his elbow. 'You staying, DG? Or do you want to check in?'

Masilela turned, placed his hand on her back and guided her towards the parking lot. 'No, let's get out of here, Marlena.'

In the car, after they had passed through the security gates and negotiated the half-tarred road, she spoke. 'You seemed distracted today, DG …'

'Distracted?'

'In the lecture.'

'Was I? I guess I was. Sorry about that. My mind was elsewhere.'

'Where?'

'At home.'

'Love matters, DG?'

'I'm afraid there's no love in my home, Marlena. I'm divorced. Well, there are my kids, of course … every alternate week, but they might be getting too old to love their daddy.'

He noticed the left dimple appear again.

They turned onto a dirt road through dense thorn-scrub, denuded acacia trees, with some dominating oaks and occasional outcrops of rock. He asked permission to open the window and breathed in the bush, the smell that reminded him of the comforting wildness of Angola, individual odours indiscernible except for the dust of the road and the faint scent of Marlena's perfume. They rounded a bend and came to a boom gate with rolling manicured lawns beyond. A guard in a khaki uniform came out of a gatehouse, saluted them and, in reply to Marlena's whisper, made a tick on a clipboarded list and hoisted the boom.

They drove on for some distance, still along a winding cobblestone driveway, the rumbling effect of which reminded him of an ancient European city somewhere in the recesses of his traveller's memory. To his left dense thorn bush in which he caught a glimpse now and again of scuttling rodents, and to the right the lawns in arrogant protest against the surrounding bush, with thatch, timber and stone chalets hinting uncomfortably of the architecture of the academy they'd just left.

'It was built in the seventies.' She turned to him with an almost coy smile.

'Really? It looks more recent. A bit like the academy actually.'

'No, it's old. One of the first lodges built around here, outside of the Kruger Park. They've probably upgraded it a few times, but owned by the same family that built it. I believe the original owner was a retired policeman, Special Branch, actually.'

'Oh, really? Interesting. Must have got a really good pension.'

She either missed the sarcasm or ignored it as she steered the car into a parking space outside a large building with a wooden sign with 'Reception' burned into it. She retrieved his suitcase from the boot and carried it into the building, ignoring the obsequious porter. Masilela followed and stood back as she checked him in. Marlena took the key from the receptionist, an old-fashioned Yale key on a carved ivory key holder, and motioned to him to follow her out into the gardens and along a stone pathway bordered by blackened wooden logs. She headed to one of the chalets, dragging his wheeled suitcase behind her.

When they reached his chalet, she, with apparent familiarity, unlocked the door and wheeled his suitcase inside. He took in the room: its dark wooden furniture, the African mask on the wall, the ochre-and-beige bedspread, the round wooden table near the sliding doors into the garden beyond. He walked past her and peered into the bathroom, all marble and beige porcelain, wooden towel racks and a large Jacuzzi. When he turned back into the room, she was standing by the bed.

'Do you want me to unpack for you, DG?'

'No, no, Marlena. That's not necessary. I'm a big boy and anyway it's only one night. Not worth unpacking.'

She didn't move from beside the bed. He looked at her. She smiled without embarrassment, both dimples now visible. 'Do you want some time to freshen up, DG? Would you like to go to the bar for a drink, or perhaps dinner?'

'Both, Marlena. Actually, all three. Just a few minutes to freshen up, as you call it, and then a drink and dinner.'

She smiled again, ran a hand through her hair and then both hands down the sides of her skirt. 'Okay, DG. Shall we meet in the bar in, say, fifteen minutes? It's on this side of the reception building, next to the pool.'

'Sounds good. See you in fifteen.'

He watched her as she left via the sliding doors into the garden, then turned back to the room, opened his suitcase, and took his toiletry bag. In the bathroom, he rinsed his mouth with mouthwash, massaged lotion into his face and sprayed cologne onto either side of his neck.

Back in the room, he extracted the folder from his briefcase, cast his eyes once more down the list and made some mental notes. He searched for the room safe, found it behind the sliding, slotted wooden cupboard doors. It was the new type of safe that could only be locked and reopened with the electronic national identity card or an e-passport and a pin number. He placed the folder and a notebook into the safe and locked it, using his daughter's birthdate in reverse for the pin.

※

'You all fresh, DG?'

He joined her at the high, round table near the log fire and slipped onto the stool opposite her.

'Yes, thank you, Marlena. All fresh.'

She waved her hand at the waiter. 'What would you like to drink, DG?'

'Whiskey, please. Double Glenfiddich, on the rocks. Water on the side. And perhaps you should stop calling me "DG". We are off duty, so to speak.'

She frowned at the lack of attention from the waiter, and got up to go to the bar. He scanned the room. It was almost empty. A group of four Afrikaner farmer types at a table in a far corner, a black couple – he much older than her – on stools at the bar, and three youthful black men at a low table across the room, all in suits.

Marlena returned with two tumblers of whiskey and a bottle of still water. 'What should I call you?'

'Pardon?'

'You said we're off duty.'

'Oh? Yebo. My name is Vladimir.'

'Not sure I can call you that.'

'Why not?'

'Don't you have a South African name?'

'Yes. Vladimir.'

'That's not South African.'

'It is now, Marlena.'

'I think I'll stick with DG – in the most off-duty sense, of course.'

He looked hard at her. She looked back, her lips pressed tightly together, though still with a ghost of a smile, her eyes were all buried laughter.

'Why don't you try "Vlad" then?'

'Nope. I'm going to stick with "DG". It's the name I have in my head when I think about you. It's got nothing to do with your title – ex-title – any more.'

'You think about me?'

'I do. Sometimes.'

Masilela ran his hand over his scalp. He put his glass down, placing it precisely on the wet circle left on the table. He looked around the room and then back at her. 'Marlena, tell me, are you trying to seduce me?'

She laughed with no embarrassment. She rested the rim of her glass just below her lips.

'Do you want to be seduced, DG?'

'Ha! That's unfair.'

'Well, your question was blunt.'

'Okay. Well, I am, for the moment, single. You're an attractive woman. And, unless I am hallucinating, I have been getting signals from you. Am I hallucinating? That would be very embarrassing.'

Masilela kissed her on the brow, the eyes, the lips, the neck. He licked the sweat from his own lips as he lay back, lifting her head gently with his left arm and resting it in the crook of his right. She bit his ear lobe.

'You hungry now, DG?'

He pulled a face. 'You know what I need now? A big plate of chips and a bottle of wine.'

She removed her head from his arm and leaned over to the phone next to the bed. He slid out of bed and went to the bathroom to dispose of the condom now clinging precariously to the tip of his deflated penis. He looked at himself in the bathroom mirror and ran the hot-water tap until the water was warm, took the neatly rolled-up facecloth from its perch on the marble shelf above the basin, wet it and wiped his groin. The warm water felt good. He frowned at himself and went back to the room. She was half-sitting in the bed, back propped up against the bulky cushions, head back on the heavy oak headboard. He slid back into bed and propped himself up next to her. She leaned her head on his shoulder.

'Okay, Marlena, now that I know you, in the biblical sense, tell me about yourself.'

'What do you want to know, DG?'

'Oh, where you're from. When did you join the Service? Stuff like that.'

She placed her hand on his thigh. 'Oh? Is this about sleeping with the enemy?'

'Are you the enemy?'

'Well? I guess I was. Until '94 that is. But I was still very young.'

'Aha. So did you spy on me?'

'No, DG.' She squeezed his leg hard. 'I joined the Service after 1990, after the ANC was unbanned. I was just a junior analyst.'

'Okay ... So, where are you from? What led you into the dark world of intelligence?'

'Actually, from around here, from what used to be called Nelspruit. How did I get into the dark world? Mmm, I'm a bit embarrassed to tell you.'

'If what we did a while ago didn't embarrass you then nothing should.'

'Ha! Well, if you must know, my father was a policeman ... a security policeman.' She gently stroked his inner thigh. He didn't

She looked at him. He couldn't believe the steadiness of her eyes.
'Yes.'
'Yes? I am hallucinating.'
'Yes, DG. I do find you attractive. Yes, I think I may be trying to seduce you, as you call it.'
'Why?'
'Why?'
'Why do you find me attractive?'
'Well, DG, you're very intelligent. Not bad looking. And you have an aura about you.'
'An aura?'
'Yes.'
'Power?'
'Huh?'
He held the glass against his right cheek, glowing from the warmth of the log fire. 'Marlena, forgive my forthrightness.'
'Sure.'
'When I was a "real" DG …' He gestured the quote marks. 'When I was a real DG, I had no shortage of women attracted to me because of my status and the power they thought I wielded.'
'Lucky you!' She grimaced.
'No, no … on the contrary. Sure, I confess I took advantage sometimes. But there's no chance of a real relationship with a woman who is with you because of your status, your power.'
'You're looking for a real relationship here, DG?' She gestured between them.
'Are you?'
'No, DG. I'm married.'
He reached for his glass but then put it down again without drinking.
'You're married? Then why the seduction?'
'Don't ask, DG. Just enjoy. You hungry?'
'I'm not sure. I think I may have lost my appetite.'
'Which appetite?'
'For food.'
'Let's go then.'

༒

Masilela kissed her on the brow, the eyes, the lips, the neck. He licked the sweat from his own lips as he lay back, lifting her head gently with his left arm and resting it in the crook of his right. She bit his ear lobe.

'You hungry now, DG?'

He pulled a face. 'You know what I need now? A big plate of chips and a bottle of wine.'

She removed her head from his arm and leaned over to the phone next to the bed. He slid out of bed and went to the bathroom to dispose of the condom now clinging precariously to the tip of his deflated penis. He looked at himself in the bathroom mirror and ran the hot-water tap until the water was warm, took the neatly rolled-up facecloth from its perch on the marble shelf above the basin, wet it and wiped his groin. The warm water felt good. He frowned at himself and went back to the room. She was half-sitting in the bed, back propped up against the bulky cushions, head back on the heavy oak headboard. He slid back into bed and propped himself up next to her. She leaned her head on his shoulder.

'Okay, Marlena, now that I know you, in the biblical sense, tell me about yourself.'

'What do you want to know, DG?'

'Oh, where you're from. When did you join the Service? Stuff like that.'

She placed her hand on his thigh. 'Oh? Is this about sleeping with the enemy?'

'Are you the enemy?'

'Well? I guess I was. Until '94 that is. But I was still very young.'

'Aha. So did you spy on me?'

'No, DG.' She squeezed his leg hard. 'I joined the Service after 1990, after the ANC was unbanned. I was just a junior analyst.'

'Okay ... So, where are you from? What led you into the dark world of intelligence?'

'Actually, from around here, from what used to be called Nelspruit. How did I get into the dark world? Mmm, I'm a bit embarrassed to tell you.'

'If what we did a while ago didn't embarrass you then nothing should.'

'Ha! Well, if you must know, my father was a policeman ... a security policeman.' She gently stroked his inner thigh. He didn't

'Yes, but from the intelligence you could have gauged the level of access.'

'Do we have to have this conversation, DG?'

'Why?'

'It feels uncomfortable. Those years are long gone. It's close to thirty years ago.'

'I know. It's just interest. It doesn't matter now. Does it?'

'Maybe not. All I can tell you is that we were getting intelligence in the early nineties about the ANC's negotiating positions that must have come right from the top – at the Groote Schuur negotiations, the Pretoria round and all the way through CODESA I and II.'

'Really? Then why did you guys do so badly in the negotiations?'

'We guys?'

'Sorry. The apartheid government.'

'Did they?'

'Did they what?'

'Do so badly.'

'What do you mean?'

He held his empty glass out to her. She reached for the bottle, her right breast emerging briefly from the folds of the duvet.

'I mean, look at the ANC revolutionary policies during the war years and look at South Africa now.'

'Meaning?'

'Let me tell you something, DG, but it's between us, okay?'

He wiped his fingers on the napkin on the tray, slipped his hand under the duvet and squeezed her thigh just below the crotch. She smiled and pouted.

'Okay, okay. My lips are sealed. Anyway, what difference does it make now?'

'My father, he had a friend – a colleague – who worked in some sort of special unit of the Security Police in Pretoria, although, if I remember, he was from around here.'

'Yes?'

'Yes. Well, anyway, I remember one evening. My father was, as usual, a bit tipsy from his after-work brandy and Coke. He and my mother and my elder brother got into a discussion about politics. I was just a bystander. I didn't understand politics then. Actually, I don't understand it now.' She laughed, a sardonic laugh. 'Anyway, they were talking about the possibility of negotiating with the ANC, I think. Something like that. I remember my father saying that this friend of his told him that, even if the ANC comes into the government, he had plenty of ANC people at the top who would do his bidding – something along those lines. I only remember because I thought, at the time, that it was mysterious and impressive.'

'Oh yeah? And who was this friend of your father?'

'Jesus, DG! Is this an interrogation? Is this why you slept with me?'

'Don't be silly, Marlena. I slept with you because you're beautiful and sexy. And very intriguing. And, anyway, it's you who seduced me. It's purely historical interest. I'm not in intelligence any more. Just interested to know if we had information about this stuff during the exile days.'

'Well, I'm not sure. I know this guy used to come to our place sometimes when he was in the Eastern Transvaal. My father always used to make me address his friends formally, as Mister, Meneer. Let me think. Meneer … something with a 'B' … Bekker? No. I'm not sure. Maybe, Bester. Meneer … Bester! Ja, Bester! That's it, I think. Meneer Bester. Or, Bekker? I don't know.'

Masilela withdrew his hand from her thigh.

'Actually, DG, come to think of it, I think my father told me this Bester-or-Bekker guy had later joined NIS. I think so, but I certainly never met him in NIS.'

They ate in silence for a while before she, gingerly, reached for his crotch. He hardened immediately. Again he slipped his hands under the duvet, touched her until she was wet and then, without the condom, entered her. He moved furiously, hardly noticing the epithets in his head that drove him. This time he didn't wait for her to climax. He grunted furiously when he reached his and rolled off her.

Chapter 10

June 2019
The teenaged Rosa Masilela entered with a tray of glasses, followed by her younger brother, Nikolai, with a platter of crisps, peanuts and biltong. They placed their wares on the low glass-topped table in the middle of the room, where their father and five other old men were seated. Rosa went over to the bar, returning with whiskey, a bottle of red tucked under her arm and an ice bucket. She placed them in the centre of the table, made a gesture resembling a curtsy, grabbed Nikolai by the arm and moved backwards with him out of the room, smirking at her father.

Whitehead was the first to extricate himself from his armchair, kneel on the floor and hobble on his knees towards the table to pour himself a whiskey on the rocks, then hobble back and settle into his chair. The other four followed suit, without the hobbling. Masilela grunted as he opened the wine between his legs.

'Comrades!'

It took a moment for the chatter to subside.

'Comrades, I've briefed each of you about why we are here. I know there's no need to repeat it, but I will anyway. This discussion is between us and us only. No wives, girlfriends, friends, comrades – nobody – should know about this. I mean this very seriously. I know this is not the first time all of you have heard this. But this time it is life or death. Understood?'

The gathering lifted their glasses in acknowledgment.

'What we've been asked to do is historic, unprecedented. Most of you will know that it's nothing new, but when we've tried to do this kind of investigation in the past we were shackled by the realities of post-apartheid exigencies.'

'Comrade Vladimir, talk English, please.'

Masilela laughed. 'Don't play, Vhonani. You know what I mean.

Our attempts to uncover the remnants of the old order in the new were obstructed because we did not know who was old and who was new. Now it's come to a head. We can't trust anyone outside this room, except those we agree to trust.'

There was a shuffling of feet, a simultaneous reach for glasses.

'But, Comrade Vladimir, we are so few. We are dealing with serious stuff here. We don't know who to trust, where to start.'

'Comrade Vhonani, I know that. But this is our last chance to clear the decks. We are going to tackle this historically. We are going to look first at who came under suspicion during the struggle. Perhaps even those who didn't at the time, and look at where they are now.'

Whitehead stood with his glass, moved over to the bar, and spoke over the back of Masilela. 'And? Are we blaming all our fuck-ups on the old order? Is that it? Are we saying that all of our captured and corrupt comrades were enemy agents?' He raised his glass to the room.

Masilela craned his neck toward Whitehead. 'You and I have had this discussion, Jerry.' He turned to the others. 'Jerry is being provocative, as usual. But he has a point.' Whitehead mock toasted again.

'We are not looking for a third force to explain away all our problems. This is a concrete and scientific investigation into who specifically may be obstructing transformation due to other allegiances.'

'How on earth are we going to do that?'

'Comrade Senzo, we have access to the old ANC security records. That's going to be Jerry's job.'

Whitehead walked over to the table for a refill.

'Vhonani's job will be surveillance. He and I have discussed this, but we're not sure yet who he can bring into his team from the old structures. We're also not sure to what extent we'll need surveillance. But we're keeping all our options open. As we all know, Senzo still works in SIGINT. Only if absolutely necessary, he can organise intercepts for us.'

Senzo scowled, raised his glass, changed his mind and placed it on the table. 'That won't be so easy. There are rules.'

Whitehead grunted from his perch at the bar. 'Fuck the rules! We're already breaking every rule in the book.'

Masilela waved at Jeremy in a gesture of dismissal, leaned forward with his elbows on his thighs and linked the fingers of his hands together. He spoke over his hands, his left thumb and forefinger massaging his chin. 'Jerry may be out of order, but he does have a point. We're operating outside of the controls governing intelligence. Even though we've been tasked by the Minister, we are in effect a private intelligence outfit.'

There was a sudden restlessness, murmuring, grunts of protest. Masilela laughed. 'Yes, yes, I know. Private intelligence has been the bane of our lives since '94. But that's, more or less, what we are. We have no legal mandate. At least we're not a commercial venture. We're not getting paid for our efforts.'

More grumbling. Velaphi, who had been quiet until now, spoke in his lazy, high-pitched voice. 'But what about our expenses? There are going to be operational costs.'

Masilela nodded, his two hands in front of him, elbows still on his thighs. 'Actually, Comrade Velaphi, that's going to be your job.'

'Oh yeah, Vladimir, you want me to rob banks, blow up ATMs?'

'No, Comrade. You're going to be responsible for, among other things, our admin. The money's coming from the Minister. Don't ask where he's getting it, but he wants us to keep strict records of expenditure. He also wants us to keep a record of all operations. That will also be your task – the operational reports. Jerry will handle the intelligence reports.'

Whitehead brandished his glass, came forward for a handful of peanuts. 'Oh yeah? And for what archive will that be?'

Masilela ignored him. He pointed his glass at the man sitting perfectly still opposite him, who got his exile nickname from his light complexion, his scarcity with words and the near inaudibility of his voice when he did speak.

'And Casper will assist me in coordinating investigations.'

They all raised their glasses at Casper. He looked down at his shirt and smoothed it over his large belly. Age had wrinkled and furrowed the skin on his face, jowls hanging down towards his near-hidden chin.

Masilela continued. 'We may all have our specific responsibilities, but we work as a team. We help each other where necessary. We're a small enough team as it is. But there is one more person I would like to bring into the team.'

He looked around as if for prior approval.

'Who's that, chief?'

'Bongi. Jerry's wife.'

'I thought you said no wives or girlfriends.'

'I said no blabbing to wives and girlfriends. You all know that Bongi is still a director in analysis in the Service. She can access records for us. If you're worried about conflict of interest, she will report directly to me.'

All raised their glasses in mock toast, this time to Whitehead who raised his glass back at them and drained it. Before he could get to the table for another refill, Masilela screwed the cap back on the whiskey bottle and pushed the cork back into the bottle of wine. He stood up. 'Okay, let's disperse. In dribs and drabs. Not all at once. We were here for a drinking session of old comrades. Let's not make it look like a meeting has just ended. Jerry, you stay behind for a bit. There's something I need to brief you on.'

Note No. 3

(i do not know what it is about you that closes
and opens;only something in me understands
the voice of your eyes is deeper than all roses)
nobody,not even the rain,has such small hands
– EE CUMMINGS, 'SOMEWHERE I HAVE NEVER TRAVELED'

July 2020
It is perhaps strange, Bongi, how, when the cacophony of life has faded and the rushed sensations of work, the commute, a young daughter demanding attention, the ever-vibrating pocket phone have subsided into the relative silence of age and exile, the memories so long subdued peek out from their slumber and rub their eyes to look upon one once more. Thus it is here in my dark London bedsit, when the memory of how we first met returns to me.

You have forgotten how we met! I know you would say. But that is not true. We have recounted the story so many times to friends, comrades, family, to our daughter, that I know it by rote. That is the problem – by rote, automated recall. But the memory, the picture, the texture, the sounds long gone into hibernation are suddenly freed by this wintry silence.

I feel first your presence sitting, through no intention of either of us, next to me in Conway Hall in London as we wait for Oliver Tambo to address us in January 1981 on the 69th anniversary of the founding of our Movement. I feel your presence first, a warmth, a naturalness, an ease. I notice your slender arm and tiny hand resting on your left thigh alongside me, with the broad bangle with the colours of the earth of our home, blending with the brown sheen of your skin.

The sounds of exile, you said, at first to no one, but then you turned to me. You smiled and nodded your head toward the stage where the ANC choir had just finished. I have always denied that that was the moment I fell in love with you, maintained that love came later, but now the sleepy-eyed memory insists that it was.

Chapter 11

January 1980
In the minibus taxi on his way back from Pretoria to Nelspruit, Amos Vilakazi used the sleeve of his blue denim shirt to wipe the condensation and grime from the window and peered out at the road eastwards and the fields, villages and roadside stalls that flew too quickly past. The taxi driver was singing at the top of his voice to the mbaqanga song on the radio, thumping his hands on the steering wheel and now and again on top of the dashboard for a change of timbre, defying the speed limit and overtaking slower vehicles, paying no heed to the solid white lines on the road, tossing the passengers from side to side. The passengers grumbled, some squealed, grabbing onto the backs of the seats in front of them.

Amos regretted wearing denim and long sleeves in the January heat in this furnace of a taxi with windows that refused to open. Sweat gathered in his armpits, around his neck, trickled down his chest so that he had to rub it every now and then to relieve the itching.

The sweat and discomfort were, however, appropriate reflections of his emotional state. Perhaps it would be better to die on this crazy taxi ride if it meant instant obliteration without terror or pain. His young life – from the moment of his entry into adulthood – had taken a sudden detour, one that he should, if he'd had more time on this planet, have anticipated. His left hand went to his trouser pocket and patted down the wad of R50 notes that made what he thought was too conspicuous a bulge. He wished he had put it in his right-hand pocket so it would sit between him and the body of the taxi.

Two months before, Amos had written his final school exams. Two weeks ago he'd received his results. Five distinctions. It had been only last weekend that his family, together with Baba Dlamini, had organised the celebration in the village. He now replayed in his head the loquacious speeches, the singing and sweaty dancing, and his having been allowed for the first time to drink in front of the adults – although they had, predictably, shooed him away from the whiskey and handed him a beer.

In his speech to the assembly of extended family, friends, villagers and schoolmates, Baba Dlamini had overdone the adjectives: 'extremely intelligent', 'obsessively diligent', 'very very disciplined', 'highly articulate', 'brilliant writer'. Amos had raised the beer bottle to his mouth for each effusion of praise and then looked down at his feet. Baba Dlamini had moved off the accolades, drawn himself up to his full stature, stared with sternness at the gathering and jabbed his fingers at the young people sitting around on boxes, plastic chairs and fallen tree trunks.

'This young man, this son of Vilakazi – as are all of you, at least those who managed to pass your matric – is entering the world of adulthood, is entering a time of life to make choices.'

He looked around again, stroked his small beard and cast his intimidating stare on each of the youngsters. He nodded at the adults. 'Yes, a time to make choices, a time in a very tricky and, yes, dangerous world. Many young men – and some young girls, I'm told – are going astray. You know what your problem is.'

He swept his arm with a pointed finger at the young people. 'Patience. You children don't have patience. Yes. You want everything now. You want money now. You want to live like the white man now. You shout slogans. You sing your struggle songs. You throw stones.'

One of the adults, swaying on his feet, jumped forward and tried to shove a bottle of beer into Dlamini's hand. Dlamini brushed it aside. The bottle fell and smashed to the ground.

'Sit down, drunkard! I'm still speaking. Some of you are running away, leaving your families, to go hide in the forests of some foreign country, to learn how to shoot guns.'

Three of the young men whispered to each other. Amos stared at Baba Dlamini.

'Yes, you go to foreign countries to learn to shoot guns, and to learn foreign ideas, from a bunch of Russians who know nothing about our country, our people, our traditions.'

Dlamini began pacing. His voice quietened a little. 'Yes, I know, life is hard for us. Yes, apartheid is unfair on us. But you will not make life better with songs and stones and, yes, guns.'

He walked up to Amos, lay his hand on his head as if to deliver a benediction. 'Life will be made better by what this young man has done and will do. By education. By patience. By resilience. When we have learned the ways of the modern world, when we have educated ourselves, when we have practised patience, then the white man will have no choice but to let us into his world. You will not defeat him with guns and stones. He is too powerful. He has more guns. But education ... You will catch up with him with education. Education! That is your AK47!'

Dlamini lifted his hand from Amos's head, waved it at the gathering to indicate that he was done, then patted Amos on the back. 'Woza, ndodana. Let me talk to you privately.'

Amos left his unfinished beer on the ground and followed Dlamini to the edges of the gathering. They stood in the scarce shade of an acacia. Dlamini put his hand on the boy's shoulder. 'Young Vilakazi, you have done well. You have excelled. Let me tell you, I know people – many youngsters have passed through my hands – and I know you are going to be a leader one day. But it is now time for the next step.'

'Yes, Baba. I understand that. I am ready.'

'Good. I hope you are ready. It is time to go and see Meneer Bester again. Here.'

Dlamini slid his hand into the inside pocket of his blazer, worn in spite of the searing heat, and slipped something into the front pocket of Amos's shirt. 'You are going to meet Meneer Bester in Pretoria. That's some money I've given you for the journey and a paper with instructions of how, where and when to find him.'

Amos patted his front pocket.

'Now, Amos, you listen to me carefully. You will listen attentively and respectfully to what Meneer Bester has to say, you hear me? Your life is about to change. You are going to do big things. Now go. Go back to your celebration ... And no more beers, you understand?'

⌇

Amos fidgeted in the taxi seat, trying to ease some comfort around the tear in the seat cushion that cut into his buttocks. His hand went to his pocket again. He wondered if he could shift the money over without the passenger on the seat beside him noticing. He decided not to risk it. He would wait until they stopped for petrol and the toilets.

It was only now, on his way back from Pretoria, from his second meeting with Otto Bester, that the full import of Baba Dlamini's public and private speeches at his graduation celebration unpacked itself in his mind. Indeed, his life had changed, but not as he had expected it. There was to be no free university education, not for now, but a promise for later, along with other promises. No, he was to leave the country. Go into exile. Join the ANC.

The taxi swept into a petrol station and squeaked to a halt next to a pump. The driver yelled at the passengers without turning around.

'Right, people! Thirty minutes break. You late; you stay.'

Amos left the taxi and found the toilet at the back of the station building. He decided to enter the cubicle to sit, although his stomach gave no indication of wanting to work. He pulled his pants down. There was no seat, and he settled uncomfortably onto the rim. There was no lock on the door so he held it closed with his foot, then gingerly removed the wad of money from his left pocket and shoved it into his right. He looked at the new watch Bester had given him to time his thirty minutes, a Casio digital, the cheapest model, Bester had told him. *We don't want to arouse suspicion.*

Snatches of the conversation with Bester in the prefab building tucked away into a far corner of the University of South Africa campus came back to him. Simultaneously, his stomach decided to start working. He grunted.

'No, Amos, I'm not asking you to be a sell-out. I'm not recruiting you to be a spy on your people. I don't want military information or stuff like that. Nothing like that.'

'What is it that you want, Mr Bester?'

'Otto, please. Surely we can be less formal now. We are going to be working together. All I will want from you is insights.'

'Insights?'

'Yes. We need to understand the thinking within the different sections and the leaders in the ANC. Who are unredeemable communists, militarists; who are the ones willing to consider some more peaceful approach – stuff like that. Not deep, dark secrets, if you know what I mean. We want you to work your way up into the leadership so that your own more sensible views can prevail. And, of course, when we finally find a peaceful resolution, you will be in a position to play a leading role in fixing our country.'

'And what if I refuse?'

'Come, come, Amos. It's too late to refuse.'

'What does that mean?'

Bester had reached into his breast pocket and pushed a scrap of paper across the desk in the otherwise empty prefab. He had turned the paper around so Amos could read it, but kept a finger on it.

29 October 1979
Received from Otto Bester
R100
Amos Vilakazi
(Signed)

Amos clenched his stomach muscles and grimaced out the last of the shit. He looked around for toilet paper. There was none. Nor were there any scraps of newspaper. He patted his pockets. Only the wad of money there. There was a moment's temptation to use a R50 note. Was it not dirty money, after all? But he found, in his shirt pocket, the half-sheet of paper from Baba Dlamini with the instructions for his meeting with Bester. He unfolded it and wiped himself. It didn't do a perfect job, but there was nothing more. He dropped it into the toilet bowl, stood and tried to rub the dents from the toilet rim out of his backside, pulled up his trousers. He turned and flushed the toilet and stood there to make sure the piece of paper disappeared along with his shit.

Chapter 12

This is the frontier – two posts facing one another in silent hostility, each standing for a world of its own. One of them is planed and polished and painted black and white like a police box, and topped by a single-headed eagle nailed in place with sturdy spikes. Wings outspread, claws gripping the striped pole, hooked beak outstretched, the bird of prey stares with malicious eyes at the cast-iron shield with the sickle-and-hammer emblem on the opposite pole – a sturdy, round, rough-hewn oak post planted firmly in the ground. The two poles stand six paces apart on level ground, yet there is a deep gulf between them and the two worlds they stand for.
– Nikolai Ostrovsky, How the Steel Was Tempered

January 1980
'Tsoga! Vuka! Wake up, S'bu! We have to leave! Now! Tsoga, dammit! Let's go, let's go, let's go …'

S'bu Dlamini stirred on the folded blankets on the floor of the sitting room in the house in Dube, Soweto. It was still dark and his head was wrapped around the dream he'd been having of his mother scolding him over an opened hole in the ground filled with hand grenades, bullets and other weapons of destruction and death he did not recognise. The sounds of the scolding and wailing of his mother escaped from the dream and hung in the air around him.

'Yini, Tshepo? What's wrong?'
'We have to leave now. We have to get out of the country. Now.'
'Why? What's happened?'
'Stop with the questions. Get up. Get dressed. Grab your things. Patrick is arrested.'

'Patrick?'

'Yes, comrade. Patrick. Your commander. The boers have him.'

S'bu leapt up, folded the blanket over four times, pulled on his trousers, buttoned his shirt and stuffed his few scattered items into his duffel bag.

'But Patrick skipped the country, comrade.' He sat on a chair to lace his tackies.

'Well, he didn't make it. We don't know the details yet. But Patrick knows you. He knows us. He knows this house.'

'Patrick will never talk!' S'bu looked around to make sure he had not forgotten anything.

'Hawu, S'bu. You know the rules. Assume the worst. Let's go!'

⁓

There were five of them in the battered Ford Anglia. Tshepo's uncle was driving, Tshepo in the front passenger seat. S'bu and the two other comrades they had picked up in Orlando East on their way out of Soweto sat tightly wedged in the back seat, the bags that would not fit in the boot held on their laps. The car might have been battered, but someone had done something to the engine. Tshepo's uncle apparently supplemented his wages as a petrol-station attendant by working on cars in the township. The car purred and roared with each change of gears, achieving speeds that would have been impossible even when the vehicle was brand new many years ago. They slipped quickly out of the sprawl of Soweto, headed northwest on the R41, used side roads to skirt Krugersdorp to avoid roadblocks, and joined the main road once again towards Magaliesburg.

It was quiet in the car, each passenger exploring his anxieties – of the dangers of being stopped on the road, of crossing the frontier and of the great unknown that lay on the other side.

Tshepo spoke once, touching his uncle lightly on the arm. 'Uncle, let's stay in the speed limit. We were told it's better not to break the little laws when you're breaking the big ones.'

The uncle sighed and eased the pressure on the accelerator.

They again skirted the town, this time Magaliesburg, by following the small roads, then joined the main road again towards Koster. As they moved further into the Western Transvaal, the small towns and peri-urban conglomerations thinned out. They were now in farming country, the fields of the white farmers spreading away to the horizon on either side of them, interspersed here and there with black villages and townships, islands of dirt and dust and ragged children in an ocean of plenitude, of wheat and maize and sunflowers and fat cattle.

S'bu stared out the window, wondering whether – with their meagre forces pitted against the might of the boers – they would ever get to take all this back. The dream came back to him: the wailing of his mother, her words of admonition repeated over and over: *What have you done, my son? What have you done?* He could take the silence no longer.

'So, we're going to Botswana? Where we going to cross?'

Tshepo turned around. 'Yes, Botswana. But it's better you don't know the details yet. Uncle Philemon knows the spot. It's not the first time he's taken comrades out.'

'Is he going to drive us across the border?'

'No. No. He will drop us nearby. We will walk across.'

'And then?' S'bu looked at the back of the uncle's head and then turned again to Tshepo.

'And then what, comrade?' Tshepo sounded irritated.

'And then? When we're across? Where do we go?'

'We make our way to Gaborone.'

'How?'

Tshepo turned towards his uncle with a slight lift of his shoulders and then faced the road ahead again. He spoke to the windscreen, dotted now with dead insects. 'Comrade, unemibuzo eminingi! Let's get across the bloody border then we'll discuss the way forward.'

S'bu faced the window, absorbing the blur of fields skimming across his vision. He tried to evade the bubbling of anxieties looming on the road ahead, the climbing of a fence, four young men trundling through the bush of a strange country looking for a town called Gaborone. When he finally managed to cast his mind back instead of ahead, two contrapuntal sounds played a discordant symphony in his head: the wailing of his mother in the dream and the song sung outside the factory gates on the day Patrick informed him of Tloks's arrest and the compromise of their unit. He tried to hum the freedom song silently to himself to drown out the sound of his mother. Thoughts of Patrick came to him.

Had he talked? Would he talk? Had he managed to get the information about S'bu's cache to the comrades in Swaziland, or had he been arrested with S'bu's instructions and map still on him? If he did talk and didn't have the instructions on him, surely he would not have been able to remember the details so the boers could find the weapons. It was buried too close to his village. The boers would be all over the place. Perhaps his mother would be interrogated?

His thoughts were interrupted by the whisper of conversation between Tshepo and Philemon. Tshepo turned to them. 'Comrades, we're going to stop in Koster for petrol. It's not safe for all of us to go into town. Uncle and I will go. I need to make a call to check the situation at home. We're going to drop you at the taxi rank outside town. You should leave your bags in the car so you look like locals. If anyone asks, your story is that you're going to Mmabatho. If a taxi comes before we get back for you, pray that it's not going to Mmabatho. Otherwise, just say that you're waiting for a relative to join you and you'll take the next taxi.'

They climbed out of the car some distance from the taxi rank and made their way over on foot. There were three locals at the rank: a scrawny but muscular older man in a worn T-shirt and faded brown dungarees, a large woman in her fifties in a floral cotton dress and shawl, and a young girl in faded jeans and yellow tank top. Only one of the three young fugitives could speak fluent seTswana. Although he had been completely silent in the taxi, staring without moving at the back of the driver's head throughout the journey, he now took the lead in engaging the locals.

After an exchange of greetings, there were questions.
'Where you going?'
'Mmabatho.'
'What you going there for?'
'Visit family.'
'Hayi, you're going to wait a long time for a taxi to Mmabatho. Most of them that pass here go to Zeerust.'
'That's okay. We will wait. Anyway, we're still waiting for a cousin to join us.'
Silence. The old man stared at them. The girl looked at S'bu: 'Why is your friend so quiet?'
'He's shy.'

'No. Black men are not shy.'

'This one is. Anyway, he's going to see his girlfriend in Mmabatho.'

'Oh? Okay. I hope he's not so shy with her.'

The old man sniggered, mumbling under his breath. He was about to say something when a taxi appeared around the bend and skidded to a halt. The driver shouted out the window.

'Zeerust! Tlokweng border! Gaborone!'

The old man guided the woman and the girl towards the taxi, allowing them to board, and then turned back to the three young men. 'You boys be careful. This place is teeming with police. Go well, wherever you are going. I hope you get there safely.'

He clambered aboard the taxi and gave them a power salute.

A few minutes later the Anglia came flying past them from the direction of Koster, did a screeching U-turn and picked them up. The mood in the car was sombre. No one spoke while they diverted around Koster to rejoin the road towards Swartruggens. Tshepo turned around. 'Comrades, S'bu, I'm sorry. Patrick is dead.'

'What! How?' The blood drained from S'bu. He wanted to scream, to punch his fist through the car window. He punched the back of Tshepo's seat instead.

'The boers ... They killed him, S'bu. I'm sorry.'

The quiet one – their seTswana interlocutor – said without turning his eyes from the back of the driver's head: 'May his revolutionary soul rest in peace.'

The fourth man, who had been just as quiet throughout the journey, but had fidgeted ceaselessly in the middle of the back seat, punched his fist into the roof of the car and shouted: 'Amandla!'

They all turned to S'bu, who sat quietly, trying to bring his breathing back to normal. His mind was slow to reach equilibrium. The wailing of his mother was gone. The freedom song outside the factory gates was gone. All he heard now was Patrick's quiet voice telling him it was time to skip the country, and how Patrick had then turned and walked away. Then a thought struck him. 'But that means he didn't talk. If the boers killed him, it must mean he didn't talk. I told you he wouldn't talk.'

Tshepo's uncle spoke for the first time. 'Not necessarily.'

S'bu started at the unexpected voice. 'What do you mean? Why would they kill him if he talked?'

Tshepo answered. 'Why? Why would the fucking boers kill anyone? Because he's black. Because he's a "terrorist". Because they were just angry, or maybe drunk. Or they just beat him harder than they intended. Or they slipped him on a piece of soap. Or made him fall out of a window.'

S'bu felt the anger rise. 'No! If they killed him, that means he didn't talk. We can go back home.'

Tshepo turned in his seat, moving his whole body to face S'bu. 'Comrade! We're not going home. You understand? We are not turning around! We have no way of knowing what Patrick might have told them before he died.'

The uncle, Philemon, chimed in. 'Look, young man. I know you are upset. The man was your friend. He was your commander. You respected him. You trusted him. But you've got to understand – everyone talks eventually.'

'No!' S'bu banged his hand against the door. 'Only cowards talk. Patrick was no coward – Patrick chose death!'

Tshepo spoke again. 'It's good that you believe in your comrade, S'bu. But the truth is, we have no way of knowing the truth. We have no way of entering those dark places into which the boers take our people. Perhaps he didn't talk and they killed him out of anger or frustration. We don't know. Perhaps he did talk, but he refused to become an impimpi, so they killed him. Perhaps he refused to be a state witness. Perhaps the boers decided it was too much trouble to take him to court, so they killed him. We will never know.'

S'bu fell silent, turning to watch as his country faded into the distance behind them. His anxieties had evaporated, leaving only anger. His thoughts raced ahead – to an imagined MK training camp somewhere in the bush, an AK slung over his shoulder, learning the art of war, of revenge.

They rode onwards in silence, past Swartruggens, taking a wide berth around Zeerust, then heading southwest to Mmabatho. Finally, they slipped onto a dirt road northward before stopping in the late afternoon near a clump of kameeldoring.

Tshepo's uncle spoke. 'Okay, boys, this is where I leave you. You have to wait until darkness to cross. The border fence is about half a kilometre that way.' He pointed. 'You see that little koppie ahead there? You pass to the left of it and you will come to a fence with a dirt road running alongside it, on this side of the fence. That is the road the border patrol uses. On the other side of that fence, you'll be in Botswana. Tshepo will know what to do from there.'

They climbed out the vehicle. The uncle opened the boot, hauled out their bags and handed them a plastic shopping bag with Kentucky Fried Chicken, cans of Coca-Cola, cigarettes and matches. He handed Tshepo a torch. 'Now, go hide in those trees until it's dark. Have something to eat and drink and a smoke, but before it gets completely dark check to make sure you will find the koppie. Just keep this clump of trees and the road we used behind you for as long as you can see them. And the koppie ahead. It should be a clear night. Goodbye, banna. Tsamayang sentle!'

And he was gone, gunning the car and throwing up dust for kilometres back along the road.

The four moved without a sound into the shelter of the trees and settled on the dry, hard ground. Tshepo motioned them not to talk. He passed around the bag of chicken and Cokes. The only sounds for the following minutes were the brief hiss of opening cans and the tearing of chicken meat from bones. When they were done eating, Tshepo collected the chicken remains and empty cans, dug a hole in the softer ground near one of the tree trunks and buried the evidence of their stay. He then passed the cigarettes and matches around, but S'bu waved his hand in the air above him, looked up into the tops of the trees and shook his head, indicating, they guessed, that the smoke may draw attention to them.

They sat in silence. The two quiet ones dozed. Tshepo and S'bu, opposite each other, looked up into each other's eyes now and then. They were getting impatient. Finally, as dusk began to settle, Tshepo raised himself onto his haunches and crept from among the trees to get his bearings. He came back and signalled by moving his finger over an imaginary watch that they would move in half an hour.

It took closer to an hour for darkness to descend. Tshepo stood up and tapped each of them on the shoulder, motioning them to follow. They picked up their bags and followed him out of the trees. They walked in single file, Tshepo taking the lead, S'bu at the rear.

The half-kilometre seemed the longest they had ever walked, but soon enough the koppie loomed ahead. They traced its contour around to the left and then bumped into each other when Tshepo stopped suddenly. He pointed at the road that ran perpendicular ahead of them and to the fence beyond. Alone, he moved to the road and looked for what seemed like forever, tilting his head left and right. He came back and motioned them over to the fence.

S'bu was surprised. The fence was low, some barbed wire on top, but otherwise much like an ordinary fence between two farms, not anything like he'd imagine a border between two countries. He wondered whether the uncle had made a mistake. But Tshepo seemed to know what he was doing. He slipped his rucksack off his back, pulled out a rolled-up blanket, unfurled it and flung it across the top of the fence. He took S'bu's arm, indicating that he should hold back, and motioned the other two to the fence and helped them over. As he did so, he whispered that they should proceed in a straight line for about five minutes and then stop and wait for them. Next he helped S'bu over the fence, whispering the same instruction. In spite of the anxiety and the difficulty of scrambling over a rickety fence, S'bu could not help but feel the import of the moment. A freedom song that he had first heard on Radio Freedom huddled around a shortwave radio in a shack in the township came blaring into his head: *Siyobashiy' abazal' ekhaya, saphuma sangena kwamany'amazwe, lapho kungazikhon'obaba no mama, silandel'inkululeko.*

But before the song could play itself out in S'bu's head, the night exploded in a riot of light and noise, as if God himself had materialised to smite his sinners. A voice blared from a loudhailer.

'Stop, julle vokkers! Bly daarso! Fucking terrorists! Ons gaan julle vokken doodskiet!'

Tshepo didn't hesitate. In one swift movement, he shoved S'bu over to the other side and then started to clamber up himself. S'bu crashed to the ground, crawled forward and looked back. He could hear the others running, crashing through low thorn bushes. He saw Tshepo struggling to scale the fence with no one behind to give him a leg up. Shots rang out – automatic gunfire. S'bu froze and tried to burrow himself into the hard earth. Dare he look back? When he did, he could see Tshepo at the top of the fence as if frozen there, a dark thick liquid oozing from his mouth. He saw the silhouette of Tshepo weakly raising his arm in a gesture to S'bu to go, to leave him. Then the hand went limp and flopped over the fence as if trying to touch the free earth.

Note No. 4

July 2020

You told me, Bongi, after our relationship began to blossom in Lusaka, that the first time you touched an AK47 your fingers tingled and your heart pounded – not out of fear, you said, but awe, even perhaps love. (I didn't want to tell you then, and now I know the telling will change nothing, but that is precisely how I felt the first time we touched. No, not as you may jump to conclude, the first time we made love, but the first time your small hand settled on my forearm as you sought my agreement in a disorganised political discussion in the crowded sitting room in Lusaka with the open bottles of duty-free spread chaotically on the table.)

Yes, you had said, the AK carried in its surprisingly trite mechanicalness the heart of you, the heart of your people, the heart of your ideas about life, the world, and our distraught corner of it. You described running your hand over its wooden butt, stroking your fingers along the length of its barrel, feeling the give of its trigger, holding it up to your shoulder as you had seen in the Soviet movies they showed us in the house of waiting in Lusaka and peering down its length through the tiny V close to your eye, to the little metal sight at the other end of it, imagining – I'd imagine – an enemy at the other end, target of your newly held power.

I slipped my arm behind your head there on the bed where we lay in the small hours as you told me of that other first love of yours: hard, powerful, metallic, with the hint of softness in the wooden butt. Your head turned towards me and you told the rest of your story with your mouth nestled against the side of my chest, the moving of your lips as you spoke giving small unintended kisses where they rested. Indeed, I told you of my own first time with an AK, the overwhelming emotion, and it struck me only later that we lay there talking about the rifle of our revolution as other lovers, in different times and circumstances, talked in that moment in a new relationship between insecurity and comfort of past lovers, comparing notes perhaps, but always with the assurance that none was like this relationship.

And, perhaps just as old lovers always hover in the bedroom of new love, after the ANC had allowed us to marry, your AK and mine – His and Hers – always leaned against the wall on either side of our bed in the house we were now allowed to share in Lusaka. Ready to be grabbed in that dreaded, always awaited, moment of mid-sleep disrupted by a raid of the special forces. Ready, as we were, always, to fight together shoulder to shoulder, just as we slept, and, yes, in those days, to die together and for each other.

Chapter 13

June 2019

The door was of wood – thick wood, to be sure – but Whitehead would have expected a steel door to protect the secrets, the lives of people, locked in a cage of history, unsure whether they would ever get out, living lives of intrigue, bravery, frailty, uncertainty, treachery. Yes, he would have expected a heavy steel door, not a door with a brass pull-down handle and a simple keyhole. Surely, with a heavy circular combination lock welded in place and a polished steel multi-armed handle that you needed to put your back into to turn once the combination was entered.

He frowned at the off-white paper, edges curled, adhering tenuously to the door stating in rough hand felt-tip pen 'Private'. Surely not, he thought. Surely this cannot be the door behind which decades of records of the ANC's department of intelligence and security have been housed for all these further decades.

He stepped back, the old key edged with rust now dangling on its ring with the soiled miniature flip-flop sandal in his hand dropping to his side. He stepped back a pace and then another, almost as though in fear of the door, the room behind it, and the contents he had been sent to investigate. He turned his head and peered down the long corridor, lit only by a wan beam that crept through a window in the alcove some metres away. He knew, having been shown around this house on his first visit, that, in reality, the corridor ended just ten paces away at another door, one of less sturdy wood that opened onto a bedroom. But the ominousness of the door before him, the thought of the contents behind it, and the paucity of light in the passage implied a length, a passage of the passage, that came to no end.

There were two framed photographs on either side of the doorframe. To the left a black-and-white one mounted on burgundy card framed by thin pine strips of Comrade Steven and his wife, Gail, the residents of this house, alongside Nelson Mandela, the old man's ever-ready smile for the camera and the face behind it (and for all the faces that would forever look at this image), his right hand appearing with a hint of caress on the shoulder of Gail. To the right of the door another photograph, also black and white – although god knows when or by whom this one was taken – of the headquarters staff of the ANC's exiled department of intelligence and security standing young and smiling on the far side of the table-tennis table in the yard of Green House in Lusaka.

Not wise, he thought. Yes, not wise that we took photographs of ourselves in those days of deep secrecy and ever-present threat, of the people who administered the ANC's intelligence operations, records and analysis outside the headquarters where it was all done. And not wise that this photo should now be hanging, slightly askew, so near the room that now housed those records.

But perhaps there had been wisdom (and a little irony) in this choice of a room in a residential house in a suburb of Pretoria East, rather than a government building, or a university archive where a searcher for these records, with mischief in mind, would start their search.

Whitehead sucked in air, moved towards the door, slotted the key in the lock. It took some jiggling to get it to settle into the mechanism and some effort to turn. The handle squeaked as he pushed it down. He had to put his shoulder to the door to dislodge it from the frame, then fell into the room as the door swung open and banged against something behind.

The room was lightless. A heavy air of must and dust seemed to rush past his head with a sigh. He ran his fingers along the wall, fumbled for a switch that took some pressure to turn on. Two strip lights on the ceiling flickered, dimming then brightening then dimming again, and then finally, with an electric gasp, came to life. At the same time the whirring of an air conditioner set high against the far wall chased the silence from the room.

The room was much larger than he would have thought, but then it would have to be to house all these records. He thought he could make out, on the far wall above the rows of metal filing cabinets, an unevenness in the plastering and a lighter shade of white paint that indicated where a window had been bricked up. He wondered at the architecture of this house and where this room fitted in. Perhaps he should go outside and take a look. Perhaps the room had been specially built, although the bricked-up window implied not.

He took in the metal-grey filing cabinets stacked tightly against the far wall. On a hook above them, where the window used to be, hung a large bunch of keys. He cursed at the stupidity of leaving the keys to the cabinets in the room for an intruder to have his day with the contents. He turned to lock the door behind him.

Against the wall to his right were three low, wide wooden cabinets, the ones in which they used to keep topographical maps. Those wouldn't be of any use to his investigation. Almost all the floor space was taken up by cardboard boxes, some wooden crates and metal trunks, the latter piled up on top of each other, blocking access to the filing cabinets. Against the left wall were bookcases on either side of an old, small school or child's desk with a hole in the top right corner for an inkwell. From his spot near the door, which was as far as he could get into the room without shifting boxes and crates, he could recognise some of the publications on the bookshelves: old government gazettes, Hansards, ANC and South African Communist Party publications, spy novels, dictionaries, map books, Soviet novels and memoirs by Soviet generals of the Great Patriotic War. There were some he would like to read again.

In the back left corner, on top of a metal trunk, stood two old Sanyo desktop computers from the 1980s, with ugly screens that tapered at the back, which made them look like some kind of wanderer of the pre-human planet. They still sat on top of their computer cases with the floppy disk drives. He wondered what happened to all the floppy disks with their coded intelligence reports that they used to receive from their units in the frontline states and their contacts inside the country. Would they still be readable and would the decoding program they had developed themselves still work? On the floor next to the computers, covered in dust, stood a dot-matrix printer. Whitehead wondered where the dust came from in this airless, sealed room.

All these objects, the school desk apart, were familiar to him. Beacons of memory of the closing years of his exile in Green House in Lilanda, Lusaka and later the move to Kabwata. In Green House, the room had been much bigger, with large wooden desks at which the processors could work, the cabinets and shelves less cluttered, with a room off their workroom where they stored the more sensitive documents, particularly the interview reports of new recruits and the interrogation reports of suspected apartheid agents. Other memories bubbled to the surface. He saw the comrades he worked with in that Green House room. Some now buried, some still in government, others discarded by the ANC, some on early retirement, trying to get rich in hopeless business endeavours. Some destitute in makeshift huts in faraway villages or urban slums. He saw the drinking and arguing sessions around the coffee table in the lounge of the house he shared with Bongi in Kabwata, a conveyor belt of comrades always passing through. And, finally floating to the surface, the feeling of those days – of family, camaraderie, hope, purpose and, yes, love.

He felt old in this room. Its derelict contents appeared an extension and accentuation of the decay of his body and the mustiness of his mind. His once soldierly muscles were now flabby and spiritless, his stubborn paunch always pushing his trouser belt down towards his hips, his once blond hair now giving more accuracy to his adopted name, the curls gone, replaced with wispy, wiry strands.

He dragged a metal trunk into a more suitable position, sat down on it and, letting his red sling bag slide off his shoulder, took out his flexi-tablet, double tapped the screen and waited the seconds while it scanned his iris. It sprang into life with a ping that startled the room. He retrieved his lightpen from the bag, pointed it at the screen, opened up his List App, looked around the room and started his list. The flexi-tab had learned his erratic handwriting, suggesting words before he'd completed them. As his first order-making effort, he took an inventory of what was there: cardboard boxes, trunks, crates, filing cabinets, for each of which he listed the number of drawers. He created categories – box, crate, trunk, cabinet – and numbered each one. He took a red marker out of his bag and moved around the room writing the item's number on each of them, breathlessly manoeuvring objects out of his way.

This took him close to an hour. He sat on his trunk again, then took a large red handkerchief from his bag and wiped his face. He looked at his list, corrected some misspellings, and looked around again. At least one of the emotions of the struggle years reignited in his breast: purpose. He was here to decipher *The Signs*. He was now a political cryptographer.

He wondered why this treasure of intelligence had been kept from them for so many decades. Who brought it back from Lusaka? When? How did they come – by truck? Under armed guard? How did they cross the border? Were they brought straight to this house? Who took the decisions? Why was it that he, a trusted member of ANC intelligence and once deputy head of the post-apartheid Service, was not trusted with this knowledge? Had Vladimir known? If not, why was he not trusted? He was head of the Service, for God's sake. Was it political? Were there secrets here that should stay secret? Damaging secrets? Or did those who made the decisions, who had custody of these things, consider them just items of historical curiosity? Did they contemplate destroying them? Were they too lazy or perhaps sentimental to do so?

Well, part one of his odyssey into this jungle of information was done. He went to the door, unlocked it. He headed to the kitchen. Although the mid-June winter dusk was starting to settle, Steve and Gail were not home yet. He made himself a large mug of coffee, was about to tip in a second spoon of sugar when Bongi's disapproving voice in his head stopped him dead. Back in the room with his flexi-tab, he swore at having to do the eye recognition thing again.

He clambered over to Filing Cabinet No. 1, reached for the bunch of keys on the wall, tried six of them before he got the cabinet open. He wrote a tiny '1' on the key with the red marker. From the top drawer the smell of stale paper and cardboard wafted up. He decided to try the keys in all the cabinets and number them before doing anything else. That took some time. He was tiring. Eventually he found himself back at Filing Cabinet No. 1 and flipped through the suspension files in the top drawer. Although the files were discoloured and frayed, everything still seemed to be in the meticulous order they had been in Lusaka. They must have shipped the stuff as was, in their containers. That was a relief, although he was anxious about the boxes, crates and trunks.

He read some of the labels on these files: 'Botswana Reports – 79/81', 'Botswana Reports – 82/83'. He checked the other two drawers: Lesotho Reports; Swaziland Reports; Zimbabwe Reports; Maputo Reports; London Reports. These were the operational reports from the regional intelligence directorates in each of the forward areas. They were organised into two-year files, some bulky and overflowing with contents, others skinny and scant. They seemed mainly to start in 1979 and end in 1989, although they got skinnier towards the end of the eighties.

He remembered these types of reports. They would have dealt with aspects such as personnel in the region, finances, meetings with contacts from home, minutes of regional directorate meetings, lists of intelligence and security reports sent under separate cover to Lusaka. He picked up the flexi-tab, made sub-lists for Cabinet 1 and listed all the folder names by drawer. That took another hour. His legs were painful. His lower back ached. He should close up for the day. Bongi would be home from work soon. It was his turn to cook. Perhaps he should suggest they go out for supper.

He locked the first cabinet, then decided he should quickly glance through the other cabinets, without making lists for now. The next few contained intelligence reports, subdivided by subject or institution: Security Police, BOSS/NIS, SADF, National Party, Detentions/Arrests, States of Emergency, Assassinations, Hangings, Missing Persons and so on. There were files for some of the big South African corporates of the time, some of which were still flourishing. The next few cabinets contained interrogation reports of suspected apartheid agents who had come into the ANC in exile. Those were cabinets he would have to come back to. And then there were cabinets tightly packed with interview reports of new recruits, interviews done in Maputo, Dukwe in Botswana, Harare in Zimbabwe, Lesotho, even London. They were filed by the person's MK name. That was going to make his job more difficult.

Whitehead locked all the cabinets, dropped the bunch of keys in his sling bag. Perhaps he should have duplicates made. He folded up his flexi-tab, picked up his mug of cold coffee and left the room. As he locked the door, he backed into Gail, who yelped. 'Jesus, Jerry! It's you! Shit, I thought we had a burglar at last!'

'Hi, Gail. Sorry. Yes, it's me. I did say I was coming today.'

'You did. Forgot.'

'Well, I guess I am a burglar of sorts. More like a grave robber maybe.'

'Indeed. What's it like in there?'

'Chaos, mostly.'

'Ja, well, sorry. We're not allowed in there. You're the first one in years.'

'Oh?'

'Yep. Steve and I are just the dragons guarding the mouth of the cave.'

'Tomb.'

'What? Oh yeah. Tomb? Grave robber. Want to stay for supper?'

'No. Can't. My turn to cook at home.'

'Okay. You back tomorrow?'

'Ja, and many tomorrows after that. Ciao.'

'Cheers, Jerry.'

And he was gone, preparing his motivation to Bongi for dinner at an Indian restaurant.

Chapter 14

June 2019

Bongi sat at her desk – one of those modular, L-shaped ones with the metal legs and frame and the formica top, more suited to a kitchen table, but at least easy to wipe off the spilt coffee. She swivelled her chair left and right, as if to a song in her head, but the lyrics consisted of just two names, repeated over and over, as given to her by Vladimir in their brief meeting at the Woodlands shopping mall the previous evening. The lyric was the names but the accompaniment, the rhythm section, was the anxiety over Vladimir's revelation.

Her desk faced the door, painted grey like the walls, with the bottle-green frame repeated, as she knew, throughout the building housing the secrets of the nation. Secrets of the nation? Not so popular any more, the notion of secrets. In the public mind – whatever that might be – an anachronism from olden days, a kind of pre-history. She remembered the campaign some years ago, in the days of Twitter, with its hashtags, the days of the student protests, of #RhodesMustFall, #FeesMustFall, #ThisViceChancellorMustFall, #ThatMinisterMustFall, #ThisPresidentMustFall. And, following another intelligence scandal, #SecretsMustFall. She felt like an artisan plying a craft long dead, for which humanity no longer had any need. She could have – should have – retired last year when she'd turned sixty. Jerry had discouraged her. They needed her salary to supplement his pension. The house was not yet paid for. The cars were not paid for. Nadine was still, in a way, dependent on them.

Her desk – the long side of the L – was bare, except for the wooden knickknack with a row of tinkling metal bells and the little wooden hammer. It had been given to her as an official gift by a delegation of visiting analysts from the Chinese service. And to her left were the three-tiered plastic filing trays, a relic she couldn't let go of from the days they used to work on paper, now with only a few notes to herself in the in-tray and a pile of magazines and journals she would never get to reading in the pending tray. The out-tray had a couple of photos of Jerry and Nadine fishing that she'd recently scanned. Today everything was digital: intelligence reports, analytical reports, submissions and leave forms and procurement forms – all signed digitally – as well as maps and images. She missed the feel of something tangible, singular, present, with a pen and highlighter in her hands.

On the shorter side of the L stood her two computers. One for the Service's internal network that she had to sign into with her fingerprint, eye scan, voice recognition and then the good old-fashioned password. The other her connection to the world, the internet. Tucked into the front left corner of the room was the large wooden table she had refused to let go of when there had been a modernisation of the office that involved some kind of scandal that lost the procurement officer – her friend – her job. On the table stood a parsley plant in an earthen pot, from which she broke a twig every now and then to take home. She didn't know how, but it survived in her office with the daily watering she gave it from the water cooler in the corridor. The rest of the table was covered with books, more magazines and journals, and the week's newspapers, which she looked at only briefly during her first morning coffee and then read online.

Behind her was the window with the green frames and small panes, metal burglar bars fixed to the wall outside, and the off-beige blinds that she opened first thing every morning and closed every evening. When she swivelled in her chair, she saw the low koppie behind the Service building, the bushes and shrubs now dry in the rainless winter. Beyond were the pale sky and brazen array of satellite dishes breaking the natural lines of the landscape. In the back left corner of her office stood a grey steel filing cabinet. In addition to its normal locks, it had welded onto the top and bottom steel slats through which fitted a flat steel rod, locked to the top slat with a large combination lock. This too she had refused to yield when they went digital. It was empty. It was still locked. Perhaps now, with Vladimir's investigation, she might have use for it.

Bongi rose, left the room, locking the door behind her, breaking the rule of always logging out of her computer before she left the room. She made her way down the corridor to the kitchen, poured herself another coffee and came back. She used to have a secretary to do that, but they too became obsolete with the digitalisation. She sat down again, placed the wireless headset on her head and turned to her computer – the internal one. It had automatically logged off. She cursed. She went through the routine, wondering if the irritation in her voice would affect the voice recognition. Indeed, it did seem to hesitate after she spoke her name, but allowed her in on the third try.

She activated the Service database app, selected the intelligence dataset and typed one of the names Vladimir had given her into the search field. *Sorry. No results match your search. Try a different spelling or modify your search criteria.* She tried the second name. Still no results. She sipped at her coffee, selected the administrative dataset and typed in the first name. The computer and the invisible network and servers behind it took their time. Eventually, red text appeared on the screen: *You do not have access to this data!* She spoke aloud, but in her head she was addressing Vladimir.

'Fuck! What IT idiot programmed in the exclamation mark? Like it's a reprimand, a threat.' She waited for Vladimir's response in her head, had an image of him shrugging his shoulders and smiling that crooked smile of his.

She cleared the screen. Taking off her headset, she reached back and untied the ochre-and-yellow scarf that held her grey-speckled hair in a bunch at the back of her head. She ran a thumb and forefinger along the edge of it in long, gentle strokes, as if soothing a child. She stared at the door, then the plant, the computer screen, then swivelled her chair to face the window, still stroking the scarf. On the grey grass outside three mossies pecked at the earth. Bongi thought of the garden in their house two kilometres away, up the Delmas Road (that, if followed in the other direction to the east, would bring you to Mpumalanga, the old Eastern Transvaal). She thought of the birds in the garden, lots of mossies and the loud hadedas. She thought of the flowers she wanted to plant in time for the spring rains, if they came this year. She wished Jerry would take more interest in the garden.

She swivelled back from the window, selected the phone app on her computer and clicked on the name of Johan van Deventer. He headed the analysis division under her dealing with the right wing, organised crime and anti-constitutional activities – the catch-all division entrusted to this very intelligent Afrikaner leftover from what they still called 'the old order' when they were among comrades. She clicked the call button. He answered immediately.

'Morning, ma'am.'

'Morning, Johan. How's it going this morning?'

'Fine, thank you, Director.' She always detected a hint of false respect in his voice. But she was used to that. A quarter of a century into democracy and some still could not acclimatise to taking orders from a black woman.

'Are you very busy, Johan?'

'I'm working on the report on the ultra-left, ma'am.'

'What ultra-left? Since when do we look at the ultra-left?'

'DG's instructions, ma'am. He set up a task team.'

'Oh, Okay. I'll clarify with him.' She paused. Brought her internet computer to life. 'Listen, Johan. Give yourself a short break and come up to my office for a few minutes.'

'Sure, Director. Be there in five.'

She logged off her internal computer and turned to the internet one. She typed one of the names into the Google search field. There were over six thousand hits. She opened the first few links but found nothing that seemed to tie into Vladimir's interests. She tried the second name. Still nothing. There was a knock at the door. She switched off the computer screen.

'Come in, Johan.'

Van Deventer entered. He was dressed in a pale blue suit, shirt of paler blue and navy blue tie, in spite of the deformalisation of dress code in the Service years ago under Vladimir's watch, the suit a size or two too big for his tall, skinny body. His hair was close-cropped to disguise the grey and the bald patch that had gradually spread over the years, which for Bongi was a measure of the passing of the twenty-four years she had been in the Service.

'Morning, Director.'

'Hello, Johan. Take a seat.'

Van Deventer slipped into one of the two visitors' chairs in front of Bongi's desk. 'What can I do for you, ma'am?'

'Can I get you some coffee or something, Johan?'

'No thanks, ma'am. I've left a half-finished cup in my office.'

'Sorry about that. I won't keep you long.'

'No problem, ma'am.'

He shifted in his chair, stared at her with the eyes that matched his shirt.

'Tell me, Johan, do you know if we have records of people who served in the old Security Police?'

'Why would we have those, ma'am?'

'No, I mean, left over from the old NIS days.'

'I don't understand, ma'am. NIS would have had no reason to collect intelligence on the Security Police.'

'No, of course not. I understand that. I meant from their liaison and coordination with the Security Police.'

'Well, ma'am, that would not have been in intelligence records – possibly operational or administrative ones.'

'And would we still have those records.'

'I very much doubt it, ma'am.'

'Why?'

Van Deventer put his hand into the inside pocket of his jacket as if looking for something that would help the conversation, removed it again, patted down his tie then let his hand drop down next to the other one on his lap. He looked down at his hands as if surprised to find them there, then up again at Bongi again. 'Well, Director, there would be no need for them now. So they would have been archived or destroyed as provided in the Archives Act.'

'Indeed, Johan, and the old NIS destroyed much of its records before 1994. Would such records have been among them?'

'Yes, ma'am.'

'Yes?'

'I mean, yes, I know they destroyed some records.'

'*They*, Johan?'

'*We*, ma'am, but I was not involved in the destruction of records.' He shifted in his seat, crossed his legs, changed his mind and reached inside his jacket again, smoothed the front of his shirt. She wondered if this was an old instinct of reaching for a firearm when threatened.

'It's okay, Johan. I'm not holding you personally accountable. Those days are long gone.'

'Yes, ma'am, they are.'

'So?'

'Yes, ma'am?'

'So? Would those kinds of records have been destroyed then?'

'To be honest, ma'am, I wouldn't know. I wasn't involved, as I said.'

'You said they might have been archived?'

'Yes, ma'am.'

'Where?'

'In the National Archives, ma'am. They might be open now. Twenty years have passed.'

'Indeed. Can you check on that for me, Johan?'

'Sure, ma'am. Anything else?' He managed to cross his legs and sat back in the chair. Bongi stared at him, looked down at her fingernails, scratched at a chip in the polish on her thumb.

'Tell me, Johan, are you aware of any former security policemen who joined the NIS before 1994?'

'You know the Security Police despised us, ma'am?'

'Yes, Johan, I'm aware of that. So? Were there?'

'I think there were some, ma'am.' The hand in and out the jacket again. 'As I recall. But I wasn't personally aware of any.'

'But you were a member of the NIS then, Johan. Wouldn't you have been aware of new members?'

'I've been in analysis my whole career, ma'am. Those that came would have gone into operations. As far as I know, to the covert collection directorate. They wouldn't have been allowed at headquarters. They had their own undercover offices. We would never have met them.'

'And did any of them stay, move over to the new Service?'

'That I wouldn't know, ma'am. The covert collection directorate was brought into the new service, so I suppose some could have come across.'

'Okay. Thanks, Johan. I'm sorry about your cold coffee. I owe you a cup.'

'Ma'am?'

'Yes, Johan?'

'May I ask why you're asking these questions?'

'Need to know, Johan.'

'Sorry, ma'am.' He prepared to stand.

'I'm joking, Johan. Relax.'

'Yes, ma'am.'

'A colleague in the Missing Persons Task Team ...'

'Missing Persons Task Team, ma'am?'

'Yes, the team that was set up after the TRC in the National Prosecuting Authority. It was tasked to trace people, or their bodies, who went missing during apartheid. People who died in combat, were hanged, killed by the Security Police, died in exile. Their main task is to try to find the bodies and provide a reburial and closure for the families.'

'Yes, ma'am. I remember.'

'Well, the team is in the process of closing its books, shutting down their cases, but they have a few unsolved cases left and they've asked for our help.'

'I see, ma'am. But why do they need to know about former security policemen?'

'Because some might be able to help them with the unresolved cases.'

'But I thought the TRC had all that information, Director?'

'Not everyone applied for amnesty, Johan.'

'I see, ma'am. Do you want me to make more enquiries, ma'am?'

Bongi scratched at the nail polish again, laid her hands on the desk and pushed herself to her feet. 'No, Johan, that's not necessary. You've been very helpful. I just wanted to get a sense of what we might have. Go back to your cold coffee and your ultra-left report. I'd like a look at the report when you're done.'

'The DG said the task team must report directly to him, ma'am.'

'That's okay. I'll discuss with the DG.'

She escorted him to the door, tapped him lightly on the back as he left. She went back to the desk, unlocked a drawer, took out her handbag and left the room. She walked down the long corridor with the wooden statuettes in alcoves and the paintings by local artists on the walls, used her access card to exit through the revolving security doors and walked to the smoking area with the concrete benches, concrete ashtrays and small trees. She thought of bumming a smoke, but remembered how she'd feel when she went for her jog in the morning. She took her cell phone from her bag and switched it on. Mobile signals were blocked in the building. She sent a text to Jerry: *Sorry about dinner last night. Let's do it tonight. TGIF. Nadine home for the weekend.*

She started a text to Vladimir, paused mid-sentence, changed her mind, deleted it, switched off the phone and went back inside.

Chapter 15

February 1980
'Welcome, comrade. Take a seat.'

Sandile Ndaba looked up from the sheaf of loose-leaf foolscap on the weathered desk in front of him and motioned towards the stool opposite. He watched the young man slip without hesitation onto the stool and place his two hands palms down on the table, as if ready to turn them over for a palm-reading. Sandile took in the handsome face, the dark skin, the darting eyes beneath overgrown eyebrows, the wisp of a smile, the unusual ease for a new exile in a strange country, in unprecedented circumstances, in this small bare room in the former colonial house in a Maputo suburb.

'Yes, comrade. How are you?'

'Good, thank you, comrade. I'm good.'

'And what's your name?'

'Senzo, comrade.'

'Senzo? Is that your real name?'

'No, comrade. That is the name the comrades told me to use – the ones who brought me out the country.'

'I need your real name, comrade.'

'But they told me not to use my real name any more, comrade.'

Sandile laughed, lifted the well-chewed ballpoint pen, removed the cap and let it hover over the blank page for a moment, then wrote *5 February 1980*.

'No. That's good, comrade. Good discipline. But it's okay. I am Sandile. I'm with the processing department. We're responsible for processing all the new recruits. We're ANC security. We need to know all about you, your background, your family, in case … in case, you know … in case something happens to you and we need to inform your family.'

'Oh? Okay, Comrade Sandile. I understand. My real name is Amos.'

'Amos? Welcome, Comrade Amos. I am Sandile. Not my real name, I'm afraid.'

Amos smiled, shrugged and leaned forward.

'And your last name?'

'Vilakazi.'

'Okay. Good. Amos Vilakazi.'

Sandile wrote the name next to the letters R/N and, with the stained plastic ruler, underlined it.

'And did the comrades give you a struggle surname, Comrade Senzo?'

'No, comrade. Should they have?'

'Not a problem. What surname would you like to use in exile?'

Amos lowered his head for just a moment, smoothed his eyebrows with his thumb and fingers, looked up and said: 'Makhanda.'

'You're not Xhosa, are you?'

'No, comrade. But I would like to use that name, if I may?'

'No, of course, comrade. Actually there are a few here on the outside who have chosen that name, but most as a first name and they spell it wrongly.'

Sandile smiled at Amos and wrote 'Senzo Makhanda' next to the letters 'MK' on the top right of the page. He took up the ruler again and drew neat double lines under the name that would, for the foreseeable future, obliterate the other one.

'And when did you arrive in Maputo, Comrade Senzo?'

'Last week, comrade. Tuesday.'

'And everything okay? Accommodation? Food?'

'Fine, comrade. I am fine. Just tired of waiting. I want to go for training, to MK. That's why I left the country.'

'Yes, yes, I understand. But your time will come. We have many new recruits leaving the country. It will take a while to process you all.'

Sandile removed four sheets of paper from the pile in front of him and handed them across the table.

'I need you to write your biography, everything about yourself, your family, where you're from, your schooling, your friends, your political activities. And, please, if there are any good people you know at home who would be willing to work for the ANC, include their names and brief information.'

'Sure, comrade. Can I have a pen and some more pages please?'

Sandile left the young man and went to find Lindiwe, who was supposed to join him. There should always be two of them for this delicate task of screening new recruits. The boers, they knew, were doing their damnedest to insert their agents into the stream of new exiles.

Indeed, there had to be at least two sitting in on these interviews, to compare notes, to balance judgements, to ensure the absence of any prejudice – ethnic or class or, occasionally, race and sometimes ideology. Any conclusion of suspicion drawn, they knew, would lead to further interrogation, perhaps life-long branding and, well, they knew of the rumoured cruelties in the detention camp in Angola.

At the half-open door Sandile glimpsed Lindiwe, who had now returned from the assignment he had given her and stood outside chatting to another wishful suitor. He beckoned her into the room.

She dragged a chair up beside him and they watched the oblivious Amos as his hand moved quickly over the page while the other alternated between wiping the Maputo sweat from his brow and smoothing the page. Sandile reached for the completed sheets.

'Comrade Senzo, can we start reading the pages you're done with?' Amos looked up. 'Sorry, this is Comrade Lindi. She's joining us for the interview. She works with me.'

Amos smiled and nodded at Lindiwe. 'Uh. Sorry, comrade. Do you mind if I finish first, so I can check it over before you read it?'

Sandile glanced at Lindiwe. She rolled her eyes.

'Okay, com. That's fine. Finish. Comrade Lindi and I will sit here and wait.'

Sandile walked over to the corner where a pile of publications lay spread on the floor. He picked up a copy of *Dawn* and one of the *News Briefing*. He handed the *Dawn* to Lindiwe and kept the other for himself. He had read it before, but it was no harm reminding himself of the unfoldings at home and abroad.

There was an article about an MK raid on a police station in Soweto, the imagined echoes of gunfire and the whoosh of a grenade spitting from an RPG7 sounding satisfyingly in his head. Did the comrades escape unharmed? He couldn't remember.

'Finished, comrade.'

Sandile would come back to it. He placed the *News Briefing* face down on the desk.

'Good, Comrade Senzo. Thank you.'

He took the sheets from Amos, straightened them and began to read, passing each page to Lindiwe as he completed it.

The first thing that struck him was the neatness and ease of the handwriting, beautifully formed letters, perfectly legible, paragraphs neatly separated, pages numbered in the top-right corners, each number ringed by a perfect circle. There were no corrections. The second thing that came to him as he read, and reread to make sure, was the language – clear, grammatically perfect (at least in Sandile's assessment), flowing logically from sentence to sentence, paragraph to paragraph, appropriately punctuated.

These observations alone, before he even applied his mind to the substance, made Amos stand out above the hundreds of new recruits Sandile had processed. Tambo could write like this. Mandela could write like this. Walter Sisulu, Govan Mbeki and the younger Thabo Mbeki could use the English language as their own.

And the substance read like a mini-memoir, logical, chronological, comprehensive and engaging. Amos's life, his family, his village, his friends, his schooling, his hobbies, his political activities, his route into exile all emerged from the pages, anticipating almost completely the normal prodding questions that other new recruits would have to be pushed for. Sandile made a few notes. He turned to Lindiwe. She seemed engrossed, although a creasing of the forehead hinted at what? Some cynicism perhaps? She made no notes.

Sandile handed the last page to Lindiwe, turned to the paper in front of him on the desk, masking with his left hand the notes he now jotted down, in a less perfect handwriting, in preparation for the report he and Lindiwe would later have to write. He looked up and smiled at Amos.

'Well, Comrade Senzo, a very comprehensive biography. Thank you.'

Amos nodded, glanced at Lindiwe and then back to Sandile.

'I have a few questions, and Comrade Lindi might have some too. For clarification, you understand?'

'Of course, comrade.'

'Your political activity at home? I don't see much.'

'No, comrade. Mainly at school, demonstrations against Bantu education.' He pointed at the pile in front of Sandile. 'And in the village – the town – organising the youth into discussion groups, giving them materials to read, discussing it. Listening to Radio Freedom.'

'Where did you get the ANC material?' Lindiwe.

'From the principal, the headmaster at school.'

'His name?'

'It's in there.' Pointing again, with eyes focused now on Lindiwe. 'Dlamini. William Dlamini. We called him Baba Dlamini.'

'And where did he get the material?'

'I'm sorry, I don't know.' He shrugged.

'Did he give the material to many students, or just you?'

'As far as I know, just me. He encouraged me to share it with other pupils and youth in the village, the ones I trusted, and discuss with them, organise the discussion groups.'

'Did he recruit you into the ANC?'

'Not directly, no. He never raised that. Only gave me the reading material and asked me to circulate and discuss.'

'Comrade Senzo, there's one thing I'm not clear on.' Sandile this time.

'Yes, comrade?'

'I'm not clear why you left the country?'

'Baba Dlamini suggested it, comrade. I did very well at school and he said I wouldn't have proper opportunities at home for my "talents", as he called them. He told me that the ANC outside would be more nurturing than the difficult politics at home.'

'Well, comrade, you have anticipated one of our questions. Earlier you said you were impatient to join MK. We give all new recruits an option, two choices: to go to MK for military training or to further their studies. Many of them have not finished school. I see you have. Most anyway choose MK, but it's not compulsory. What's your choice?'

Again Amos pinched his thumb and fingers across his eyebrows.

'MK, comrade, as I said. I would like to go for military training.'

'To go home and fight?' Lindiwe.

'I'm not sure, Comrade Lindi, that I'd make a good soldier. I guess I'll know when I've finished my training.'

'What else, then? Further your studies?'

Amos turned his smile on Lindiwe.

'Again, Lindi, I'll be in a better position to say when I've finished my training.'

Sandile winced. 'In MK, Comrade Senzo, we address each other as "Comrade", not first names.'

'Apologies, Comrade Sandile, Comrade Lindiwe.'

Sandile made as if to shuffle through the pages of the biography again, and check his notes.

'Okay, comrade, fair enough.'

Lindiwe took advantage of the pause. 'Have you ever had any contact with the boers?'

'The boers? You mean whites?'

'No. I mean security – the Special Branch?'

'No, comrade.'

'You ever been arrested?'

'No, comrade.'

'The boers ever try to recruit you?'

'Recruit me?'

'Yes, recruit you. To spy on the ANC or organisations at home?'

Sandile intervened. 'Comrade Senzo, we ask this question of everyone. If you've ever been approached by the boers to spy for them, tell us now. There will be no repercussions. The ANC has a big heart. It understands the pressure on our people. So, better you tell us now than we discover later, because later we will have to assume that you are a committed sell-out.'

'No, Comrade Sandile. I've never been approached. Never recruited. Selling out is not in my blood.'

Sandile looked at Lindiwe. She lifted her shoulders almost imperceptibly.

'Okay, comrade, good. Good. I think that's all for now. We may have more questions later, but we'll call you if we do.'

'Thanks, comrades. And … when do I leave for training?'

'As I explained, we have a lot of people to process. Anyway, it's not our department that arranges transport for training. It's the military comrades here in Maputo. You'll be informed. Be patient. Use the time to read and discuss, as you used to do at home.'

Amos stood and left the room. Sandile and Lindiwe remained huddled at the desk to discuss the biography and interview. There was some debate, some concern about the relative lack of political involvement, but they eventually reached consensus. It was lunchtime.

Later Sandile began his report.

This is a remarkable comrade. He is very intelligent, writes very well, very articulate, confident. Definite leadership material. No reasons for suspicion found.

Chapter 16

*We left our parents at home. We departed and entered
other countries, places that our fathers and mothers
do not know.
We are following freedom.*
MK Freedom Song (translation)

January 1980

S'bu had no idea of how far and how fast and for how long he had crawled, like a snake, after the shooting of Tshepo. He had no awareness of the hard, dry ground that had torn through his trousers and shirt and caked his elbows and knees with blood and grit. His shorter leg now felt like a dead appendage, dragged along with him. He had not heard the shouting at the fence behind him. Nor had he seen the flashlights that peered into the darkness of the scant thorn bushes in which he sought to disappear. Only two thoughts occupied his mind: the image of Tshepo slumped over the fence and the singular desire to get as far away as he could from that place. The rest was instinct – the alternating movement of his knees and elbows forward, hugging the ground.

It was only with the sudden silence behind him and the murmur of voices and metallic clinking in front of him that a consciousness began to re-emerge, to swirl like river water in S'bu's mind. He lifted his head and became aware for the first time of the pain in his neck, down the muscles of his back and the burning in his elbows and knees. Against the night sky he saw the silhouettes of men in uniform, rifles held in front of them, two standing before him, others spread out in kneeling and prone positions to his left and right. He stretched his arms out, his palms upwards in supplication, one leg bent ready for the next crawl forwards. He waited for the bullet.

'Wena, o mang?' The soldier in front of him raised his voice just above a whisper.

'S'bu. Ke S'bu.'

'O tswa kae?' The voice a little louder now.

'Kwa.' S'bu pointed his thumb behind him. He raised himself on his elbows. The soldier switched to English.

'What's happening here? What's going on?'

S'bu tried to gather his thoughts, the words coming from his mouth in staccato. 'Tshepo. My friend. They killed Tshepo.'

'Who killed your friend?'

S'bu waved his hand behind him. 'The boers. The boers killed him.'

The soldier knelt down in front of S'bu, lowering his voice to a whisper. 'You a fence-jumper? Letlolaterata?'

S'bu could not assimilate the word. 'I'm trying to get out of South Africa. The boers are after me. My friends ...'

'What friends?'

'My other two friends. They jumped the fence with me. I've lost them. They're gone.'

The soldier stood up and walked over to two others and whispered to them. They, in turn, motioned to others and they fanned out through the bush. The soldier came back to S'bu and knelt again. 'And your other friend, what was his name? Tshepo?'

'They shot him ... on the fence. They killed Tshepo.'

'Yes, we heard the shots. That's why we're here. We're the BDF.'

S'bu looked up. 'BDF?'

'Yes, Botswana Defence Force.'

'I'm in Botswana?'

'Yes, of course. Where did you think you were?'

S'bu's body first went limp and then the trembling began. Tears burned his eyes. He sobbed into the sand. The soldier put his hand on S'bu's shoulder. 'You're safe now, refugee. Come. Stand up.'

The soldier motioned one of his men closer. S'bu struggled first to his knees, balancing himself on his hands, then slowly stood up and then promptly toppled over again. The soldier and his colleague stood either side of him and lifted him up by his elbows. He winced.

'Take him to the truck. I'll go help find the others.'

As S'bu followed, his knees still half bent, his limp attenuated, his torso leaning forward, his arms swinging at his sides, his senses began to come alive. He breathed in the dusty air, mingled as it was with the scent of green life from the thorn bushes and the trees, and the pungent odour of his own sweat. He heard the uneven sound of his feet on the hard ground in counterpoint to that of the man in front. Although the night air was warm, his skin felt cold. His eyes were fixed on the dark swaying form ahead, fearful of losing him, noting the shifting creases in the man's uniform as he walked briskly, pausing every now and then to make sure S'bu was keeping up. Gradually his legs straightened, his limp back to normal, his torso more erect and the obsessive swinging of his arms calming.

They came to a dirt road, a military truck and a Jeep parked one in front of the other. Two soldiers with rifles slung over their shoulders stood between the two vehicles talking quietly and smoking. S'bu's escort went over and whispered to them, then led S'bu to the back of the truck and helped him climb in.

'Wait here, refugee. We'll be back when we've found your friends.'

S'bu slid onto the bench along one side of the inside of the truck. He now noticed the caked blood and mud on his hands, his trouser knees. He touched his knees and the pain stabbed at him. He felt faint. He lay back on the bench and closed his eyes, but opened them quickly again to stop the images. He sat up, dropped his head between his knees, then lay down again, closed his eyes. He was unconscious in seconds.

He dreamed he was on the Botswana side of the border fence. Tshepo walked beside him, his hand on S'bu's shoulder. He looked down at Tshepo's feet. Although they were making walking movements they did not touch the ground. 'We're okay, S'bu.' Tshepo was speaking. 'We're safe, comrade. We're in exile now. We're going to go now to learn how to fight. And then we're going to go home and kill the racists who shot me.'

S'bu was about to answer when a sudden clambering up the tailgate of the truck stirred him from his dream and he woke. His two comrades stood stooped and weary. He sat up, paused a moment for the dizziness, then got to his feet and gave them each the three-part handshake and an embrace. They were about to say something when a group of eight soldiers climbed up behind them and spread themselves along the two benches.

The soldier who had found S'bu, framed by the opening of the truck, spoke loudly.

'Okay, matlolaterata. They're going to take you to Gaborone, to the central police station. You will sleep there tonight and they will process you in the morning. Good luck.' And he was gone.

The truck spluttered to life, did a U-turn, and bumped its way up the road. S'bu tried to monitor the journey through the opening at the back but all he could see was dust. As they bounced along, his head kept banging against the metal strut that held up the canvas covering. Eventually they reached a tarred road and he could make out a long, dark road behind them, occasionally broken by the approaching lights of cars that eventually sped past. There was silence. S'bu leaned back, trying to find a comfortable place for his head between the metal strut and the canvas. He fell asleep and the dream returned, but this time Tshepo was sitting on top of the fence facing him and slowly receding as S'bu walked backwards away from him. Tshepo was smiling and waving. Every now and again his arm went limp, his smile faded, and then the smile and the waving arm started again. Finally, S'bu fell into a deep, dreamless sleep, but it wasn't long before he was startled awake by a sudden stop and the grating sound of the tailgate being swung open.

'Okay, matlolaterata. We're here. Gaborone Central Police Station. Climb out.'

S'bu and his two comrades climbed out of the truck and were led into the police station where a sleepy officer showed them to a cluster of cells, gave them each a dusty, rancid blanket, which they unrolled onto what floor space they could find between the other sleeping prisoners who grumbled and swore at being disturbed.

In the morning there was a clanging of the heavy metal door.

'Where are the three refugees?' a voice shouted.

S'bu, his comrades and four other inmates gathered at the door.

'No, no!' the officer policeman grumbled. 'Just the three who came in last night with the army.'

The three were then led into the main building and made to sit on a narrow bench outside a green door with a small white sign that read 'Interview Room 3'. S'bu whispered to the others. 'Don't tell them too much. Just tell them we ran away from apartheid and want to go and study.'

The door opened and a man in civilian clothes, with a large stomach and thick jowls, leaned out and motioned to S'bu. They all stood up.

'No, no, one at a time!'

Inside the room another man, very skinny, with a patchy beard, sat on the other side of a large wooden table. The first man motioned S'bu to take the single chair. The thin man spoke. 'So? You a refugee?'

S'bu hesitated, scratched the back of his neck. 'I've left South Africa, yes.'

'Why?'

'I want to go and study. I can't under apartheid.'

'Which party do you want to join?'

'Sorry?'

'Which party? Liberation movement? PAC or ANC or Black Consciousness?'

'I'm ANC.'

'You want to join the ANC?'

'I *am* ANC.'

'You are ANC? What do you mean?'

S'bu realised his mistake. 'I mean. I was a trade unionist at home. My union supported the ANC. I got fired after we went on strike. I'm unemployed now. I want to further my studies.'

S'bu hesitated between sentences, looking down at his hands and then up at the two men opposite. They shot questions at him, starting the next question before he'd had time to finish answering the previous one. They asked his name. He made one up. He coughed into his hand. They asked if he had any identification with him. He said not. They asked where he was from. He lied by a few hundred kilometres. They asked about his political activities at home. He said he was just a factory worker and a member of a union. He didn't mention the shop steward bit. They asked if he was wanted by the South African police. He said no, not that he was aware of.

All thought of the past or future had gone from his mind. This was a now he had to cross.

Eventually the pace of the questions slowed and then stopped. The man with the jowls stopped writing. The emaciated one pushed a printed form across to S'bu and passed him a pen. 'Fill that out. With the truth!'

S'bu did, slowly and carefully, making sure that what he filled out complied with what he had said. When he was done, he pushed it back. The thin one glanced at the form and spoke, his eyes narrowing, his mouth set in a contrived grimace. 'You South Africans are all bullshitters!'

'Why? Why you say that?'

'You refugees don't trust anyone.'

'But this is Botswana, a free black country. Why shouldn't we trust you?'

'Exactly. A free country. No apartheid here. But you answer as if you're being questioned by the boers.'

'I've told you the truth.'

'Sure.' He looked into S'bu's eyes, then turned towards his colleague. He took the sheaf of papers, dug into his shirt pocket and brought out a paper clip and clipped them together.

'Okay, young man, you say you're ANC. Are your friends also ANC?'

'I'm not sure. I only met them in Soweto on my way out.'

'Well, we'll see. But at least for you we'll arrange for the ANC rep here to fetch you and take you to Dukwe.'

'Dukwe?'

'Yes, the refugee camp up north.'

⁓

At Dukwe, S'bu squatted on the ground under a towering, wizened old tree, a baobab they'd told him. His legs were spread in front of him, a tin plate of rice and bean stew balanced on his lap. A mug of bitter coffee was placed on the ground beside him. His two comrades sat nearby, a corner of relative familiarity in a sea of strangers – fugitives from Namibia, Zimbabwe, Angola, more from South Africa, and some from places further north who seemed to S'bu like remote foreigners with very dark skins who talked in alien tongues.

Dukwe refugee camp is roughly 130 kilometres north-west of Francistown on the main road to the far north of Botswana where the borders of Botswana, Zimbabwe, Zambia and Namibia converge, a little to the east of the Sua Pan. The nearly 600-kilometre drive from Gaborone to Dukwe a week before in the dirty white Land Cruiser driven by the boy from the ANC office in Gaborone, who hardly seemed old enough to have a driver's licence, had been long and hot. The trip was debilitating, the only respite being the sense of getting somewhere – further away from the threat of incarceration back home and the terrors of the crossing, and progressively closer to the life of a fighter for freedom. But the week of waiting in Dukwe, sleeping on the ground in a musty tent at night and dozing under the big tree by day, had killed the momentum.

S'bu spooned the food into his mouth, tasting nothing. He sipped at the coffee between mouthfuls. From the direction of the weather-blanched administration building a girl approached, in her mid- to late teens, faded jeans clinging to her body, eyes that smiled perpetually, whatever shape her mouth took. Her presence in the camp had filled S'bu with a deep longing for Lizzy, the woman he had left behind in KaNyamazane without warning or farewell. He wondered what Lizzy thought. He guessed her first assumption would have been that he had left her for another woman. Or perhaps she'd assumed he'd been arrested for not carrying his pass, or was a victim of a road accident or a knife fight in a shebeen in Nelspruit.

The girl spoke to S'bu. 'They're ready for you.' She jerked her thumb towards the building.

'Who? Who is ready for me?'

'ANC. Security. They ready to interview you.'

'Can I finish my lunch?'

'They're waiting for you now.'

S'bu quickly spooned the rest of the food into his mouth, gulped down the coffee and followed her back to the building.

She ushered him through a door, touching his arm as he passed. 'Here. Give me your plate and mug.'

Much of the room was occupied by a long, fold-out metal table covered with peeling blue paint. On the walls were posters, some faded with curled corners. S'bu recognised one of the Freedom Charter, another with bright red lettering: 'Free Mandela' over a background of prison bars. There were a couple of others, official-looking posters.

Behind the table sat a coloured man, possibly only a few years older than S'bu, with curly blond hair and dark eyes and skin a few shades lighter than S'bu's. He smiled and pointed to the chair opposite.

'Hello, comrade. Come. Sit down.'

S'bu hesitated. He did not expect to be interviewed by a coloured. He did not know there were coloureds in the ANC. He did not know any coloureds back home. As far as he'd heard, all coloureds lived some kind of preferential life in Cape Town. There were certainly none in or near his village, unless you counted the few albinos that the villagers treated with mean superstition. There were few coloureds in Nelspruit, except perhaps for one of the foremen at his factory who might as well have been white.

'It's okay, comrade. Sit.' He motioned to the chair again. 'I'm from ANC intelligence and security. Based in Lusaka. The comrades sent me out here for a couple of weeks to help with the processing. There are lots of you coming out.'

S'bu sat down slowly, placed his hands on the table in front of him.

'They call me Whitehead.' He ran his fingers through his hair and giggled, hoarsely. 'The clown who interviewed me when I came out the country decided to give me that as my MK name when I couldn't think of one of my own fast enough. Now I'm stuck with it. I suspect it's the name that will be on my tombstone. But that's actually my surname. First name Jerry. You are?'

Jerry stood and held his hand out. S'bu took it after a moment, noted that the grip was firm and the execution of the triple handshake natural. S'bu gave him the name he had given to his Botswana interrogators, sat down and averted his eyes. Whitehead picked up a ballpoint pen, opened a small notebook and wrote the name, drew a circle around it and an asterisk next to the circle.

He dug his hand into the pocket of his African-print shirt. 'Ufun'ugwayi, comrade?' Whitehead held out a packet of cigarettes. S'bu mumbled and took one. Whitehead leaned over with a box of Lion matches, struck one, cupped his hands and lit S'bu's cigarette, sat down and lit his own. He reached below the table and brought up a tin cup that he placed between them. It was full of butts.

S'bu drew heavily, now able to look across at Whitehead through the smoke billowing between them in the airless room.

'Is this your real name, comrade?' Whitehead tapped his finger on the notebook. S'bu looked at the end of his cigarette and leaned over to tap ash into the cup.

'Yes, sir.'

'Sir? Sir! You can't call me "sir"! I'm your comrade!'

'Sorry, c-c-comrade.'

Whitehead pulled on his cigarette, holding it between thumb and middle finger. He brushed the smoke away with his other hand

and looked at S'bu. 'I think I know what the problem is, Comrade Whatever-your-real-name-is.'

S'bu looked at him.

'You don't trust a half-larney.'

S'bu exhaled a cloud of smoke.

'Is that it, comrade? You want me to fetch a darkie to interview you?'

S'bu mumbled: 'No, comrade.'

'Ufun'utshwala?' Whitehead reached for something below his chair. S'bu wondered what kind of bottomless container was hidden there. Whitehead came up with a three-quarters-full half-jack of Martell VO brandy. He held it out to S'bu who hesitated. Whitehead drew the bottle back, screwed off the cap, and took a long gulp, then held out the bottle to S'bu, who drank. The brandy went down his throat like hot oil. He hadn't touched alcohol since he'd left Nelspruit. He took another drink and handed the bottle back to Whitehead who placed it in the middle of the table.

'Okay, comrade, here's the story. I am a comrade. You can trust me.' He leaned back in his chair, ran his hand through his hair again, and placed his hands on either side of the notebook. 'I left the country in '76. Before the student uprisings. I'm from the Cape Flats. Cape Town?'

S'bu nodded.

'I was in my last year at UWC.'

S'bu looked puzzled.

'University of the Western Cape, the bush college for coloureds. You heard of it?'

S'bu shrugged.

'Yes, well, I was recruited into an ANC underground unit at varsity. Propaganda. We distributed leaflets and ANC publications. I had to leave when one of our unit was arrested. I also left via Botswana.'

S'bu reached for the cigarettes, looking questioningly at Whitehead. 'Sure, comrade, take one. Have another swig.' He pushed the bottle towards S'bu, who lit a cigarette, burning his fingers, then took another sip. Whitehead reached for the bottle and emptied it. He bent again to place it at his feet and came up with a full half-jack.

'Anyway, com, I was first sent to Lusaka who sent me to London to help with solidarity work and debriefing visitors from home. Then

I went to Angola, to MK, then to the GDR. You know GDR?'

S'bu shook his head.

'German Democratic Republic. DDR in German. East Germany; the communist half of Germany.'

S'bu nodded.

'There I did further military and intelligence training. Now I'm based at the Department of Intelligence and Security headquarters in Lusaka. I'm an analyst. They call us processors. Okay?'

Whitehead opened the half-jack and pushed it towards S'bu. S'bu drank and felt the warmth of the brandy move up to his head. He felt okay. For the first time in a long time, he felt okay. He needed to talk. And so he did. Whitehead picked up the pen and wrote without looking up. S'bu noted his untidy scrawl.

He started with his dreams. Whitehead didn't seem to mind. He wrote. S'bu couldn't stop talking, initially telling his story backwards, from Dukwe, the interrogation, Tshepo, the crossing, the trip from Soweto, Tshepo's uncle, the death of Patrick.

'Okay, comrade. Good. But let's start from the beginning now.'

And so S'bu went back. The factory. His union work. The referral from Tloks to Patrick. The underground secrecy and weapons training. The burying of weapons. The arrest of Tloks. The move to Soweto. Whitehead wrote furiously. He never asked questions. S'bu reached for the brandy and a cigarette again and said: 'My real name, Comrade Whitehead, is S'bu. Sibusiso. Dlamini.'

And then he told of buried weapons, a rural road, a white man and his Cressida and Baba Dlamini and an exchange of envelopes.

Note No. 5

For we are like the green earth that waits for snow
And like the snow that waits for the thaw
— Paul Ernst, *Brunhild*

April 2020
It snowed in London last night. Quite out of season. Not this time the common sound of rain gurgling in gutters and drainpipes and whispering against windowpanes that enters sleep and insists on its presence. I was, nonetheless, awoken in the dark hours. A cold white silenced the room, seeping through the dank walls and the cracked window. I did not know what had woken me – I assumed last night's pints of bitter in my bladder. I rose and padded on bare feet across the stained wooden floor to the door and down the passage to the communal bathroom. Coming back to the room I was struck by the absoluteness of the silence and some quality of light. I went to the window and parted the faded curtains.

All was whiteness outside. Kilburn was gone. London was gone. The streets, the cars, the pavements, the lampposts, the bicycles chained to lampposts, the rooftops, the eaves – all transformed. Through the dim rays of the street lights floated tiny feathers of snow.

I stayed at the window for a long time. The first feelings of something true in the early months of this, my second exile. I took the coat off the back of the door, shrugged it on over my tracksuit pyjamas and put on the black sneakers with the pink trim that Nadine had given me for my sixtieth birthday with the card that said, simply, 'Forever Young'. I went out into the streets.

All was quiet. Empty. I stepped quickly, regretting the scars the footprints left behind me. I don't know for how long I walked. I was reminded of walks in the snowed streets of East Berlin, the quietness, the clarity, the absence of commercial gaud.

I walked home, no, I walked to the bedsit, careful to place my feet in the footprints I had already left. It was still dark when I got back, slipped out of the coat and sneakers and climbed back into bed. I slept more deeply than I had in a long time, like I used to sleep after making love with Bongi, her head in the crook of my arm and her legs wrapped around mine.

In the morning I went back to the window. Cars and buses and motorcycles and pedestrians had violated the snow. It had turned brown. The garishness of Kilburn and London and the world had reasserted itself. I didn't wash. I didn't eat. I made a cup of instant coffee with two sugars. I opened this red notebook and began to tell this story. But this story will not begin here. It will begin at the beginning of the end.

Chapter 17

Friday, 10 May 2019
This gathering of the National Executive Committee of the African National Congress was different to earlier such gatherings. For one, they could use a much smaller meeting room at the Saint George Hotel and Conference Centre outside Pretoria, just off the R21 that served as a pumping artery for commuters between OR Tambo International Airport and Pretoria. The 2017 elective conference of the ANC had reduced the main committee from over eighty to just thirty-two members. There were those they now called 'The Big Five' – the president, his deputy, the secretary-general, her deputy and the treasurer-general. There used to be a chairperson, but conference had done away with that. There were the thirty-two main members and the nine chairpersons of the provincial executive committees.

The forty-six individuals sat around tables arranged in a large rectangle, with the Big Five at one short end of the rectangle. A large black, green and gold banner took up most of the wall behind them, emblazoned with the shield, spear and wheel symbol, and big letters saying 'African National Congress – Ke Nako!'

Behind them stood a lectern at which the secretary-general, Thembi Masondo, just managing to show her head above the rim, was now gathering up her notes from the organisational report she had given. She paused, tapped the pile of papers, raised her fist and shouted 'Amandla!' The members lifted their fists and responded in partial unison, 'Ngawethu', then waited for her to proclaim the next slogan, but she was quiet, picked up her notes and spoke: 'Comrade President, can you please come and give the political report?'

President Moloi leaned over to say something to his deputy, raised himself up with his hand on the deputy's shoulder, and moved to the lectern. The deputy turned to whisper something to the treasurer-general sitting to his left.

Moloi raised his fist and proclaimed, 'Ke Nako.' About half the gathering raised their fists enthusiastically. He waved a sheet of paper at the gathering. 'Comrades, these are my notes. I have not prepared a speech. Nor have I allowed my office to draft something for me. This is not the time for jargon, for prepared speeches, for slogans.' He turned and looked at the banner on the wall behind him, laughed and pointed to it. 'Except, of course, for this slogan – Ke Nako! Now is the time for speaking from the heart. For brave thinking. Ke Nako!'

This time more than half the room responded. Moloi folded the sheet of paper and squeezed it into the side pocket of his black, green and gold tracksuit top. Someone in the room laughed.

Moloi placed both hands on the lectern, bent his elbows, leaned into it until his chin almost touched the top of the lectern, then pushed himself back upright, dropping his arms to his sides.

'We've been given a second chance.' Pause. 'Perhaps a last chance.' He paused again, walked over to his chair and placed his hands on the back rest. 'Just under two weeks ago, the people, the electorate, asked us to rule, at least one more time.' Murmurs in the room. 'Yes, comrades, we all hope it is not just one more time. But that depends on us. We scraped through in the April elections.' Murmurs again. 'Why? You don't think we scraped through? Forty-eight per cent. We got forty-eight per cent! That is not a landslide, not with our history of close to two-thirds. If it wasn't for the votes our coalition partners garnered' – he nodded towards the observers from the Communist Party sitting against the far wall – 'the bloody opposition would be in power. We just held onto Gauteng, reduced majority in Eastern Cape. The opposition still controls Johannesburg and Tshwane and Nelson Mandela Bay. And they've retained Western Cape. Yes! Scraped through.'

Moloi turned to look at the banner, and walked slowly back to the lectern. 'We are only back in power again because we took steps. We took steps to save our Movement. In 2017 we took steps, with the help of our ANC veterans.' He waved his hand in the direction of the two representatives of the Veterans' League in the far corner of the rectangle. 'And the MK veterans – the real ones.' He gestured again, this time with a wide sweep of his hand. 'And the Party.' He smiled broadly. 'We took steps to reclaim our Movement. That's why we are here. All of us. We took steps and we made promises.'

Moloi moved again from the lectern and walked slowly around the room, around the back of the chairs of the gathered executive members, every now and then, as he spoke, stopping behind a chair and resting his hands on the shoulders of the occupant, then moving off again with a tap on the person's right upper arm.

'We made promises. Firstly to cleanse the ANC. To rid ourselves of factions and slates and the buying of votes. To recapture the ANC and the state from those who'd captured us – old and new capturers.' The person he was standing behind laughed, raised a fist and quietly said, 'Amandla!'

Moloi moved off. 'Amandla, indeed. We promised to deal with corruption. We promised to tackle, more ambitiously, the rise in crass materialism.' He laughed. 'And I don't mean historical materialism, comrades of the Party.' General laughter. Moloi grunted, then sunk for a moment into thought. He closed his eyes, swayed on his feet, then opened his eyes widely as if jerked out of sleep. 'We promised many things to ourselves, to our members and to our people. And now, ke nako – now is the time! We are in government. We are in power. And this time ...' He moved quickly back to the lectern, again put his hands on either side of it. 'And this time, this time we are going to keep our promises!'

A few of the members began to applaud. Others joined in, until there was a crescendo of acclamation. Thembi shouted 'Matla!' The response was instant and loud.

Moloi stood back and watched, his face inscrutable. He waited for the slogans to subside. 'Thank you, comrades, but I'm not done yet.' Laughter. 'This might be the shortest political report in the history of such gatherings, but it might be one of the most crucial for the survival of our Movement and the achievement of the goals we set ourselves from the earliest days of struggle.' He paused, moved his eyes around the room, taking in the expressions of each one present. 'So, I am not done yet. We are not done yet.'

Moloi retrieved the folded sheet from his tracksuit pocket, placed it on the lectern, unfolded and flattened it with his right hand, but did not look at it. 'Yesterday, I was inaugurated as president of the Republic. Today is Friday. On Monday we must announce and swear in our new cabinet. Early next month we announce our plans to the new parliament. We have these three days to get ready.'

Moloi walked to his chair and sat down. A few people started to applaud. He held up both his hands. 'As I said, I'm not finished yet. Just thought I'd sit down amongst you. And, anyway, my war wound is starting to throb.' Someone sniggered.

'Here's my thinking on the way forward. After I've finished my input and we've had some time to discuss, we'll break up into commissions. For the rest of the weekend, until teatime on Sunday morning. After that we'll take reports from the commissions and take decisions. We're only going to deal with governance issues. We've been dealing with organisational issues since conference. And here's what I think commissions should deal with. First, a commission to look at all ANC conference resolutions relating to governance and policy, especially those from last conference – to prioritise those for urgent implementation and make suggestions on how.'

He stood up, made his way back to the lectern, retrieved his page of notes and returned to his chair.

'The second commission – and this might upset some of you – should look at the size and make-up of cabinet. And also at the issue of official cars, blue-light brigades, presidential jets and other extrava—'

Loud voices, raised in frenzied chanting breached the walls. Something large and heavy banged against the ceiling-high wooden doors. Moloi stood up, pushing his chair back.

'Comrade Sandile, go see what's going on.'

Sandile Ndaba walked to the door and opened it gingerly. It opened inwards. The opening was blocked by a large presidential bodyguard in a black suit and opaque sunglasses.

'Don't come out, sir!'

'What's going on?'

'A demonstration, sir.'

'How did they get in?'

'We're not sure, sir. They just suddenly were here.'

Sandile craned to look over the outstretched arm the bodyguard was using to hold him back. Now he heard the chants. 'Moloi must fall! Down with Moloi!' He caught sight of placards – professionally printed – and banners with similar injunctions. Behind him the hall was quiet. The president still stood at his chair looking towards the door.

The bodyguard turned his head towards Ndaba. 'We've called for reinforcements, sir – the riot squad.'

'The riot squad? Do we still have such a thing? This is not a riot! We don't want any violence here. Let me speak to them.'

'I don't advise that, sir.'

'How many are they?'

'About a hundred, sir.'

'Let me talk to them!' Sandile tried to push past the bodyguard. The man leaned back. 'Don't do that, sir!'

Sandile stepped back, closed the door and turned around.

'Well, Sandile, what is going on?'

'It's a demonstration, Comrade President.'

Moloi twisted his head as though from an involuntary tic. 'What are they protesting about?'

'About you, Comrade President.'

'Me? Why?'

'They want you out …'

Moloi stepped back from his chair and faced the banner behind him. He laughed, from the belly. 'Hawu! They want me recalled? I've only been president since yesterday and they already want me out. Wiser people tried for two years to get my predecessor recalled and failed. What have I done since yesterday?' He paced between the lectern and the chair. 'Who are they? How many? Are they ANC?'

Sandile returned to his seat and stood behind it. 'They're apparently about a hundred, Comrade President. I don't know who they are. They seem to be well resourced, though – professionally printed placards, T-shirts and banners. They seem to be wearing ANC colours.'

'Are we safe?'

'They've called the riot squad, Comrade President. They won't let me talk to the protesters.'

'They? Who won't let you?'

'Your bodyguards.'

'But we can't have violence.'

'Yes, I told them that, Comrade President.'

Moloi started circumnavigating the room again, hands clasped behind his back, head down. He mumbled to himself. As he completed one half-circuit, he began to limp. All eyes in the room followed him. At last he stopped and spoke in a curt, staccato voice: 'Okay. That's it. We're going to continue. Take your seats.'

Moloi picked up his sheet of notes and went back to the lectern.

'Right! Where were we?'

Through the heavy wooden doors the sounds of chanting, the stamping of feet, shouts and scuffling insisted their way into the room.

'I was saying that the second commission must ask and answer some hard questions. We need to reduce the size of cabinet by at least half. We need to reduce expenses on fancy cars, battalions of bodyguards, flotillas of blue lights, lavish entertainment. We need to wrest the moral high ground back from the opposition. Where they govern they have done some of these things. Why? Why did we not retain the moral leadership we built with such difficulty in the struggle? We faltered. We fell. We failed. Now is the time to put things back where they belong. Ke Nako!'

The muted response from the gathering was smothered by the scuffles outside.

'The third commission will look thoroughly and finally at real economic transformation. If the country is not yet ready for socialism, let's at least do some real social democratic things. The fourth commission—'

Three rapid-fire shots rang out, reverberating through the hollow room as if fired within the four walls. From beyond the door a sudden silence. Members of the national executive started, scattered towards the wall furthest from the door. Moloi stared at the door. The deputy president, who appeared calmer than most, went up to him and took him by the elbow and guided him towards the others. Sandile Ndaba moved again towards the door. Moloi shouted: 'No, Sandile!'

Sandile carefully opened the door, just wide enough to peer out. The large bodyguard, perspiration dripping down his face, held his arm in the air with a pistol pointed to the ceiling. He quickly extended his left arm to stop Sandile from coming through. 'Please, sir, don't!'

'What the hell happened?'

'They were trying to storm the room, sir.'

'Who fired?'

'I did, sir. They were trying to storm the room.'

'Jesus, man! We don't want a Marikana outside an NEC meeting! Is anyone hurt?'

'I fired into the air, sir. They were pushing. The police are here now, sir. They'll disperse them.'

'Please, no violence! Let me talk to them.'

'Please, no, sir. The police are here. They will talk to them, together with the hotel management. The main thing is to protect the president. Please go back to him, sir.' And with his left hand he nudged Sandile back into the room, his right hand with the pistol still up in the air. The noise from the crowd, which had subsided following the gunfire, had risen again to an angry rumble, with only occasional outbursts. It reminded Sandile of a sudden, brief lull in a gale-force Cape Town southeaster. He closed the door. The executive members formed a static tableau. President Moloi stood slightly apart, his eyes fixed on Ndaba and the door. Sandile went up to him and reported back.

'Okay, comrade. Thanks. Let us let things cool down a bit before we continue.' Sandile was about to move off when the president called him back. 'Sandile, wait ... When we break into commissions, there is something I need to discuss with you. Let's meet in the holding room later.'

Chapter 18

April 1980
The LAM Airlines flight from Maputo to Luanda in April 1980 was the first such experience for Amos Vilakazi, aka Senzo Makhanda. He watched from his window seat as the plane ascended and Maputo, its peri-urban slums, the dense green countryside and the Mozambican coastline grew smaller. He turned to Lindiwe, appointed to escort the new recruits to Angola, and noted her hands clenched on the seat arms.

'You okay?' She couldn't hide the tremor in her voice.

'I'm fine. Thank you.' Amos smiled, laying his hand on hers. She waited a moment, then retracted her hand and let it rest on her lap. Amos turned back to the window and watched as the plane banked away from the coast and headed northwest. He traced the route in his mental geography: over Zimbabwe (just now changing its name from Rhodesia), across Zambia and finally upwards to the Angolan coast at Luanda.

~

For S'bu Dlamini the two flights, also his first, on Air Botswana from Francistown to Lusaka and on Aeroflot from Lusaka to Luanda, were rough. He clung to his seat arms and kept his head turned from the window except when he felt the plane finally begin its descent into Luanda and he turned to watch the bay grow large and foreign in the tiny window. This would be his first time near an ocean.

~

Vilakazi's and Dlamini's planes landed within an hour of each other and they were bustled with the other new recruits through the Luanda airport. They assembled in an untidy group while their ANC escorts stood with sheaves of papers for half an hour in front of a darkskinned immigration officer, speaking in a strange language.

'I know you.'

S'bu turned to the voice that had spoken to him.

Amos spoke again. 'I know you. You're a Dlamini.'

S'bu recognised the dialect but not the individual. He looked around. No one seemed to be paying them any attention. The new recruits stood in small groups composed of those who had spent some time together waiting in Maputo, in Dukwe or in Lusaka. They talked in quiet mumbles, looking around, pointing at items of interest, of strangeness.

S'bu turned back to Amos. 'Sorry?'

'Dlamini. You're a Dlamini.' Amos put out his hand. The corners of his eyes wrinkled. 'I'm a Vilakazi.'

S'bu took Amos's hand, but said nothing.

Amos spoke again. 'Aren't you a son of Baba Dlamini, the teacher? Did he also send you out?'

S'bu took his hand back. He looked down at his feet then up again into Amos's eyes.

'Hey, comrades! You two know each other?' Lindiwe paused next to them, her feet apart and hands on her hips.

Amos smiled and put his arm across her shoulders. 'Yes, this comrade here and me are from the same area.'

Lindiwe moved away far enough for his arm to drop off her shoulders. 'Asibuzi eMkhontweni! We don't discuss our personal backgrounds in MK, comrades!'

'Sorry, com.' S'bu looked at Lindiwe. He took a few steps backwards.

Amos smiled. 'Sorry, Lindi. It's my fault. I was just excited to see someone from home.'

'Hey, Comrade Senzo, we're all from home here. Let's move.' She took them both by the elbows and directed them back into the gathering of fellow recruits and then ushered them all towards the exit. S'bu moved away. Lindiwe followed him. 'You know Senzo, comrade?'

'No, I don't. But I can hear he's from my area. Maybe a nearby village, but I've been staying in town the last few years. He says he knows me.'

'What's your name?'

'My real name?' S'bu's head jerked up.

'No. No, com. Your MK name.'

'Paulo.'

'Paulo? A Portuguese name? Paulo who?'

'Paulo Freire.'

She laughed. 'Hawu! Paulo Freire? Who gave you that name?'

'Uh, Jerry. The coloured comrade.' He passed his hand over the top of his head. 'With the white hair.'

'Whitehead? Jerry Whitehead? You were processed by Comrade Jerry? Where? In Lusaka?'

'No, no. In Botswana. In Dukwe.'

They were moving out through the airport doors and into the sunlight and a wave of heavy, wet air rushed at them. S'bu smelled damp salt and something else, something fecund. They were ushered towards two open-backed army-green trucks and herded aboard with their assortment of suitcases, duffel bags, rucksacks and plastic bags. Some carried just a roll of clothing under their arms. Lindiwe placed her hand on S'bu's back and coaxed him onto the truck, passing him his duffel bag and her small suitcase. She clambered up and led him to the front of the truck and stood, with him holding onto the railing behind the cab. Two men in camouflage stood on either side of the cab, watching the new recruits board. One had a rifle slung over his shoulder, the other a holstered pistol. S'bu nodded towards the two men. 'Angolan army?'

Lindiwe laughed. 'No, no, South African army.'

S'bu slung his duffel bag over his shoulder and made a move towards the rear. She pulled him back.

'No, Paulo, MK. Umkhonto we Sizwe. The South African peoples' army. These two are your comrades.'

S'bu massaged the back of his neck. 'And that rifle he is carrying? What is it?'

'That, Comrade Paulo, is the AK.'

S'bu felt a tightness well up from the gut and into his throat. He coughed. 'When do I get one?'

The truck trundled off, and he toppled backward. Lindiwe grabbed him and pulled him back towards the railing and smiled. 'Be patient, Comrade. You still have to go for training.'

'Is that where we're going now?'

'You're going to a transit camp just outside Luanda. You'll be processed there before you move on into the deep bush for training.'

They were silent for a while. S'bu looked out at the streets of Luanda as they rolled by. Colourful posters and hoardings in a strange language with images of revolution. Pockmarked walls where some gunfight had taken place. Broken, potholed roads. People in tattered, dirty but colourful clothing. And soldiers, women and men, in uniform, everywhere he looked. He looked back at the others in the truck – all his new comrades, some in bright-coloured clothes, some fashionable, others more worse for wear. Amos caught S'bu's eye and smiled as if in mutual conspiracy. S'bu turned to savour the wind in his face.

Lindiwe leaned towards him. 'Why did you leave the country?'

'I thought asibuzi eMkhontweni?'

'No, no, com. I don't want details. Just in general. But, I am, by the way, from ANC security, like Comrade Whitehead. So just give me the general idea.'

'I was in a unit. My commander got arrested. The boers killed him. I had to leave.'

She looked at him for a long moment.

'What kind of a unit?'

'I buried weapons. I was also a shop steward.'

'So you're not really a kursant?'

'A what?'

'Kursant. It's Russian. A new recruit … a cadet.'

'Does that mean I can get my AK now?'

'Ha-ha! Your time will come. But it is good to have someone come out who was already in the underground. Most of the kursants are from political organisations, or from schools or universities, or just running away in general.' She waved at someone in the truck in front of them.

Amos approached and stood beside her, wrapped his arm around her waist and whispered into her ear. She laughed and pushed him away. He went back to lean against the side of the truck to continue his conversation with a group.

Lindiwe raised her hand with the thick cardboard folder and held it in front of them to stop the wind from drowning out her words. She spoke quietly. 'When we get to Viana I'm going to introduce you to one of my colleagues from NAT.'

S'bu had to bend to make himself heard. 'To where?'

'Viana. That's the name of the transit camp we are taking you to. We would like you to help NAT.'

'Who is Nat?'

They bumped heads as they tried to switch ears and mouths.

'ANC intelligence. They call us Mbokodo.' She leaned closer and lowered her voice further. 'If you could keep your eyes and ears open. Report to us anyone or thing suspicious among the kursants, anyone who may be impimpi. Just quietly, you know.'

S'bu raised his thumb and said loudly: 'Sharp!'

Lindiwe moved back through the truck, using the shoulders of the others to steady herself, and squeezed next to Amos.

S'bu leaned into the wind just as they slowed and turned through a large gate that was swung open by two men in camouflage with AKs over their shoulders. Lindiwe called out 'Welcome to Viana, ma-comrade!'

The men scrambled off the trucks, their luggage tossed down after them. There was chaos as each tried to gather their belongings and form a tiny safe space for themselves.

'Fall in!' A deep, loud voice.

No one moved, apart from a few who shuffled awkwardly around their luggage.

'Comrades! Leave your things and fall in! I want two platoons! One here and one here. Three lines each. Eight in a line.'

S'bu stepped forward into an open space and stood facing the loud voice. Others followed and lined up alongside.

'No! No! Not like that. Stand behind this comrade in a row of eight, then another row and a third. The other platoon over there.'

Eventually, they got it, the second platoon managing to muster only one and a half lines. There they stood, facing the front, waiting. The voice spoke again.

'Okay, good. Now wait while we consult.'

The voice, Lindiwe, the others who had escorted them from Lusaka and Maputo, plus a few more in uniform, huddled in a group some metres from them and whispered together. Lindiwe and a couple of the others held card folders in front of them and ran their fingers down the pages inside, every now and then nodding or pointing towards the assembled recruits. Lindiwe talked animatedly.

Eventually the group dispersed and the voice took his place in front of them.

'Comrades, welcome. Welcome to Viana. Welcome to Angola. Welcome to MK.'

The recruits stopped fidgeting, some emotions welling up in S'bu at the last welcome. His eyes scanned the groups for Lindiwe, but she had disappeared. Amos, standing at the head of the line alongside S'bu's, smoothed down the front of his shirt.

The voice spoke again.

'Comrades, my name is Mandla. I am the commander of this camp. This here is Comrade Lucky. He is camp commissar.' He moved over to a young man in perfectly pressed uniform and put his hand on his shoulder. 'He is responsible for your politics and your welfare while you are here.'

There were murmurs in the ranks.

'And this is Vusi, chief of staff. And over there, Comrade Velaphi, chief recording officer.' He gestured with a loose-wrist hand at a young man wearing a brand new uniform, a pistol on his belt, olive green peaked cap tilted over a pair of sunglasses.

S'bu noticed someone in a pale green uniform and peaked cap approach. Another woman comrade. She approached the commander, raised her cap for a moment to smooth her hair ... Lindiwe, now transformed into a soldier. She carried a clipboard and handed it to the commander, who turned back to the assembled group.

'And, comrades, I assume you know Comrade Lindi and the others from the recording department that escorted you.' He let the arm holding the clipboard fall to his side. 'You comrades will be here for a few days while we process you and arrange your transport to Quibaxe.' There were murmurs in the ranks again.

'Quibaxe. That's the camp up north where you will do your training. Now ...' – he lifted the clipboard – 'you are Platoon One.' He pointed to the formation in which S'bu and Amos stood. 'You are Platoon Two.' He pointed at the other.

'Okay! Order, comrades. Each of these lines is a section. Three sections to a platoon. Each platoon must have a commander and a commissar. Same with each section. After consultation with the recording officers, we are making temporary appointments.' He looked down at the clipboard and began to call out names and assign their responsibilities.

'Comrade Freire? Who is Comrade Paulo Freire?' A wave of sound rippled through the gathering.

Commissar Lucky repeated: 'Hawu! Paulo Freire?' S'bu put up his hand.

'Comrade Paulo, you are commander of Section 1, Platoon one. That's your section behind you.'

S'bu turned and looked down the line behind him. Some nodded at him.

Mandla spoke again. 'I see we have another Makana. Who is Senzo Makana?'

Amos raised his hand and stepped forward.

'It's Makhanda, Comrade Commander.'

'Makhanda? Why?'

'The whites mispronounced it, Comrade Commander.'

'Okay, Comrade Makhanda. Still, however it's pronounced, there are a lot of you in MK. You are going to be commander of Platoon One.'

Amos stepped back into line.

'Hey, Comrade. Step forward and take your place in front of your platoon.'

Amos turned to his platoon, smiled and turned again to face the front.

Chapter 19

March 1980

Unusually, for someone eliminated by the security forces far from witnesses, as Tshepo Tau was killed trying to cross the South Africa–Botswana border with S'bu Dlamini and two others in January 1980, his perforated body was brought back to his family in Soweto. More specifically, it was brought to his widowed mother and her brother, Philemon Tau. It took the security police three weeks to do so, but they returned the body and quietly provided the uncle with money for the funeral.

Now, with Tshepo duly buried in Avalon Cemetery, Philemon Tau, his uncle, sat in an obscure room of the Protea Police Station on one side of a large wooden table, with Sergeant Ndlovu and Corporal Msimang of the security police opposite him, their eyes avoiding his, except when he stopped speaking.

He was speaking now. 'You killed my nephew! You killed Tshepo! My sister's only child! That wasn't in the plan.' He shifted in his seat, trying to find comfort on the wooden chair.

'Calm down, Ntate Tau.' It was Corporal Msimang who spoke. He seemed the engaged one. The sergeant appeared as a spectator. Msimang continued: 'It was not us who killed him; it was the army.'

Tau half stood but then sat down again. 'Army. Police. Same thing. What's the difference?'

'There's a big difference, Ntate Tau. The soldiers, they are cowboys.'

Tau flicked his tongue against his upper teeth and waved his hand dismissively.

Msimang placed his hands, palms together, under his lips. To Tau, it looked like he was praying. 'It's true, Ntate. It's true. We alerted the soldiers to the crossing of the boys. We told them to catch them before they crossed and bring them to us in Zeerust.' He turned his head towards Sergeant Ndlovu. 'Me and the sergeant drove down to

Zeerust specially. We told the soldiers just to scare the shit out of the boys before they brought them to us.'

Tau's chin was bent towards his chest, his arms stretched in front him, hands spread out on the table. He sat upright again with a loud expulsion of breath. 'You bastards told me you were just going to scare them, turn them, and send them out to the ANC.'

'Yes, Ntate Tau, that was the plan. But the soldiers were late – just by a few seconds. Some of the boys had crossed the fence already. Some crazy soldier just opened fire. Tshepo was on the fence.'

Tau slumped forward. The two policemen watched. He stayed like that for a few minutes, then sat up.

'You fucking idiots! You've killed him. My sister's boy. Her only child. She's already a widow. Now she has no one, only me. And how long will I last? It won't be long before the township tsotsis suspect me. They will kill me. I drove the boys to the border. I picked the spot.'

Sergeant Ndlovu stood up and left the room. Tau didn't notice his departure. He continued: 'Even my sister is asking questions. I keep telling her I don't know how the boers found out. I told her I had taken other boys to the same spot to cross, many times, without problems. I don't know.'

Msimang spoke quietly: 'That's because the other boys were ours.'

Tau turned his head away and stared at a Wanted poster on the wall. Msimang stayed silent for a while, turning periodically to look at the door. He continued: 'We didn't know who Tshepo's friends were so we couldn't send them ourselves. We had to catch them in the act of leaving the country first.'

Tau, his chin on his chest, didn't respond. When the door finally opened, Ndlovu hovered there for a moment, then motioned to Msimang to leave. Msimang's brow creased. He left, closing the door a little harder than necessary.

Ndlovu pulled a chair up next to Tau and sat down close to him, quiet for a long time, then put his hand on Tau's back and spoke quietly.

As Philemon Tau walked from the police station back to his Anglia, which he'd parked some distance away, beneath his anger and sorrow an idea was forming. He would accept Sergeant Ndlovu's offer.

Note No. 6

June 2020
I have two pictures: the photograph I hold in my hand, and the image I retain in my head. In this one in my head, you are seated next to me on the rock that slopes down towards the dam, your short bare legs spread out in front of you, your shoes long discarded, the water lapping up against your feet. The child-size fishing rod is clutched tightly in your right hand, while your left is stretched out to my rod, helping me, as you say, 'to catch a very big fish, Daddy'.

Our picnic basket and cooler box stand a little behind us, where the rock provides a slight levelling before it continues its downward slant past us to the water. I can still conjure up the smell and the taste of the egg-mayonnaise sandwiches you insisted on making yourself before we left home to spend our father-and-daughter day together at this dam on the outskirts of Pretoria. Yes, you left one helluva mess behind in the kitchen for your mother to clean up, but she chased us away, steering us out of the front door with our fishing rods, tackle box, bucket for the fish we never caught, picnic basket and the cooler box with juice for you and cold beers for me.

Yes, Nadine, it all comes back to me with an unexpected clarity that only serves to put in painful relief the distance of time and space, confusing the pathway between joy and misery: joy at the closeness of you perched next to me on our rock, your left hand on my fishing rod, your eyes turned up to me with the care and wonder of a child, the smell of you – the scented lip-balm your mother taught you to use – the smell of the water, faint wafts of fishiness, of the minty scent off the pine trees, the hint of decay off the flotsam brushing back and forth against the rock just below our feet; misery at the absolute distance of it all, distance from this cold space in which I now find myself.

Lying here on this bed, with the rain whispering incantations against the window, the bare light bulb swaying under no obvious causal force from the ceiling of this apartment they call a 'bedsit', I hold up the photo I found in a pouch of my hurriedly packed suitcase. In it, you smile, not at the camera, but at me behind the camera. You were always like that in front of cameras, more interested in the person behind it than the lens that would stamp your image forever onto the pages of family history. You hold your tiny fishing rod in your hand as if an irrelevant prop. Behind you I see the dam, the pine trees along the far shore, and – miraculously – a gull of some sort swings into the picture behind your head as if swooping to snatch you up and disappear with you into the cobalt sky.

I close my eyes on this bed of misery and hear once more the gentle wind in the pines and nearby shrubs. I hear the swish of the fishing-rod spool and the tiny splash as you once more cast your line far out as I taught you. And, most of all, I hear the music of your voice, your laughter, your silly questions and surprising observations. I hear the clink of bottles in the cooler box as you dig for another juice and offer your dad another beer with a 'Don't get drunk now, Daddy. Drunk people don't catch fish.'

Chapter 20

August 1986

The first time, perhaps, that S'bu Dlamini felt like a real guerrilla was with the crossing of the Zambezi River in a rubber dinghy at the confluence of Zambia, Zimbabwe, Namibia and Botswana. Sure, he had fought against Unita in the bushes and forests of Angola, survived ambushes, killed and been wounded in battle. But that was somehow different – a foreign battle field in someone else's war.

As the boat carrying him and the three members of his unit was pushed into the water from the northern, Zambian bank, and their armed escorts splashed on board, he looked out towards the southern bank and remembered photographs and movies of freedom fighters elsewhere fording rivers, homeward into battle. He looked up at the dark sky. It must be close to midnight. As their escorts rowed the dinghy mid-stream, and he felt the pull of the river eastward towards the Victoria Falls, he held with one hand onto the rope handles laced through the side of the boat and with the other onto his duffel bag wedged between his wet boots, and savoured the sounds of the quiet splash of oars, the tinkling of rifle straps against gun metal, the whispered instructions between oarsmen, the distant roar of stronger waters. His thoughts travelled.

On the flight from Luanda to Lusaka, the wait in the safe house in Lilanda, the briefing there by comrades JM and Chris, the Land Cruiser drive down to Livingstone and then west to the crossing, and now on this dinghy on the river of crossing, his one thought had been 'I'm going home – I'm going to fight!'

It was six years and four months since his arrival in Angola, six months' basic training in Quibaxe, then the long wait for the next order which, when it finally came, had him on a flight to Moscow and ten months' intellectual and physical slog in Odessa.

Now the dinghy lurched, listed slightly, then calmed itself when the escorts shifted their weight. One of them spoke: 'Hippo.' The rhythm of the crossing slowed again. S'bu's thoughts migrated again.

After the Soviet Union, it was back to Angola, again to Quibaxe, as a tactics instructor. Then the deployment against Unita in the Angolan bush; the patrols, the ambushes, the battles, the deaths. Then the battle to take back Pango camp from the mutineers, followed by three months' harsh survival training until, finally, this – this grand crossing.

He was roused by the scraping of the shallows against the bottom of the dinghy. Two of their four escorts jumped out and dragged the boat through the reeds onto the bank.

'Okay, comrades, climb out, move away from the water.'

S'bu and his unit stepped into the shallows and onto the bank, crouched to avoid providing silhouettes to possible watchers – the boer army occupied the Caprivi Strip, only a few kilometres west. Once everyone had disembarked, the dinghy was dragged further up the bank, S'bu wincing at the clatter. The lead escort came up to him and crouched alongside. He motioned to the others.

'Come, comrades,' he whispered. 'Get ready to walk.' The others shuffled to them with bent bodies. 'We're in Zimbabwe now. We've got a bit of a walk to get into Botswana. Single file. Stay close.'

They stood and moved into single file, the escort commander in front, followed by S'bu. Two of the escorts stayed with the dinghy. The fourth took up the rear. As they set out, he cautioned: 'Careful of wild animals, comrades. One comrade got mauled by a buffalo around here.' The line hesitated. 'He survived, comrades, but now they call him Buffalo Soldier.' The sniggering went down the line like a tremor.

They steered away from the wetland along the riverbank and into a forest of tall trees and shrubs, slowing to scramble over fallen branches and trunks, pushing aside wayward vegetation that intersected their path. S'bu moved mechanically, his shorter leg following the other with minimal limp, without thought or volition. He wished he were carrying a weapon, even if just to complete the mental picture of the real guerrilla, but there were no likely enemies here. They would be issued weapons in Botswana before infiltration into South Africa.

After about an hour they crossed a fence and came to a tarred road. Parked on the opposite verge was a Cressida. S'bu cringed. The lead escort turned to him.

'We here, comrade. Botswana. Wait here.' He started to make his way to the road then suddenly turned back. 'Here, mfowethu, bamba la,' and handed S'bu his AK, returned to the road, crossed to the car, and bent down to the driver's window. The door opened and a figure emerged – no more than a silhouette in the dark, but short, warmly dressed against the bite of the August night. As the shadow approached across the road, S'bu saw she was a woman.

She and the crossing commander came up to them.

'Comrade Paulo, this is Thembi. She's the commander of MK, la eBotswana. Thembi, this is Paulo Freire, the unit commander.'

Thembi put out her hand. 'Aha! The famous Paulo Freire. Welcome to the Front, comrade.' S'bu took her hand and gave the triple handshake. Thembi raised her left hand to his shoulder and pulled him in for an embrace. Her head came up to just below his shoulder. With short steps, purposeful, energetic, she headed over to the others, standing back under the protection of low trees, and greeted each of them with the shake and embrace. Then she motioned them forward and returned to S'bu. 'Let's go, comrades. Into the car.'

They moved to cross the road, S'bu beside her. The escort commander beckoned the others to join them. He called out in a stage whisper: 'Hey! Yima, Comrade Paulo.' S'bu stopped and turned.

'Isibham' sam', comrade!' S'bu started, reached for the strap of the AK still hanging from his shoulder, and returned it with a laugh. 'Sorry, com. Bamba. Hambani kahle.'

They shook hands and the escorts disappeared back into the forest. At the car, Thembi pointed S'bu to the front passenger seat. The rest of his unit climbed into the back, their bags on their laps. Thembi turned from the driver's seat.

'No man, comrades. Put your bags in the boot. We're going to go through roadblocks between here and Gabs. You can't look like damn refugees I've just picked up.' They did as instructed and when they clambered back in, Thembi switched on the interior light and faced them. 'Right. Who are you, comrades? Me, I'm Thembi Masondo.'

Her voice had a warmth, but her words were clipped, spare, economic. Her face was dark under the overhead light. Her eyes darted, looking from one to the other, then to S'bu in the seat next to her. Her hair was short, in Afro style. A dark-coloured polo-neck sweater came up to her chin, seeming to throttle her.

151

S'bu turned and reached his arm out to each of his unit members in turn. 'This is Jackman. He's the unit commissar.' Jackman nodded. He was big, the top of his head touching the car ceiling.

'And eto, eto tovarishch Tolstoy.' S'bu slipped easily into the Russian. 'On nash inzhener.' Skinny and lanky, Tolstoy gave a smile that was warm, his eyes crinkling and reflecting light. 'And that,' S'bu reached his hand to the far corner of the back seat, 'that is Comrade Vusi, our logistics man.' Vusi nodded. He was short and stubby, his skin was lighter than the others, even in this subdued light.

Thembi nodded and smiled, then turned off the light, and checked the road and behind. She started the car and spoke again. 'Khorosho, tovarishchi. Now listen. We're going to drive to Gaborone where we'll put you in a safe house until you cross. It's about nine hundred kays south from here. We'll stop in Francistown for a bit. There'll be roadblocks after Francistown. You are students, coming from Francistown back to university in Gabs. Niyangithola, ma-comrade?'

They grunted and nodded consent. She put the car in gear, did a U-turn and pushed the speed up to 140kph on the long, straight road. The back-seat contingent put their heads back and went to sleep. S'bu sat silently watching the road.

Chapter 21

August 1986
Now that Senzo Makhanda was out in the open, so to speak, as secretary of the ANC Economics Desk based in Lusaka, he could – he wanted to (needed to for his degree certificate) – revert to his real name. His Ghana-supplied passport indeed named him as Amos Vilakazi, but many still referred to him as Makhanda. Now, in this August of 1986, on this British Caledonian flight from Lusaka to Gatwick, he looked out the window at the darkened continent passing below. And as the plane traced its path northward, his mind traced his own path through Angola as platoon, then company commissar, his brief stint as a political instructor, then Party School in communist Russia, then – at his pleading – a degree in Economics from the London School of Economics, culminating in his appointment to the Economics Desk and assurance of an upward path to the future.

Indeed, the future was on his mind now on this flight, as it was for many who watched – perhaps too optimistically – the apparent unravelling of apartheid. It had been just under a year since South African business leaders had defied their government to meet with the ANC in Lusaka. And a month or so later, the Commonwealth leaders, meeting in Nassau, had appointed an Eminent Persons Group to plumb the possibility of a negotiated end to apartheid. And only earlier this year, in the same month that Olof Palme was murdered in a Stockholm street, the UDF travelled to Stockholm to meet with the liberation movement. Yes, it was the time of imagining the possibility of a new South Africa and, in the spirit of such imaginings, there arose interminable gatherings about South Africa after apartheid. And Amos Vilakazi was on his way to one such gathering in London to ponder the future economy of a future country.

Turning now from the window, from the splattering of pale lights in the vastness below, Amos turned on the overhead reading light, reached for his briefcase between his feet and took out the conference discussion papers to continue his reading. He fell asleep, faint smile on his face, while reading a paper on the need for a mixed economy and awoke only to the sudden grind of wheels unfolding in the air above a dim morning London. Unusually fast through passport control, baggage collection and customs, dragging his wheeled suitcase behind him, he took the train to St Pancras and, having lost some of the fitness and inclination of the Angola days, eschewed the walk and took the 73 bus up Pentonville Road and alighted at Penton Street where the ANC had its London office. After the warm handshakes and Russian bear hugs, a courtesy call on the chief representative, much waiting around being ignored, an early lunch at the pub up the road with a briefing on the conference, he was given directions to his modest hotel back down Pentonville Road into Euston Road and off into the side streets opposite Kings Cross.

Amos checked in at the glass window with the hole that looked more like the counter of a bank teller than a reception desk, then wound his way with suitcase in tow down the uneven and confusing corridor to Room 43c. He threw his briefcase onto the only flat surface in the room – a dressing table – and heaved his luggage onto the bed. He undressed, squeezed into the bathroom for a shower, then, dried and perfumed, took out the remainder of the conference papers and lay back on the bed. He was soon back asleep.

A timid but insistent knock on the door woke him from one of those disturbed travellers' dreams. He groaned, rolled off the bed in his underpants, grabbed a towel just in time to see a blue envelope appear beneath the door and to hear the sounds of retreating footsteps. He let the towel slip to the floor as he stooped for the envelope and slipped his finger under the flap to open it. A blue card emerged:

Greetings. Welcome back to London.
Meet me at The Old Bell, Kilburn.
Tomorrow 19:30.
O.B.

Chapter 22

August 1986
Preparing for his first firefight on home ground, S'bu was instinctively calm, a stillness born out of past experience, of battle in the chaos of the Angolan bush. But, after the Angola experience, there was something incongruous about this terrain. Here there were no vast tracts of forest, no empty mountain ranges, no plains where the eye could wander vastly without sight of occupation. Here it was farms, villages, towns, fences and roads everywhere. And everywhere white farmers, black farmworkers, policemen, soldiers and a more or less bustling population. You had to work hard, be constantly on edge, to stay alone, to stay unremarked. And, if you were noted, you had to have a damn good explanation for being and for being there – not just a wordy explanation ('Nee, baas. I'm from Jo'burg, baas. I'm visiting my auntie in the village, baas. What's in the bag, baas? It's just my clothes, baas.'), but a total dramaturgy, with costume, gait, accent, hairstyle, props, the works. All had to stave off suspicion and idle curiosity. Here there was no respite, no dark endless forests in which to be yourself.

As he and his unit lay in wait on this fortunately dark August night behind a small bushed mound beside the patrol road that ran along the Botswana–South Africa border, S'bu ran the battle through his head, tucked the butt of his AK into his shoulder and cast his eye once more down the barrel, then looked across to Jackman in prone position to his left and Tolstoy and Vusi to his right.

The crossing the night before had been surprisingly easy, almost boring, mundane – a night's outing. As the Gaborone night dropped suddenly from the sky, Thembi had driven them the sixty-or-so kilometres from the safe house to somewhere near the Sikwane border post, with their weapons hidden in a false petrol tank in the 4x4. She had been quiet during the drive, had done all the talking over the past days as she prepped them for the crossing – checking their luggage for traces of their time outside the country: ticket stubs, receipts, clothing labels, snacks, letters, photographs, cigarette packets. She had given them their money, their instructions, their pep talk, which they didn't really need – they were fully pepped.

She had also expressed her disquiet about their first planned mission, but S'bu had remained adamant. 'Listen, Sis' Thembi, we are going to do it. I know it's risky, but it's what the boers will least expect.'

Thembi spoke slowly. 'Yes, Comrade Paulo, I know. But they will expect you to retreat into Botswana and put us in shit.'

'That's the point, Sis' Thembi. They will expect us to withdraw into Botswana and we will be on our way the other way – deep into the country.'

Thembi sighed, pulled at a twist of her hair above her forehead. 'And if they cross into Botswana?'

'But, would they do that, Sis' Thembi, without preparation, without planning? I don't think so. They will complain to the Botswana government who can genuinely claim that no MK unit crossed back into their country after the attack.'

Thembi lifted her shoulders and rolled her eyes, silent for a moment. She ran her right hand up and down her left arm. 'I have an idea. We have a senior contact in the BDF, the Botswana De—'

S'bu coughed. 'I know what the BDF is.'

'Okay … We have a contact. We'll tell him we have intelligence about a possible boer incursion at the border close to your operation.'

Tolstoy cleared his throat. 'Why? What will they do?'

Thembi looked at him. His eyes belied the naivety of his question. 'Well, comrade, if the boers are stupid enough to follow in hot pursuit across the border, they will get the surprise of their lives.'

S'bu worked hard on rationalising his guilt. He knew that planning an attack on a boer army border patrol one day into his unit's sojourn inside the country and right next to the border was, by most measures, lunatic; except by the measure that he was applying: revenge. It was one of these border patrols that had killed Tshepo and nearly himself and there was no more fitting a closing of the circle of exile than to hit where he had been hit. He could not tell his unit that. He could not tell Thembi that. He had to use his powers of persuasion and cash in on the respect he had earned in Angola and the Soviet Union. After all, one of the tenets of guerrilla warfare – of all warfare – was surprise and, damn it, those boers were going to be surprised!

And so Thembi had, voicelessly, driven them the sixty kilometres to the border, helped them unpack the weapons from their concealment, and herself cut the fence and silently ushered them through. S'bu, emotionless at this momentous crossing, turned back one last time to see the dark shape of Thembi crouched at the fence with a faint torch held in her mouth, diligently fixing the breach they had made.

And now, lying in wait to execute 'Sibusiso's Revenge', the first rumble of an approaching truck reached S'bu's ears and he whispered: 'Niready, madoda? Wait for my first shot.' And he felt for the two hand grenades fastened to his belt.

And then, just as the truck crested a slight mound in the road about two hundred metres to their right, the moon, as if bestowing its blessing on the coming battle, emerged from behind the bank of clouds, providing S'bu with an eerie but clear view of the truck and its occupants: what looked like two white officers in the cab and four black soldiers on the back. He lowered his eye to his rifle sights and aimed at the windscreen in front of the driver and, when he was sure of himself and of all the shooting he had done, in and out of battle, he tightened his finger and pulled the trigger. Five rapid shots. Jackman to his left, Tolstoy and Vusi to his right, opened fire on automatic. The truck stopped dead. There was a silence, a sudden lull, as if all nature had gone quiet to listen to this thing of humankind. Then Vusi leapt up and half crawled towards the truck, tossed a grenade into the back and dropped flat. The explosion shook the night. S'bu saw the passenger door of the cab fly open and an officer stumble out, pistol pointed at S'bu. He opened fire again and the man fell and went still. Then all went still, except for the faint tinkle of grenade shrapnel still falling from the air onto the metal of the truck.

S'bu stood. 'Forwards, comrades.'

The men rose and approached the truck, Tolstoy and Vusi to the back, S'bu and Jackman to the front. Jackman kicked at the officer on the ground. 'Dead.' S'bu looked at the driver. All five bullets had hit home, perforating his head and chest.

Three rapid shots rang out. S'bu and Jackman ducked and crept around to the back. Vusi was standing with rifle pointed into the back of the truck. 'One of the sell-outs was still alive,' he whispered. 'He tried to shoot me.'

S'bu stood up, stretched his back, looked up at the sky. The moon was gone again, spectacle over. 'Right, comrades, follow me.' And he walked with a deliberate step to the border fence.

'Hey, komandir, where the fuck we going? I thought we weren't going back into Botswana.'

S'bu stopped and turned to them. They huddled around, none of them sure how to deal with the post-battle high.

'No, comrades, we're not crossing. We're going to leave tracks as if we did. We're going to cut the fence again as if we left that way.'

And so they followed, seeking ground for their feet that would make the clearest tracks. At the fence S'bu pulled wire cutters from the side pocket of his trousers, cut the fence and pushed the strands outwards. Then he turned. 'Right, men, go back using the tracks we just made.'

They moved carefully back, past the silent truck and back to the other side of the road where they had lain in wait. S'bu cut a leafy branch from a low thorn bush and used it to sweep their tracks as they moved off. They found their way back to the clump of trees where they had left their bags, packed away their weapons, and moved swiftly in the dark, southeast into the interior.

Chapter 23

August 1986

When Amos entered the pub in Kilburn at precisely 19:30, Otto Bester was seated on an upholstered bench in the far corner, his back to the wall and a three-quarters-full pint of lager on the table in front of him. He watched the young man, immaculate in a grey suit, sidle over to the bar, stand for a while, then make his way over to Bester with an ice-frosted glass of white wine in his hand. He sat down.

'Bester, I had to forego the conference reception to be here. You need to plan better.'

'And hello and how are you to you too, Amos? Sorry about that, but opportunities were limited.' He pointed at Amos's glass. 'You drinking girls' drinks now, Mr Vilakazi? What happened to the whiskies?'

'Ha, meneer Bester, I can't afford whiskey any more. We get 14 Kwacha a month in Lusaka, you know.'

'Yes, I know. And the money we give you.'

Amos scratched at his eyebrows. 'Otto, you know I can't be seen to be spending money I can't explain. Anyway, this wine is bought with the forex allowance I get for these trips. And wine is more distinguished for an international jet setter like me, no?'

Bester had travelled to escape a highveld winter in favour of a northern summer, but this August was a little cooler than usual for a typical London summer. He rubbed the evening chill from his bare arms below the sleeves of his short-sleeved shirt. Amos sipped at his wine, keeping his eyes on Bester over the rim of the glass.

Bester took a swig of his beer, kept his gaze fixed on Amos and spoke quietly. 'Welcome to London, Amos. It's good to see you, as always. How you been?'

Amos pushed his glass forward on the table. Leaned closer. 'I've been good. Very busy. Always busy.'

'Yes. You're going up in the world. Very good.'

Amos lifted his glass at Bester. Bester raised his mug. 'Cheers!'

Amos pointed at Bester's bare arms. 'Aren't you cold, Otto?'

'Actually, I am. This blerry place can't even do a proper summer. I have something in my bag.' He bent down to the knapsack under the table and fished out a green tracksuit top. As he pushed his arms into it and pulled it over his head, he reached into the side pocket and pressed the record button on the hand-held tape recorder.

'Jesus, Bester! You want people to see the secretary of the ANC Economics Desk talking to a boer wearing a Springbok jersey?'

'Sorry, man. It's all I've got. No one here will notice.'

Amos fidgeted on his chair, eyes darting around. The pub was sparsely populated. Unusual for a London pub at this time of night. 'So, Otto,' he turned back to Bester. 'how things at home?'

'Hey, Amos, you know ... Hotting up. Your guys are giving us a hard time.'

'My guys?'

'You know what I mean. Making the country ungovernable. Students. Unions. Terrorist attacks. PW extended the state of emergency to the whole blerry country in June.'

'Yes, I know, Otto. And in May you guys tried to bomb me in Lusaka and hit a UN refugee camp. You screwed up the Eminent Persons Group mission. More sanctions are coming. Thatcher can't stop them now. Damn stupid.'

'I know, I know ... That was the military. Bunch of idiots, led by idiot politicians.'

'You mean the police are not idiots, Otto?'

Bester lifted his glass. 'Actually, Amos, they are. I've left them.'

Amos put his glass down, looked around the pub and back at Bester. 'You've what?'

'Ja, I've left the vokken police.'

'So, who am I talking to then? You really work for Unisa now?'

Bester brushed a fringe of hair from his forehead. It was longer than usual. 'Ha-ha, Mr Vilakazi. Nope. Me and my unit have been moved to the NIS – National Intelligence Service. And they *are* more intelligent, I can tell you. They better understand what you and me are doing. And their head, Niël Barnard, is a bright, bright man; damn bright man.'

'And what is it you and I are doing, Otto?'

'You know, Amos. Finding a middle way.'

'Middle of what?'

'Come on, man, don't play. Middle of the extremists. The commies on your side, the Nazis on mine.'

Amos picked up his empty wine glass, stood up and walked to the bar, returning with a refill to continue where Bester had left off.

'Yes, I know, Otto. I just like provoking you. But you've got to understand, on my side there's no thick khoki line between what you call extremists and the rest. It's gradations, shades.'

'Yes, but ...'

'No, Otto. In a sense, we're all extremists on my side, all communists or communist sympathisers. That's the ideological frame your side has laid down for us. Extremism begets extremism.'

Otto drained his beer. 'Hey, Vilakazi, that soutpiel university has made you clever, hey? An ANC intellectual. That's good, that's good. Give me a sec.' He hoisted himself from the bench and picked up his empty glass. Amos stood. 'Whoa, Bester. You're not going to the bar with that top on. Give me your glass. What you drinking?'

When Amos returned, Otto nodded his thanks and sipped at the lager.

'So, what you saying, Amos? You an extremist now?'

'Actually, Bester, in technical terms, from your viewpoint, I am.'

'What do you mean "in technical terms"?'

'I've been recruited into the Party.'

Bester lowered his glass. 'You've joined the SACP? Jirre!'

'Hawu, Otto, I thought you knew better: nobody *joins* the Communist Party – you are recruited, spotted.'

'So you a blerry commie now?'

'Meneer Bester, I'm used to more sophistication from you. I told you it's in "technical terms". I'm a member. That doesn't mean I'm a believer. It's a career move. You keep encouraging me to advance. Well, I'm advancing.'

Bester tugged at the neck of his tracksuit top, letting some air in.

'Yes, yes, Amos. I'm sorry. You're right, of course. You just hit me with it so sudden; I thought you'd defected.'

'Defected, Otto?'

'Well, you know ... I thought for a minute there you'd gone over to the extremists.'

'I told you, Otto, the boundaries are woolly. There are some sensible communists who know that South Africa, even if apartheid is gone, is not ready for communism; who understand the need for some talking, compromising. There are some of those.'

'Who, precisely?'

'All in good time, Otto. All in good time.' He patted at the left breast of his jacket.

Bester curled his thick fingers around his glass and stared at Amos, quiet for now. He longed for a cigarette but he had chosen a bloody pub that now banned smoking inside. His mind traced the trajectory of his relationship with Vilakazi over the years, like a finger moving with nostalgia over a route map to fathom the road travelled from A to B and all the stops in between. In two months it would be seven years since his first meeting with Vilakazi. This boy was only – what was it? – twenty-four years old, ten years his junior, and already well on his way. Seven years ago he had struck a golden seam. And the mining was going well. He took his eyes off Amos and glanced around the pub. Diagonally opposite, a few metres away, at a table in the middle of the pub, sat two pallid but attractive young English women. They were looking in their direction. He raised his glass and turned his smile to them. They turned away. He put his glass down and turned back to Amos. 'Two pretty chicks at two o'clock, Amos.'

Amos didn't turn. 'You seriously want us to pick up women in an English pub in these circumstances? Zip your pants, Otto. And, anyway, I'm married now.'

'Shit, Amos! I forgot. Congratufuckinglations!' He held out his hand to Amos, who hesitated for a moment then took it limply.

'You forgot? I never told you, so how can you have forgotten?'

'Amos, you're not the only friend we have in Lusaka. I heard about it.'

'From who?'

'Never mind who. One of our friends over there. They were at your wedding party.'

'Ha! That narrows it down. The place was packed.'

'So who is she, Amos?'

'I thought you knew everything.'

'Just that you got married.'

'Her name is Lindiwe.'

Bester raised his glass. 'Ah, nice name. How d'you meet?'

Amos raised his glass in return, then drained it. 'Actually, strangely enough, she was the one who interviewed me when I arrived in Maputo.'

'She with security? Jeez! So you arrive in exile and the first thing you do is screw your interrogator?'

'Please, Otto. Cloak your prejudices. She didn't interrogate me. And I didn't start anything with her until much later, when I came back from varsity.'

'Okay, okay, but does she know about me?'

'Jesus, Bester! Is jy mal? Of course not!'

Bester noted the slip into Afrikaans. 'So you have secrets from your wife?'

'We all have secrets from each other in this turmoil of ours. Of course I can't tell her about us. I can never tell her about us. And you'd better make sure she doesn't find out from some slip on your side.'

'And where's she based now?'

'She's back in Maputo.'

'So you guys are living separately. And, by the way, after the Nkomati Accord, you guys are not supposed to have trained people in Maputo.'

'And you guys are not supposed to be providing support to Renamo. And, yes, we are living apart. Many ANC couples are.'

'It's not us, it's the military.'

'Yeah, sure.' Amos stood and returned to the bar, taking the opportunity to assess the two young women. They were attractive but looked out of place in this pub. When he returned to his seat, Bester was taking off the tracksuit top.

'You not cold any more?'

'A bit sweaty, actually. So … what's her real name?'

'Who, Otto?'

'Lindiwe, your wife, of course.'

Amos pushed his glass away. 'Look, Otto, you told me a long time ago, when this … this thing started, that I was not going to be your spy. I was going to be your advisor on trends and tendencies in the ANC and the chances of a negotiated settlement. My wife has nothing to do with that. Don't ask me to give you information about her. Don't.'

'Okay, Amos, jammer. But where does she fit in the political scheme of things? You must have married her for a reason, some sort of empathy?'

'I married her because she's pretty. She's intelligent. She's a good woman. And being married in the ANC is good for me.'

'Good for you?'

'Yes. It makes me a complete ANC family. A closed unit.' Amos pulled his glass closer again and took a long swig. He smiled with a hint of mischief. 'And, anyway, being married in Mbokodo is a good thing. If suspicion is ever raised about me, she will no doubt protect me.'

'Ha, Amos, you're a real Machiavelli. You'll go far. Okay, what have you got for me today?'

Amos reached inside his jacket and took out a long thick envelope and pushed it across the table. 'Lots for you there. My party unit members; summaries of party documents; some analysis of likelihood of accepting negotiations; and the programme of this conference I'm at. Should be interesting. Everyone wants to talk these days of South Africa after apartheid. But I guess I'm not the only friend you guys have got there.'

Bester grunted, then smiled, his dimples accentuated by the shadows thrown by the dim pub lighting. 'No comment, Amos.' He held up the envelope – 'Thanks for this' – then bent to slip it into his knapsack and came back up with a smaller envelope in his hand.

'And this is for you. Five hundred quid – British quid.'

Amos slipped the envelope into the pocket vacated by his envelope.

'Okay, Amos, you leave first. It's been good to see you again. In the envelope with the money is a note with instructions for our next meeting, as well as some questions we'd like you to try to get answers to. Go well.' He stood up and put his hand out. Amos didn't look up. He slowly drained his glass, then took Bester's hand, turned and left.

Bester sat down again and sipped slowly at his beer, glancing across at the two women. One got up to leave. The other didn't look back. He tipped his glass up and let the remains of the lager slip in one stream down his throat. Outside, he looked around, crossed the street to the bus stop and waited there to see if anyone followed him out of the pub. After a minute, the other woman came out, hesitated at the door, looked around as if unsure which way to go. Bester looked at his watch and then turned towards the tube station, crossing the street now and then. The woman also seemed to be going to the tube station. He ducked into a shop doorway and lit a cigarette. She walked past.

⁕

Back at the MI5 Gower Street headquarters the next morning, Sandra Collingwood and Judy Hutchins briefed the Security Service's South Africa desk officer and her MI6 counterpart, Martin Simmonds, about their previous day's surveillance of Amos Vilakazi. A manila envelope lay on the table before them.

When they were done, Simmonds, in an almost caricatured Eton drawl, spoke. 'And who was this fellow the target was meeting?'

Sandra looked at Linda and back to him. 'We don't know, sir,' she shrugged. 'He's not been of interest to us before.'

'And? What did you make of the nature of the meeting?'

'Nature, sir?'

'Yes, nature. Was it two old pals meeting for a pint? Or something more sinister, eh?'

'Well, sir ...' Sandra looked across at their desk officer, who nodded assent. 'Well, sir, they were unlikely friends.'

'Indeed? Why not?'

'Well, for one, it is a bit unusual for a black and white South African to be friends.'

'Oh yes? And how do you know the other fellow was a South African?'

'He looked it, sir.'

'Looked it?' Simmonds ran his thumb and forefinger across his moustache. 'And you can tell a white South African by his looks, can you?'

'Actually, I can, sir. He looked like an Afrikaner. We've had to do surveillance on enough of them.'

'Indeed. And what else?'

'What else, sir?'

'Yes. What else might have led you to conclude this was not a meeting of old pals?'

Sandra looked at her desk officer again. She raised her eyebrows.

'The envelopes, sir.'

'Envelopes?'

'Yes, sir. The subject and the other man exchanged envelopes.'

'Oh, really? Interesting. Anything else?'

'Well, the target left the pub first. Judy followed him. He went back to his hotel. I followed the other gentleman.'

'You did? Excellent. And where did he go?'

'Don't know, sir. He took countermeasures. I lost him.'

'Mmm ... You don't by any chance have a photograph of this other chap, do you?'

Judy pushed the envelope over to Sandra who took out a wad of black-and-white images, flipped through them and handed an enlarged one showing the back of Amos's head and the full face of Bester.

The MI6 man picked it up, tilted it for better light, and grunted. 'Goodness! We know this fellow. We have him on file. Former South African special branch. Now with NIS. Well done, girls!'

The MI5 desk officer spoke. 'Excellent. Can we have his name, please.'

'Sorry, ma'am, can't do. Need to know.'

'Really?'

'Really, ma'am. No can do.'

The desk officer stood up, gathered the photos together and stuffed them into the envelope. 'So, this is the nature of the collaboration between our services? One way, is it?'

'Not at all, ma'am. I can tell you this. This Vilakazi fellow is going places in the ANC and, from what we know, this fellow he met is a mover and shaker on the other side. If Vilakazi is his source, this could be good for us. This could be something we could use down the line.'

Note No. 7

*And memory transforms the continual struggle
into a process which is full of mystery and interest
and yet is tied with indestructible threads to the
present, the unexplained instant.*
– GEORG LUKÁCS, THE THEORY OF THE NOVEL

June 2020
I have begun reading again. Yes, the scorched skin of the passed years has blistered and peeled away. To a younger, fresher veneer. To a time when I read all I could. History. History of thinking. History of creating. History of history. In the intervals between writing, I am reading again. I go each day to the Kilburn Library in the misspelt Salusbury Road that I have renamed, in my interior map of this space, Harare Boulevard. The Kilburn Library, with its orange-brick façade, white-framed portico and bay windows, the black-painted metal railings bounding the raised frontage. It's only a half a mile walk (yes, I am already thinking imperially) from The Old Bell and another half-mile back for a post-study bitter.

I joined the library trepidatiously (is there such a word?), unsure whether my ancestry visa status allowed library privileges. Yes, thanks to my Scottish grandpa I have a tenuous hold on imperial residence. The old man kicked the bucket before I dropped into the world. Married, as they used to whisper in family kitchens, a young Xhosa beauty who worked in the factory where he supervised at a time when it was frowned upon but not yet totally illegal. And Grandad and Grandma begot my mummy, who, with my third-generation Cape Flats daddy, begot me. And here I am, forsaken in the land of my forefathers two or three times removed. So, yes, thank you, Scottish forebear, for my access to the Kilburn Library.

And I am reading again. Old reading. Flaubert. Tolstoy. Dostoevsky.

Eliot. cummings. Kant. Hegel. Marx. Lukács. Yeats. Lenin. Sartre. Achebe. Ostrovsky. Fanon. Nietzsche. Serote. Zhukov. Gordimer. Reaching back to when the mind was lush. When it all made sense.

Chapter 24

August 2019
Whitehead glanced at his watch, tapped the screen. Nothing. He fished out his phone. It was just gone 9am as he stood at the front door of the house in Pretoria East. In his mind, he ran over the work ahead. Today would be the real start of his research after the month of organising and preparation. He drew his windbreaker more tightly against the August wind that had now returned after years of succumbing to climate shifts. He reached into his red sling bag for the growing bunch of keys and unlocked the door.

He headed straight to the kitchen for his first brew of coffee before starting in the room. At the kitchen door he stopped in his tracks. Gail sat at the table, a finger through the handle of the glass mug before her at least a third full of herbal tea. He bent to greet her but, closer up, her drink was clearly something stronger than tea.

'You're home?'

'Yes. As you see. I'm home.' She pushed the mug away from her, changed her mind and took a sip.

Whitehead sat down. 'What's up? You sick?'

Gail heaved herself up from the table with a sigh. 'You want coffee?' She didn't wait for an answer and headed straight to the coffee machine. She spoke without turning to Whitehead. 'No, I'm not sick. I'm fucked!'

'What d'you mean? What's going on, Gail?'

'I'm fucked. I'm unemployed.'

'You're what?' Whitehead started to rise, but sat down again.

'Unemployed, Jerry! Jobless. Laid off!' She fetched a mug from the corner cupboard and came back to the table.

Whitehead half stood again, an old gentlemanly instinct. 'What you mean laid off? Why?'

'No more money for NGOs, Jerry, not an activist one like ours

169

anyway. Closing us all down, that's what they're doing. Shutting us up.'

'Who's shutting you up?'

'Them. The evil ones.'

Whitehead stood to get the coffee himself. As he passed her he lay a hand gently on Gail's head. She placed hers on his.

'Come on, Gail,' he said. 'Tell me what's going on.' He poured his coffee and sat down opposite her. Gail went into the pantry, half-closing the door behind her. Whitehead heard the quiet pop of a cork and the gurgling of liquid leaving a bottle. She came back, sat and cupped her hands around the mug.

'Okay, Jerry. Sorry … Listen, with the move to the right in the West and the recent move to the left here, money for outfits like ours is drying up. Most of our funds came from Europe and the US.'

'Yes, I know. And you were accused of being the lackeys of the imperialists, part of the regime-change agenda.'

'Yes. We were popular with the donors when we attacked the government, even though it was from the left. We were seen as the balance in civil society, a human rights watchdog of sorts.'

'So? What happened?'

'Now that the ANC and the government have moved to the left, we have to be on their side, encourage them, make sure the interests of the workers are guarded. That doesn't suit the ideologies of the West. They can't have civil society and the ruling party working together on a left agenda. So they've basically withdrawn their funding and … and we're fucked. I'm fucked.'

Whitehead looked at her for a moment. Her usually green eyes looked a pale grey this morning, her auburn hair hanging limp. The first creases of her approaching fifties had made an appearance below her eyes. He lifted his mug to her as if in a toast. *'The Signs,'* he whispered.

Gail toasted back. 'The what?'

'The Signs. Less esoteric now than they used to be, but signs nonetheless.'

'Jerry! What you talking about?' Her words were becoming garbled.

'Back in the day, when I was in government, we – I – coined this word, phrase: *The Signs*. It was about a whole lot of things that were happening that we couldn't put our finger on, but seemed to signify that although we were in power, we weren't in control.'

'Things like?' Her eyes glistened, then glazed.

'Like? Jeez, Gail. Like what? Like spurts of violent protests against the ANC as elections approached. Like partly true, mostly fake intelligence reports leaked into the public space calling into question the integrity of key leaders. Like the bloody Meiring Report, the NIA email saga, the VAG allegations, the Browse Mole Report, the report that got a finance minister and his deputy fired. Like constant, unproven allegations of crime and corruption, especially – sometimes – against those who were actually doing a good job. Like the reemergence of old-order securocrats in the police and intelligence organs, in the justice sector. Like those we knew or suspected to be enemy agents in the struggle days suddenly rising to influence, being appointed to senior positions.'

'But what's all that got to do with my unemployment, Jerry?'

Whitehead tapped his mug lightly on the table in time with his oratorical rhythm. 'It's a whole matrix of local and international forces, dynamics, things happening behind the scenes, outside of the obvious, beyond public view. Things we can't control.'

Gail's eyes penetrated him. 'You blaming everything on a Third Force? All our fuck-ups?'

'Did I say "Third Force"?'

'No, you didn't, but sure sounds like it.'

'Forget it!' He bent to pick up his sling bag.

Gail put her hand on top of his. 'No, I'm sorry, Jerry. Didn't mean to belittle your passion.' She left her hand there.

'No, Gail. It's okay. Let's forget it for now. It's too complicated and my mind is elsewhere. It's not about a Third Force. It's about many forces; many pushes and pulls against us as we tried to do the progressive thing. And, yes, we made our own fuck-ups. We collapsed morally – many of us politically. But still.'

Gail started to softly caress his finger, eyes looking directly in his. She gestured towards the door. 'You want to go to the bedroom?'

Jerry jerked his head round to look at the door and back again. 'Pardon?'

'Don't worry, Steve isn't here. He's still got a job, the bugger. There's always work for engineers, even lefty ones, or perhaps specially lefty ones nowadays.' She was talking too much.

'Gail! What are you saying?'

'For god's sake, Jerry! I'm saying I need a fuck! I'm discarded and miserable and I just need a simple fuck!'

Whitehead removed his hand from hers, and went across to the coffee machine. This time he put in sugar. 'Gail, I'm sorry about your job. Really, I am. And you know I like you. And Steve. I can't do that.'

'It will be only once and between us, Jerry. Just this once. Steve will never know. Nor will Bongi.'

He looked at her. 'Listen, I know you won't believe this, but I've never been with anyone else since Bongi.'

Gail's mouth shaped itself into what looked like a sneer, uncharacteristically. 'You're right. I don't believe you.'

'It's true, Gail. I'm not claiming the moral high ground. It's just that the temptation has never been stronger than my fear of losing her. Simple as that.'

She looked at him now, a softened look, eyes sad. 'Okay ... I understand. I do. I'm sorry, Jerry. I'm just messed up today. First working day as a non-worker.' She held up her mug. 'And this is brandy.'

'I know ... I know it's brandy.' He smiled. 'Will you be okay? I need to get into the room now.'

'Yes, I know you have a mission. Lucky you. I'll go lie down anyway, until my head stops spinning.' She left the room, leaving the door open for him.

At the door to the room, the photograph of Mandela, Steve and Gail was gone. The photo of the comrades in front of Green House was gone. The scrap of paper with the felt-tip 'Private' was gone from the door. The door was gone. In its stead was an alcove with a moulded plaster cornice decorating the arch. It was backed with a shaped mirror filling the whole space.

Whitehead stood back a moment to admire his and Steve's handiwork – well, mostly Steve's actually. During a week he had taken off from work in July, he and Whitehead had designed and constructed this new aperture into *The Room*. Steve could make, break or fix anything – of metal, of stone, of plastic, of electricity, of water. As a very young man in exile, he had endeared himself to the ANC and to his comrades as a genius at doctoring vehicles and other receptacles for the hiding of weapons and propaganda that had to cross into

South Africa and make their way through innumerable roadblocks. It was rumoured that none of his mobile hiding places had ever been found. He never confirmed this when asked. He just smiled. Yes, Steve was a man of the hands, but he was also a man of the mind. As the two of them worked through that week on replacing the door, Steve did not stop talking about his views on all the philosophers of all known time – through the Greeks, the Europeans, the New-Worlders, the Africans, the Latinos.

Whitehead placed his thumb on a spot to the right edge of the mirror where a hidden fingerprint reader whirred its approval and the alcove swung outwards to reveal a door, which he unlocked with a plain, old-fashioned key, swung the alcove back into place and entered. The lights and the air conditioner came on automatically.

The inside of the room too was transformed. The long topographical map cabinets were gone. The bookshelves and most of their contents were gone, except for a few books Whitehead had kept back for his own purposes – some spy novels, Georgi K Zhukov's *The Memoirs of Marshal Zhukov*, Nikolai Ostrovsky's *How the Steel Was Tempered* and a few copies of the MK journal *Dawn*. The old Sanyo computers and the dot-matrix were gone. In the spaces left by these there now stood brand-new metal filing cabinets, taking up all the wall space. The cardboard boxes, wooden crates and metal trunks were gone, their contents now meticulously ordered in the new cabinets, with the exception of one metal trunk with a bright yellow 'O' painted on it. He had not been able to open it yet – it had a combination lock. The children's desk was gone. Now, in the centre of the room under the bright strip lights, stood a large metal-legged desk with lockable drawers, a brown leather swivel chair before it. Piled on one corner of the desk were the books Whitehead had kept back. He sat down now and paged through one of them, then slipped the Zhukov autobiography into his sling bag for home reading. It was a thick, heavy tome.

He sat for a while, looking around, his hands around the coffee mug. He took the flexi-tablet out of his bag and opened his List App. As he ran his lightpen down the lists of filing cabinets, their drawers and their contents, he lifted his eyes to each cabinet as if to make sure it was still in its place. He now had to decide where to begin. With all the organising and reorganising of the past weeks, he had a good idea of where everything was, but the mission was so vast, so open-ended, he could start anywhere and get nowhere. There was the methodical, logical approach – the slog: start with the known, make suppositions, follow those through the morass of primary material, eliminate, confirm, follow tangents, go back, retrace, draw diagrams and charts. And then there was the dip and dive approach: open your heart to hunches, dive in, if no-go, step back, hunch and dive again. Whitehead knew from experience that both approaches delivered results, but he hankered after good old-fashioned luck – the fast way.

With Vladimir's help, he had prepared for the slog. From his flexi-tablet he called up the copy of *Mandela's List* with Vladimir's markings and notes on it. From his bag he took out the hard-copy list that the two of them had compiled of all the known ANC members of the struggle days, from exile, the underground and the Mass Democratic Movement, who today held positions of influence in the party, the government, the corporate world and civil society – anyone who might be in a position to block, stymie or sabotage the new radical programme. Compiling that had indeed been a slog. He took out his red marker and, although he had done this mentally before, compared the two lists, marking the names on the new list that appeared on *Mandela's List*, but he felt as if a rock had settled on his solar plexus. Mandela's list was so old, so unreliable, so likely to contain disinformation. But when the dead, obscure and forgotten were removed from it, there were no more than twenty marked up on the other list.

Whitehead went to the cabinets that housed the files on suspected apartheid agents and fingered his way through. Of the twenty, only five had files. He took the files over to the desk, placing cardboard markers in the space left in the drawers. Next he took the list over to the cabinets holding the intelligence reports and ran his fingers through the section filed by person. Three more files joined the pile on the table, of people who'd been active in the United Democratic Front. Lastly, he tackled the files of recruits into the ANC, the reorganisation of which had taken most of his time since his first foray into the room. There were thousands of them. They had been filed according to the MK names. He'd had to refile them by real name. It had taken him many long days and late nights and Bongi's approbation. He looked through these for the remaining names on the list – only three more joined the pile on the table.

Back at the table, he felt the effect of the coffee on his bladder and made for the door. He looked through the one-way spy hole onto the back of the false alcove to make sure no one was in the passage, and opened and closed the contraption behind him. He hastened down the passage to the bathroom, stood over the bowl for a long time until he was sure of the last drop. On his way back, he peeked into the master bedroom. Gail was sprawled on her back, her mouth drooped open, soft snoring emanating from her throat. He backed out quietly.

Back in the room, he stood over the desk and the pile of files, uninspired, incurious. He looked around for a glimmer of inspiration in this dark room with its catacombs of history hidden within prosaic cabinets. He extracted an old *Dawn* from the pile of books on the corner of the desk. It was from 1982. He ran a finger down the contents, instantly struck by an article by Paulo Freire. How on earth had *Dawn* solicited an article from Freire? He turned to it. It was titled 'Lessons of the Soviet Partisans in the Great Patriotic War against Fascism'. Didn't sound like something Freire would write about. At the end of the article it stated that 'Comrade Paulo Freire is a tactics instructor in Camp 31'. Something stirred, idly but curiously.

Whitehead logged in again to his flexi-tablet, and back in his List App he found the two lists he had made when reorganising the files of new recruits into the ANC – both with the real and MK names, one in alphabetical order of the one and the other vice versa. He scrolled through the MK names to *Freire, Paulo,* found the real name and extracted the file from the cabinet. The first document in the folder, dated February 1980 in Dukwe, was the initial interview he himself had done with the comrade. Suddenly he remembered, and laughed. It was he who had given the MK name – he had been reading *Pedagogy of the Oppressed* at the time. He was about to put the file back, his curiosity sated, but a moment of self-indulgence sent him back to the desk with the file. He read through his interview report. Right at the end it stated: 'Subject reports on an apparently clandestine meeting he witnessed on a rural road in Eastern Transvaal between his uncle, a Charles "Baba" Dlamini, principal at the local school, and an unknown white man driving a white Cressida. Subject observed an exchange of an envelope from the white man to Dlamini.' This sentence was highlighted in yellow with a red circle around the name of Charles Dlamini.

In the cabinet with the files of suspected agents he found a very thin folder for a Charles Dlamini, which cross-referenced the Paulo Freire file with a note from one of the Green House processors: 'Nothing further found on Dlamini or unknown white man. No registration provided for Cressida.'

Whitehead pondered this false lead, a dead end. Perhaps there'd been too much else, material that had been more concrete than this snippet, for it to have been pursued at the time. He sat for a while, the other lists and files on his desk forgotten, usurped by thoughts of the small, curious trail, unrelated, to be sure, but it was now an itch. He took out his phone, opened WhatsApp at the MK Veterans chat group. Struggling with his thick fingers, he typed:

> *Hey comrades! Anyone know the current whereabouts of Cde Paulo Freire (MK), Sibusiso Dlamini (R/N)?*

Chapter 25

May 1994
Lindiwe Vilakazi was late. She had waited at home for Amos to return from his meeting – always negotiating – but when the sky had paled, reddened and darkened, she gave up on him and made her own way into town for the celebration. But first, she drank a mug of coffee to evict the sleep from her head. They had arrived in Jo'burg at lunchtime, returning from Amos's village in the Eastern Transvaal where he had insisted they cast their first vote, and had stayed a few extra days so Amos could once again enjoy the prodigal attention from family, childhood friends, the community and the man he called his mentor, Baba Dlamini. (She had wondered at the relationship, the frequent huddling in deep discourse away from others, the apparent disdain with which Dlamini related to her, but, she guessed, she was the village outsider who had, without the requisite permission, nationalised one of their own.) She'd had a nap after they got home, and Amos had gone off to his meeting.

Now, as she entered the Grand Ballroom of the Carlton Hotel, the gaud lessened somewhat by the pervasiveness of black, green and gold – on banners, posters, T-shirts and dresses – she helped herself to a glass of Champagne just as Mandela took to the podium. She slipped back through the throng to a space of relative calm, keeping an eye out for comrades she knew. It seemed every constituency of the ANC was here tonight: returned exiles, leaders and cadres of the mass democratic movement, unionists, Party leaders, church leaders in their smocks and nuns in theirs, the lumpens in dirty T-shirts faced with faded pictures of Mandela, every hue of skin and creed. She glimpsed Amos as a space opened up momentarilyy across the room; he stood in a group with the leaders – Joe Slovo, Thabo Mbeki, Cyril Ramaphosa – his eyes lit up with a laugh. She cursed, not quite under her breath, and moved to the edges of the room where she found gathered, as always, her colleagues in ANC intelligence. They had that look on their faces that made her question whether it was natural or practised, a look she could not quite decide was all-knowing or disdainful or both. She joined them just as Mandela began to speak.

Fellow South Africans – the people of South Africa:
This is indeed a joyous night. Although not yet final, we have received the provisional results of the election. My friends, I can tell you we are delighted by the overwhelming support for the African National Congress ...

Lindiwe joined in the cheering, the ululating and slogan shouting. She squeezed herself back against the wall, with Jerry and Bongi to her right and Vladimir Masilela to her left. They shifted to let her in, nodding their heads in greeting. Masilela squeezed her arm. They were all here, the Green House boys: Comrade Sandile over there, others whose faces lingered even though the names were gone. At any rate, many had reverted to their real names on their return, eager, she supposed, for some semblance of normality, of the repairing of a broken continuum.

South Africa's heroes are legend across the generations. But it is you, the people, who are our true heroes. This is one of the most important moments in the life of our country. I stand here before you filled with deep pride and joy: pride in the ordinary, humble people of this country. You have shown such a calm, patient determination to reclaim this country as your own – and from the rooftops proclaim – free at last! ...

Bongi leaned over Jerry and whispered to Lindi: 'Coretta is here. And her son?'
Lindi replied: 'Who?'
'Coretta. Martin Luther King's widow. And their son, King Junior.'
Jerry shushed them.

For we must, together and without delay, begin to build a better life for all South Africans. This means creating jobs, building houses, providing education and bringing peace and security to all.

> *This is going to be the acid test for the Government of National Unity. We have emerged as the majority party on the basis ... on the programme which is contained in the Reconstruction and Development Programme ...*

The hubbub in the room subsided. Both Masilela and Jerry nudged Lindi at the same time and gestured towards Mandela, whose voice became sterner, almost threatening.

> *And I appeal to all the leaders who are going to serve this government to honour that programme. And to go there determined to contribute towards its immediate implementation. If there are attempts on the part of anybody to undermine that programme, there will be serious tensions in the Government of National Unity ...*

Applause, cheering, more slogans. Lindi missed Mandela's next few words. She picked them up again at:

> *And nobody will be entitled to go to that, to participate in that Government of National Unity to oppose that plan.*

Next to her, Whitehead raised his fist and yelled: 'Batshele, Madiba!' Bongi laughed and gently pulled his arm back down and held his hand. Their attention wandered after they'd heard what they wanted to hear. At last Mandela ended with something about welcoming sports teams and proposed the toast. Champagne glasses were lifted and emptied. Whitehead sidled over to a chair against the wall and retrieved a plastic bag from under it. The Green House boys gathered around him and proffered their glasses. Lindi and Bongi both rolled their eyes and sighed, but joined them. Whitehead poured Johnnie Walker Black from the bottle in the bag. They toasted again, a private one this time, like the survivors of a combat unit remembering the fallen and celebrating their own outliving of the war.

Whitehead raised the plastic bag toward Lindi. She emptied her glass and held it out. As he poured he said: 'We are having an after-party at our place.' He nodded towards Bongi. 'You coming?'

'Sure. Can I bring Amos?'

'Konechno. If he doesn't mind slumming it with Imbokodo.'
She laughed, weakly, and walked off to find Amos.

※

Later, at Bongi and Jerry's home in Yeoville, with its varnished Oregon floors and doors, high ceilings and textured glass windows in leaden frames, they spread out across the lounge – on an old sofa, one armchair, some kitchen chairs and two new beanbags. Amos and Lindi shared a beanbag. Masilela sat back in the armchair, Sandile straddled a backwards-facing kitchen chair, his chin resting on his arms across the chair back. Bongi and Jerry moved between the lounge and kitchen, serving crisps and nuts and biltong and cheese, and juice for the one teetotaller, the ever-quiet Casper. Finally Jerry brought in a cooking pot filled with ice and the bottle of Black now liberated from its plastic bag.

Amos laughed. 'Wait, I have something better in the car.' He held his hand out to Lindi for the keys, grunted as he lifted himself out of the beanbag and was gone.

Whitehead looked at Lindi. 'Better than Black?'

Lindi lifted her shoulders to her ears with a slight tilt of her head, her eyebrows arched. Whitehead went back to the kitchen for glasses. Masilela sat forward and pulled the bottle and the pot of ice closer. 'Let's drink, comrades ... To our revolution.'

Sandile raised an imaginary glass. 'Not yet uhuru, comrades.'

Lindi lifted herself out of the beanbag and asked directions to the bathroom. Bongi stood and accompanied her. Whitehead returned with a tray tinkling with glasses. The doorbell rang. He left the room. Masilela poured himself a shot from the Black and settled back into the armchair. 'Okay then, comrades ... To the not-yet-revolution!' All leaned forward to help themselves. When Amos and Jerry entered Amos was carrying a canvas bag, which he set on the floor next to the beanbag.

Masilela lifted his glass to the room again. 'What you have there, Comrade Amos?'

'Empty your glass of that cheap stuff, Vladimir.' He bent and, with a flourish, pulled out an embossed box that looked as though it belonged in an art gallery rather than a Yeoville lounge. 'Voila, ma-comrade, Blue Label!' He removed the bottle from the box and placed it ceremoniously on the table.

Sandile scraped his chair back from the table. 'Jesus, Amos! Where d'you get the money for Blue Label?'

'I didn't buy it, com. It was a gift.'

'A gift? Who do you know who can afford to give away a bottle of Blue?'

Amos opened the bottle, poured himself a shot, and sank into the beanbag. 'You should know, Sandile, everybody wants to be our friend now.' He raised his glass.

Sandile took a glass and poured from the Black. 'And who are these everybodies who want to be our friend?'

'You know … Businessmen. Professors. Old bureaucrats. Everybody.'

Bongi helped herself to whiskey and some crisps. 'And? Why?'

'Why?'

'Why do they want to be our friend?'

Jerry sat forward on the couch and touched his shoulder to Bongi's. He reached for biltong and the Blue. 'Yes, Comrade Amos, why?'

'It's obvious, Whitehead. Because we're going to be the government in a few days. That's why.'

Bongi let her body drop back into the couch. Whitehead fell back beside her. Bongi looked at Lindi and turned again to Amos. 'And what do your business people, professors and bureaucrats want in return for their Blue Label?'

Lindi looked into her husband's eyes. 'Yes, Amos, what do they want?'

Whitehead: 'They want what Madiba was talking about tonight.'

Sandile laughed. 'Huh? What you talking about, Jerry?'

'They want to sabotage the RDP. These bureaucrats and businessmen of yours want to obstruct revolutionary transformation.'

Amos raised himself from the beanbag, using the edge of the coffee table as a lever. He moved over to Lindi and spoke quietly into her ear. Her eyes lifted towards him. He moved away and stood, glass in hand, at the edge of the circle with the other hand in his jacket pocket.

'Comrades, let's not go overboard. Let's cut the conspiracy theories. There's no clean slate here. We're going to have to work with these people to execute our transformation. Look at you intelligence guys.' He waved his glass in a wide sweep in front of him. 'You are negotiating with your old enemies to plan for the new intelligence service.'

Masilela grunted. 'They don't fucking buy us Blue Label!'

'Well, perhaps I've been negotiating with a different breed.' He laughed and poured himself another whiskey, first pointing the bottle at Lindi.

She shook her head and spoke. 'Tell them about your negotiations, Amos. Tell them about the economic haggling.'

'Haggling?'

'Negotiations.'

'I'm sure these spooks don't need me to tell them. They know everything.'

Masilela leaned forward for another handful of ice. 'Actually, we don't. Believe it or not, we didn't bug your subcommittee sessions.' He poured whiskey and lifted his glass to Amos. 'Of course, we can't guarantee that the boers didn't.'

Amos stood his ground. 'It was a tricky negotiation. But we got the best deal.'

'Best deal?' Sandile stood up.

'Yes, com. Best deal in the circumstances. A mixed economy is the only option.'

'Yes, I guess it is. The question, though, is how mixed? What are the proportions of the mixture?' He moved towards the door. 'Toilet this way, Bongi?'

Halfway out the room, Bongi turned to look at Jerry. She shrugged – just as a loud explosion shook the windows. For a split second, there was a stunned silence, immediately broken by the ring of Jerry's brick-sized cell phone. He picked it up and ran to the door. Then the house phone in the kitchen began to ring. Bongi ran to that.

Masilela stood, emptied his glass and moved to the door. 'Bloody right-wing again, I'm sure. Bombing couldn't be that far away. Let's go, comrades. Back to work.'

Chapter 26

> *... the night that the old South African flag came down for the last time, celebrated in secret by a number of special operations officers in a Pretoria-based safe house known as Eikeboom, counts as a monumental moment ... because while we celebrated this historic occasion, we were also imbued with a sense of foreboding at the possible consequences of our actions ... Were we possibly wrong about the strategic significance of the collapse of Communism, the disintegration of the Soviet Union and the ending of the Cold War? Could we keep control of the wildly bucking bronco that we had helped unleash? ... These thoughts pulsed through our minds as the whiskey flowed and the officers toasted an uncertain future they had helped to create but could no longer control.*
> – ANTHONY RICHARD TURTON, SHAKING HANDS WITH BILLY

May 1994
On the evening of the day Mandela was inaugurated as president, Marie – girlfriend to Otto Bester and secretary to the NIS Covert Collection Directorate – was early arriving at the Service's safe house in a verdant suburb of Pretoria a little off from the N4 highway that started the journey east towards the newly named Mpumalanga province. She was early because, unusually, she hadn't got lost – Otto's directions had been precise and, being her first visit to the house she'd heard so much about, she wanted some time to explore before the others arrived. She stopped before the imposing wrought-iron gates, smiled into the camera over the gate-phone and called her name. The gates swung open with some reluctance, and as the tyres of her yellow Beetle scrunched up the driveway and around a bend, she glimpsed

the façade of the house: a stern, white watchful gable flanked by a sloping thatched roof, and underpinned by what she thought was excessive whiteness. There was something familiar about the style, but she was no aficionado of architecture. As she moved towards the front door, she was reminded of a holiday visit with Otto to the wine farms in the Cape.

Before her hand could reach the doorbell, the heavy wooden door swung open and she immediately assumed it was electronically controlled, like the gate. But as the dusk light slipped in through the door she noticed the dark-skinned figure standing just beyond the light, made somewhat iridescent by the white double-breasted chef's jacket, without the *toque blanche*, but instead a head of long, dark hair tied behind and – as the light allowed her now to see – covered with a black hairnet. Patel, the house chef and caretaker. Otto had talked about him – recruited in the seventies to spy on Indian organisations, found out and saved from certain death or severe mauling, and hidden here for years cooking and caring for the Service's foreign intelligence visitors and sometimes top management when they came to plan and plot in suburban sumptuousness. Patel was reputed to be a wizard in all manner of cuisine, except Indian – he refused to cook curries.

She held out her hand. 'Meneer Patel?'

'Yes, madam. Welcome. Please come in, if you will.'

'Anyone here yet?'

'You are the first, madam. You are somewhat early. I was told to expect the guests at seven.'

'Ja, sorry about that. It's my first visit. Didn't want to get lost. Maybe I can look around for a little bit?'

'Please yourself, madam. I must return to my kitchen.'

He ushered her in, shut the door behind her and disappeared. Marie wandered through a large open-plan sitting room with lush furnishings, purchased and tastefully placed, she was sure, to impress (and influence) the foreign intelligence dignitaries from America, the UK, Germany, France and elsewhere who had visited to exchange intelligence on the ANC terrorists and their communist handlangers. At the far end of the lounge stood a heavy, ostentatious mahogany bar with shelves of liquors and spirits, many of which she'd never heard of. She moved out onto the cobbled patio, the stones polished to a near glassiness. Beyond the patio, in the far reaches of the garden, she wandered into a thatched lapa with a built-in stone braai and bar area. The autumn night air might be too chilled to sit out here tonight. She went back inside, found the kitchen where Patel was moving swiftly between pots and pans on the stove and dipping now and then to the oven.

'What we eating tonight, Patel?'

He looked up, wiped his hands on a dishcloth. 'Mr Bester asked me to prepare finger food, madam. Just finger food.'

'Sounds good.' She headed over to his pots, but he stepped in front of her, arms stretched out to the sides. 'Sorry, madam. Just boerewors, lamb chops, roast veg and things. Light snacks, madam.' A chime sounded. 'That will be the others.' She followed him out and waited in the lounge.

They entered noisily, at the tail end of laughter, lewd by the sound of it, at a joke told on the threshold. Otto led the way, with Graham Kline and Johan van Deventer close behind. Otto whispered to Patel who tilted his torso forward and stepped backwards like a nineteenth-century butler, closed the front door and walked sideways to the kitchen.

Marie greeted with outstretched hand and did that hardly perceptible curtsy that women in the Service couldn't seem to get out of their systems. 'Is that it? Is this all of you? Who else is coming?'

Otto placed his hand on her back. 'Oh, they'll be around later. Gonna be a long night. Some of them have to work. The war isn't over yet.' He sat himself in the easy chair they called 'The Throne' – the one in which they always seated visiting heads of service, partly to give them a sense of false superiority, but mainly because it was the closest to the listening device in the table lamp alongside with the imitation papyrus shade decorated with meaningless hieroglyphics (at least that's what the Service's resident Egyptologist said).

Kline marked a chair for himself by placing a folded copy of the *Pretoria News* on it and moved to the bar. Marie sat opposite Otto, Van Deventer next to her. Kline came back with a handful of assorted glasses.

Otto glowered. 'Why don't you get Patel to serve us, Meneer Kline? That's what he's here for.'

Kline set the glasses down clumsily on the marble-topped coffee table, cracking a wine glass in the process. He did his false cough.

'No, no. Not tonight. This is our space tonight.' He circled his hand around the room. 'And that ...' – he pointed at the door to the kitchen and mimed an invisible border with his hand – 'that's his space. And the twain shall not meet. Not tonight.' He went back to the bar and returned with four bottles, one under each armpit and the other two in his hands, placing them gingerly on the table. Marie noted the choices: a Rémy Martin; a whiskey with a name with too many consonants; a red wine and Stolichnaya vodka. Kline opened all the bottles and placed the appropriate glasses next to each, then helped himself to a shot of vodka and sat down.

Otto reached for the Rémy Martin and a brandy goblet. 'So, meneer Kline, you're drinking vodka now. Your end-of-the-Cold-War poison of choice? That's what the commies in the ANC are drinking.'

Kline downed his tot in the Russian fashion. 'Hey, chief, Stolichnaya is readily available now. We don't have to sneak bottles any more from our secret Russian contacts. Now it's made by the new Russian capitalists!'

'Corrupt Russian capitalists.'

Kline laughed. 'Yes, Marie, corrupt, but passionate. Nothing more passionate than a new capitalist.'

'And more corrupt ...' Marie brushed a strand of hair from her forehead.

Otto held the goblet up to the light from the ornate chandelier. 'Yes, nothing more corrupting than sudden freedom.' He raised his glass to Marie and took a sip with exaggeratedly pursed lips. 'Don't look at me like that. Watch and see what happens here.'

Kline fetched a bigger glass from the bar. 'Corruption is the loam of betrayal.'

Otto snorted. 'Jesus, Kline! Did you make that up?'

'No, chief. Wish I had. I was told it by one of the instructors when I was doing the course in the States. He liked to say that it was easier to recruit agents in a corrupt society.'

Marie sipped her wine. 'It would work the other way round too.'

'Huh?'

'You could say that betrayal is the seed of corruption. It is corruption.' She turned to Van Deventer. 'You're quiet, Johan. What do you say?'

Van Deventer fiddled with his suit jacket. He was the only one wearing a suit and tie. The others had changed into casuals. 'I don't know, Marie. It cuts both ways, I guess. To spy on your people needs a kind of corruption.' He only now reached for the whiskey bottle. 'But once you've crossed that line you've lost your moral compass, I guess. The rest is easy.'

Otto caught Marie's eye. 'Are you saying the people who spied for us have no morals?'

Van Deventer looked startled. He ran a finger along the rim of his glass. 'I don't know. Do they?'

Otto paused before he answered. 'You forget that some of them cooperated with us because they shared our vision, respected us, hated communism like us. You guys should remember your training – the hierarchy of betrayal.'

Kline coughed. 'The what?'

'The hierarchy of betrayal – the different reasons for someone to cooperate with us – from shared values at the top to plain old-fashioned blackmail at the bottom.'

Marie heard the chime of the doorbell somewhere in the recesses of the house. Patel emerged from the kitchen and went to the front door. He opened it a fraction, spoke to someone, then closed it again. He came to the lounge and hovered close to Marie. 'Excuse me, madam. There's a Philemon here who wants to speak to you.'

Marie stood. 'Thanks, Patel. That's the courier.'

She went to the door. Philemon Tau stood on the threshold, a cloth cap in one hand and a large brown envelope in the other. 'Evening, madam. I've brought reports from headquarters for Meneer Bester.' He proffered the envelope.

'Thanks, Philemon. You want to come in?' She gestured into the house.

'It's okay, madam. Will there be anything to take back to HQ?'

'Come inside, Philemon. You can wait in the hallway. I'll check with Mr Bester.' He crossed the threshold and waited, his cap held in front of his crotch, in the hallway.

'Reports for you, chief,' Marie said to Otto. 'Philemon's waiting for a response.'

Otto stripped the seal from the envelope and pulled out the sheaf of pages. He read quickly. 'It's okay. He can go. No need for a response tonight.'

Marie returned to the hallway and ushered Philemon out. She watched him amble down the driveway to the couriers' vehicle disguised as a Telkom van. He was a good sort, our Philemon. Recruited by Otto from the Special Branch in Soweto as part of an effort to bring some colour into the NIS before the ANC monopolised that innovation. Back in the lounge, the men were still arguing about the ethics of their spies. Before she could sit down, the door chimed again. Turning to answer it, she almost collided with Patel who glided out of the kitchen door as if on skates. She stood back while Patel opened the door to a sudden rush of sound ushered in with the night air – laughter, yelps, loud words. The five men, all carrying opened beer cans, pushed Patel aside and entered.

She recognised Willie Oberholzer and Booysens, the one they still called Sarge, both from the old Special Branch special unit Otto had brought with him into the NIS. She had advised against it, but for Otto camaraderie trumped ability. The other three she didn't recognise – probably from one of the outlying covert units, breaking security protocol on this historic night. They all smelled and acted as if this wasn't their first beer of the evening. She steered them toward the lounge where Oberholzer, forever on the move, stopped at the fridge behind the bar to extract more beers. Patel had disappeared.

'The boys have arrived!' She sat down and sipped at her wine, as the newcomers arranged themselves on the available chairs, sofa arms and scattered poufs.

Otto leaned forward on The Throne. 'So? Where you guys been?'

Oberholzer drained his beer can, crunched it in his left hand and cracked open another. 'Monitoring the inauguration banquet, chief. Very fancy. Place is full of commies and blacks feasting it up. We opened a can of worms there, hoor my lied.'

'It's a new world, Willie. Get used to it.' Marie smiled, but she didn't feel it.

Patel sidled in and hovered near Marie. 'Snacks are ready, madam. Where would you like me to serve them?'

'Oh, Patel, you're asking me? Mr Bester is the boss.'

Otto grunted, then turned on his smile. 'In the dining room, Patel. Set it up in the dining room. We'll move there when you're ready.'

Marie watched as Patel opened a door in the hallway she had assumed led to a bathroom, and was astonished by the cavernous space beyond. He then moved between the dining room and the kitchen, carrying trays and bowls.

'Actually,' Otto continued, 'the world is only as new as we allow it to be.'

Marie turned to him. 'Meaning?'

Otto took his brandy goblet and stood with his back to the French doors that opened onto the cobbled patio and the dark garden beyond. They all turned to look at him.

'I mean, the world is as new as we allow it to be. What's not to understand about that? It's this Service that advised De Klerk to talk to Mandela, to the ANC. It's this Service that kicked off the talks about talks. We did it because we knew that we could not sustain forever the fight against the resistance to apartheid. And the economy was in dire straits.'

Marie noted with some pride this new side of Otto. Otto the orator. Otto the politician. She watched as he gathered up steam again.

'And we knew that, with the collapse of the Soviet Union and the death of communism, the ANC was less to be feared, more pliant, more malleable.' He moved back to the table and poured himself another brandy. 'But mostly we know that we have our people in the highest places in the ANC. They can't move without us knowing and we have many strings to pull.'

Kline leaned forward. 'But to what end, chief?'

'It should be obvious, Meneer Kline. To protect our way of life. To protect our businesses. To protect our people.'

Patel waited in the wings until Otto had finished. 'It's ready, meneer. The food, it is ready.'

They all stood and followed Patel to the dining room, allowing Marie to enter first. It was a long, rectangular room, dominated by a heavy oak dining table fringed with high-back oak chairs with brown, beige and burgundy patterns on the seat cushions and backs. Two large silver candelabras stood on the table, one at each end. A narrow woven runner ran the length of the table of the same pattern as the seat cushions. Spaced along this were the dishes Patel had prepared.

Otto seated himself at the head of the table, placing the brown envelope on his side plate. 'You can leave us now, Patel. We'll look after ourselves. Thank you.'

Two bottles of Pinotage were passed around. Hands and forks

stabbed at the grilled chops, boerewors, roast veg and other dishes. Otto let them eat and drink for twenty minutes, then sat back, picked up the envelope and withdrew the papers inside. The clatter of cutlery and glass stopped. He waved the pages in the air. 'This is a report on a meeting between Mandela, Joe Nhlanhla and other leaders of ANC intelligence.' No one spoke.

Otto put the report back in the envelope. 'Mandela has instructed Nhlanhla to speed up the amalgamation of ANC intelligence with us. It looks like, before the year is out, we're going to have new masters.'

Kline removed a half-eaten piece of boerewors from his mouth. 'Come on, chief. We have to discuss this tonight?'

'Yes, Meneer Kline, we do. As of a few hours ago, Mandela is in charge. What are we going to do about it?'

Marie looked around the table. No one seemed interested in answering.

Otto continued. 'I've had some thoughts. We need to place ourselves strategically before it is no longer in our hands. We're the ones who know who's who in the ANC. We're the ones with the levers to pull. We need to spread ourselves accordingly.'

Oberholzer spoke, a fork halfway to his mouth. 'Like where, chief?'

Otto pushed his plate and glass away. 'This is how it's going to be.' He gestured towards Van Deventer with the envelope. 'Johan, I'm having you transferred to the Research Directorate. That way we'll have access to the incoming intelligence. Kline, you're going to Foreign Liaison.'

Kline choked on the wine he had just gulped. 'What? You want to turn me into a bloody diplomat, chief? I'm an operator. Always have been.'

'Meneer Kline, it's strategy. We still have our friends among the Brits, the Yanks, etcetera. We need you there as a conduit to them.' Kline wiped his mouth with a napkin and went quiet.

Marie raised her glass. 'And what about you, chief?' She, of course, already knew the answer. They had discussed it for months in their private spaces.

Otto stared at the painting on the opposite wall, one of an orderly from the Boer army standing next to a bicycle with some dispatches in his hand – the first Afrikaner intelligence officer, it was claimed.

He stayed quiet for a minute, then looked around the table. 'Me? I'm going to take the package. I'm taking early retirement. I'm going to go back to my late father's farm and coordinate things from there.'

Note No. 8

July 2020
So, I ask myself, with my left hand circled around this pint, and my right loosely holding the fork that I dip into this soggy shepherd's pie before me on the stained and cracked table, whether I have anything to thank you for, Bongi. Now that I am The Outsider. Is gratitude an appropriate word for what you shared with me and have now withdrawn?

I look around at this motley clientele in my Kilburn pub, all of them, each with someone else. Over there a noisy gaggle of young black youth, laughing, arguing, spilling beer. And to my right, on stools next to the high bar, an incongruous white couple in their forties, drinking white wine (it's expensive and tastes like piss here) and whispering to each other, their thighs touching. All around me are people whose lives I know nothing of, but who seem to me to have something to feel gratitude about.

But you, you have been my companion, comrade, lover, colleague, wife, mother of my daughter and, finally, co-conspirator. And yet, you are not here. All you have given me – all the nimbus clouds of memories that float between my head and the odours of this pub – all gone, stolen, taken back, denied.

How do I feel thankful for a gift taken back? How do I summon gratitude for something passed that is now no more? Sure, if you had died, dropped dead while we still shared the same life, yes, then I would have been able to tell myself – others would have told me – to be grateful for the time we had together.

Time we had together ... Huh. There was a mess of times we had together, when time and space were indeed relative, when one did not metamorphose without the intertwining of the other – London, Lusaka, Luanda, Harare, Johannesburg, Pretoria – all carrying their own time.

I feel ill, Bongi. Something gnaws at the gut. I can't finish this pie. There is an ache that won't go away. Look. Look at the touching thighs again. Why? You and Vladimir? Why? And I, the outsider. Estranged. First from your heart. Then from your bed. Then from your home. And now? And now from your land. Again. You and Vladimir. First the looks. Then the prolonged handshakes. The whispers. The travels together. This pie is soggy. My guts are soggy. These drinkers are noisy. This city is raucous. I need quiet, Bongi. I need to lie down quietly. Pull. Pull. Pull yourself together, Whitehead. The thighs touch. Touch. Whisper. You and he. You and he pushed me out of the circle. You dropped into your language. You descended into your traditions. You left me tottering on the abyss. A man of no traditions. No certainty. No solidity. Mixed. Mixed up. I have come unstuck, Bongi. Unstuck.

Chapter 27

April 2017
'You get what I'm saying, Comrade Sandile?'
'Yebo, Comrade Thembi, I get it.'

Sandile looked down at the flowered plate with a mound of rice drowning in a pallid beef stew before him on the cramped kitchen table, relieving himself for a moment from the gently intense eyes of Thembi Masondo. He wondered at the banality of this location for this discussion. The kitchen, like the table, was small. Thembi was not a great cook, but the walls, the shelves, the nooks and hooks were inundated with instruments of culinary provenance: pots, ladles, measuring cups, pans, spice racks – wooden, metal, teflon, plastic. Through the window to his right, beyond the half-closed floral curtains, the dusk light was beginning to fade on the riot of trees, shrubs and flowers in Thembi's Bez Valley garden. He was impressed that she had remained in her first post-exile house and not followed the other newly entitled to Sandton, Houghton and Waterkloof. On the wall behind where she sat opposite him at the white-painted wooden table were posters mounted on cork frames of the Freedom Charter, one of a young Oliver Tambo and another of a frowning Chris Hani.

He scooped another forkful of rice and stew up to his mouth. The rice was at least ten minutes over-boiled. The stew bland and spiceless. No, Thembi had many good qualities – courage and a dogged stubbornness, among them – but, sadly, it seemed, cooking was not one of them. Sandile lifted his glass of wine to his mouth and was forced to look into Thembi's eyes. They conveyed an air of expectation, awaiting further comment from him. Perhaps the four years as ambassador in Paris had spoiled him, had rubbed the last faint pencil marks of the village from his book of life, the village where this rice and stew would have been only an annual luxury, if at all. That was the thing about Thembi. For all her sophistication, her

195

intelligence, her urbane beauty, she still carried the village in every molecule of her being. But he? He had perhaps become that which he despised: the nouveau bourgeoisie.

'Ukuphi, Sandile?'

'Huh?'

Thembi pointed the bottle of wine at his glass. 'Where are you? You're far away. Is this discussion boring you? Or bothering you?'

'Sorry, sisi. No, not boring. But bothering, yes. My mind was just wandering. Sorry.' He held the newly filled glass up to the light from the window, admiring the deepness of the colour.

'Hawu, Sandile! You've picked up a few French mannerisms in your time there. How was it?'

'The wine?'

'No, comrade, Paris.'

'It was okay. It was good to get out of things for four years.'

'Things?'

'Come on, Thembi, you know what I mean. Out of the country. Out of the infighting. Out of the backstabbing. In short, out of the shit.'

Thembi got up to switch on a floor lamp in the far corner of the kitchen. 'What happened with you? You left the NEC. You left Cabinet. I missed all the fun. I was in my own diplomatic exile, you remember, when the fan blew the shit?'

'I remember. At least you got a socialist country.'

'Yeah, no fancy wines and cordon bleu food for me.' She drizzled more Tabasco on her stew. She ate with a spoon. 'So? What *did* happen?'

Sandile reached for the Tabasco. 'You know, Thembi ... My deployment as deputy minister of social development in 2004 was, for me, the apex of my career. A job, at last, where I could make a difference to the people. And I think I was. Making a difference, I mean. Then, of course, 2007 happened. I was voted out of the NEC and, come the 2009 elections, I was out of Cabinet.' He didn't look up for her response. He stirred the sauce into the stew and took a forkful, silenced now by the necessity of masticating. The Tabasco was an improvement. He took some wine.

Thembi fetched another bottle, unscrewed the top and placed it on the table, throwing the empty bottle into a bin built into a cupboard under the sink. 'So? You became one of the coalition of the wounded?' She held her hand up as she sat down. 'Don't answer that.' Then, 'And the posting?'

'Well, after I became non grata, UJ offered me an adjunct professorship in Political Science, and I became, let's say, critical; academically critical, mind you, of what was going on; and then, just before the Mangaung conference, my branch nominated me as a delegate. I got called to the president's residence and offered the ambassadorial post. Was sent for urgent diplomatic training, missed conference, and by February I was in Paris.'

The house phone rang. Sandile didn't think people still used landlines. The floorboards squeaked under her as Thembi made her way to the entrance hall. Sandile made sure to empty his plate before she returned. He was leaning back in his chair with the glass to his lips when she did.

She took a handful of tissues from a box on the kitchen counter and sat down. 'Sorry about that.' She blew her nose. Hard.

'Bless you!'

'That wasn't a sneeze.'

'I'm blessing you anyway. You deserve to be blessed. You're a good person, Thembi. One of the stalwarts. MK commander in Botswana. You were a legend.' He paused.

She looked at him. It looked like sympathy.

Sandile raised his glass. 'So? What is *your* story, comrade?'

She finished dabbing at her nose. 'My story? Came back from Havana in 2011. Elected onto the NEC at Mangaung. Now a Luthuli House bureaucrat.'

'We have bureaucrats in Luthuli House?'

'Well, I organise, administer, facilitate. I don't take decisions. I don't influence policy.' She blew her nose again. 'Excuse me.'

'Bless you, again ... So, you're not part of the shit?'

She was silent while she finished wiping her nose. 'No, I like to think that I'm not. I like to think that I'm part of the solution.'

Sandile reached for the wine, but she was quick to get to it first and pour for him and for herself. 'The solution, hey? And what is the solution?'

She carried the empty plates over to the sink. 'You want dessert? Tinned peaches, and cream, if you like.'

He stood to help her clear, but she gestured back to his chair and, in Russian, told him to sit. 'No thanks, comrade, no dessert for me. I'm trying to stay off the sugar.'

She sat again. '*We* are the solution. You and me. And many others.'

'We? How?'

'Look, we can't go on like this. We're now opposition in three major metros, cities that we governed less than a year ago. We will be out of power in 2019 if we don't do something decisive.'

'Decisive? Like what?'

'Like mobilise all the good forces to ensure that the December conference elects the right people into office and the NEC.'

'Good forces?'

'Yes, comrade. There are still good people in the ANC. There's the veterans and stalwarts. The MK veterans. The Party …'

'The MK vets?' Sandile imagined that he'd suitably smirked.

'The real ones, comrade. The real ones!'

'And how do we ensure that the right people get elected to the NEC? We all know it's the branches that decide and they are all bought.'

Thembi went to the kitchen dresser, returned with a sheet of paper and placed it face down on the table. 'Then we buy them back, Sandile.'

'Oh yeah, sis Thembi. So we do evil to defeat evil?'

'Not with money, mfowethu. Not with money.'

'Then, with what?'

'With politics.'

'Oh yeah? You going to go round to all the branches and teach them the Freedom Charter?'

Thembi laughed, ladled some peaches for herself and smothered them in cream. She went silent as she ate, looking up every now and then to Sandile with eyebrows raised. What was she waiting for?

He spoke. 'We talk a lot these days of going back to the values and ethics of the ANC of Oliver Tambo.'

She looked up at him, her eyes indicating she was waiting for him to continue.

'I just wonder if that's possible, that's all … What were the values and ethics of the ANC in the struggle days? Yes, we were anti-apartheid, pro-poor, pro-worker and, at least some of us, anticapitalist. But mostly, our ethics were based on the need to hold the moral high ground, both for our people but also for the international community we had to mobilise.'

He stood up. 'Can I borrow your bathroom, Thembi.'

'Sure, as long as you promise to return it. Down the passage behind you. First door on the left.'

Standing over the toilet bowl, leaning forward with one hand on the wall to support himself (the wine was well ensconced in his head), Sandile wondered what he was getting at on the issue of values and ethics. It came to him as he flushed and put the seat back down. He washed his hands and went back to the kitchen. Thembi was still busy with her peaches and cream.

'You see, Thembi, our values and ethics were built on the need then to conquer the moral high ground. But now?'

'Yes, mfowethu? And now?'

'Now, Thembi … Now that we are the government, the high ground comes, not from values and ethics, but from power.'

Thembi looked at him for a long time. There was something about her eyes that stirred forgotten feelings in him. 'That's precisely it, Sandile! We will buy the branches back with the politics of fear.'

'The politics of fear? You're going to threaten to beat them up? Assassinate them?'

A look of sorrow crossed her face. 'No, comrade. The fear of loss of power. With the poor showing in last year's local elections, the loss of some councils, a lot of comrades lost their jobs as councillors; lost their income. And some comrades, working as civil servants for the local municipalities, were booted out by the new opposition mayors. If we lose the national elections in 2019, and perhaps more of the other provinces, there will be a helluva lot of comrades who will suffer, who won't get seats in parliament or the provincial legislatures. So, it's change or die!'

Sandile digested that for a moment. 'Yes, you have a point. The rifts, or should I say panic, have already taken grip of the ANC since the local elections. You have a point. The politics of fear, huh?'

Thembi picked up the sheet of paper, turned it over and handed it to him. The phone rang again. 'Have a look at that. Those are the comrades we're suggesting for election to leadership at the end of the year.' She left the room, then stuck her head back through the door.

'Your name is there, comrade.' She disappeared again.

Sandile scanned the names on the list. Indeed, his name was there – and many others too. Good comrades, those he knew. Interesting suggestion for president – Moloi, one of the best of the slightly younger crowd. And, surprise-surprise – Thembi for secretary-general. That's a good one. He would support that.

Thembi returned. 'So, what do you think, comrade?'

'It's a good list. I like the proposal for SG!'

'Be serious, Sandile.'

'I am serious. I fully support the proposal for SG. And a good suggestion for president. He's been doing great things in the province. But I see only about forty names here. The NEC has over eighty members.'

'Yes. We're planning a resolution at conference to reduce the NEC to around thirty.'

'And I see you've got Vladimir on the list?'

'Who?'

'Masilela.'

'You don't agree?'

'No, no, I agree. Excellent proposal, but he'll never accept. He sees himself as a backroom boy. He doesn't like the political realm.'

'Ha! Isn't it time for all us backroom people to come into the front room?'

'It is, but I guarantee you Vladimir won't.'

'And you?'

'And me, what?'

'Will you accept nomination?'

Sandile looked at her for a few moments, then down at the list. 'Aren't you doing what we've criticised all along. You're creating a slate. You're encouraging slate politics.'

'Sandile, this is the slate to end all slates. Answer my question.'

'Look, Thembi, I very much doubt you can pull this off, but if you can, you can count me in, yes.'

The doorbell rang. 'That's the SG.'

'You'd better hide the list.'

'No, he supports the list.'

'But his name's not on it.'

'He wants out after December. He's had enough.'

Chapter 28

*Messages you send to this chat and calls are
now secured with end-to-end encryption.
Tap for more info.*
WHATSAPP

August 2019
It was Whitehead's habit to check messages on his phone while on the treadmill at the gym, although 'habit' is perhaps the wrong word as he was by no means a regular at the gym. When he did go, he went to think, to placate Bongi, and/or to fool himself about the state of decline of his corporeal self. He only really used the treadmill and the stretching machines, and, on the treadmill, he confined himself to no more than a brisk-ish walk. He detested jogging. Always had. Had suffered in MK for it.

Now, headphones on and his eclectic music collection humming in his ears off of his phone, he opened WhatsApp to check for replies to his message of yesterday to the MK Veterans chat group about the whereabouts of Paulo Freire. There were many messages to wade through, although he did note that the group seemed to be shrinking as members shuffled off the mortal coil, or just got too damned depressed to bother any more.

Paging through he came across a debate between two old comrades evaluating President Moloi. One seemed to think that the fact that Moloi was never in MK or in exile disqualified him from leading the 'revolution' (that was the word used). The other replied with a rather nasty questioning of the other's politics. 'That is not the politics we learned in the camps, comrade!' The debate went on a bit, until some moderator made a 'speech' about uniting behind our elected leader and closed the thread down. There were the usual complaints that the ANC was doing nothing for the veterans and some were living in

misery while others did something or other with the fat of the land.
Then he came to the first reply:

Cde Paulo Freire and his unit were killed in a skirmish with the boers near the Bots border just after crossing into the country. May their revolutionary souls rest in peace.

Whitehead turned down the treadmill speed. He looked up at the gargantuan picture on the far wall of a young woman in a bathing suit with an impossibly contoured body. He looked down at the phone again. He switched off his music app, and flipped back to WhatsApp. He reread the message. A kind of sorrow crept up from his stomach and settled in his chest. At least that's what he thought it was. He copied the message and pasted it into an email to himself. He continued scrolling, even if it was just to get to the end of the messages to eradicate the red number on the top right corner of the app logo, but on the way down he found that someone had replied to the previous message on Freire:

That's not true. Paulo and his unit attacked and annihilated a boer border patrol after entering the country and escaped to fight on. The other members of the unit were comrades Tolstoy, Jackman and Vusi.

Copy. Paste. Send. Whitehead turned up the treadmill speed and upped the gradient a notch. He switched the music back on. He was working up a sweat and the hated shortness of breath was growing. He slowed down and levelled out. He scrolled down the rest of the messages, and came upon another:

Paulo Freire and his unit carried out a number of ops in Eastern Transvaal in the late 80s. Then they had a skirmish with the enemy and Jackman, Tolstoy and Vusi were killed. Freire surrendered and became an askari.

Whitehead took his eyes off the phone. He felt something that resembled anger, or was it sadness? He looked at the blurred limbs of the lithe young woman running on the machine next to his. She stared straight ahead. He looked back at the phone. Another one, three messages down:

> *Hey comrades! You can't mess with a comrade's reputation like that!!!! Cde Paulo Freire never sold out. He wasn't an askari. He was arrested and sent to the Island. He came out in 91 and joined the Defence Force in 94.*

Whitehead took his sweat towel off the treadmill bar and wiped his face and head. He continued to scroll down the messages until the end. There were no more. Just some more argument about the ridiculous ages of some so-called MK veterans. He exited the group and saw that there was a direct WhatsApp message to him from a number not in his contact list. He opened it:

> *Cde Whitehead, if you want to know the truth about Sibusiso Dlamini phone this number*

Whitehead switched off the treadmill, stepped down and walked to a far corner of the gym. He called the number.

Chapter 29

February 2015
Just two months after Masilela took early retirement and vacated his post as director-general of the Service, Jerry Whitehead sat in the management boardroom at the head of a long glossy table, to the left of the new DG. Spread around the table sat all the heads of the specialised units of the Service. In the style inculcated by Masilela, all were casually dressed – Madiba shirts, guayaberas, light cotton frocks, jeans, chinos – except for the new DG, Brixton Mthembu, who wore a fawn suit, lemon shirt and dark brown tie and pocket kerchief. He looked like he should be the Minister. Whitehead had that feeling in the gut, somewhere between indigestion and fear.

Mthembu ended his maiden speech. 'So, officers, that will be my style and those will be my priorities: discipline, respect and efficiency. As I said, clean audits will be my legacy.'

Whitehead looked around the table. All heads were turned towards the two of them, but the faces were without expression, although his familiarity with each one of them, his subconscious antenna, accurately discerned questions and comments swirling around in their minds. We've had clean audits for the last four years; what about focusing on decent, accurate, useable intelligence?

There was no applause, although none was really called for. This was a management meeting, after all, but Mthembu looked like he was expecting some, or at least some sort of reaction – nods, grunts, smiles, anything.

Whitehead broke the silence. 'Thank you, Comrade DG. All clear.'

Mthembu turned his whole body toward Whitehead. 'Uh, DDG, we don't call ourselves "comrades" here. We are colleagues in a government department, not in a branch meeting.'

'Sorry, DG. Old habits.' Whitehead looked around the room. With one exception, everyone in the room came from an ANC struggle background; the exception was one individual from the old PAC intelligence service. It was a natural evolution from the early days after '94, with the delicately negotiated balance between the old state service and the liberation intelligence services. It boiled down to the simple factor of trust. Of course, a struggle pedigree was no guarantee of competence (nor of loyalty), but sometimes a balance had to be struck – a balance between efficiency and trust. Never perfect.

Mthembu stood up and walked towards the door. For a moment, Whitehead thought he was leaving. But Mthembu placed himself in front of the white screen and spoke. 'Okay, DDG, Mr Whitehead, tell me about your most significant intelligence concerns.'

Whitehead shifted in his seat, opened the file in front of him and thumbed through the pages to the wad of notes he'd been making for an upcoming briefing to the Intelligence Coordinating Committee. He looked up and around the table, eyebrows raised in an appeal for support. 'Sure, DG. I'm using notes I've prepared for a briefing to the ICC.'

'The ICC?' Mthembu waved his arm over his head.

'Yes, chief. The Coordinating Committee.'

Mthembu waved his arm again. 'Get on with it, Whitehead.'

'Well, DG, much of it is the usual stuff: organised crime, espionage, the extreme right wing, political murders. Then there's the spurt of service-delivery protests, the violent protests, the students – these we only monitor, as you know, DG, in case of any unconstitutional activities.'

Whitehead looked around. All the heads around the table were facing Mthembu, gauging perhaps his response to this tenet of democratic intelligence – a debate among them that was lively and sometimes rancorous. It was Masilela who had persistently insisted on a clear line between legitimate protest and real threats to democracy. The debate was always where to draw the line.

Mthembu cleared his throat. 'I don't hear you mentioning the left wing, Whitehead.'

'The left wing, DG?'

'Yes, the left wing or do you prefer "ultra-left"?'

'Such as who, DG?'

Mthembu completed a circuit of the entire room before settling back in front of the whiteboard. 'Well, like the new unions, the new crazies who want us to nationalise everything, the new parties, the ones who are rubbishing our president. You know … the lefties.'

A thought formed itself in Whitehead's head. For a moment, it took him from this room. He would go down to Bongi's office after this meeting.

'But, DG, unless they are a threat to democracy or the Constitution, we can't spy on them.'

Mthembu waved his arm at the room again, as if it was a branch he had just torn off a tree and was brandishing at an assailant. 'We will discuss, DDG. What else?'

'Well, DG, there's the old issue of *The Signs*.'

'The what, Whitehead?'

'*The Signs*, DG. That's what we've been calling them here.' The others around the table looked at Whitehead as if to dare him to let it all hang out.

'You see, DG, we've been concerned for a long time about the persistence of networks of the old apartheid security into our democratic period, in our institutions – government, business, private security, political parties.'

Mthembu paused mid-stride from another foray around the room. 'And we have intelligence on these so-called networks, DDG?'

'That's the problem, DG. It's very hard to put our finger on this. We don't know for sure who were apartheid agents – as you know, the boers destroyed all the files.'

'DDG! That's another word we will not use here!'

'Sorry, DG? Which word?'

'We don't say "comrade" any more and we don't say "boer". The struggle is long over, Whitehead.'

'Well, I'm not quite sure of that, DG, but you're the boss.'

Mthembu resumed his perambulation. 'So you have no intelligence but you think there are these so-called networks.'

'That's why we call it *The Signs*, chief. Strange things go on that we can't explain; things that seem to obstruct government's transformation programme, strange characters with no struggle history found in senior positions in sensitive areas, even old apartheid securocrats being appointed into leadership positions in the justice and security sectors.'

'Hold it right there, Whitehead!' Mthembu stopped pacing and waved his arm again. 'You have no intelligence. You see "signs". This is nonsense. We are twenty-one years into democracy and you are still seeing ghosts of the past. Nonsense. Conspiracy theories. There will be no conspiracy theories under my watch. You got that?' He looked straight at Whitehead, then around the room. No one nodded or spoke. 'This meeting is over. We will discuss our intelligence priorities further when I've had a chance to study recent assessments. Whitehead, you will certainly not include this nonsense in your briefing to the ICC.'

And so they filed out. Other management members tried to gather around Whitehead in the lobby outside, but he waved them off. He went down to Bongi's office and walked in without knocking. She was at her desk, reading something off the screen. She looked up.

'Bongi, I'm taking retirement.'

'When, Jerry? Why?'

'Now. Immediately. I can't work with this guy.'

'But you still have a year to go before you turn sixty.'

'I don't care. I'll lose a year of my pension. I can't work with this guy.'

Bongi stood up, walked around the desk, and put her arms around Jerry. He sunk his head into her shoulder.

Note No. 9

The language of the absolutely lonely man is lyrical.
— Georg Lukács, The Theory of the Novel

August 2020
Like clouds coagulating above a jagged horizon, the drooping of the air pressure felt in the tendons of the gut awaiting the drag inwards, so I sense the gathering of tempest. The air becomes, first, luminous, visible; then, a darkening, a thickening, a weightfulness.

What, erstwhile cohabitants of the proverbial trenches, is to become – has become – of our revolution? The distant woodland, promising shade, now effaced, lumbered down, the bleeding trunks genuflecting to the cold wind.

Does revolution, does love, like the flesh, all droop and die?

Chapter 30

All changed, changed utterly:
A terrible beauty is born
– WB Yeats, 'Easter, 1916'

August 2019
Masilela thought it was a wild goose chase motivated more by Whitehead's need to close a personal loop than furthering the investigation. But he was also well aware of Jerry's theory of investigative dialectics – 'the slog' versus the 'dip and dive' – and so he finally relented. But he sent Casper, with clear private instructions, along with Jerry to KaNyamazane.

It took Jerry and Casper a long hour to find S'bu Dlamini's one-roomed shack in the township. Now they sat in it around S'bu, Whitehead on an upturned banana crate, Casper on the single wood-and-steel kitchen chair and S'bu on the immaculately made bed. As his eyes accustomed to the dull light, Whitehead tried to connect the S'bu before him with the Paulo Freire he had known and named. He could not. This one seemed aged beyond his years. In Whitehead's calculation, he must be in his late fifties at most, but his hair was the colour of fresh ash, the skin on his face and hands creased and patched, his eyes jaundiced.

But his room, with its corrugated-iron walls and roof, stretched plastic window and wood-and-cardboard door, had the perfection of a lifer's prison cell – everything placed for maximum utility and neatness: the bed tucked into one corner, raised on bricks; the formica-topped kitchen table with scarred and stained but neatly stacked pots, pans, plates and cutlery; against the wall behind him, a bookshelf with books stacked according to size and, above the bed, behind S'bu's head, a dark-framed holographic picture of a very Aryan, pale-skinned Jesus which, when you moved your head, metamorphosed into a picture of a beautiful young woman holding a luminescent baby. Must be one of the Marys, Whitehead thought – either the virgin one or the girlfriend.

Whitehead raised his hand towards the picture. 'You become a Christian, Comrade Paulo?'

S'bu did a half-turn of his head, without looking at the picture. 'I don't use that name any more, sir.'

'Sir? You call me "sir"?'

'I can't do the "comrade" thing any more, Mr Whitehead. Can't do the Paulo thing either.'

'Okay, S'bu. Sorry. So?' He nodded towards the picture.

S'bu's words came out as if in a painful limp. 'Yes, I came back to Jesus. Many of us came back to Jesus when we came home. The things we believed in those days, in umzabalazo, they are gone now. The things we hoped for, the dreams, inkululeko. We must wait now. We must wait for the next life.'

S'bu broke into a paroxysm of coughing. He took a perfectly folded white handkerchief out of his jacket pocket and held it to his mouth with a strange daintiness. When the coughing stopped he took a long time unfolding and refolding the handkerchief before he returned it to his pocket.

Whitehead looked at Casper, who looked back and shrugged. He turned back to face S'bu. 'So, S'bu? What happened to you? Some comrades said you were dead. Some said you sold out. Some said you went to the Island. What happened?'

S'bu ran a knuckled hand across his face. 'Come, let's sit outside. It's time to light a fire.'

They followed him out, his limp now greatly accented, carrying their seating with them, and settled down around a brazier that S'bu quickly fired up, before seating himself on an upturned metal drum. The August air was warm, but the fire comforted. S'bu went inside and came out with a metal grid and kettle and placed them over the fire. 'You guys want something to drink? Tea? Coffee?'

Whitehead shifted on his crate. 'Nothing stronger, comr— Sorry ... S'bu.'

S'bu laughed for the first time, but still it sounded painful. 'Brandy, if I remember? Your drink? Brandy.'

'Good memory. Yes, it used to be. More of a whiskey man now.'

'Sorry, Whitehead, I don't do that any more. Haven't touched utshwala since I came home in '86.' He went pensive. 'Hawu! What month is this? August? Hawu! It's exactly thirty-three years without!' His eyes became glassy.

Jerry and Casper sat still while they waited for S'bu to return from the past. Whitehead broke the silence. 'It's okay. I'll have coffee. Black.' Casper gestured agreement. S'bu went back inside and returned with metal mugs and a tin of Ricoffy. Casper pretended to check messages on his phone and switched on the recording app.

Whitehead coughed. 'So, S'bu, tell us your story.'

S'bu held his hands to the fire. 'It was August '86, thirty-three years ago this month. Me and my unit – Jackman, Tolstoy and Vusi – I don't even know their real names. Sies! We came into the country via Botswana. A good unit. Good comrades.'

He lifted the kettle off the flames and swirled the water around, spooned coffee into the mugs and poured. Whitehead and Casper leaned over for their mugs.

S'bu sipped at his, his eyes once more disappeared into the past. 'Soon after crossing we ambushed a border patrol – killed them all. Then we moved over some weeks to Eastern Transvaal – as it was called then – now Mpumalanga. We carried out a few missions on the way: police roadblock, a dompas office. We kept moving so the boers always looked for us where we'd been, not where we were going.' He sipped his coffee, eyes cast downwards into the mug, searching for the next memory.

Casper spoke, startling Whitehead and S'bu. 'You were heroes.'

S'bu looked at Casper, then back into his mug. 'Forgotten heroes.'

Whitehead stretched his legs out in front of him to shift the pressure on his buttocks. 'And? When you got to Eastern Transvaal? What then?'

'We settled here.' S'bu waved his arm around him then let it drop. 'Here, in the township. We set up base here. But …' He went away again.

'But what, S'bu? What?'

'We lost contact, with the outside, with the comrades. We were isolated. We carried out some ops, closer to Jozi, and then come back here so they looked for us in the wrong places. But we ran out of ammo.'

S'bu took a single cigarette out of the breast pocket of his jacket, stuck it through a hole in the side of the brazier to light it, and pulled hard at it, blowing the smoke back into the fire. After a few drags he held it out to Jerry and Casper as if it were a zol. They shook their heads.

S'bu sipped loudly at his coffee. 'You know, before I left the country – had to leave the country – I was a unionist, and ANC underground.'

'Yes, I remember. You told me.' Whitehead shifted his legs again. 'A plastics factory in Nelspruit, wasn't it?'

'You got a good memory.'

'Well …' Whitehead couldn't tell him he'd recently re-read the interview report.

'It's still there.'

'What is?' Whitehead put his hand out for the cigarette.

'The factory. It's still there. Still in the same white family. The son runs it now. The union has died.'

'If I remember, you were responsible for DLBing weapons.' Whitehead passed the cigarette back. It tasted so good. He would have to gird himself against temptation.

'Yes, that's correct. Uyakhumbula. Only a few times though, before I had to leave. And my commander – uPatrick – was arrested. Killed.' S'bu puffed long on the cigarette and stared into a distance that was not there, their tiny fire-lit space bounded by other shacks, sagging fences, car skeletons, blackened stovepipes and white satellite dishes. There was no distance. S'bu's eyes dropped down to his coffee mug. 'I think that's how we got caught.'

'Who got caught?'

'My unit.'

'What happened?'

Casper looked at his phone to check the sound level. He scraped his chair closer to the fire.

'I made the classic mistake, that's what … that's what happened.' S'bu looked at Casper, at Whitehead, then back at the fire. He spoke to the flames. 'My mother passed. 1989. October. I went to her funeral. In the village. Mistake. People saw me.'

'You were arrested?'

'No, no. On my way back from the village I passed the spot. I remembered it – the spot where I'd buried the ammo.'

214

Whitehead looked at Casper and gestured with his eyes at the phone. Casper looked at the screen and nodded. Whitehead turned to S'bu. 'Is that where you saw your uncle and the white man?'

S'bu looked up and hard at Whitehead. His eyes narrowed and glazed. 'Yes.'

'Was your uncle at the funeral?'

'Of course.'

'So, what happened?'

'When?'

'You said you remembered the spot where you'd buried the ammo.'

'Yes. But it'd been nearly ten years. But I stopped and went to check. The rock I used to mark the spot was still there. The soil looked undisturbed.'

'So you dug out the weapons?'

'No, not then. I came back here, to the location. I gathered my unit and we went back to the spot together, with our weapons. Although we had no ammo.'

'So you dug it up? It was still there and still okay?'

'Yes, we dug it up. We took it back to the car. It was night. We had to use torches.' S'bu looked into his coffee cup, paused, emptied the dregs onto the earth. He swirled the kettle again and put it back on the fire. He took out another cigarette and puffed long.

Whitehead sipped at his own coffee. It was cold. He waited until S'bu seemed to stir. 'And then?'

S'bu started. He looked at Whitehead. 'And then? And then the night lit up. Bullets flew. Boers. Everywhere. They fell.'

'Who fell?'

'The comrades. All of them. Tolstoy. Jackman. Vusi. They were standing in the road next to the car. They all fell with the first bullets. I was behind the car, holding the plastic bag with the ammo and my AK. I dropped into the donga next to the road. I tore open the plastic, managed to load a magazine. There was quiet. The boers started approaching the car, so I opened fire. I saw three fall, I think. Others dropped to the ground. I fired on auto until the magazine was empty. Then I climbed out the donga … into the bush behind me. And I ran.'

'And? Did they catch you?' Whitehead hankered for a drag on the cigarette that rested forgotten between S'bu's fingers, a long tube of ash precarious at its tip.

S'bu came back from his memory. He clucked and flicked the cigarette at the brazier, but the ash fell to the ground. He rubbed it into the earth with his foot. 'No.'

'No?'

'No. They didn't catch me. I came back here. To the township. And then I moved around for a few months, sleeping in different places, sometimes in the bush. Until ...'

'Until?'

'Well, until 1990 came. The ANC was unbanned. The comrades started coming home.'

'And you? Did you make contact with the ANC?'

'Hawu, Whitehead! Yes, I tried. Here at first. But the ANC was becoming otherwise. Everybody was suddenly ANC. Even the bantustan people. No one was impressed with me. Maybe saw me as a threat, competition. Maybe. I don't know. I helped out with campaigning for the elections. In '94. Even voted. Yebo, voted.' S'bu lifted the kettle and grate off the brazier and stirred the fire with a metal rod. He went into the shack and came out with an armful of rough-hewn logs and placed them in the fire.

The rich smell of woodsmoke approached Whitehead. He breathed it in deeply. Still longing for a cigarette. 'And after the elections?'

'In '95, I think, I went to Jozi. Hung around Shell House. Saw many comrades, but everybody was busy with their own things, their own ambitions, schemes, survival strategies. But I did manage to link up with Sis'Thembi – you know her? She was the one in Botswana that crossed us into the country.'

'Which Thembi?'

'You know? The short female comrade.'

'Masondo? You mean Thembi Masondo?'

'Yes, that's the one.'

'You know she's SG now?'

'She is? No, I didn't know. I don't follow ANC things these days.' S'bu looked into the fire as if searching for something that had fallen in there. Whitehead thought he caught a smile.

'She's SG? That's good. She's a good woman.'

'So? Did she help you?'

'She tried. She arranged for me to go to Wolmaranstad, for the Brits to rank me for the new army. I went. They ranked me sergeant, but I refused. I took demob.'

'How much you get?'

'Hayi, Whitehead! I thought I was rich. I came back here. I went to the white boy who owned the factory where I used to work. I told him I wanted to buy shares in the factory. When I showed him the money, he laughed, chased me away. I tried to buy a taxi – not enough money. I rented myself a flat in town, bought some furniture. Got a job driving a taxi. Then I had an accident, so the owner fired me. Fired me. The money ran out, so I lost the flat, lost the furniture.' He thrust his thumb over his shoulder. 'Except the few things I kept – in there.'

Whitehead stood to stretch his legs. Casper too. S'bu looked from one to the other. He put the grid and kettle back on the brazier. 'You leaving?'

Whitehead sat down again. 'No, comrade. Just stretching.' He held out his mug for more coffee. What he needed was a whiskey and a smoke. 'How d'you survive after that, S'bu?'

S'bu poured and stirred the coffee and handed the mug back. 'I moved back to the township ... Back here.' He circled his hand above his head, then waved away a gust of smoke from the brazier. 'I opened a smous, here in the location.' He pointed into the distance. 'And I've been surviving on that.'

'But how did you get the money to buy stock for the shop?'

'It's not a shop. It's a smous.'

Casper laughed. S'bu and Whitehead started and looked at him.

'I borrowed it from my uncle.'

'Your uncle? The same one? Baba Dlamini?'

'Yes, Whitehead, the same one. By that time he had finished with the school. He got a job in the provincial government. Senior. He did well.'

'I see. Were you close, you and your uncle?' Whitehead looked at Casper who was checking his phone again.

'Close? He was my uncle. Family. Not really close. He never asked me about my time in exile, my MK stuff.'

'You said he "was" your uncle. Is he late?'

S'bu looked thoughtful for a moment. 'No. No, sorry. Was talking about the past. Got confused. He's still alive, in his seventies now. Retired from government with a good pension, I'm told. Still active, though. Chairman of his ANC branch.'

Whitehead glanced at Casper. 'Tell me, S'bu ... You trust him?'

S'bu looked at Casper and then back at Whitehead. 'Trust him?' He nodded towards Casper.

'No, no ... Your uncle. Your story. The one you told us when you came out. About your uncle and the white man. And then the boer ambush after your mother's funeral, when you dug up the ammo. Do you trust your uncle?'

S'bu lit another cigarette. 'Does it matter now? It's over. Umzabalaz'uphelile.'

Whitehead bristled. 'Is it? Over, I mean ... Is it really over? I wonder.'

All went quiet. The light was completely gone. The flames from the fire cast strange slicks of shadow and light through the holes in the sides of the brazier, ever moving, twisting, jiving. The sounds and smells of the township wafted in: voices, dogs, chickens, TVs, more smoke, mbaqanga, grilling meat, car engines, hiphop, fumes.

Whitehead hoisted himself up from the banana crate, and nodded towards Casper. 'Comrade S'bu, we think it's very possible that your uncle was recruiting for the SBs, maybe from the school, maybe sending spies out to us.'

S'bu looked languidly at Whitehead and then at Casper. 'That was a long time ago. If it's even true. Does it matter now?'

Whitehead put his hand out and took S'bu's. The grip was firm. 'It may matter if those spies are still among us.' S'bu did not respond. He held out his hand to Casper.

Whitehead said goodbye, and then turned back: 'Where can we find Baba Dlamini?'

Note No. 10

Spying was forced on me from birth much in the same way, I suppose, that the sea was forced on C.S. Forester, or India on Paul Scott. Out of the secret world I once knew I have tried to make a theatre for the larger world we inhabit. First comes the imagining, then the search for the reality. Then back to the imagining, and to the desk where I'm sitting now.
— JOHN LE CARRÉ, THE PIGEON TUNNEL

August 2020
Just when did the synapses reach, grasp, cling and weld? When?

I write this now in this red-covered notebook in the Kilburn Library, oppressed by the ranks of books glaring accusations at me. On the table in front of me, open at a new chapter where I have paused before, another Le Carré book. Why? I have read them all, have I not? Twice? Thrice? Why? Because I was – I am? – a spy, an officer of intelligence. Yes, Intelligence needs intelligence. It should. Le Carré knows this, knew this. He also knew that we are fallible. Sometimes wasted. Often wasted.

Yes. Synapses. In my case, in my grappling with the realness behind phenomena, I have an image of synapses flailing about restlessly, angrily, each seeking out a mate. And when they do – if they do – I hear them exhale quietly, like a gentle zephyr, relieved finally. Connected. Joined in holy ...

But when, I need to remember, when did these particular synapses wed? The visit to Freire? The trunk with the yellow 'O'? A meeting on a dirt road with an envelope? Should I have got it sooner? Would that have changed the world, changed history – the red pen doing its thing?

But I knew. There was a moment when I knew. Unproven, yes, but I knew. I guess, as I've always known. The Signs. *The Signs.*

Chapter 31

August 2019
'I still don't understand!'

Bongi did not look at Jerry where he stood on the opposite side of the bed. She kept her eyes down to the travelling bag she was packing, carefully tucking two pairs of panties into a corner. 'You still don't understand what, Jerry?' She laid a pair of slacks, folded precisely, in the bag and moved back to the cupboard behind her.

'Why you have to accompany Vladimir.'

'I told you, Jerry … I'm not accompanying Vladimir; he's accompanying me!'

'Same thing.'

'No, it's not, Jerry. The cover story is centred on me. He's going to be the hanger-on.'

Jerry didn't respond. Bongi looked up. He was looking at her with a sorrow she could not fathom. Or was it sorrow? It was not a look she associated with Jerry. She smiled. But he turned away, stood looking out the window at the wintered garden, then left the room.

⁓

Later, on the N4 east in Vladimir's near-silent A4 hovering around the speed limit, she looked across at Vladimir, his eyes narrowed on the road, his forehead furrowed, the late-winter sun painting shards of light on his shaven scalp. She had always thought that he had an innate look of wisdom; in fact, not so much a look as an overall demeanour. In his speech, his body language, his eyes, he was the calm, reasoned one. Jerry was the fervent one; not unreasoned, not unreasonable, always just hovering on the edge – in work, in life, in love, in his appetites, always edging it.

Vladimir turned suddenly to her, caught her gaze. 'What?' he asked with raised eyebrows before turning back to the road.

'Nothing, Vladimir. Just thinking.'

'About?'

'I was comparing you and Jerry – the Jekyll and Hyde of intelligence.'

Vladimir turned briefly again. 'Oh, really? Which one am I?'

She turned away, to the window to her left, eyes blinking at the sun and the blur of the passing fields. 'Actually, I don't remember which character is which. But, anyway, it's an inaccurate comparison. Life is not that dichotomous.' Speaking to the window, she continued. 'Jerry and I had a bit of a fight this morning.'

Vladimir did not turn this time. He too looked out the side window. 'Oh? About what?'

'I think he's jealous of you.'

'Of me?'

'Of us.'

He took his foot off the accelerator as if he was going to stop, then pressed it down again, going well past the speed limit, overtook a truck on a solid line, and pulled sharply back into lane. 'Of us? Should he be?'

Bongi regretted starting this conversation. 'I don't know. Should he?'

Vladimir didn't reply. He didn't look at her. But his mouth appeared to twitch, in and out of a smile.

Bongi looked back to the window and the passing scene, mountains emerging around them, replacing the spreading fields. They were coming down the hill now towards the Watervalboven tunnel. She turned the dial on the radio up. Pop music. She turned it down again, turned to Vladimir, put her hand on his thigh and took it back again. 'I think my perfect man would have been an amalgam of you and Jerry. You can't always get want you want, but if you try sometime, you just might find, you get what you need.'

Vladimir laughed. 'Hawu, sisi, you quoting the Rolling Stones! I would never have imagined.'

'That's Jerry's influence. I'm into all kinds of music, and literature. I'm a multiculturalist. Jerry calls me an eclecticist.'

'A what …? Oh! Yebo, I get it. Eclecticist.'

They went quiet. She turned up the radio again. It was news. The end of the news. Exchange rates and weather. The rand was going down; the markets didn't like the new president much. The weather news was good – spring approaching; the gods, it seemed, liked the new president. She ran her hands down the top of her slacks, shifted her legs, held out the coffee flask to Vladimir. He refused. She poured herself a cup, bending forward and pouring between her legs to avoid a spill on the slacks. She sipped at it, rehearsing their story in her head.

~

Their hands touched as they pushed simultaneously at the small metal gate to the front garden of the house in this suburb of the provincial capital, formerly known as Nelspruit, then as Mbombela, now more recently re-renamed after a former, late provincial premier who had died under suspicious circumstances two years before. It suddenly occurred to Bongi, as she quickly removed her hand from the gate, that it was quite likely the town would soon get a new name. The former premier was not a loved one of the new administration. Vladimir ushered her through the gate and followed behind her. The garden was all lawn – scrawny kikuyu grass – dry, patchy and ashen. There were no beds, no trees, no shrubs – just the poorly paved path to the front door. The house itself was box-like: square whitewashed face, square windows, square front stoep; the front door was rectangular, but only just.

She rang the bell. Silence. Vladimir stepped forward and rapped hard. It echoed into the house, followed by footfalls limping down a passage. The door opened. The man before them was tall and stooped, tight grey curls forming a crescent around a wrinkled bald patch on his head, the skin of his face folded over itself, his lips large and wan, his eyes much younger than the rest of him.

'Ah, Miss Nkambule, I presume. And ...?' He turned to Vladimir.

Bongi put out her hand. He took it with hesitation, looking at Vladimir for permission. 'Doctor, actually, Mr Dlamini. Dr Nkambule. But you can call me Thando.' She retrieved her hand and gestured to Vladimir. 'This is my colleague, Professor Manzini.'

Dlamini took Vladimir's hand and shook it with some vehemence. He looked long at him, some effort etched on his face. Silence for a moment, then he looked beyond them to the street, stepped back and ushered them through the door much like a butler. 'Ngicela ningene.'

They walked past and then stepped aside to allow him to lead them into the lounge and point them to two armchairs as he sat on the sofa. There was something about the furnishing of the room that irritated Bongi – heavy, light-coloured wooden frames to the seats with purple upholstery, uncomfortable lumps in the wrong places; scattered cushions of devious colour; imitation ceramic statuettes, large and small, on a cluttered mantelpiece, dark-wooded side tables and a bookshelf empty of books.

Baba Dlamini stared long at Vladimir again, rose suddenly and, without a word, left the room to busy himself, Bongi assumed from the emanating sounds, in the kitchen. He returned with a tray with china teapot, cups, saucers, sugar bowl and milk jug that Bongi later described on the drive home as English daintiness. He poured without offering, held out a cup to each of them and pushed the sugar and milk first toward Vladimir.

'You look familiar ... so familiar. But my old brain. My old head.'

Bongi leaned forward, pushing away the sugar and milk that Vladimir proffered. 'Professor Manzini here is retired now. He is supervising my research. He is quite a well-known academic. Perhaps you've seen him on TV? He used to be their favourite expert on historical things.'

Dlamini sipped his tea and looked at them over his cup. 'Yes, perhaps, on TV. Yes. Professor, eh? Which university?'

Bongi answered. 'Wits. As I explained on the phone, Mr Dlamini, I am with the History Workshop at Wits. Professor Manzini is an associate now. I am doing research, collecting narratives, about the resistance to apartheid in local communities. My current project is focused on the former Eastern Transvaal. Mpumalanga.'

'Yes, yes, Mrs Nkambule, I understand. Funny thing ... In my long life – I am seventy-nine now – I have not met many professors. Funny. You might be only the second ... yes, the second one. I knew one, a while ago. But he was a white man. Yes. I don't think there were any black professors in those days. Yes.' He sipped at his tea.

Vladimir leaned forward to speak, but Bongi motioned to him to sit back. She took a digital recorder from her handbag. 'May we start the interview, Mr Dlamini? Do you mind if I record?'

He looked at her as if surprised to be called back from his reverie. 'Yes, yes. Of course, Madame Nkambule. The interview. Go ahead. More tea?'

'No thanks, Mr Dlamini. If we can begin?' She switched on the recorder. 'Why don't you start with a brief summary of your life ...? Perhaps start with the present, what you are doing now.'

He suddenly preened, back up straight, as straight as it would go, chest out. Bongi only noticed for the first time that he was wearing a sports jacket and tie. She was reminded of the old men of the village of her childhood, on a Sunday late afternoon, sitting around the fire, drinking the brew, dressed as if for the city far away. She nodded her readiness.

'Yes, well, now I'm retired. Yes, sometime now. Was a director in the province's education department under the old premier. Yes. I miss him. Good man. Tragic ending. He was assassinated, you know.'

Vladimir spoke. 'I thought it was suicide.' Bongi glared at him. 'Sorry, Dr Nkambule. Sorry.' He sat back.

'No, no, sir. It was murder. His political enemies.' Dlamini paused, looking to Vladimir for a response. Bongi spoke. 'Please continue, Mr Dlamini.'

'Yes, well, I retired – had to retire ... Age, you know. But I'm still active in my branch – ANC, you know. I'm branch chairman. But not happy, no. Not happy with this new ANC, this new leadership. I miss the former president, the premier. They were for us rural folk. Yes, us out here in the bushes. This new lot is for the city folk, the workers, the lazy workers – always striking ...'

'And before that?' Bongi poured herself another cup of tea. 'Before the provincial department.'

'Before that? Yes, I was a teacher, a headmaster.' He named the school. Vladimir took a piece of paper out of his shirt pocket and wrote it down. Dlamini stared at him. Bongi glared. Vladimir lifted his shoulders in part apology: 'Old habits. Bad memory. I don't trust technology.' He pointed at the recorder. 'She does.' He pointed at Bongi.

And so the interview continued, Bongi allowing the old man to ramble, her own mind drifting too, back to the tiff with Jerry that morning, the discussion in the car with Vladimir, and back, now and then, to the obvious fabrications of his past by Baba Dlamini – well, if not quite fabrications, at least a re-remembering in deference to the required narrative that the present demanded of the past, of him, his past. Now and then, she prodded with a question, but there was hardly need. He seemed flattered with the interest in his history. She almost felt a little guilty for the deception.

At last his voice slowed and quietened. He paused, looked at her. She thanked him, promised him a copy of the transcript and the final research. She looked to Vladimir for small talk. There was more, she thought.

Vladimir obliged. 'Baba, you said I'm only the second professor you've met. Who was the first?' Bongi pretended to switch the recorder off.

'The first? Yes. I said, didn't I? A white man, Afrikaner actually ... From Unisa, the University of South Africa.'

'Oh? How did you meet him?' Vladimir wore a look Bongi recognised – disinterest in his own question, more like feigned politeness, pretended interest. He was good at that.

'He was one of those, you know ... Liberal whites. His university was looking for bright students – yes, that's right – exceptional students.'

Vladimir looked out the window, then lazily back at Dlamini. 'I see. Exceptional students, hey? Why was that?'

Dlamini seemed flustered. 'They wanted to support them. You know, to study further after matric, sponsor them for university studies. Yes.'

Bongi stepped in. 'That's interesting. I never knew about that. And? Did you recommend anyone?' She saw Vladimir turn away again to hide a smile.

Dlamini scratched at the crescent of hair. He looked into his empty teacup. 'Oh dear, now you're asking things of an old man, an old brain. I can't remember. I might have. There were so many pupils over the many, many years.' He trailed off, looking to Vladimir for support.

Vladimir put on his smile, his famous smile. 'Very nice. Very good. Is he still alive, that professor? You remember his name? We should look him up. It will be very good for our research.'

Dlamini seemed to warm to the smile and the question. Bongi wondered why. 'Oh yes. Very good, yes, but I think the professor is late. I believe so. I forget his name. I used to call him Prof. He called me Headmaster. Very polite man. Very polite.'

Later that evening, in Vladimir's room in the rustic lodge he had chosen, he and Bongi sat at the small round table just inside the wood-and-glass French doors, listening to the recording of the interview with Dlamini. On the table between them the bottle of Glenfiddich Vladimir had retrieved from his overnight bag, as well as two glasses. They sipped as they listened, both taking occasional notes. Every now and then Vladimir looked up at her, his eyes narrowing quizzically. She pretended not to notice. The recording finished. They sat in silence for a while, each going through their notes, Vladimir with a yellow highlighter.

He spoke first. 'It's him, I'm sure. The same one.'

Bongi looked up, pulled her glass closer. 'Who is *him*?'

'This so-called Professor. I'm sure it's the same Bester or Bekker I asked you to look up … I'm sure.'

'But you never told me why I should look him up.'

Vladimir looked at her over the rim of his glass. He rubbed his scalp vigorously. 'I got information that there was a Bester or Bekker in the security police here in the old Eastern Transvaal who boasted about having sources high in the ANC.'

'You got information? From who? How reliable?'

'Does it matter from who? Very reliable. I was also told that he later left the police and joined the old NIS. That's why I asked you to check, to see if he was amalgamated in '95.'

Bongi pushed her glass away. 'I'm hungry.'

'I'll order some hot chips, and a bottle of wine.'

Bongi laughed. 'Hot chips? You wanting to fatten me up?'

Chapter 32

September 2019
Whitehead had few day-to-day principles on which he stood firm, but one of them was not working on weekends. This weekend, though, he was going to make an exception. With Bongi gallivanting with Masilela in Mpumalanga, the house was not a home. It had taken him years to entrench this resolution, which he attributed to the need for work-life balance. In reality, it was an official-work-private-work balance.

When he was still employed, his weekends were spent reading, making notes and concocting fragments for the memoir he was never to finish. It had become a habit. Saturday and Sunday mornings he would have a breakfast in bed, always two slices of toast, thick butter, cheese and marmalade, with a cup of coffee; read in bed for an hour or two, and then spend time in the study, pretending to write but mostly embroiled in perpetual research. It – his work, his life – all needed a context, and context was his rationale.

Of course, once he retired, the weeks had no end and the weekends no boundaries either, but still he divided them in his mind and in his habits, measured by Bongi's absence on weekdays. Now, with the investigation, weekends were back to their old format. Some weekends, instead of the toast and cheese in bed, he and Bongi would walk to the nearby House of Coffees for the full-on breakfast of bacon, eggs and all the trimmings. But, over time, Bongi had weaned him onto smoked salmon, rye bread, one poached egg and avocado, no sugar in the coffee.

This Sunday, with Bongi departed the day before, he left early for House of Coffees, ordered extra bacon, two fried eggs, hash browns and baked beans; coffee with cream and sugar. He read the Sunday papers. The *Sunday Times* ran a front-page story about a group calling themselves the RETD – the Radical Economic Transformation

Detachment – who were claiming that President Moloi's so-called radical agenda was no more than a cover for his own corruption. They were demanding his recall. Whitehead had heard about them. He wondered about their provenance – a strange collection of acolytes of the former president, former bantustan bureaucrats and securocrats, the recently discarded of the ANC Youth League and others. The social media sympathisers with the new regime had dubbed them the #RETarDs.

Whitehead finished his breakfast, sent a text to Steven while he waited for the bill, paid and then walked to the nearby hardware store that stayed open for a few hours on a Sunday for the still mainly Afrikaner men in Pretoria East who DIYed on Sundays. He bought a bolt cutter, walked home and took the car to Steven and Gail's place.

As it was a Sunday, he didn't let himself in. Gail answered the door. 'What's so urgent, working on the weekend? The counter-revolution about to start?'

'Hi, Gail. No, Bongi's away for the weekend. Home is boring.'

She ushered him in. Steven was on the couch watching TV, a James Bond movie guessing by the soundtrack. Gail went to sit next to him.

Whitehead waved. 'Okay, let me get straight to it then.'

Steven paused the movie. 'With bolt cutters?'

'Yep. One more lock to open. No key.'

In the room, Whitehead dropped his sling bag, cleared the desk and, bolt cutters in hand, went straight over to the trunk with the big yellow 'O'. He struggled to cut through the tempered steel of the combination lock. He twisted his arms and his body this way and that to seek better leverage, but the thing wouldn't give. He thought of calling in Steve, but that would be a breach of security. He sat down on the trunk, breathing through his mouth, big breaths. He dabbed at his hairline with his red handkerchief. He ran his hands around the edges of the trunk, hoping to find a secret 'Open Sesame' latch. Then, suddenly, he stood up, took the bolt cutters to the hinges at the back of the trunk and sliced through them like butter.

The trunk was full to the brim with files, cardboard folders, some borrowed or pilfered from the Zambian civil service, it seemed, others newer and more colourful, with the CNA logo. Whitehead picked up a file on the top with the neatly stencilled letters on the cover – 'The Oracle Project'. He took it over to the desk.

Four hours later he had not moved, except once to drag the trunk closer to the desk and then to bend now and again to extract another file. The desk and floor around his chair were now strewn with folders, just a small space kept clear for his notebook. He had abandoned his flexi-tab for the older technology of pen and lined paper, his barely legible handwriting already covering tens of pages of notes.

'The Oracle' – this was a trove of treasure, but why hidden for so long? He had heard whispers of it in the Green House days in Lusaka, but, coming as the whispers did during drinking sessions, he put it down to wishful thinking or boastfulness – after all, ANC intelligence sources in the heart of apartheid security? Really?

What intrigued him now, though, was that the stream of intelligence had continued to flow after the return from exile and even, from some of the files, into the early years of democracy. Who knew about this? He knew at least one person who did, and that was perhaps the bigger surprise: the quiet, apparently evanescent Casper, had been the handler of the primary source, The Oracle himself. The Oracle, who had visited Botswana in 1980 and made contact with Casper in the regional underground intelligence machinery there, offered his services, having taken the decision to infiltrate the security police after they had killed the only child of his sister.

Chapter 33

September 2019

Although not planned, it happened on the following Sunday that Vladimir Masilela and Mr and Mrs Whitehead arrived simultaneously early at Rietvlei Dam, perhaps both in deference to the old trade craft of arriving betimes to a secret assignation. Jerry and Bongi's car appeared behind Masilela's as he pulled up to the gate and spoke to the guard. They did not acknowledge each other. Once inside the reserve, the Whiteheads followed Masilela at a discreet distance to the spot he had previously chosen.

Once unpacked, they began to set up. It would be at least half an hour before the rest of the team arrived. Jerry set up the Weber braai, placed the firelighters and charcoal and lit the fire. Masilela unfolded the metal table, set up the camp chairs and unpacked the drinks – beers and wine; he had banned the hard stuff for today. Bongi set the bowls of salad and the containers of marinated meat on the table.

Jerry picked up a beer from the cooler bag, but Bongi took it from him and pointed at a bottle of wine. He poured and sat down next to Masilela, reached into his sling bag and handed Masilela two typed documents. 'You know about The Oracle Project?'

'Heard about it, but I wasn't privy. Lusaka once sent us some reports when I was in the forward area, but that's all I saw – reports about meetings between the boers and the Swazi police.' Masilela flipped through the first document, a summary of Whitehead's notes. 'Jesus, Jerry! This is gold! Where d'you find it?'

'In the archives – The Room. It was in a trunk that I only managed to open last week. There's a lot more. Read the second document.'

Masilela read.

15 May 1994
IO: CSP
S: ORC
RE: NIS INAUGURATION MEETING

Source reports that on night of inauguration he delivered envelope to members of management of NIS Covert Collection Directorate at NIS safe house (c/f). As trained, source, before delivery, securely opened and resealed envelope. It contained report on meeting of President Mandela with JN and other DIS members on amalgamation process. Source of info was not included. [Note: to check present in meeting]

Source reports following present at safe house:
– Mr Patel (safe house caretaker)
– Ms Marie (secretary to Covert Directorate)
– Mr Otto Bester (head Covert) [Note: Bester recruited source from Soweto SB to NIS in 1988. Source says Bester was previously SB]
– Mr Cline [sp?]
– Mr Johan van Deventer

Source says others arrived as he was leaving, but too dark to identify them ...

Masilela looked up. 'Bongi, what was the name of that subordinate of yours you asked about former SBs in the Service?'

Jerry looked at Bongi and back at Masilela. His forehead crinkled.

Bongi balanced her glass of wine on the ground. 'You mean the Van Deventer fellow?'

Masilela grunted. 'Johan?'

'Yes. Johan. He's a unit head in my directorate. Why?'

Masilela waved the report at her. 'The bastard lied to you. He was part of the Covert Collection management before amalgamation.' He turned to Jerry and waved the report again. 'And this one? Cline? Is that not Graham Kline?'

Jerry cradled his glass. 'I suspect so, chief. Must be. We only had one Kline.'

Masilela walked over to the fire, peering down at the coals. 'Check your fucking fire, Whitehead!' Jerry stood.

Masilela went to the table for more wine. 'Kline! We were told he had an impeccable career in liaison, a string of foreign postings. That's what his bloody CV said. When we interviewed him he told us that, because he was English-speaking, he was not really accepted in the NIS, so they kept sending him abroad to keep him out of the way. That's what the bastard told us.'

Jerry laughed, a dry, hoarse chuckle. Masilela grunted again. 'Shit, man! We deployed the bastard to London as station chief!'

Jerry stirred the coals with the braai spatula. 'Here come the others,' he said, looking up at the sound of a car engine. 'Shall I start the meat?'

Masilela's head was back in the reports. He reread both. Bongi took the container with the boerewors over to Jerry and watched while he placed them on the grid. 'These will take longer, so do them first. Is the fire not too hot, Jerry?' He didn't answer.

The car pulled up. Doors and the boot opened and slammed. Vhonani, Velaphi, Senzo and Casper approached, lugging more camp chairs and a large cooler box.

Masilela greeted. 'What you got in there, madoda?'

Velaphi spoke. 'Drinks and ice, chief.'

'What drinks?'

'The usual, chief?'

'I said no hard stuff!'

'Jesus, chief, what kind of a picnic is this?'

Masilela glared. 'This is no fucking picnic, comrade!'

The new arrivals looked at each other and at Bongi. She raised and dropped her shoulders quickly. Masilela noticed. He motioned them to the table to get drinks. When they were done, he pointed Casper to a chair opposite him. 'Sit, Comrade Casper.'

Casper sat and pried open his can of beer.

Masilela raised his glass at him. 'You're a real spy aren't you, Casper? A real fucking spy. The perfect spy. Invisible. Sit down, the rest of you. Listen to this. When were you going to brief us about The Oracle Project, Casper?'

Casper pulled at his jeans to loosen them over his knees. He turned to Jerry at the fire behind him, to the others, then back to Masilela.

'Huh? chief? I didn't think it was relevant now?'

'Not relevant? You've been in this task team for …' – he looked at his watch – 'yes, for three months, a team investigating old-order agents in our new order, and you didn't think it relevant to tell us you ran a source in apartheid intelligence?'

The other newcomers turned to Casper. Velaphi let out a dark breath. Casper dropped his chin to his chest. 'It crossed my mind, chief. It did. But I don't know what happened to the reports, the files. There was so much detail. There's no way I could remember that stuff.'

Masilela rolled the report into a tube and pointed it at Casper. 'You remember this?'

Casper pulled himself out of the canvas camp chair and took the report. Masilela watched him as he read. He wondered how on earth this diffident comrade had managed to successfully handle such a sensitive source. Perhaps it was, indeed, his near invisibility that had instilled confidence, a sense of safety, in Agent Oracle.

Bongi handed the container of lamb chops to Jerry. He pushed the wors to the side of the grid and used the tongs to carefully place the chops. They wouldn't all fit.

Casper finished the report. He gestured with it to the others, but Masilela stood and took it back from him. 'Where did you find this, chief? Is there more?'

'Jerry found it. All of it.' He waited for that to sink in, watched memories flit across Casper's eyes. 'So? Where is this Oracle now?'

'He's late.'

'When?'

'I think, 2014. Yes, 2014. Just before you retired.'

'Just before I retired?'

'Yes, chief. You were at his funeral.'

Masilela suddenly regretted forbidding stronger drink. 'I was at his funeral? Who?'

'He was in the Service, chief. He stayed on after amalgamation. But he asked to be redeployed out of covert. We put him in counter-intelligence, investigations. Then he served as one of your protectors for a while. In 2012, I think.'

'For chrissake, Casper! Who?'

'Meat is ready!' Jerry waved the tongs.

Everyone stood. Masilela yelled. 'Hlalani phansi, ma-comrade!' He turned back to Casper. 'Who?'

'Tau, chief.'

'Philemon?'

'Yes, chief.'

'You put a former collaborator as part of my security.'

'He was *our* collaborator, chief. Very loyal. The boers killed his sister's only child. He never forgave them. Never.'

Masilela reached for a paper plate. 'I wish you'd told me this at the time.' He went over to the braai, cursed under his breath to Jerry.

There was silence as they ate, near silence, or rather, as Masilela observed, an entry into their space of the sounds of eternity: birds chirping, the soft slush of languid water against the dam banks, a gentle spring wind and the flapping of wings. Strangely, these sounds provided a kind of choral resonance to the sounds of clinking bottles, glasses, the bursts of beer cans opening, and the scraping of plastic cutlery on paper plates.

When they were done, they cleared plates, shrank the circle of chairs and took out notebooks. Under Masilela's stewardship, they each recounted the outcomes of their own investigation, such as he was willing for them to share, enough to decide on the next steps.

Bongi spoke of her attempts to find records of a Bester or Bekker in the Service. They all offered various versions of 'Aha' when she described the message 'Above your pay-grade' on her computer.

Masilela added the titbit about a Bester or Bekker boasting about top agents in the ANC, and then Jerry described the lists he was making of potential suspects. He left out the interview with S'bu Dlamini. Casper looked at him, but said nothing.

As the light began to dim, Masilela returned his empty glass to the table, signalling the others that it was over. 'Right. You all carry on with what you're doing, but the next big thing is to find this Bester fellow.'

Casper spoke. 'I think I can help.'

They all turned to him. He continued. They weren't used to so many words emanating from Casper's mouth in one go. 'He's on his farm in Mpumalanga.'

Masilela: 'How would you know that?'

'Philemon told me. Bester and his secretary – also his girlfriend or his wife – left NIS just before amalgamation. They moved back to his farm. He actually invited Philemon to visit. Recruited him to give him stuff on what was happening among the darkies in the Service after '95. I encouraged him. Advised him on what to say.'

Masilela turned to Jerry. 'Those reports in the files?'

Casper answered. 'No, chief. They wouldn't be. This was after amalgamation. The Oracle reports are from exile and early nineties.'

'So? Where are they? The reports, I mean.'

'I didn't submit reports, chief. Philemon didn't trust the old-order people in the Service. He didn't want his past double life to be known. He liked to say it was "our secret".'

Masilela began folding the camp chairs he had brought. Bongi helped him. He snapped one shut. 'So, how the hell do we find this Bester?'

'Philemon told me the name of the farm, chief. I wrote it down somewhere, at home. I'll find it.'

Note No. 11

> *I must die. But must I die groaning? I must be imprisoned. But must I whine as well? I must suffer exile. Can any one then hinder me from going with a smile, and a good courage, and at peace?*
> – Arrian, *The Discourses of Epictetus*

July 2020
Bongi! Nadine! I am ephemeral.

Yes, I have it on the impeccable authority of the apparatchiks of the NHS of the St Mary's Hospital of Paddington, with its façade of musty stone, dark arches and red brick redolent of Gothicness, churchiness and death. I write this on a bench in a corridor, clumsy fingers penning across my notebook. I feel this corridor should be dark – a dank tunnel to oblivion – but it is light-buzzed from the strips above, shimmying off white walls and acid green tiling.

I write now to keep my eyes from the beckoning tunnel, but I am disturbed by the rumble of passing gurneys – sick ones on their way to theatre, their pre-medded eyes displaying a pale trepidation; and the ones returning from the slicing, eyes of doped surprise at consciousness returned.

The pain in the gut will not subside. I clutch at it, fists pressed in, as one would jab a finger into a toothache, but there is no relief. No crescendo and diminuendo. Just a constant clutch of corporality, of endedness.

The oncologist, who waits down the tunnel for my time, is young. She is a dark beauty. She exudes the opposite of what I have become, am becoming, am to become. She speaks quietly. Talks of hope, of options. She, with a white smile against dark lips, bats off the 'how long' question.

Bongi! Nadine! You are all that is left of what I love, of what I need now. Who else is there? Who will care? Parents? Gone. Siblings? None. Friends? None here but nodding acquaintances in the passages of my bedsit, in the pub, the musty librarian who fathoms my tastes. And at home? Friends? None, only comrades. But comrades, comradeship, have dissipated into the obscure interstices of survival, disappointment, dread.

Chapter 34

September 2019
'I can't believe Google Maps can now find boer farms.' Vhonani flicked a fingernail at the screen of the smartphone hooked up to the dashboard. The image was all a pale green depicting the farmlands spread around them, with just the one skinny squiggle of the road they were on. He looked to Casper, but Casper, eyes straight ahead and hands tight on the steering wheel, remained silent. The hum of the road was all, amplified through the metallic acoustics of the cab of the Nissan. Vhonani turned to look out the back window at the rest of the surveillance team on the back of the bakkie, dressed, like him, in the suitable rags of farm labourers and general rural hangers-about. He raised his thumb at them. The four waved back. One mimed shivering.

He turned back to the side window and watched the farmlands pass by as the road curved, dipped and rose through groves, plantations, passed farmhouses and outbuildings, ever narrowing as they slipped turn by turn from the major arteries to the roads less travelled, as instructed by the stern, clipped American voice emanating from the phone. Casper spoke. Vhonani jerked his head back from the window. 'You saying something, Casper?'

'Not all the farms here are owned by boers any more.'

'Oh yeah? You think so? Check out all the farm names. Any darkies who own farms here are probably city boys farming remotely, employing white farm managers. Hey, you can't make a quick buck from farming. We are all after a quick buck these days. Planting money to grow money. Shit! Who wants to wait a season to reap rewards?'

Casper slowed the bakkie. 'Here it comes.'

Vhonani lifted the camera from the seat next to him and held it at the ready. The entrance to the farm appeared on the left, a gravel road disappearing between two concrete curved walls into the vegetation beyond. At the end of the promontory of one of the walls, a wooden pole was planted, a brass hinge at the top, from which swung a wooden sign. Cut through the sign, so that they could only be read with the light behind, were the words:

Duquesne se Rus
Otto en Marie Bester

Vhonani motioned to Casper to slow right down while he zoomed in on the sign, clicked away, then zoomed back out and clicked away at the gateway, the road beyond, the barbed fence on either side. Casper spoke. 'Take of the other side of the road, for a possible OP.'

Vhonani turned the camera across Casper in the driver's seat and focused the lens on the road opposite. He spoke with the viewfinder to his eye. 'There's some good, big trees there. Could be okay for OP. Let's move on.' Casper coaxed the bakkie back to rural-road speed until Vhonani motioned to him to pull over a kilometre further on. 'Okay. You wait here with the others. I'll take one of the guys back on foot to set up the OP.' He placed the camera back into his cloth shoulder bag, slipped out the door, beckoned to his companion, and began the walk back, careful to tread on dried tufts of grass and stones off the road close to the opposite fence.

At the farm gate, Vhonani walked up to each of the three trees standing like arbitrary sentinels, ran his hand along the bark and looked up into their branches and then back at the gate. His companion fidgeted with his torn shirt, his eyes darting up and down the road, then back at Vhonani, who eventually motioned to him and pointed him to the tree set a little behind and between the other two. 'That's the one.'

His companion looked up at the tree, assessed its nodules and branches, and began to climb, careful foothold first, then arms up to the next graspable branch and then levering up, until he got to the long, thick branch that stretched out as if pointing suggestively at the farm gate. Vhonani watched from below, his aged neck cricking as his head bent back to follow the progress of the climb. At last the thumbs-up from above as his companion straddled the stretched branch at the edge of its safest thickness.

Vhonani thumbed back and reached into his bag as a skein of

fishing line with a small sinker on the end descended down to him from the man above. He brought first the artificial bird's nest out of his bag and fastened it to the line, then watched it disappear upwards and get placed securely in the cleft of the branches. The line came down again. Vhonani next fastened to the line the aerial camouflaged as a tendril of bark and watched it go up. Finally he fished out the tiny digital video camera with transmitter and swallowed hard on some post-nasal drip as it went up into the tree. When the cricking got too much, he looked down at the ground, rubbed the muscles at the back his neck and carefully twisted his head from side to side.

A grunt from above forced him to look up again. There was a thumbs-up and a finger pointing to his bag. He reached in and took out the new flexi-tab, unfurled it and went through the switching-on ritual. At last the video app opened and there, bright as a floodlit stadium, was the perfectly framed gate to Duquesne se Rus. He looked up, smiled, gave a power salute.

They walked quickly back to the waiting bakkie. Casper was on the phone. He hung up when they got near, and turned the ignition. Vhonani climbed onto the running board of the bakkie. 'Kulungile, madoda. Masiyeni.'

Casper pulled off even before Vhonani had flopped into the seat and closed the door. He cursed. Casper ignored him, turned to look behind and did a quick U-turn. He looked straight ahead when they passed the farm entrance. Vhonani had taken out the flexi-tab and watched their bakkie pass on the screen. He pressed Replay and showed Casper, who looked, nodded and turned back quickly to the road.

They drove about five kilometres until the T-junction – the town to the right and Kruger Park and Mozambique to the left. Casper pulled up on the verge, and they all clambered out. Vhonani indicated the chosen spot. Two climbed back onto the bakkie and handed down a pocked and stained wooden trestle table and boxes of fruit, vegetables, cigarettes, toiletries, household cleaners. The other two covered the table with a hessian cloth, laid out the wares, positioned a couple of upturned wooden boxes as stools behind the table and a small cash box at the table's inner edge.

Vhonani stood back and observed. 'Xorosho, gents. Looking good. Great spot. When the target leaves the farm to go to town for shopping or even further, he has to come this way. And any visitors he gets will have to pass here too.' He reached into his bag. 'Here's the camera. Take a photo of any car that passes.' He paused. 'And write down the time, licence plate number, occupants, direction – any car, you hear?'

They nodded and grunted assent. He pointed at two of them. 'You guys, in the bakkie. You'll do the next shift.' The two climbed on the back. Vhonani put his hand out to Casper. 'Okay, com, let me drive now. It's my op from now on.'

Back in town he dropped Casper at his car and saw him off on the road back to civilisation. 'Go well, com. We'll be okay. Tell Comrade Vlad the reports will start coming in soon.' He watched Casper's Toyota disappear over the rise, went back to the bakkie, and drove the two to the township shack they'd rented for the duration, and himself back to the boarding house. In his room, he set the flexi-tab up on the bedside table and watched the image of the farm gate, the only movement the faint bowing of leaves to the wind.

Chapter 35

As someone long prepared for the occasion
In full command of every plan you wrecked
Do not choose a coward's explanation
That hides behind the cause and the effect
— Leonard Cohen, 'Alexandra Leaving'

September 2019
Masilela was already there at the house in Pretoria East when Whitehead arrived and let himself in. He had noticed Masilela's A4 parked discreetly down the street, and found him in the kitchen with Gail. Their conversation paused when he walked in.

'Heita, Jerry. You're late.'

'No, Vladimir, you're early.' He glanced at his fitness watch, the watch he used to check his heart rate and count his daily steps. He had forgotten to charge it again. 'Hi, Gail. Still no work?'

'Hi, Jerry. No, don't be stupid. I wouldn't be here in the middle of the week if I was working.' She poured him a coffee without asking.

Masilela drained his mug, took it over to the sink and rinsed it. 'Poydem. My dolzhny rabotat.'

Gail's forehead furrowed. 'Huh?'

'It's Russian, Gail. I'm saying it's time to go do some work. Thanks for the coffee.'

'You still know Russian?'

Masilela turned back from the door. 'I talk to myself in Russian to retain what I learned in the Soviet Union.'

'But, why?'

'In my heart, Russian is still the language of revolution.'

Whitehead sat down, and sipped at his coffee.

Gail snorted. 'Revolution? After what happened? You're joking.'

'Yes, the Soviets messed up,' Masilela retorted, clearly a little irritated. 'They messed up badly. But they had a revolution that shook the world. Perhaps all revolutions are destined to mess up when they face such vicious opposition. Look at ours.'

'Our what?'

'Our revolution.'

'What revolution?'

'Exactly! Come Jerry. Let's go.'

'Thus your name? You've kept "Vladimir" because it's revolutionary?'

Masilela turned from the door. 'Yes, Gail ... My MK name is my badge of honour. I wear it proudly, unlike those who've discarded their politics and analysis for the comforts of capitalism. It's easy to rationalise what you're enjoying. Much harder to stick to your principles and your history in spite of the temptations of sophistry.' He ushered Jerry out, turned, smiled and waved at Gail.

At the entrance to the room, Masilela clucked his admiration for the security procedures. Inside, he remarked on the orderliness – rows of filing cabinets, bookshelf, desk and, on the far wall, above the row of cabinets, four large sheets of newsprint joined together and covered with multicoloured diagrams, arrows, boxes, circles and text. To the right, something large attached to the wall but screened by what looked like a tablecloth – chequered green and white.

He pointed at the newsprint. 'And what's all that? You been busy, Jerry?'

Whitehead walked over to the far wall, picked up a long wooden pointer, the kind from the old school days that doubled as a cane. He pointed to a set of red squares with text to the left of the diagram. 'These are the names on the Mandela list. The ones with black crosses are dead. The ones circled in blue are the ones we already suspected in exile and have dealt with one way or the other. These, the ones with blue crosses, are retired or out of active life. And these ...' He ran the pointer from left to right from one of the squares along an arrow to circles with text. 'These are the ones who are still active – red in government, green in the ANC, blue in business, and black in civil society or academia.'

Masilela stepped closer to the diagram, slipped on his spectacles and quietly read out some of the names in the different-coloured circles. 'You've really been working, Jerry. Impressed. And your conclusions?'

Whitehead waved the rod in circles on the left of the diagram. 'Basically, chief, I think the Mandela list leads nowhere. These names to the right here – in the circles – I've checked their files. We had nothing on them of any concern. I've unpacked their bios; nothing to arouse suspicion or even curiosity. I've researched their activities and views in the past decades – nothing to indicate anything worrying. Sure, one or two went over to Cope, or criticised the ANC as stalwarts, but if those were criteria there are hundreds we'd have to paint as sell-outs.'

Masilela removed his spectacles and waved them at the wall. 'Conclusion?'

'The list the boers gave Madiba was a mix of truth and lies; truths we mostly already knew or were mainly harmless, and lies – these in the circles here – good comrades they wanted us to doubt and suppress. As we suspected all along. The research seems to confirm this.'

Masilela stepped back and nodded towards the rest of the newsprint diagram. 'Good. As we suspected. And the rest of the diagram?'

Whitehead tapped on the diagram, rhythmically, more as an accompaniment to his words than to point to anything in particular. 'Here, chief, what I've done is this ... Similar to the Mandela list, but more complicated. I've been through the old files of all those we suspected or discovered were enemy agents. Again, I've eliminated all the dead and inactive. Also, those where I thought the basis of suspicion was flimsy. We were cowboys in those days. But if I included all that remained, my diagram would not fit it all, so these squares and names here are those who are still alive and active – same colour scheme as for these on the left. Red for—'

'Yes, yes, Jerry, I got that. Have you written this up in a report that I can give to Sandile?'

'Not yet, chief. Will do.'

'And when you do, include a brief assessment of the likelihood that the individuals are still serving agendas of their old masters.'

Masilela's phone beeped. He looked at the screen. He went silent, moved over to the desk, sat down and stared for a long while at the phone, his thumb scrolling down.

'What's up, chief?'

Masilela held his palm up, and continued reading. Eventually he looked up. 'It's the first reports from the surveillance team. Curiouser and curiouser.'

Whitehead walked over to the desk. Masilela handed him the phone. 'Our friend Baba Dlamini visited Bester's farm. That's *after* Bongi and I met him.'

Whitehead's stomach muscles contracted. Masilela continued. 'And it seems, after that visit, Bester came up to Gauteng.'

Whitehead looked up from the phone. 'Gauteng? Where in Gauteng?'

'They don't know that. Vhonani couldn't follow him all the way. Only one vehicle. Too conspicuous. You'll see in there – he followed him on the N4 up to the Mpumalanga border. So, Gauteng it was.'

Whitehead finished reading. 'You'll send me a copy?'

Masilela took the phone back, punched the keys and Whitehead's flexi-tab pinged in his bag. He ignored it.

Masilela walked back to the far wall. 'And, Jerry, what's that behind the dishcloth?'

Whitehead picked up the pointer. 'Tablecloth, chief. Bongi donated it to the struggle.' They laughed, Whitehead nervously. He dislodged the tablecloth with a flourish to reveal a mounted and laminated 1:1,000,000 map of the northern half of South Africa: Gauteng, Limpopo, Mpumalanga and portions of North West and KwaZulu-Natal. Dotted over the eastern side of the map, all in Mpumalanga, there were felt-tip markings and Post-it Notes, a few arrows pointing towards the Zimbabwe border and to Gauteng. 'I'm working on a theory, chief.'

Masilela groaned and scratched his scalp. 'A theory, Jerry? A theory? What? *The Signs* again?'

Whitehead sniggered. 'No, chief. No. We're moving beyond *The Signs* now.' He paused. 'Or maybe "beneath" *The Signs*?' He stroked his beard with his right hand, a mannerism reminiscent of Thabo Mbeki. 'There was something in philosophy about that – signs, semiology, I think ... Yes, Augustine. St Augustine.'

'Hey, Jerry. Come back to the present. What's this theory of yours?'

Whitehead pointed with the rod at the board. 'We have moved beyond signs now, chief. We are moving to cause and effect. Look here.' He tapped at the denser markings on the map to the east of Mpumalanga and then turned away to face Masilela. 'I know it's a bit of a crude categorisation, but it's useful to characterise the roles of the apartheid security institutions in two ways – the military and the police were largely focused on what the Soviets called tactical and operational intelligence ... Potential targets: our camps, personnel, houses, offices, training methods, who's who, etcetera. Their main purpose was the short-term destruction of the ANC.'

Masilela sat down. 'Okay, Jerry, makes sense, broadly speaking. And?'

'And, chief, the main focus of the NIS was strategic, long term. Yes, they collected tactical, operational and strategic intelligence on us, but – and this is the issue – their aim was also, perhaps even mainly, influence; to influence the movement in a certain direction – then and in the future.'

Masilela mimed applause 'And the map? How does the map illustrate your theory?'

'I'm coming to that, chief. The map deals with the one manifestation of my theory that we are currently dealing with. You see, I believe that the NIS, apart from all the other stuff they did, had a project to inject high-quality agents into the movement, with the long-term aim of placing them in the leadership not just for the period of struggle but for the post-apartheid era ... for now. Why d'you think they were so willing to push Botha to negotiations?'

Masilela shifted his buttocks on the seat, trying to rid himself of an itch. He stood up and walked towards the map. 'Yes, yes, Jerry. Very feasible theory. But the map. What's on the map?'

Whitehead pointed at the markings and Post-its on the right edge of the map. 'You're not going to like this, comrade.'

'Just tell me, Jerry. Get on with it!'

'I believe, chief, that our friend Bester was part of this NIS project ... the long-term project. We know that he moved from the security police to the NIS, probably because his strategic vision didn't suit the police, as I've said. What would make sense if you're looking for high-quality agents to infiltrate the ANC? Finding the brightest among black people who could be persuaded, or otherwise pressured, to do their bidding. And where to find such people? At schools – young, malleable. At schools.'

'Jesus, Jerry! Dlamini. Baba Dlamini. A headmaster. Seen meeting Bester. Envelopes. Confirmed to us he knew Bester. Shit! He was Bester's spotter at his school.'

'Exactly, chief.' He dabbed with the pointer at a flag drawn towards the outer edges of the map. 'That is, or was, Dlamini's school. These arrows to these Post-its show the four people I've managed to identify who came to the ANC from Dlamini's school.' He dabbed at the first Post-it. 'This one died in exile, of malaria in the camps, according to the ANC submission to the TRC.'

Masilela moved closer.

'These other two are also dead. Inside the country after '94. But this one ...' He struck at the last Post-it with vehemence. 'This one is still alive.'

Masilela put on his glasses and moved closer still. 'But there is no name on this one.'

With a flourish, Whitehead peeled off the Post-it to reveal another beneath it, one with a name in dark black ink.

Masilela fell back. 'Shit, Jerry! He's not only still alive, he's ... Fuck!'

Chapter 36

October 2019
'We have no choice now. None. We have to move to Plan Z.'

Otto pronounced it the American way – *zee*. Marie assumed the habit had come from his six months' FBI training at Quantico in the seventies when he was still a young, and perhaps impressionable, security police officer, part of the intelligence collaboration between the Americans and the old services in the good old days; collaboration that continued into the new regime – the old Scorpions were trained at Quantico. When he wrote too, in English, he occasionally used American spelling, lots of *zees*.

Marie looked around at the motley and aged gathering, sitting on camp chairs in a semicircle on the deep wooden stoep Otto had built along the entire front façade of the farmhouse, surprisingly in the old colonial style, his last great DIY project. The views through the wooden railings extended across the farmland that rolled from the house to fields of grazing, mealie and potato plantations and citrus orchards against the hill near the dam. Otto was old now, his features still handsome, but more sag in the face; his blond curls now gone, grey strands struggling to cover a tanned pate. But the rest of him belied his sixty-seven years – still sculpted and straight-limbed, weather-beaten, although more hairy.

The others too showed signs of the years, most just short of retirement, which seemed to impose a kind of desperation as they discussed what to do next. Of the old crowd there was Kline, Oberholzer, Booysens, the younger ones including blond twins from the Afrikaner Vryheidsbeweging, as well as Johan van Deventer, still in his fifties, and Tertius Botes from the provincial office of the Service. The only black there: Brixton Mthembu.

They all held cans of beer in one hand and the boerewors rolls she had prepared in the other, just like the ones you used to get on a weekend outside the butcher in the Castle Walk shopping centre in Pretoria in the old days – her perfectly grilled boerewors, fried onions, bright yellow mustard, tomato sauce and the long white bread roll. No servants to help her this Sunday, all given the day off, unusual, perhaps suspicious, she thought, when they were expecting 'guests'.

'Plan Z, Otto? You sure? So drastic?' Kline looked pained, the lines on his face puckering together.

Otto sneezed, white handkerchief to nose, then wiped the residue with long, exaggerated movements. He tucked the hanky back into the pocket of his shorts. They all waited. 'Yes. Drastic, but necessary. These Moloi Bolsheviks are going to undo everything. Everything ... all we've achieved over decades, in fact, since the last millennium.' He waited for a laugh. None came. 'And I'm afraid his old commie spooks are getting closer.'

This was news to Marie. Otto let her sit in on these meetings, at least this one, because it was in their home, but he never shared anything with her when they were alone. She looked at him. 'How so, Otto?'

Otto's lips tightened, his eyes narrowed. 'How so? Well, for one, old man Dlamini came to see me. He was visited by two people – a man and a woman.' Otto took a small notebook out of the breast pocket of his safari jacket. He thumbed through the pages. 'Yes, a Dr Thando Nkambule and a Professor Manzini. They said they were from Wits, doing research.'

Marie paused in the bite she was taking from her boerewors roll. 'And so? What's the significance of that?'

'The significance, Mrs Bester, is that they asked about me and about the project.'

'They asked or the old man blurted?'

'Well, not sure about that. He might have. But he said, to use his words, "they showed an interest".'

Marie heard a creaking from the camp chair Mthembu was sitting in. 'Did he describe them, Mr Bester?' he asked.

'Who, DG?'

'This Dlamini ... Did he describe the two visitors?'

Otto looked at his notebook again. 'Both blacks.' Mthembu's chair creaked again. 'Both in their sixties, maybe late fifties. The man, short, stocky, clean-shaven head. The woman, grey hair, a bit plump, but quite pretty, according to Dlamini.'

Mthembu stood, walked over to the railing, stared out at the farm for a moment, then turned to face them. 'Sounds like ... Could be ...' He paused.

Otto stood up too. 'Could be who, DG?'

'It could be ... The man could be Masilela. And the woman—'

'For God's sake, DG! Which Masilela?'

'My predecessor. Vladimir Masilela.'

Otto's face contorted. 'You sure? Sure-sure?'

'I can't be sure, of course. I can't. But ...' He turned to face the farm again. 'But the description fits, and, in June – June this year – I got information that Masilela had visited the new minister in Cape Town, had a meeting with him.' He turned back to the assembly. 'The Minister has been in office six months and he's still not met me, still not visited the Service. I don't know what he's doing, but it's certainly not supervising us. I suspect – no, I'm sure – he'll replace me soon. Masilela denied he was being asked to come back, but I have my suspicions. Not good. Wouldn't be good.'

Booysens grunted. Oberholzer cursed.

Mthembu held the beer can to his cheek, then rolled it against his forehead. He sat down again. 'And the woman? I wonder ... The description could fit. She's a director in the Service – Sibongile Whitehead. Could be. I don't know. Her husband was Masilela's deputy – also retired. But they are family friends, the Whiteheads and Masilelas.'

Van Deventer held his beer can up as if signalling a request to speak. No one noticed. He coughed. 'Chief, there's something ... I work in Mrs Whitehead's directorate. She called me to her office one day, a few months ago, to ask me about any former Special Branch people who'd joined the NIS.'

Otto went to the fridge, took out a beer, and came to stand behind Marie. 'This is adding up. This is all adding up.' He paused. 'Yes, Botes? You want to say something?'

Botes placed his half-eaten roll on the table and was tapping the beer can against its rim. 'My wife, Mr Bester, you know ... Marlena. She works at the Service training campus here.' He waved his arm over the stoep railing in the direction of the land beyond.

'Yes, Tertius, we know.'

'Well, sir, she told me this Masilela oke, he gives talks at the campus sometimes.'

251

Mthembu nodded. 'Yes, he does. I bumped into him there.'

'Well, sir, she mentioned she had dinner with him once, after a lecture. She says he was asking questions.'

'About what?' Otto put his hand on Marie's head, an uncharacteristic show of affection in public.

'Well, that's it, sir. About you.'

'About me? You sure?'

'Well, sir, I don't know the context, but your name came up.'

Otto removed his hand and went to sit down. 'You see, gentlemen, as I said, it's time for Plan Z. Plan Z or else we are in trouble.'

Kline had been quiet, sipping at his beer, taking bites of his roll, his eyes moving from speaker to speaker, expressionless. He spoke now, softly, but all turned to listen. 'I still think that's a bit drastic. We're talking conjecture here. Nothing concrete. But I can say, if we go ahead, at least I know the Brits will support us. I had a meeting with Simmonds, their station chief in Pretoria. They are ready. And he thinks the Americans will support, and the French. They're ready for a change.'

Otto stood up again. 'Conjecture, hey? Big word, Kline. Conjecture. Wait here. I'll show you conjecture.' He went into the house and came out with a Spar plastic bag. He sat down and placed the bag on the floor next to him. Marie was talking, offering more boerewors rolls or coffee or rooibos. There were no takers. She relaxed back into her seat.

Otto put the bag on his lap and reached inside. 'Here's your conjecture!' He retrieved something that looked like a miniature camera with a long tendril attached to it. 'I found this in the tree opposite the farm gate.'

There was silence. He held it up. 'I took my horse for a ride around the perimeter to check the fences. When I was near the gate I saw a ka— black man jump down from the tree and onto a bakkie that sped off. I suspect he was changing the batteries. So I checked the tree and I found this. It's a surveillance camera. Looks like one of yours.' He handed it to Mthembu.

'Mmm, it does look like one of ours – digital, broadcast camera – no on-board memory. Broadcasts the images to a base station up to 10 kays away.'

'So? The Service is doing surveillance on me?'

'Of course not, Mr Bester. I would know. I have to approve all surveillance ops. Must be someone else. Someone who has access to our equipment. Or has stolen it.'

Oberholzer stood up. 'Jesus, Otto, we're under surveillance, everyone who's come to the farm in – we don't know how long – they know ... Whoever it is, they know. Fuck! Sorry, Marie. How about a brandy, Otto? Brandy and Coke?'

'No, Willie, no hard stuff today. This is serious. Plan Z. We have to go to Plan Z. Our man – Duquesne – is well placed now. Very well placed. It's time. It's time to pull the bull by its horns. And, it's got to be big, dramatic, in their face. After this, they must know that their time is once and for all over.'

Marie found herself taking deep breaths to dislodge the tightness in her solar plexus, while Otto dished out instructions, sotto voce. She both admired and feared the sudden gestures and intonations of purpose in Otto. She knew the years, the decades, had wound their way around to this, to this ending. The quiet life was over.

Chapter 37

February 2020
Masilela lifted his foot off the pedal and allowed the Audi to glide up to Gate 10 of the Bryntirion Estate, a gate he had passed through times beyond remembering in the older days. He applied languorously the counter-surveillance tricks of the trade, tired of them all, but given that he was not supposed to be here at all, nothing seemed to matter now, not with a president dead. He turned his head in time to see the tenacious cream Ballade slow momentarily and pass the turnoff from Dumbarton into Nassau Road. When he turned his head again, the black iron gates had opened, no blue-clothed policeman at his window, no request for an ID, no call to the ministerial house he was visiting – just an open gate and men in black military gear with unknown insignia on their shirts waving him through with what, to him, looked like knowing nods. He passed through, with one final glance in the mirror, but the gates had closed with no one else behind.

He followed the long curve of the road as it veered to the left, passed the ancient trees through which peeked, as if in apology for the intrusion, the whitewashed walls and red-tiled roofs of the ministerial homes. He took the wind right around until the turn into The Rotunda Circle. Across the circle stood majestic and old Mahlamba Ndlopfu. He wondered what happens to a presidential residence with a president recently dead. Was it locked up until the successor was elected? Where did the family, the comrades, the colleagues go to hold vigil until the interment? Here, in this ghost house, or in his family home in some pockmarked street in Soweto?

He turned off the circle into the driveway of Sandile Ndaba's ministerial residence, more squat and spread than the others, with a garden that seemed boundaryless. No security at the gate. No housekeeper at the door. Sandile himself let him in, spatula in hand, white apron over a maroon tracksuit, bedroom slippers on his feet.

'Ai, Comrade Vladimir, caution to the wind. Bad, bad times. Come in, I'm making breakfast. You'll join? Fried eggs. Sausage. Coffee. Come in. You've got something for me? Later. Let's eat.'

'Morning, Minister. Yes, I have. Something. Not good. Zimb'izindaba. Okay for the breakfast.'

'Okay then. Let the bad wait. Go out onto the patio. I'll bring breakfast there. I'm home alone.'

Masilela, with black folder tucked under his arm, followed the direction of the pointing hand to the oak-and-glass doors to the patio beyond, with its red-tiled floor, wood furniture and corrugated perspex overhang. He sat at the table, the dark folder to one side. He watched the hadedas swoop, settle and peck, their calls slicing the morning silence, the unusual quietness of the estate – no sound of cars on tarmac, no approaching or receding blue-light sirens, no distant laughter of the children of the estate; only the keening of the birds and the other quiet, gentler sounds of humanlessness.

Ndaba came out with two plates with eggs, sausage, white bread and grilled tomato. He placed them on the table, went back into the house and returned with a tray with cutlery, napkins, mugs and coffee. They ate, adding new, subdued sounds to the morning.

Masilela kept his eyes down to the plate, lifting his head only to sip at the coffee. When he did, he saw Sandile's eyes on him.

At last, the final scrape of fork on plate. Masilela dabbed his mouth with a napkin. 'So, Comrade Minister of Intelligence, who killed Moloi?'

Sandile lifted his coffee mug. 'We all know, Vladimir, don't we? The late MEC for Education in Mpumalanga killed the president.'

'Yes, yes … But really? Who?'

'What do you mean?'

'Who killed the late MEC?'

Sandile stood up. 'The great RC, that's who.'

'The great RC?'

Sandile placed his napkin on his lap. 'Regime Change, comrade. Regime Change – RC. I'll show you. Wait here.'

Masilela turned back to the garden. The hadedas were gone. He pushed his plate away, drew the black folder closer. Sandile returned with an A4 brown envelope, and handed it over. 'Here. Read this.'

Masilela took out the document, then immediately put it down and covered it with the envelope. 'This is marked Top Secret. I no longer have such rights.'

Sandile made a noise that sounded like a groan, or perhaps a gasp or a giggle. 'Rights, Vladimir? Rights? You've been running a secret investigation for me that breaks all the rules of "rights".' Ndaba's arms extended wide to either side of him in an exaggerated mime of quotation marks. 'Read the bloody thing! I got it from my dear DG, Mthembu, yesterday. The Service's official report on the assassination of our president.'

'Okay, Sandile. All rules of right to know waived! Perhaps, all rules in abeyance. A president is dead ...' Masilela read, his right hand rhythmically stroking his shaved scalp. Sandile kept his eyes on him, rolling his head slightly as Masilela turned the pages. At last Masilela turned the last page, placed the document back in its envelope and pushed it across the table, pulling his hand back as if scalded.

'So? The Americans did it? Regime change? So the MEC was a CIA agent, was he? And I suppose it was a Marine sniper who shot the MEC outside parliament?'

Sandile laughed, then stopped himself. 'Well, none of that is in there.'

'Exactly! This is all speculation.' He tapped at the envelope. 'Of course the Americans don't like us. They never have. We were terrorists in the old days. In the new days we were friends with Castro and Gaddafi, with Iran and Iraq and Palestine and China. And, sure, it is theoretically possible that they'd like to change our government, but ...' Masilela poured more coffee. It was cold.

'But what, Vladimir?'

'But there's no intelligence in there.' He pointed at the envelope. 'How do we know the MEC was an American agent? When was he recruited? By whom? And why kill the president? There are other ways to effect regime change. And who shot the MEC? Why? How? There's no intelligence. It's what I call "pampering intelligence".'

'Pampering intelligence?'

'Yes. Intelligence that pampers to the biases, the predilections of the client. We have a gut distrust of the Americans, of the West, the former colonial powers, so we are happy to have their evil confirmed.'

'So you don't believe it was the Americans?'

'I didn't say that. I'm saying that that bloody report doesn't contain anything to confirm or even strongly suggest it. There's no intelligence in it – not in the sense of our trade or even the more generic meaning.' Masilela paused, pulled the black folder closer again. 'I have my own theories.'

Sandile seemed not to hear. 'And what hard intelligence would you like to see in this report.' He, too, tapped the envelope.

Masilela opened the folder. 'Well, for one, I'd like to know what school the MEC went to in Mpumalanga and when?'

'Huh? School? Why?'

Masilela took a folded A3 sheet of paper out of the file. He unfolded it in front of Ndaba. On it was replicated Whitehead's diagrams with the squares and arrows and circles and labels. He explained about the Mandela list, the old Green House files, who was alive and who was dead, who was active and who harmless. He traced the arrows with his fingers, explaining all, although he appeared mechanical, somewhere else. Ndaba listened and followed the finger. Occasionally he sighed, sometimes clicked his tongue. The hadedas started up again, unnoticed in the inner silence.

After a pause a few seconds longer than Masilela's usual rhythm, Ndaba spoke. 'So, that's it? These are the possible izimpimpi? Good. Well done. Is that it?'

Masilela stood up, pushed his chair back, the scrape on the tiled floor loud and resonant. 'No, chief, that's not all.' He pushed the folder over. 'I have to go now. It's not safe. Nothing is safe any more. In there …' He pointed at the folder. 'In there is a narrative report. You won't like it. You won't like it at all.'

Masilela stood up and left. Outside Gate 10, as he turned back into Dumbarton Road, the cream Ballade was back, closer now.

Note No. 12

March 2020
The Doldrums

I surprise myself by taking up the red notebook to write in these conditions. Or, perhaps it is the conditions themselves that allow this – the sudden calm in this cockpit, on this yacht, the sails twitching idly from side to side above me as the swells tense and unwind, the wind that drove us madly here suddenly gone, two degrees north of the equator, somewhere in the pit of Africa's bulge. I would like to believe, but the Skipper tells me otherwise, that, with the unceremonious crossing of the equator, we are halfway, a majestic sail up the Thames just a few weeks away.

This calmness stands in stark relief to the beating of the winds, the cracking of the sails, the slapping of lines against the mast, and the deep groaning of the joints of this vessel. Stark relief, too, from the ceaseless disgorging of my stomach for a week after we left Table Bay and entered the deeper regions of the vast Atlantic. Now, leaving some sort of remnant in the gut, a knot, a nodule, a pressure that will not subside.

Why do I write, apart, if anything, from the celebration of quietude? Perhaps, being beyond the turmoil now, there is a story to tell. Or is it to keep a record? For whom? Is there anyone who will listen, who will believe? No, I write now to tell of the storm in the moment of becalming.

The Storm. History has disgorged its gut into the tide. The president has fallen. The rough beast has slouched. Hope has stumbled, teetered, sunk. And I was there. And I know why; I know what comes next.

The swells are soporific. I am on watch, the Skipper sleeping below. But there is nothing to watch. I cannot sleep, for who knows when the winds rise again, perhaps a storm, that needs a reefing.

To record: After our world disintegrated with the slaying in parliament, I headed straight for the hotel, packed quickly, checked out. I took the hired car back to the airport, and then a taxi to the yacht club to meet the Skipper. I was pretty sure the surveillance was lost. I was quick, lithe.

The Skipper – comrade, colleague, retired from the fray – heard me out, agreed to my crazy plan. Who would have thought? In the old days, the days of the first exile, who would have thought of an escape by sea – no fields to trudge, hills to climb, fences to ford? A liquid border, in fact.

The Skipper hid me on his boat moored in the yacht basin, taught me the basics of sailing, as they say, taught me the ropes, prepared the boat, purloined the supplies. Within a few days we were off, out the harbour, hauling close to Robben Island, then pointing northwest into the Atlantic, just the two of us, alone on the boundaryless sea, taking turns at the tiller, tracking our progress on the electronic and paper charts, squiggly lines leading into a vagueness beyond.

Chapter 38

February 2020
Sandile Ndaba fell back against the cushions of the mustard-coloured couch in the second sitting room of his residence, slamming shut Masilela's black folder on his lap. He closed his eyes, right hand to his forehead, and let the breath out of his lungs with a hiss like the sound of the steam trains that had passed the village of his youth.

He hadn't expected this. Any of it. This was beyond expectation, beyond suspicion, beyond comprehension. This cleaved the very roots of the tree of friendship, comradeship, trust, loyalty that spread its branches to all the open spaces of the forest that was his life, his world, his country, his organisation.

The report was clear. This was, at last, the unearthing of the tendrils that had reached into South Africa's underbelly from the darkness of apartheid into the modern years of peace – of relative peace – of justice, democracy, freedom, decay and recent resuscitation. This was the making translucent of the grey mists that had swirled beneath the seemingly obvious, the assumptions, the easy causal tracks. This was not one of those intelligence reports of earlier years, his predecessors' years, of insinuations and allegations and pandering to fears and concerns to fight factional battles, to take sides, to ruin reputations, to serve self.

But what was he to do with this? What possible outcome could come out of this? Where was he to place his trust? The line of accountability had been severed. With whom could he share this information? Who was not infected by the disease of decades-long treachery? How do you report treachery to the treacherous? And with the knowledge now revealed to him, the possibilities of the extent of the treachery were theoretically infinite.

He rose from the couch and, in spite of the earliness of the day, for the first time since his appointment as minister for intelligence, he walked over to the well-stocked entertainment cabinet and poured himself a double whiskey. But he would never taste it. The blast that shattered his sitting-room window took away the glass, together with the hand that was holding it and much of the rest of him.

Chapter 39

February 2020
Despite her self-defined status as the estranged wife of the deputy president, Lindiwe Vilakazi was seated in the VIP section of the parliamentary gallery for President Moloi's state-of-the-nation address at this gaudy opening of parliament. Alongside her sat the two ageing former presidents with their wives. One of them had taken time off from his court hearing, perhaps cheekily, to make an appearance in this ritual that had once been his.

Lindi looked down and across at Amos in the front row of the ANC benches, next to the seat that awaited the arrival of President Moloi. She wondered again why on earth she was here. Discipline? Decorum? In this age? But, she had been – had had to be – persuaded to keep up appearances, if not to actually reconcile. She wondered at that word. Reconcile? Reconciliation? Mandela's word. Being reconciled implied that there was a previous conciliation that had to be recaptured. Had she ever been 'conciled' with Amos? Yes, she supposed, in the very early days of exile, of hope, love. But she learned, painfully over time, that Amos was a man of outward conviviality and inward fathomlessness. In short, he was a charmer, but when you were close to him that charm hid a stickiness, a murkiness, a secretness she did not understand. Apart from anything else, the charm also made him an incorrigible womaniser. And his status, surrounded by bodyguards and personal assistants and other factotums, created a wall of protection against the approbation of his comrades, his family, his society.

But not against her. She had had enough and she told him so. She walked out on him. He did not plead. He did not apologise. She was, however, summoned to his village for a family intervention. They pressed her for a reconciliation, but she was emphatic, told them it was not possible. Then Baba Dlamini took her aside to ask her, to tell her, that she had, for appearances' sake and for the sake of political stability, to play her role of second lady. She did not understand when he said, 'Amos will rise all the way to the top sooner than you think.'

Now the voice of the Sergeant-at-Arms boomed the arrival of the Speaker and the president. All stood. Lindi looked down on the procession, Moloi striding down the carpeted walkway, his head turning from one side to the other, smiles and gesticulations. Amos appeared lethargic. She lifted her eyes to the opposite gallery. She caught sight of Jerry Whitehead, seemingly alone, no Bongi at his side. He looked dishevelled, wrinkled. She wondered what he was doing here. Being long out of government, he had no need. Perhaps some nostalgia? Perhaps some hope for what would emerge from Moloi's coming words. She missed that crowd of him and the other ANC intelligence comrades. Memories crowded in – deep discussions at the departmental planning sessions in Lusaka, raucous drinking sessions afterwards, the bottomless barrel of anecdotes, the camaraderie that lasted into the early post-struggle years. But now they had all drifted apart, away, into discreet corners, some down into the earth. She missed them. She missed those days. Now all that was left her was playing wife to a husband she despised, a traitor to her heart.

The Speaker called on the president to deliver his address. The ANC benches stood, cheered and ululated. The opposition benches stood politely, some heckling from the back, somewhere below Lindi's vantage point. She sat down again, and waited for the wave of sound to recede. Moloi spoke, it seemed off the cuff, although perhaps there was a teleprompter – she couldn't see.

Speaker of the National Assembly
Chairperson of the National Council of Provinces
Deputy Speaker and Deputy Chairperson
Deputy President Amos Vilakazi ...

He paused, looked around, pushed something away from him on the lectern. He waved his arm around the chamber.

Come, come. Let's forget all this imbibed pomp and ceremony, for goodness sake ... all protocol dispensed with ...

Lindi saw the cabinet ministers in the front row of the ANC benches fidgeting, glancing surreptitiously at each other. In the directors-general box, alongside the Speaker's podium, facing into the hall, she noticed the director-general in the Presidency fiddling with the pages before her as if looking for the place in the script. Obviously, Moloi had gone off script, abandoned the carefully prepared and meticulously consulted address. As for Lindi, she was pleased.

> *This is a small change. It is time for a big change. It is time, fellow South Africans, that we go back to basics; back to the things we struggled for, the things we dreamed of when our miracle was unfolding nearly thirty years ago.*
>
> *It is time, indeed, to rid ourselves not just of the pomp that we inherited and took as our own, but also of the trappings, the indulgences of power.*
>
> *Let us be honest with ourselves. Not only did we inherit a country, a society that was grotesquely unequal; we ourselves, yes, all of us, basked, bathed, lavished in that inequity. We got ourselves big cars, big houses, big bank accounts. We thought it was our birthright, or rather, our struggle-right. We were sucked in and we descended with fervour, with passion, with new philosophies and theories to explain, to justify our descent.*
>
> *And the result? Lascivious greed, corruption, naked individualism.*

Moloi appeared to drift back to the script, tinkering with something in front of him.

> *Our Party and our Government have been pondering these challenges for the past year and, with great difficulty and great self-reflection, we have decided on a number of steps to, apart from anything else, dramatically transform the morality of our government and, in fact, of the country as a whole ...*

Leaning against the railing, Lindi peered down at the gathering below, trying to assess their responses; she had a good view of the ANC benches opposite, partial glimpses of the opposition below her, and the seats in the middle especially set up for the premiers and

MECs of the provincial governments. She noticed an MEC from the Mpumalanga benches rise, perhaps with an urgent biological need, although it was admittedly a measure of discipline to sit through the president's speeches. But the man did not sneak to the exit as she had expected; instead, he approached the president at the podium, drew something from his jacket pocket and jabbed repeatedly at Moloi, who swore and crumpled to the floor. Only then did the man turn and run out the chamber.

It took a moment, but it came upon Lindi, like a wind wave through wheat approaching from across a field, what the recent words of Baba Dlamini had meant. She felt the blood snap in her head and all go dark.

Note No. 13

And what can I tell you my brother, my killer?
What can I possibly say?
I guess that I miss you. I guess I forgive you
I'm glad that you stood in my way
— Leonard Cohen, 'Famous Blue Raincoat'

September 2020
Coming back from my pub, this evening, dear Bongi – yes, I call it 'my pub' now as it serves really as my sitting room, my bedsit having sparse room to sit – tipsy as I was, I would never have even glanced at the rack of pale wooden post boxes in the narrow, dark passageway that serves as an excuse for a foyer to this boxed tenement they call an apartment block. There's never anything in my post box other than leaflets calling me to the local supermarket for better prices, or begging my vote in an election I don't know about, or another unctuous announcement from my landlord about new occupancy rules or a scribbled reminder that my rent is once again late.

Tonight, though, as I moved wearily towards the stairs preparing to summon some momentary sobriety to get me up the two flights to my room, my eye was caught by a flash of white protruding from the slit of my mailbox, top right of the bank of boxes just before I was to mount the stairs. It did not look like the usual junk. I snatched at it with my left hand as my right gripped the banister for the long haul upwards. I held the envelope out in front of me like a torch.

In my room, in the dim light of the single shadeless lamp, a cracked glass of cheap whiskey on the over-varnished round table that held the lamp, I see now that this is a letter. A letter. A real old-fashioned letter, such as we used to write in those early years of exile. A letter, with a stamp (digital, I'm sure, but designed to look like the ones I used to collect as a boy), and with an address, my address, handwritten as we used to write addresses. Handwritten and in your handwriting, Bongi, that jumped out at me, dragging from the thin paper on which it was affixed sudden memories such as the ones that would come from a long-forgotten photograph found in the recesses of a cupboard during a move of house or some other packing or unpacking – there were so many of those.

My dearest Jerry it starts – the letter, I mean – after I have managed to slip my crooked finger under the flap and gently pry the contents loose in fear of damaging the words inside.

My dearest Jerry

What should I read into that? Why not just 'Dear Jerry'? A little formality to represent more accurately the time and space between us. But the possessive pronoun 'My' signifies a continued ownership that I thought had long been surrendered. And the 'dearest'? That implies the upper limit of dearness, the superlative. Did you think about these opening words? Or was it a sop to diplomacy, to kindness?

> *My dearest Jerry,*
> *First, I must say, don't worry. I have used a safe route to get this letter to you. And don't ask me how I got your address. That too is safe.*
>
> *I write to raise some things with you, and there was no other way but this letter. Some of these things are not good, very bad. Things here are very very bad. I don't know what you know, what you've heard from where it is that you're hiding. I don't know how you are, what you are now, what you are thinking, feeling. Jerry, I miss you. Yes. I love you. I still do not understand what happened, what dragged or pushed you away from me. I have never stopped loving you. And, no, I have never been unfaithful to you, if that is what you still believe.*
>
> *This is a difficult thing to tell you. I'm not sure how much of our news you're able to follow. Do you know that Sandile is gone? Dead. He was blown up by a bomb, right in Bryntirion, not long after the president.*

Bongi, I read your words. I hear your words – your voice is here in a space in my head, a special vault or device, perhaps, that vocalises the written word, like computers do for the challenged of sight. You love me, you say? Ndaba is dead? No, I didn't know. I do not follow the news. I am shackled to the more distant past. Sandile gone? I mourn, but I am not surprised. And Vladimir? What of Vladimir?

I don't know how to tell you this, Jerry, but Vladimir is not doing well. In a coma, for many months now, since February. The story is that he was hijacked, shot in the head. They say he was on his way back from seeing Sandile, just before Sandile himself was killed. They say Vladimir won't make it, and if he does, if he does wake up, he will be a cabbage. That's the word they use. I'm sorry, Jerry.

Vladimir a cabbage? No! They have shot a hole in the revolution, the trajectory of the bullet erasing our history, our memory, our story. Bongi, I too have a hole that is killing me, a dank hole, a dark, diseased pit in my stomach. We all go down the road to journey's end.

There are more bad things, Jerry. Terrible news, I am sorry. Stephen and Gail burned to ashes in their house, their house burned down, nothing left. The Room, as you called it, is gone, ashes and molten metal, they say.

Not surprised, Bongi. Not surprised. Ashes to ashes. Slime to slime.

I am okay, Jerry. I am safe. I am in hiding. I have left the house, our home. I have left it empty. I am not going into the office. After the president and Ndaba, DG Mthembu set the counter-intelligence investigators on me. But I am safe.
 And, Nadine is safe. For some reason they do not visit the sins of the father (and the mother) on the child. I am glad to tell you that your daughter, as part of her training, has been posted to the London station as an intern for six months. You will see her soon. That is the real reason I am writing to you now. And that is how this letter has got safely to you …

Nadine is in town!

Chapter 40

And you who were bewildered by a meaning
Whose code was broken, crucifix uncrossed
Say goodbye to Alexandra leaving
Then say goodbye to Alexandra lost.
— Leonard Cohen, 'Alexandra Leaving'

October 2020
Nadine Whitehead returned to her father's bedsit from the Kensal Green Cemetery, her head still struggling with the images of the dark green poplars, the paler green barrage of trees she did not recognise, and the too-large dirty-grey stone angels reaching unrequited towards the heavens from the graves beneath them. The images were incongruous with the dank earth that she and the two undertaker's boys had spooned into her father's grave.

A grave it was, in spite of Jeremy's insistence to her, as he lay skeletal and translucent in the St Mary's Hospital bed, that he be burned. When she had eventually managed to communicate the news to her mother, Bongi had pleaded that he be buried, for it would take her a while to extricate herself from the country and she needed, she must have, when she finally arrived, a concrete space on the planet where she could say goodbye to him, a place to which she could return now and again, over what years were left to her, to report developments to him, where her tears could fall, where the fact that he had once been could, so to speak, be written in stone.

Nadine now let herself into her father's room, her second visit since finding him just in time to ferry him to hospital. In the far right-hand corner, a single bed with a faded green sheet and pillow case that she remembered as a brighter, spring green, on her childhood bed, and an unzipped stained blue sleeping bag as blanket. The bed was unmade. Next to it, an antique chest of drawers spilling underwear, shirts and jerseys; an off-white tracksuit dropped on the floor between bed and chest. In the middle of the room, a round wooden table with a bare-bulbed lamp on it, a cracked and stained whiskey glass, a wicker chair alongside. In the near-left corner of the room a sink with unwashed dishes with a table alongside holding an electric hotplate, a chaos of bottles and packets of spices and condiments and empty whiskey bottles tucked away beneath. And in the far-left corner, beneath a grimy, cracked window with soiled green curtains, a desk with straight-backed chair on which lay Dad's laptop, flexi-pad and a large red-covered notebook and, on closer look, a much-handled letter.

Nadine made the bed, though who would sleep in it? Perhaps her mother as a last touch with fabric that had brushed her husband. Her mother would arrive soon, just hours too late to bury Jeremy, from her circuitous route overland to Gaborone, flights to Lusaka, Addis, Dubai, Paris and chunnel to London. Nadine washed dishes, wiped surfaces, tidied; conscious of an attempt to sanitise, to make order of the dust, grime and chaos of her father's last abode.

She poured herself a cup of coffee and sat on the wicker chair with her father's red notebook. She paged through. Notes, it seemed, for a book. About being at the president's assassination; the sail into exile; snow in London; and – the tears now finally fell – fishing with a much younger her at the Rietvlei Dam. She closed her eyes, did not wipe the tears, allowed them to funnel down her face and drip off her chin onto her lap, her shoulders shaking, her arms crossed over her breasts, her hands clasping her upper arms, her torso rocking forwards and back.

She stayed like that for a long time, slowly stilling and then drifting into some form of unconsciousness, perhaps sleep, until the shrill chime of the access phone next to the door of the bedsit startled her back to this room. It must have been, she surmised, only the second time it had ever rung during her father's occupancy. He had told her that the first time was when she visited. She answered. It was her mother. She buzzed Bongi in, went downstairs to help with the bags, and, when they were back in the room, fell into her arms and they both wept.

Eventually, Bongi disentangled herself, held Nadine by the shoulders at arms' length and smiled weakly. 'Dad leave any whiskey for us?'

Nadine grunted. 'You don't want to visit him first?'

'Ntombazana, ngikhathele. It's been a long road. You will take me to him tomorrow. He will wait.'

Nadine went over to the table with the hotplate. She looked below it and came back with a half-empty bottle of Teacher's and two frosted glasses. 'There's no ice, Mama. No dash. No fridge.'

'Then what did Daddy eat?'

'I don't know, Mama. There's tinned stuff, but I think he ate mostly at the pub.'

'The pub? How do you know that?'

Nadine pointed at the table by the wicker chair. 'It's in there. The red notebook. Papa was writing notes. I think he was writing a book about what happened.'

Bongi sat in the wicker chair and picked up the notebook. Nadine poured single tots into the glasses. Bongi, eyes down to the opened notebook, motioned for her to continue pouring. Nadine sat on the bed and sipped at her glass. There was a long silence, backgrounded by the hum of Kilburn – cars, buses, the far-off rattle of passing trains, and, now and then, shouts from the street, slamming doors, and, somewhere distant, music, indiscernible music.

Nadine watched her mother, saw her eyes moisten without losing their focus on the turning pages, running her finger down the pages as if tracing braille. Nadine reached into the pocket of her black cotton jacket and pulled out her father's passport. She opened it again at the page with the photograph of a much younger father, but under it glared up at her a name she did not know, but had to use on his death certificate.

'Mama, who's Alexander Sebastian October?'

Bongi paused in her reading. She got up and went over to Nadine, held her face in her hands. 'That was Daddy's birth name.'

'His real name? Why was I not told?'

Bongi pulled Nadine's head to her breast. 'Daddy always insisted that Jeremy Whitehead was his real name. He said it was the name he was given when his life became real. He had it officially changed when we came back from exile.'

'Then why is the October name in his passport?'

'Because he had to use his birth name to qualify for the UK ancestry visa, that's why. You, though, are officially a Whitehead.' Bongi let go of Nadine's head, looked into her eyes. Nadine fell silent, returned the passport to her pocket, and went over to the table for more whiskey. Bongi returned to the chair and the notebook. Nadine drifted to the window and looked out at the bleak autumnal streets, sipping at her whiskey, sniffing at it before each sip – it reminded her of the smell of her father when he kissed her goodnight on those Pretoria evenings.

At last Bongi closed the book, held it on her lap, her hands spread over it as if in protection. 'Yes, ntombazana, Daddy was writing a book. Definitely. Where's his laptop?'

'Over there, Mama – on the desk. Also his tablet. You want to get into them? I'm sure there's a password.'

Bongi stood and went to the desk. She sat down, opened the laptop and pulled it towards her, switched it on. It asked for a password. She tried one. It refused. She tried again.

'I'm in!'

Nadine walked over. 'How? How did you get in so quick?'

'I know your father. I know … I knew his heart. His password is "enidan".'

'"Enidan"?'

Bongi laughed. It was not a dry laugh, but it was not merry. 'Enidan is Nadine spelt backwards, girl.'

Nadine sniffed back the tears, stood over her mother, hands on Bongi's shoulders. Bongi searched the laptop's folders until she found what she expected. 'Yes. Daddy was writing a book. It looks like it's about what happened at home – everything. He nearly finished, too, it seems.' She paused, squinting her eyes at the screen. Nadine peered over her shoulder.

Bongi shut the computer, stood up. 'This needs to be finished. Come, let's go to Daddy's pub.'

Inothi Yokugcina

I know you need your sleep now, I know your life's been hard, but many men are falling where you promised to stand guard.
– Leonard Cohen, Field Commander Cohen

London
April 2021

My name is Sibongile 'Bongi' Whitehead, nee Dube. I was the wife … no, I am the widow, of Jeremy 'Jerry' Whitehead, born Alexander Sebastian October, a man from the flatland below the mountain named after a table, of Scottish, Xhosa and Khoi lineage – and author of this book. A man who wandered the globe not, I must say, as an aimless itinerant, but as a believer, an ardent believer that things could be better. A lover. A revolutionary. An officer.

I commend him to you. I commend the man. And I commend the work.

Yes, he wandered from the southern extremity of Africa, through the world, and, eventually, back again and – finally – to return to the land of his forebears … one of them … to be buried in lush English soil a few kilometres from where I write this.

The tale he tells in this book is substantially and despairingly true. It must be told. The treachery he depicts must be unravelled, put out to air, a harsh wind blown through it.

I commend it. I commend it.

Author's note

This book is, emphatically, a work of fiction. I know some of you will not, or are not willing to, believe that. And that, I confess, is at least partly my doing. When my non-fiction book, *Songs & Secrets*, came out, at book launches and talks I was invariably asked: Why are there not more secrets in *Songs & Secrets*? I deflected the question by saying: My next book will be a novel and all the secrets will be in there, accompanied by the standard disclaimer 'Any resemblance to real …'

Sitting one day at a table on the pavement outside Poppy's in Melville nursing a glass of Johnnie Black with a media friend of mine, I outlined for him the plot of the novel I was working on. He probed how much truth there would be in it. To my insistence that it was a fiction, he retorted: 'Barry, no one will believe that a novel that comes from you is not factual.'

Be that as it may, I do hereby disclaim:

This is a work of fiction. Names, characters, businesses, places, events, locales, and incidents are either the products of the author's imagination or used in a fictitious manner. Any resemblance to actual persons, living or dead, or actual events is purely coincidental.

That is an interesting word – 'coincidental'. It implies some sort of happenstance. The reality is more complex. Many novelists (some may deny it) base their fictional characters on people they have known, in terms of physical description, mannerisms and other traits. I confess, in some instances, I have done the same. But, as an alert to the guess-who addicts, let me assure you that guessing who, even correctly, will not add anything to your understanding of the novel or the story it depicts.

The real persons on whom some of my characters are based serve as shop mannequins, whom I dress and display as I want according to the demands of the fictional world I am creating. Or, perhaps a more apt metaphor: the novelist is a robotics engineer, creating his humanoid robots with the physical appearance of people he has known, but whose internal programming is designed for the functional services they will perform. Actually, in my own experience, much as in the robots-who-take-over-the-world cinematographic genre, some of my 'robots' reprogrammed themselves to take over the world I thought I was in charge of.

There is one thing I must say. This novel was conceived in broad outline in 2013 and writing completed in early December 2017, before the outcome of the ANC's December 2017 elective congress, and nothing in it has been changed as a result of the real-world developments since the completion of its near-final draft. It was conceived as a narrative of an imagined future, which, at the time, was seven years away. Now that 'future' is upon us, and some of it nearly upon us, and, for some of you readers, will possibly be in the past. It – the novel – is thus a genuine work of imagination, even if possibly of an 'informed' imagination.

This novel has had a long gestation. The idea for it first came to me when I was working on *Songs & Secrets*, perhaps because it raised issues for me that couldn't be dealt with in a non-fiction work. But the first fragments of it were crafted during creative writing classes I attended when I was temporarily resident in New Delhi during 2013 and 2014. The classes were led by Aditi Rao, a wonderful poet. She used to tell us that writing was a muscle that needed to be exercised and, during the many exercises she gave us, I found myself crafting little bits of what would later go into this novel. So, my very warm appreciation to Aditi and to the other participants in the class for your insights and encouragement: Amruta, Kandala, Neha, Nikhil, Mallika, Manvendra, Priya, Sapnu, Saloni and the others whose names time has stolen from me.

When I returned from India, hungry to continue writing, I joined a writing group in Johannesburg that met monthly. My warm thanks to the past and present members for their detailed comments on draft chapters, for the writers' camaraderie, and the totally unwriterly gossip we sometimes engaged in: Makhosazana Xaba, Christa Kuljian, Karen Hurt, Catherine Hunter, Madeleine Fullard and Terry Shakinovsky.

It was members of this writing group who put the thought into my head of undertaking a creative writing degree. So, I now have to formerly state: This novel was completed in partial fulfilment of the requirements for the degree of Master of Arts in Creative Writing at the University of the Witwatersrand. (I passed – with distinction.) My thanks, therefore, to my supervisor, Bronwyn Law-Viljoen for meticulous editing, provocative ideas, and support through forty chapters and two broken limbs in the course of the two years. Warm gratitude, too, to the other course lecturers: Phillippa Yaa De Villiers, Elsie Cloete, Gerrit Olivier, Ivan Vladislavic and Kgafela Magogodi. And, of course, to my fellow students: Noluthando Ncube, Stanley Hermans, Mehita Iqani, Dane Bowman, Sarah Roberts, Rachel Solomon and Sheena Magenya. Thanks, guys.

I also want to thank Hélène Pastoors and Alison Lowry for very useful comments on very early draft outlines and passages from the novel.

Warm and loving gratitude to Reneva Fourie for her read of the near-final manuscript, astute comments, enthusiastic support (she wanted it published before the ANC's December 2017 conference!) and continued encouragement and balm. (She gave the novel its title.)

And to Mandla Langa, also for reading the near-final manuscript, praise and encouragement, and for fine-tuning my vernacular. Ngiyabonga mfo! (I am told Mandla credits me for encouraging him to also undertake the Wits Creative Writing Masters.)

My fatherly gratitude and pride to my daughter Neo Gilder for her inspiring design of the cover artwork of this novel. She is truly a great photographer. Visit her at http://neogilderphotography.squarespace.com.

Thanks go, too, to my publishing friends Bridget Impey and Maggie Davey for so quickly and passionately taking on this novel as another Jacana project. And, of course, to all the people at Jacana involved in this project, especially to Sean Fraser for his sensitive and professional edit.

Final words of gratitude go to Joel Netshitenzhe and the Council, Board, management and staff of the Mapungubwe Institute for tolerating my distractedness during the birth of this work and the couple of broken limbs.

About the author

Barry Gilder went into exile in 1976, joined the ANC and MK, underwent intelligence training in the then Soviet Union, served in the ANC underground leadership in Botswana in the 1980s and returned to South Africa in 1991. He served the democratic government as deputy director-general of the South African Secret Service, then as deputy director-general of the National Intelligence Agency, as director-general of the Department of Home Affairs and as South Africa's Coordinator for Intelligence. He retired from government in 2007. He is currently Director Operations at the Mapungubwe Institute for Strategic Reflection. He has a BA in English and Philosophy and a Masters in Creative Writing from Wits University. He is the author of the non-fiction work *Songs & Secrets: South Africa from Liberation to Governance* (Hurst, Jacana 2012).

Acknowledgements

Every effort has been made to trace copyright holders and to obtain their permission for the use of copyright material. If the publisher has used copyright material where permission has not been granted, we will credit this material in future reprints or editions of this book if the permission status changes.

The following texts have been reproduced with permission:

Page vi: Lines from 'The Second Coming' by WB Yeats, reproduced under fair dealing permission from AP Watt Ltd.

Page 1: Eliot, TS. 2002. 'The Waste Land'. *Selected Poems*. Faber & Faber Ltd, London.

Page 79: cummings, ee. 1994. 'somewhere I have never traveled'. *100 Selected Poems*. Grove Press, New York. Used by permission of Liveright Publishing Corporation.

Page 183: Turton, Anthony Richard. 2010. *Shaking Hands with Billy*. Just Done Productions – Publishing, Durban.

Page 211: Lines from 'Easter 1916' by WB Yeats, reproduced under fair dealing permission from AP Watt Ltd.

Page 243: Cohen, Leonard. 1993. 'Alexandra Leaving' © Leonard Cohen and Leonard Cohen Stranger Music, Inc. Used by permission of The Wylie Agency (UK) Limited.

Page 267: Cohen, Leonard. 2011. 'Famous Blue Raincoat'. *Leonard Cohen: Poems and Songs*. Alfred A, Knopf, New York. Used by permission of Everyman's Library, an imprint of the Knopf Doubleday Publishing Group, a division of Penguin Random House LLC.

Page 271: Cohen, Leonard. 1993. 'Alexandra Leaving' © Leonard Cohen and Leonard Cohen Stranger Music, Inc. Used by permission of The Wylie Agency (UK) Limited.

Page 275: Cohen, Leonard. 2011. 'Field Commander Cohen'.

Leonard Cohen: Poems and Songs. Alfred A, Knopf, New York. Used by permission of Everyman's Library, an imprint of the Knopf Doubleday Publishing Group, a division of Penguin Random House LLC.